HURRAH FOR THE NEXT MAN TO DIE!

Samuel J. Winter

The characters and events portrayed in this book are fictitious. Any similarity to real persons, living or dead, is coincidental and not intended by the author.

ISBN: 9798637869671

Cover design by: Art Painter
Front Cover by: Unknown Author - http://arkarthick.com/2011/04/19/incredible-antique-omg-photos/, Public Domain, https://commons.wikimedia.org/w/index.php?curid=24084664

Library of Congress Control Number: 2018675309
Printed in the United States of America

The Western Front, and millions of men are locked in a life and death struggle, knee deep in Flanders mud. High above them, swooping and jousting, are the knights of the air, the world's first fighter pilots, pratting about looking damned heroic but having no real impact on proceedings. Slightly below them are the observation aircraft. Slow, lumbering two seaters, taking photographs, directing artillery fire and dropping bombs. These men wield enormous influence over the battlefield. This also makes them flying targets.

April 1917 and the allied forces prepare to launch a massive ground offensive around the town of Arras and the Royal Flying Corps throw large numbers of men and machines into supporting the infantry, regardless of the cost. The slaughter in the sky reaches a crescendo and the month will ultimately become known as 'Bloody April.' The average lifespan of an airman is two weeks.

CHAPTER 1

1st April 1917

He sat hunched over, eyeing the window critically from beneath a half-raised eyebrow, and tugged at the dregs of a hipflask that had been two-thirds full when he had woken. The day's fifth cigarette burned slowly between his fingers, wisps of smoke curling through the stale air. Somewhere in the blackness, he remembered something about 0500 take-offs and 'dud-weather,' and reluctantly concluded that he should probably find out whether he was going to die this morning. Morning, was it? Blasted time of day to die if ever there was one. He started scraping around his skull in a vain attempt to find two working brain cells to rub together.

The bed opposite his own lay vacant and unmade, a tangled mess of sheets. From the other end of the hut, a loud, rasping fart reverberated and caused a flicker of disgust to momentarily cross his face. Carefully, he placed the cigarette between his pale, peeling lips and screwed the lid back onto the flask. The fear began to rise again, creeping sickeningly up his gullet, and he drew half the cigarette in an effort to subdue it, before choking on the acid smoke that bit into his lungs. The noise provoked a muttered grumble of irritation from the bottom of the hut.

Letting his head drop into his hands, his eye fell upon the tumbled pile next to his bed that resembled the filthiest, bedraggled beggar or sloppy pile of effluent, and smelled worse than both. God, how he hated that pile. It was fear, hatred, despair and comfort, anathema yet essential. No, it was none of these things, it was just a coat. A heavy leather coat, soaked through with sweat, petrol, engine fumes and oil. And urine, from the time he had pissed himself when a burst of anti-aircraft fire had flipped his aeroplane onto its back. The romantics, he had once mused, would have said that its smell was as comforting to him as a woman's scent. But the only women he had known were the local French whores who smelled of cheap cologne and musty semen.

With a herculean effort, he levered his body off his bed, and moved towards the Nissen-hut door. Two pigeon-steps were enough to tell him that his balance was shot and his left foot became tangled up in his flying coat. Slowly, he toppled over and measured his length on the floor with a resounding thud, and another irritable grunt rose from the back of the room. Julian Canning could not have cared less. From under his bed, a half-full bottle of scotch winked at him, and with something loosely resembling a smile on his face, he reached out to it.

In another hut fifty yards away, another young man sat on the corner of his bed, steadily scraping the night's growth of stubble from his strong, lean face. His clear blue eyes peered back at him from the gloom of the shaving mirror. He felt alive, awake and alert. And very soon, he would be soaring above the earth, looking down upon his fellow man. William Hendley-Bart was a natural pilot, approaching one month at the front now, and getting on famously. He had been singled out during a base inspection the previous week for his 'parade-ground dress' and 'noble bearing.' The fact that he had been standing next to Canning at the time had only heightened the impression.

'He was,' the visiting Colonel had remarked, 'fighter-pilot material. Full of spunk and dash and a uniform that had been painted onto him.'

The Colonel had something of a special appreciation for the male form, it was why he had joined the Army, that and to get away from his wife. There was nothing quite so masculine, quite so *right*, as another man. His seedy little eyes slid over Hendley-Bart and his immaculate pencil moustache twitched imperceptibly. Here was a ready-made hero, a fighter who would always stand out from the next man. The next man being Canning, who stood slouched to attention, and had been deliberately ignored. Too surly-looking to rebuke, no idea how the fellow might react, and he looked positively *uninterested* in dying. No, leave him be, the Colonel thought, the blighter would never get anywhere with a uniform like *that* anyway. Father was probably new money, a businessman or something equally horrifying. The notion had caused him to choke on his own saliva, and he had been shepherded away to get a glass of water.

Julian Canning was the compost that helped flowers like William Hendley-Bart grow all the sweeter. As far as military institution allowed, the men were polar opposites, but there was only one difference that really mattered, Canning was lucky. In three hours' time, the body of Julian Canning would be collapsed back in bed, reeking of scotch and petrol, and sleeping soundly. The tall, sculpted form of William Hendley-Bart, which three months ago had slid into uniform to fall under the approving eyes of Brigadier (ret.) Sir Rupert William and Lady Hendley-Bart, would be roasting slowly in a smouldering pile of canvas and plywood, south of Lens. The tanned, handsome skin that had never had to face the troubled onslaught of acne, blackened to a crisp. Birds would begin to gather, waiting for the heat to subside, beaks salivating at the prospect of cooked meat. In a few days' time, William Hendley-Bart would exist in ink form only; a name, on a list, printed in *The Times*. Back in England, Brigadier (ret.) Sir Rupert William Hendley-Bart would place the newspaper on the breakfast table, nod gently, and remark that he had raised a good boy. And his wife would hate him for it.

At 0530 however, Hendley-Bart was more pre-occupied with where his morning coffee had got to, and Canning was engaged in the delicate balancing act of drinking away his hangover whilst trying not to vomit. Gravity lost, and he stumbled out the door to deposit a sickly brown spew around the side of the hut. At 0550 the hut's steward, having failed to find his officer in his bed, gently shook the dew-soaked lump that was snoring loudly in the long grass near the doorway.

'Sir, weather's cleared. Take-off in ten minutes at oh-six-hundred.'

Canning's grunted reply seemed to condense the words 'piss' and 'off' into a single syllable. The steward knew this ritual well enough and proceeded to coax some of his own rather rough brandy into Canning's mouth, whilst rolling his officer onto his back. Lying in the ghostly half-light, Julian opened his right eye slowly and looked up at the sky. It was grey. Just grey. Five more minutes of half-dragging, half-lifting, along with half a flask of brandy, saw Canning on his feet, and beginning to walk towards the hangars. After four steps, he promptly fell over again.

Julian's stocky figure, right arm draped over the steward, shuffled up to the two aeroplanes sitting patiently on the grassy runway, facing into the gentle morning breeze. His appearance prompted Albert Burton, his irrepressibly cheerful Welsh observer, who was known throughout squadron as 'Two Berts,' to burst into a fit of laughter. His cesspit of a flying jacket dwarfed him, like a child in his father's coat. His boots were different colours, the steward having hurriedly grabbed whatever spare kit he could find lying around in the hut. And his flying helmet sat at what, for a healthier figure, might have been considered a jaunty angle on top of his head.

Burton's mirth subsided to a chuckle, 'Jesus Christ, Canning lad, were you drinking petrol last night?'

Julian opened his mouth to fire back a retort but only succeeded in belching. He swayed slightly.

Hendley-Bart was less impressed, officers like Canning lowered the tone of the whole war. He glared at the diminutive, shrouded figure, good God he could smell the man from here. He twisted his frown into the most disdainful expression possible. But all he got in return from Canning was a brief look of bewilderment as he lurched forward and grabbed desperately at an interplane strut to steady himself. Hendley-Bart shook his head sadly. As far as he was concerned, Julian Canning had no business fighting alongside him. War was about courage, brotherhood, and comradeship, whereas Canning merely appeared to be drunk most of the time. Moreover, he could barely fly an aeroplane and was hopelessly inept at the various duties that the squadron was tasked with. His bombs always missed, his photographic plates always spoiled, and he had the unsettling habit of overshooting the aerodrome when landing, and finishing up in the adjacent turnip field. After four months of war flying, Canning had been awarded a Distinguished Service Order. Hendley-Bart could only assume that this had been for simply surviving those four months by chance alone. War, he believed, like sport, was a competition, survival of the fittest, and Julian Canning was not the fittest. Not even close.

Canning gripped the strut tightly and tried his utmost to stop the grass from spinning. Slowly, the rushing green blur separated itself into individual blades once more. Still holding on, he raised his head to survey his aeroplane and felt instantly worse. Two Royal Aircraft Factory BE2s stood quietly inanimate, glistening as what little morning light able to filter through the dense layer of cloud, reflected off the myriad of tiny dew-drops. To Hendley-Bart the aeroplanes resembled great, new-born dragonflies, with long slender fuselages and a double layer of slim, rounded wings, just waiting to take flight. Canning thought the BE2 was an abomination. Canning was right. The machine was ungainly and thrown together, two huge exhaust stacks reared up vertically from the engine like antlers, apparently in direct defiance of the laws of streamlining and aerodynamics. The wings were too small and the struts too weak and the whole contraption had the endearing quality of catching fire rather easily. It had won a military trial in 1912 for its ability to fly in a straight line. In 1912 flying in a straight line was a wonderful attribute for an aeroplane to boast. In 1917, it was a death sentence. The Germans now employed the deadly-nimble Albatros scout with a top speed of one hundred and twenty miles an hour. The BE2 puttered along at a steady eighty miles an hour if the engine was new. None of the engines in 33B Squadron's aircraft were new.

But the worst flaw, and to its crews, the one that was criminally inexcusable, was that the gunner was seated *in front* of the pilot. This meant that to defend the vulnerable rear of the aeroplane, he was either forced to fire his Lewis machine gun over the top of the pilot's head and shoulders, or move his gun to various alternative mounting points around the cockpit. Canning could remember the squadron once losing an aircraft when an over exuberant observer had swung his gun around to continue firing at an enemy scout, and succeeded in blowing his pilot's head off. What had possessed its designers to make it this way was a mystery, the general consensus amongst the aircrews, was that they had felt that British airmen needed a bit of a challenge to make the war more sporting. It made about as much sense as any other reason.

It took Two Berts and two mechanics to heft Canning into the cockpit, threading him through the web of flying wires strung between the wings, and a further couple of minutes to get him pointing upright and forwards. Once Julian was seated, Two Berts climbed up and adjusted his hat and goggles for him, clapped him on the shoulder, which almost made Canning hurl again, and clambered up into the front seat.

Canning thoroughly disliked how his cockpit smelt, a sickly mix of oil and petrol fumes combined with the occasional waft of piss that still lingered, and got caught up in the back of his throat. He stared at the instrument panel in front of him, struggling to make out any of the numbers. Instinct led his hand to switch off the ignition as the mechanics prepared to turn the great four bladed propeller in order to suck air into the engine cylinders.

'Switches off!' called his fitter.

Canning nodded heavily, unable to speak without vomiting.

The mechanic pulled on the heavy wooden blades until he had completed three rotations, 'Contact!'

Canning flicked the switches back on, lolled his head again, and the fitter swung his leg and threw the propeller in the opposite direction. It came up against the compression, paused and fell back. Canning began to hope that his engine was foxed. The mechanic pulled again and this time the tired old motor sputtered into life. The vibrations instantly shot through Julian and began to trouble his sphincter. He sat in the wicker chair, clenching desperately.

'Contact!' Hendley-Bart's voice rang out through the crisp morning air.

His engine was a couple of months younger than that of the other BE and sprang to life first time. He played with the throttle, checked that the control surfaces were all responding, and then, satisfied, turned to wait for Canning to taxi out. That he was junior to that...man on the basis of mere time-served experience continually rankled with Hendley-Bart, it was bad enough just having to fly with him. Damnation, why didn't he take off?

Having spent a nervous couple of minutes concentrating intently on the contractions of his anus, and satisfied that he was now unlikely to soil himself, Julian turned his mind to taking-off. He groped unsuccessfully for the throttle, frowning perplexed, and then tried his left hand instead, giggling to himself. The needle ticked up towards the higher end of the blur of numbers that formed the tachometer, but the BE refused to move. He revved the engine further, but still it remained stationary. In front of him, Two Berts seemed to be exercising his arms.

'Chocks away!' he hollered in a flash of understanding and had to quickly choke back the bile that had flown up his throat as a result of his gleeful exclamation. Realising that none of the mechanics could hear him above the roar of the engine he threw his arms laterally in imitation of Two Berts. Suddenly, the BE leapt forwards and began to barrel down the runway as the wooden blocks were pulled from beneath the tyres. The steadily increasing soreness in his head was magnified by every little rut and bump, and it was with some relief that he was eventually able to lift the wheels from the damp turf. There was no physical sensation of having taken to the air, the BE was too slow to generate the notion of leaving one's stomach behind, something that Canning was infinitely grateful for, as he began the laborious task of circling the aerodrome for height.

The BE had a painfully slow rate of climb, six-thousand feet in twenty minutes was the factory reckoning, which meant that half an hour later, Canning had just passed the five-and-a-half thousand mark. The constant turning was making him feel rather nauseous, so he decided to set off for the Front Lines at a height that was rather lower than safety demanded. As he levelled out, it slowly dawned on him that he had no idea where he was going or what he was meant to do when he got there. He couldn't remember seeing any bombs on the aircraft, which left either reconnaissance or artillery spotting, but he had no recollection of a camera or a radio either. No, wait a minute, there was a camera attached to the fuselage, on the opposite the side from where he had entered the cockpit; a large, dark metal box with several levers and protuberances. How the hell had he missed that? It was up to him to work the blasted thing as well since Two Berts was seated directly between the wings, and consequently could not see downwards. Stupid aeroplane.

Having solved one mystery, he turned his attention to

where he was meant to be going. He noticed that bloody idiot Bendley-Hart had flown in close and was waving at him from near his left wingtip. Sod him. He peered at his map, pasted onto a sheet of wood that he held on his knees, and thought how unfamiliar France looked, even after all this time. After another minute of staring, he turned the map-board the other way up, and felt quite gratified as the names and terrain he was more accustomed to began to materialize. Although, he reflected, sitting in a wicker chair, strapped to an underpowered box-kite, six-thousand feet above the earth, he couldn't be *quite* sure that the world wasn't upside down at the moment...

By now the BE had drifted rather further north than it should have and Two Berts, glancing round, guessed the problem. Reaching for his own map he cross referenced their position with the compass in his instrument board and turned to Canning, pointing in the direction of their target. Julian nodded appreciatively and swung the aeroplane around. Two Berts smiled to himself and began to sing.

Hendley-Bart stared in wide-eyed exasperation at the other aircraft, as it began to slide aimlessly across the sky. Muttering curses, he flew in close and waved desperately at Canning but received only the briefest of glances in acknowledgement. Beneath his heavy woollen scarf, he chewed on his bottom lip in frustration. He reckoned the only reason he was on this mission was to ensure that a clear photograph came back. Usually machines flew solo on reconnaissance, but he was pretty sure that Canning's habit of exposing his plates just as he was flying over a cloud, meant that he had been detailed to accompany him. Eventually, after what felt like an age, the lead BE turned its nose toward their destination, a supply area behind the front-line trenches at Vimy, which Headquarters wanted information on in preparation for the secret offensive that everyone, including the Germans, knew was coming. His relief at finally pointing the right way was short lived as he realised that Canning actually intended to cross the Lines at six-thousand feet, flying just under the cloud layer that was only a few yards above them. German scouts would be lurking in the grey morass, waiting for an opportunity to dive down upon any unsuspecting two-seaters. It was like entering a lions' den with their eyes shut, dressed in bacon. Again, he flew in close to Canning waving frantically and jabbing his finger upwards. Again, he got the briefest of looks and then, with a shake of his head, the pilot of the second aircraft ploughed straight on. William Hendley-Bart said a quiet prayer.

Having finally ascertained where they were heading through a brief but animated map and finger waving session with Two Berts, Julian was feeling rather pleased with himself, despite his uneven gut and throbbing head. All he had to do now was fly in a straight line, take a photograph and come home again. He noticed with a certain amount of chagrin that the other machine had come in close again. Dash it all what did Bendley-Hart want now? Up? No. No, no. Above those clouds was a stinging, searing sun and Julian Canning was in no fit state to cope with that. The clouds helped to muffle his hangover. He shook his head and carried on, only an hour or so now and he could go back to bed.

The rhythmic drone of the engine and warmth of his jacket, combined with the fact that Canning had only managed three hours sleep the night before, meant that he started to doze. Due to its inherent lack of manoeuvrability, this was not a major issue when flying the BE2, indeed he had heard that there was a popular story going around the Front about a BE that had returned to its base and landed perfectly with both pilot and observer dead in their seats. So as Julian drifted in and out of an uncomfortable sleep, the BE continued steadily on its course. Compared to his aeroplane however, Canning's own progress was far less serene. His dreams were broken and twisted, and his mind protested against the situation by continually returning him to consciousness. Shapes and colours mutated and twisted as his brain struggled through a mist of alcohol, attempting to forge some coherent visions. He started to become aware of a dull thudding that began somewhere in the back of his head before quickly forcing its way forward until it was clashing loud and red against the blackness behind his eyes, an incessant pounding tearing through his brain. Suddenly he found himself back in the cockpit of the BE, looking at Two Berts who was standing up and firing his Lewis gun at something over Julian's right shoulder. The staccato crackle continued to hammer into his skull, rolling around the inside of his head and jarring his retinas. The sensation was awful, hellish, and Canning screwed up his eyes in a futile effort to make it stop. He really did not care who or what Two Berts was shooting at, and made no attempt to find out. Instead he pushed his head downwards, onto his knees beside the instrument board, and just wished that it would all go away.

In the second aircraft, Hendley-Bart was rather more concerned with what was going on. He had been the first to see the streamlined, torpedo shaped fuselage of the Albatros emerge from the cloud layer and had alerted Callow, his observer, to the danger with a yell. Callow had spun round, following his pilot's outstretched arm and swung his gun about to bear. His first shots were intended more as a warning to Two Berts than to frighten the German fighter, and in a couple of seconds, several dark pencil lines of tracer ammunition appeared from between the wings of the other BE. Hendley-Bart continued to watch the Albatros in a detached fashion as it hurtled toward him. He could not help but admire how the other pilot handled his machine. It swooped down onto the two BEs, a double stream of tracer pouring from its twin machine guns, whilst continuing to dive at a speed and angle that made shooting back increasingly difficult for the observers.

However, what impressed Hendley-Bart perplexed Two Berts, it wasn't the skill of the Hun that worried him, but the tactics. The way the Albatros was being flown told him that the enemy airman was capable, but any pilot who knew his stuff never bothered shooting at anything more than two-hundred yards away, and the German had opened fire at well over four-hundred. Sensing danger, he ceased firing himself and quickly scanned the sky. Sure enough, he spotted the shark-like outline of another Albatros that was approaching from underneath the second BE, targeting the blind spot below and behind the tailplane, where the two-seater was defenceless. He desperately flailed his arms in an attempt to attract the attention of the other aeroplane, but both pilot and observer were too intent on the first fighter firing at them from above. The decoy had worked perfectly.

From his cockpit, Hendley-Bart watched as Callow's shots whizzed past the Hun scout. They missed, but appeared to have the desired effect as the Albatros banked away, displaying large, black Maltese crosses painted on standard brown-green camouflage wings, and he chuckled triumphantly to himself at how they had sent the Hun packing. It was then the second Albatros opened fire. Hendley-Bart searched about frantically as tracer bullets flashed past, tearing his aircraft to pieces around him. Shots ripped through canvas and plywood, a flying wire cut loose and, relieved of its tension, lashed him a bloody weal across the face. Gingerly, he touched the wound with his heavy leather gauntlet as the altimeter flew to pieces, scattering tiny shards of shattered glass into his lap. It dawned on him that very soon he was going to die, and yet he could only feel strangely detached about it all. He supposed that he should attempt some kind of evasive manoeuvre but saw little point. The BE was too sluggish for anything he did to make a difference, the Hun would follow him and be there waiting. No, he thought, Hendley-Bart had been bested and it was much better to stand...well, sit and face death like a gentleman. Everything grew increasingly dreamlike as Callow collapsed over his Lewis gun and slid slowly into his cockpit. He barely noticed the shot that hit the BE's petrol tank, and the flames that billowed up around him seemed positively unreal. William Hendley-Bart only started screaming when what little fat was in his lean cheeks began to melt and drip onto his jacket.

When Canning had finally mustered the strength to look up again there was no more noise and Two Berts was watching the sky like a cat tracking a fly, his head never still for more than a second. The constant motion made Canning feel sick so he decided to put his head back down for another couple of minutes. When he next arose, the sky appeared to be clear apart from a dusty trail of oil smoke that was dispersing itself among the clouds and he glanced around quickly for the other BE. Oh well, he thought, Bendley-Hart's dead. Julian made a quick mental note to have a drink for his fallen comrade and cranked his aeroplane round in an agonisingly slow turn, wincing as it put up a creaking protest at every degree, and headed back to the airfield.

Two sets of mechanics ran out to greet the lone aircraft that steadily circled the aerodrome but they quickly deduced from the piloting that only Canning had returned. Because, unless Hendley-Bart was grievously wounded, only Canning would land an aeroplane in such a fashion. The BE lurched toward the ground in an ungainly sidestep and, after several heavy hops, came to rest forty yards from the airfield boundary hedge. His mechanics were rather pleased, since Julian regularly landed in the adjoining fields, and today they had a far shorter distance to push the aircraft back to the hangars. As the machine was pulled towards the sheds, Julian let his head fall backwards against the fuselage. The BE slowed to a stop, and a team of gasping, breathless mechanics collapsed about it. Two Berts hopped down from his cockpit and stood grinning at him.

'You all intact, Canning?' he asked jovially, cuffing Julian on the shoulder.

Slowly and painfully Canning raised himself up, hooked a leg over the side of the cockpit and, with what his observer considered to be a surprising amount of grace, fell out. Two Berts and his flight sergeant hefted him onto his feet.

'Not hit are you, Sir?' Asked the NCO anxiously.

Canning shook his head briefly and pulled off his hat and goggles. The bottom half of his face was dark with a liberal coating of oil, exhaust fumes and gun-muck. As the photographic sergeant began to tinker with the camera, Canning suddenly realised that he had forgotten to take any photographs. Bollocks to it, he'd deal with that later. The senior Captain, Stuart, jogged across to him,

'What happened to Hendley-Bart, Canning?'

Julian shrugged his shoulders laconically and turned to weave his way back to the Nissen-hut, and bed.

CHAPTER 2

2nd April 1917

It was 0430 the next day when Canning finally awoke, and the entire aerodrome was shrouded in quiet darkness. A gentle snoring, emanating from one of the cots at the back of the Nissen-hut was all that broke the silence. There were six metal-framed beds, laid end to end in two rows, under the low rounded roof. The other occupants of the hut were all fast asleep when Julian slowly slid his feet out from under the covers. The cold air shocked him as it bit into his toes but he left them hanging. It had been the first time in days that he had felt anything with any intensity. He swung his bare soles to the floor and gasped audibly as they touched the freezing surface. Shivering, he sat on the edge of the bed and reached out for his flying jacket that lay in its usual crumpled heap, and threw it across his shoulders. Clamping his jaw to stop his teeth from chattering, he silently got up, eased the door handle and stepped out into the night.

Canning stood out in the field in his piebald pyjamas, which he had no recollection of donning, and hugged himself, gradually diminishing into the great leather folds of his coat. His feet sunk into the wet turf. Mud and moisture seeped in between his toes, oozing marvellously as he squeezed them together, curling them towards the balls of his feet. It was wonderful to be able to feel again. A chill, whirling wind whipped around him, pulling at his coat and making his eyes water. He stood there in the darkness, shaking with cold, feet soaked and plastered in mud, enjoying every second of discomfort, it was horribly cleansing and refreshing. The last dregs of alcohol were pushing to leave his system and, feeling utterly at one with the earth, he threw open his jacket, dropped his pyjama trousers and urinated freely. The chill of the night caused his stream to burn and steam as it flowed, and it felt fantastic. He raised his eyes to the heavens, to the gaps in the clouds that the wind had blown and saw layer upon layer of universe stacked atop one another. There was no blackness up there, it had been lifted from pitch into the darkest inkiest blues, the deepest of greens, and subtlest purples by the millions of stars that lit the up sky and promised hope. The nearest and brightest burnt with a ferocity that brought more tears to his eyes, the smallest and farthest stood regal and magnificent, untouchable in their infinity, and all the more beautiful for it. The wind twisted playfully through Julian's loose brown hair as he stood and basked in his insignificance. All seemed right in the world.

A rumble of thunder shattered the miasma. Shaken from his reverie, Canning turned towards where the sound had originated. Thunder again, and this time with an accompanying flash that outshone some of the weaker stars. Against the horizon the first imperceptible flush of dawn was creeping. Julian crashed back down to earth as the rumble of the howitzers sending the massive explosive shells designed to shatter earth and body intensified, the accompanying muzzle flash continuing to light the skyline. The whole world was at war, so Julian Canning pulled up his trousers and went back to bed.

Canning was woken later by a smiling Two Berts proffering a cup of coffee. He grunted and rolled away to face the curved tin wall. Two Berts, not easily dissuaded, persevered.

'Come on Joo-lianne, drink up, there's a good boy!' He crooned, sarcastically.

Canning turned his head and fixed his observer with an icy stare out the corner of one eye.

'Fuck off.'

'That's not very polite now, is it? And you, an officer and a gentleman! What would your mother say?'

Julian rolled towards him irritably, 'She'd tell you to fuck off too. And then charge you an extra shilling for being Welsh.'

Two Berts hooted with laughter and held out the coffee. Canning took it, spilling greasy brown drips over his bed sheets. He gulped at it, found that it was at scalding temperature and swore viciously in a spray of brown saliva. Two Berts chuckled. One day, thought Canning, he would find something to make the bloody man stop smiling.

'What time is it?' He growled.

'Thirty minutes past the eleventh hour, on the second day of our good Lord's glorious month of April.'

'Our good Lord can go and swing for a shit,' Julian muttered, puzzling over how long he had been asleep.

He had gone to bed at around 0830 the previous day and barring his early morning sojourn, had slept straight through.

'Fuck me, I've been asleep for twenty-eight hours!'

'Twenty-seven,' Two Berts cocked an eyebrow, 'The rest of the day was a washout so we didn't wake you. In fact, there was a pool going on whether or not you were dead.'

Julian made a snorty-grunting noise that was something akin to amusement.

'And since you're alive, I've made some money, although I can't help but feel that the world overall is a little poorer...'

Canning ignored his observer and tried the coffee again. This time it only stripped the taste-buds from his tongue instead of melting his teeth.

'Shame about Hendley-Bart and Callow though.' Two Berts continued.

'Who?'

'Oh sod off, you know damned well who they were, they had been here almost a month!'

Canning retrieved a brief memory of tall scorn and a smoke trail and nodded in pretence that he remembered who Bendley-Hart and the other fellow were. The former had despised him and the latter was his inconsequent lackey. He raised his head to survey the hut.

'Where are the others?'

'Flying, fighting, fulfilling their duty to King and Country.'

'Poor bastards,' he lit cigarette and proffered the open pack to Two Berts, who selected one, and lit it in turn off Canning's.

'The CO wants to see you by the way.'

'Oh shit,' Julian winced, remembering his failure to use the camera, 'Any idea what about?'

'Sounds like you've got a fair idea already,' Two Berts countered shrewdly.

'I forgot to take the bloody photos on yesterday's recce,' he blurted.

Two Berts stared at him for a couple of seconds then burst out laughing again, 'You great ass, Canning.'

Julian rapped briefly on the open door of the squadron administration office. Pouilly Yvredon aerodrome (known colloquially to all of 33B Squadron as "Pull-the-other-one") had been established in the remains of what had once been a farmstead of the same name. The landing strip was a large, flat plain of good grazing land, well suited to aviation, which was bordered by trees and light woodland scrub. It was surrounded by arable fields, heavily tilled over the years, which were far less welcoming to the BEs' spindly undercarriage legs.

The squadron office was situated in the dilapidated, flint-clad farmhouse at the corner of the airstrip. Canning tramped up the stone steps and down the corridor, pausing briefly to rap on the open door before stepping through. The office was erratically lit by a collection of light bulbs that appeared to have been installed at random intervals across the ceiling, each one dangling from a different length of flex. The small window in the far wall was black with neglect, and served only to add a token scintilla of daylight that somehow seemed unhealthy. The adjutant, Billington, whose duties were exclusively clerical, was seated at a mealy, woodworm peppered desk that had a liberal covering of paperwork, and was frowning at a sheet of brown foolscap. Piles of files and folders, many of them water damaged by the leaky ceiling, were stacked about him.

'Hello Billy, the CO wanted to see me?'

'Go straight through, he's expecting you,' replied a voice that was laced with cream teas and arsenic.

Julian scuttled past, head down, avoiding the adjutant's cobra green gaze. He knocked once upon the wooden door opposite and opened it without bothering to wait for a response.

The room was far darker than the squadron office and it took Canning a couple of seconds for his eyes adjust to the gloom. The Major had been sprawled on his bed, reading a book in the sleeping alcove that was separated from his 'office' by a small curtain. He got up quickly and paced over to his desk, slumped into his chair, and motioned for Julian to take the seat opposite.

'Ah yes, Canning,' he stared down at his yellowed fingers and ragged nails as he spoke, 'what happened with yesterday's reconnaissance?'

'Well, Sir,' began Julian, 'we were just approaching the...er... objective when a couple of Albatroses jumped us, one of the bastards, sorry Sir, Huns, dropped on us from up high as a decoy and the other attacked from below,' Julian had made Two Berts quickly fill him in on the details of the previous day's combat, 'And I'm afraid that Bendley-Hart was caught off-guard and shot down.'

'Hendley-Bart.'

'Him too, Sir.'

The furrows in the major's brow became ever so slightly more pronounced.

'And the photographs, Canning?'

Julian attempted what he hoped was a look of uncomprehending innocence.

'The photographs, Sir?'

'There weren't any, Canning,'

Julian did his best to look mortified, 'There weren't any, Sir?'

He parroted.

'No, Canning, there weren't any. Have you any…ah…any idea why?'

'Well the plates must have been spoiled, Sir, I don't remember any bullets hitting the camera…'

'The photographic sergeant informed me that none of the plates had been exposed.'

Julian persevered with a guppy-like stare. The Major sighed.

'Could it be that you…ah…forgot to take them?'

'I'm really not sure, Sir, I mean, in the heat of battle, possibly. Well obviously, *you* know what that's like, Sir.'

It was a spiteful little jab and stung the Major as Canning had intended, who began to back down, putting Julian in mind of a hermit crab scurrying back into its shell.

'Yes, well…ah…it…ah…really must not happen again, Canning…'

His voice trailed away to silence, and Major Thomas Frost, MC, DFC, DSO and Bar, lost any remaining semblance of authority. As his eyes dropped from a smirking Julian, he caught a glimpse of himself in the tarnished gilt picture frame that contained a photograph of his fiancée. In the warped reflection, he saw a face heavily lined and haunted by shadow, eyes that were bathed in darkness, and dark hair, greying at the temples. Shoulders, that at one point had been proud and squared, were now stooped and rounded. At twenty-three, he was only four years older than Canning.

The silence in the room extended as Frost continued to study his reflection in the frame. Seizing his opportunity, Julian threw a smart salute, stated with confident affirmation, 'It won't happen again, Sir,' turned on his heel and double timed it, out the office, past Billington, and towards the mess bar.

Which was where Two Berts found him shortly afterwards, with a full glass in his hand, preparing to dive into the day's first glorious whisky.

'You do know we're flying this afternoon?'

Julian, having slept through yesterday's briefing, looked

confused.

'We've got a shoot to do over Arras,' his observer continued, 'Some supply depot that wants a pasting, should be a couple of Pups topsides to look after us.'

Canning snorted derisively, fighter escorts rarely bothered to show up, they considered protecting the lumbering two-seaters too boring and would rather be off hunting Huns. Which meant they would almost certainly end up pursuing the mission alone and, since the mission was a shoot, they would be in aircraft Number 8, as it was currently the only available aeroplane with a serviceable radio fitted. Number 8 was a horrid machine, it had developed a persistent left-wing lean since Julian had flown it into a tree a couple of months ago and nothing the riggers tried seemed to fix it. And to compound matters, the weight of the radio added to what was already a rather lacklustre, engine meant that it struggled to break seventy miles an hour on a calm day. Canning hated Number 8.

'Take off in half an hour,' grinned Two Berts, walking towards the door, 'I'll show you where we're going when we get to the hangars. Oh, and we're in Number 8 by the way.'

CHAPTER 3

2nd April 1917

Two Berts was waiting by the BE as Julian stalked up in full flying kit and frowned at the faded figure eight that was painted on the fuselage.

'So, which bunch of Huns are we helping them to miss today?' He asked grumpily.

'There's a supply dump around Guemappe, ammo and barbed wire mainly, but big enough to earn the ire of our brass.' Two Berts jabbed a gauntleted finger viciously into the map that was spread out on the wing. 'Battery is the...' he paused to glance at a heavy, leather-bound notebook, 'the 20th CFA at Neuville, Canadian outfit, they're expecting us at about 1230.'

'Fat chance,' muttered Julian, whose watch was already showing 1220.

'Better get moving then,' replied Two Berts and swung himself up into his cockpit. Canning managed to clamber into his seat unaided, provoking wry smiles among the mechanics as they began to prepare Number 8 for take-off. Two Berts secured his gun, checked it, double checked it, and gave Canning a thumbs up,

'Switches off!' came the call.

'Switches off.' Julian replied irritably. The large propeller was swung slowly round.

'Contact.'

'Contact!'

True to form, Number 8 refused to even splutter on the first swing. Or the second. It let slip a slight cough on the third but by now the sucking-in process had to be repeated.

'Switches off!' came the call.

Canning sighed and shook his head, he hated Number 8. Pulling off his right gauntlet, he flicked the ignition switch and fumbled inside his coat for a second, before happily producing his hip flask.

'Contact.'

The warm liquor slid down his throat, burning wonderfully as the world became blurred at the edges and took on a familiar, comforting fuzziness.

'Contact!' He replied and the engine spluttered into life with a belch of blue exhaust.

Julian toyed with the throttle for a moment then waved away the chocks. The BE bumped forwards and rumbled toward the airstrip. The wind was strong and he could see it gusting in the canvas windsock as Number 8 turned its ugly snub nose into the face of it. His Flight-Sergeant gave a final wave to indicate the all clear and the engine rose to a somewhat tepid growl. The BE's walk broke into a trot, then a run and Julian felt the tail lift from the ground, but he waited until the engine was guttering at full strength before raising Number 8 clumsily into the sky.

The strong following wind meant that they arrived above Neuville at just after 1300 and at seven-thousand feet. Since the cloud ceiling was at ten-thousand Julian decided to stay at this height, partly from laziness and partly because the intervening patch of clear sky between the BE and the clouds could provide a valuable couple of warning seconds should anything nasty drop out. Below, he could just about discern the outlines of the four camouflaged 8-inch howitzers that made up the battery, and Two Berts reached out to fire a red flare from his Very pistol to notify the Canadians below of their arrival. Carefully, the observer replaced the signal gun back into the canvas pocket in his cockpit, his role in proceedings effectively over. From now on his duty was to constantly and painstakingly watch the skies for danger and the job of the shoot fell to Canning. Hanging over the side of his cockpit,

Julian saw a red ball of smoky light floating towards them in reply, and he turned away to find the target.

The shoot or artillery observation ('art obs') for which he had been detailed followed a standard operational procedure. Canning's BE was equipped with a basic wireless radio that could transmit signals but not receive them. The battery that he was spotting for would communicate via a series of flares, and the task of the aeroplane was to coordinate the fire of the battery's guns onto a specific objective. This was done by placing the target in the bullseye of an imaginary set of concentric rings that were spaced at hundred-yard intervals. These rings were denoted by letters, beginning with A, which was one-hundred yards from the target, B was two-hundred yards away, and so on. Direction was determined by placing a clock face on the target with 12 o'clock due north. Therefore, a shell which landed five-hundred yards away north of the bullseye would be expressed as E12, a shot three-hundred yards south south-east as C5. Julian would then transmit this information in Morse code, the battery would acknowledge receipt of the signal and the gunners make the necessary adjustments. All signals were sent three times for clarity and a triple letter G meant that that particular gun had scored a direct hit on the target and the rest of the artillery pieces were to range upon it. The same process of correction would then be repeated for every gun in the battery until each was accurately trained, at which point a triple X would signal 'fire at will.' Julian found the work boring and dangerous, throughout the shoot he had to fly continuous figure-eights over the target area to sight the exploding shells. Essentially, he was a floating target for enemy anti-aircraft guns and any passing fighters that fancied having a crack at him.

In theory, the information from the aircraft allowed for quick and effective corrections. In theory, the war was meant to have been over by 1915. In theory, Julian Canning should be dead several times over. War did not always follow theory.

Julian found it a laborious and inaccurate process, affected by gusts of wind and tired gun barrels, and, when this was coupled with his inability to properly judge distances, the process could end up taking several hours. Two Berts and Canning had once spent eight hours (returning and refuelling twice) just trying to accurately range one gun. Eventually Julian had lost patience, and the battery had ended up destroying a small forest south of Lens. Art obs was universally unpopular among the squadron, serving mostly, it seemed, to increase the airmen's contempt for their ground bound brethren, whereas many of the infantry were convinced that the Flying Corps were intentionally feeding them duff information in order to show them up. However, it seemed to both sets of participants that as long as the occasional German lost a limb, Headquarters were content to let the practice continue.

The presence of a nearly full hip flask in the inside pocket of his coat however, meant that today's shoot promised to be marginally more bearable for Canning. Potter about calling in the misses for a couple of hours, he thought, then toddle back home and plead inconsistencies in the engine to make sure he wouldn't have to return later in the afternoon. After a quick tug of scotch he proceeded to unwind the great wheel of copper wire capped with a lead plummet that acted as an aerial. He was beginning to warm up from the inside out now and the cool rush of air from the propeller backwash did nothing to disturb the cobwebs that the whisky spiders had started to spin.

His hand sought the Morse tapper and he sent out the T-test signal, three brisk dashes in quick succession, to see if the battery's own wireless was receiving him. Glancing over his shoulder, the rough leather of his coat scraping his neck, he saw a green flare in acknowledgement. A few desultory puffs of black anti-aircraft fire, scattered and wayward, told him that he had crossed the Lines and a couple of miles behind the winding mass of trenches he could see a poorly disguised collection of barbed wire and buildings, nestled among the interminable sea of brown.

'Okay then you Canuck tossers, let's see you shoot,' he muttered as he sent the triple O signal to fire.

A brief flash and a flower of smoke and dust blossomed some way short of the supply dump, prompting a snort of derision and causing him to take a quick suck from his flask. F9 – F9 – F9 he sent, not entirely sure how far short the shot had dropped but six-hundred yards seemed a good enough guess. A green light flickered briefly on his right in acknowledgement as he swung the BE round over German territory to curve through the apex of an erratic figure eight.

The next shell fell, Julian's best guess, four-hundred yards north-east and his left hand rattled out D2 – D2 – D2 on the signal button. Useless bloody Canards. Already he was bored, although at least he had now had enough whisky inside him to also feel annoyed at the potential threat to his life rather than just outright scared. As long as he was drunk enough to ignore the fear he could work, could do his job. Not very well, but at least well enough to eradicate any question of cowardice. Not that Julian Canning was a coward, he just couldn't really see a point to the fighting. He had no cause to go to war. The Germans that he was doing his level best (or at least going through the motions) to obliterate, destroy and eviscerate had never offered him personal threat or insult. He stood to gain no riches, certainly not on a 1st Lieutenant's salary, and his family were all safely ensconced in England (not that he particularly cared for them either). However, neither did he have any justification, other than to protect his soft pink body, *not* to go to war, and that was an infinitely more damning reason to wear the khaki and put a premature end to what so far, had been an unfulfilling time on earth.

Three-hundred yards east. Wankers. C3 – C3 – C3. Canning had been seventeen when war broke out. Half of those his age had dropped out of school in an attempt to join-up. Canning had not. Not until he was nineteen, and the advent of conscription made serving an inevitability, had he gone to fight. The Flying Corps had seemed a good bet though, far enough above the earth to avoid the mud and slaughter, and enough glamour to finally acquire the women that had eluded him throughout his youth and young manhood. So he had volunteered for the Flying Corps before they could process him as an infantryman. Unfortunately, all he had found had been BE2s and whores and no good reason to die. South this time, bloody hell! C6 – C6 –C6.

At least being a pilot meant that he got to be an officer though, which was good, it meant that he got to drink whisky, rather than the gut-rotting Army issue rum. And it also put some distance between him and the rank and file, who made him uncomfortable. He always felt that somehow, they were getting the better of him, without ever being quite able to pinpoint why. It was a phenomenon that those born into the upper or officer classes seemed not to notice or simply ignored but Canning, whose modest lineage boasted no patrician family or military service of mention, sensed it acutely.

He gazed dispassionately as another shell blossomed, a bit closer but still too far north. B12 – B12 – B12. Seven thousand feet below a thirty-year-old German Corporal, who had been crouched in a sentry picket when the wayward shell landed, lay screaming, clutching like a baby at the ragged, bloody stumps where his legs had been, images of his children flashing before his eyes.

Canning shook his head, Christ this was impossibly infuriating, and to cap it all the anti-aircraft fire was beginning to creep closer to him as the Huns got their eye in. The world began to swim and Julian became immersed in his routine, the constant figure-eights, and tapping on the wireless. He wasn't particularly bothered if his information was accurate and a couple of times he sent back made up results to see if it had any noticeable effect. It didn't. An hour later and work had begun on the second gun. The first howitzer had just about landed a shell on the perimeter fence, which prompted a now rather comatose Canning to rap out a relieved G – G – G along with a muttered, 'Thank fuck for that.'

Two Berts was stood up in front of him, head darting around incessantly, scouring the sky for the first signs of danger, and Julian couldn't help but stop and admire his observer's concentration for a moment, before realising that he had neglected to watch the shells and he signalled for the battery to fire again. This time the crump came just past the depot and he decided to attribute its extra length to a gust of wind and call it in as a hit. Only two to go now and a third of a tank of petrol left, he might just get them all ranged.

He signalled for the next gun with a smidgen more anticipation, which evaporated seconds later when the shell burst six-hundred yards south-west. F7 - F7 – F7... Another half an hour followed with the gunners tip-toeing around the supply dump but apparently hesitant go anywhere closer than a hundred yards. Exasperated, Canning glanced at the petrol gauge, decided he had pushed his fuel far enough, and sent the triple H that informed them he was returning home.

'Useless bastards,' he grunted, ignoring the gunners' waves as he flew over them, 'useless Canuck bastards.'

He settled lower in the cockpit as the icy wind dug into his face. He had, he reckoned, slightly more than enough petrol to get him home even with the headwind. What Canning did not know, however, was that the wind, which had been strong enough when he had taken off, was now pushing gale force. But he soon realised with alarm that the airspeed of the BE had been reduced to around forty miles an hour. Fantastic. He'd look a complete prat having to ditch in a field and would probably break his neck in the process, what a completely arse-headed way to die.

The bubble in the glass fuel gauge was resting on empty by the time the aerodrome swam into view and Julian pushed the nose down into a dive to maintain flying speed. The engine began to splutter on approach and then, just as Canning made his final preparations to land, gave a final cough and died. He saw Two Berts look round at him nervously as the big propeller slowed to a stop in front of them and Number 8 decelerated alarmingly. The aircraft actually ceased all forward momentum when it was still ten feet off the ground and flopped straight down into a crunching pancake landing.

For a couple of seconds, it stood there, groaning in protest at the treatment it had received then with a final splintering crack, the undercarriage fixture gave way and the BE slumped to the ground like a boxer falling face first onto the canvas, two of the prop blades snapping as they hit the turf. Sighing, Julian unscrewed the cap on the now nearly empty flask, grimacing at the bruising in his buttocks. How he hated Number 8.

'Ye great bollock, Canning,' Stuarts lean face was red and a small vein bulged from under the corner of his light brown hair where it was beginning to recede. 'Yee've been oot here how long? And ye manage to crack-up the only bloody aircraft wi' a working bloody radio.'

'Ran out of juice,' replied Julian laconically, lighting a cigarette, 'engine cut out on approach, lucky to be alive really…'

Stuart snorted, 'How on earth did you manage to run out o' petrol?'

'Because,' began Julian with careful deliberation, 'my dedication to God, King and Country was such that I used it all trying to get those useless bloody Canucks to shoot straight. They, I, and God's own will failed. Quite miserably too. Look on the bright side, Jimmy, now I've buggered the aeroplane you won't have to go back and teach 'em how to either.'

Stuart balled his fist in exasperation, his anger exacerbated by the alcohol fumes that wafted pungently towards him and for a second he seriously considered thumping Canning but instead waved him away despairingly and Julian stumped off to the mess bar. The damage to Number 8 was yet another problem for Captain James Stuart to deal with. It was not the first time Canning had broken an aeroplane, would certainly not be the last, and usually he would endeavour to find at least some amusement in it. But combined with yesterday evening's loss of yet another aircrew to the German Albatroses, an official complaint from the Lamaincourt gendarmerie about the behaviour of several squadron members during the last piss-up in the town, and the recent arrival of two replacement crews who had undertaken less than eight hours' solo flight, and who had apparently also yet to begin shaving, it annoyed him. It was unnecessary and would seriously impair the squadron's performance for the upcoming offensive.

The senior flight commander glared at the battered aeroplane then turned away with a sigh. His eyes scanned the sky anxiously, partly from habit and partly because one of his replacement crews should have returned from their patrol over an hour ago.

Having deposited his flying gear on his bed, Julian was making his way leisurely over to the mess, content at having survived another day. He heard the tramp of feet momentarily before his name echoed across the airstrip, called out in a voice that was parade-ground crisp.

'Lieutenant Canning!'

Julian quickened his pace.

'Mr. Canning!'

Louder this time, closer, and quite impossible to ignore. He did his best though and only stopped when a firm hand descended on his shoulder. He turned to meet short-cropped black hair shot through with silver, and a viper green stare.

'Why hello, Billy.' He smiled cheerfully, dreadfully forced, 'What's new?'

'Problems with your hearing, Canning?'

'Pardon?'

Green fire seared his retinas.

'Busy, were we, Lieutenant?'

'Well yes, as a matter of fact I did have plans…' he

answered truthfully, they mainly involved making up for being interrupted at the bar earlier.

'Nothing that can't be postponed temporarily, I'm sure. Those photos, Canning, the ones you were too...ah... preoccupied to take yesterday.'

Oh fucking hell thought Julian,

'Oh yes?' he answered.

'They need to be retaken.'

'I see.'

'By you.'

'Ah.'

'I've had your plane fuelled and a fresh set of plates sent up for the camera.'

'Oh, come off it, Billy, I've just been up for three and a half hours playing pin the bomb on the battery with the Canadians.'

'Headquarters need those prints, Canning. *You* failed to take them once so it doesn't seem fair to ask someone else to risk their life to remedy your mistakes now, does it?'

Julian thought that actually it sounded eminently fair. He shrugged.

'Put it this way, Lieutenant, the assignment is for a set of oblique photographs taken from nine-thousand feet, I can always volunteer you for a series of six-hundred feet mosaics...'

Bastard. 'I'll get my coat. Oh Billy...ah just one other thing...'

'Yes.' Billington made the word both a statement and a question.

'Whose orders are these?'

'Major Frost's, of course.'

'Of course,' he smiled politely and turned away. All the way back to the Nissen-hut he could feel twin viridian bolts boring into his back.

CHAPTER 4

2nd April 1917

Back in the hut, Canning found that Shellford, the owner of one of the beds at the back of the room, had just awoken from an afternoon snooze, and was sat up on his cot, blinking owlishly. He greeted Canning with a crooked smile.

'What cheer, young Julian?'

'What cheer yourself,' came the grumbled reply.

'My my, how the weight of the world hath piled itself upon this young aviator's shoulders, pray tell what ails thee?'

'Well for a start its four-thirty and I'm still worryingly sober, I've spent most of my day pissing about above a battery, my crotch has felt itchy ever since that last time in Lamaincourt and, now damn it there was definitely something else, oh yes, I've just got to nip off and die before dinner. So, if you'll excuse me...'

Shellford chortled and smoothed his tousled, wispy hair, which was thinning to the point of baldness, before raising himself off his bed. Drawn to his full height, he towered over Canning, although looking up at him, Julian reckoned that they must have weighed about the same.

At twenty-seven, Shellford was on the old side for a pilot and the laughter lines around his eyes crinkled as he cracked an enormous yawn, 'And for what noble cause must you lay down your life in sacrifice?' he drawled.

'I've got to retake some photos.'

'Didn't come out first time?'

'Didn't take 'em first time.'

'Ah yes, I recall young Albert mentioning something of the sort at lunch. Bad ones?'

'Just a couple of line shots.'

'Shouldn't be too hairy then, Jerry's not quite so adventurous these days, rarely comes within three miles of our side.'

'He was there the other day,' Canning replied, recollections of a fading smoke trail flashing across his mind. 'Bollocks to it all. Where's Two Berts?'

'Follow the sound of distressed sheep, dear boy.'

'Hah, I thought they enjoyed it.'

'And that, in a nutshell, is your problem. You struggle to make the distinction between pleasure and discomfort, it's why you've got the pox.'

'Piss off. And it's an itch not the pox,' he made to leave.

'Oh, before I forget, a few of us are heading over to 240 Squadron tonight, bit of a piss-up to welcome them to the war if you fancy it? They're a new lot so they probably haven't heard of you.'

Julian hesitated for a moment, 'Maybe, if I'm back in time, I'm still trying to keep a low profile after erm…'

'Quite understand, old boy.'

The 'erm' to which Canning was referring had occurred at the beginning of February, when a group of 33B squadron officers had paid a visit to 242 Squadron, who flew Nieuport scouts. Julian had been grumpy from the outset, since he felt that the fighter pilots had more in common with their German counterparts than with the British two-seater crews who they were tasked with protecting. The fact that his escort had failed to turn up for his morning shoot had only served to salt his irritation. The evening had started well enough though, the 242 squadron pilots seemed a decent bunch and, more importantly, the alcohol was plentiful. There was, however, one particular Captain who had shot down sixteen German aircraft and was, to say the least, rather pleased about it. Throughout the course of the pre-dinner boozing he managed to irritate most of the BE squadron, especially the observers, as he constantly harped on about the importance and simplicity of straight, effective shooting. Stuart's observer, Marshall, had attempted to impress upon him the myriad problems that came with trying to fire a machine gun at a faster, more manoeuvrable opponent, whilst cloistered deep between a working propeller, airframe and pilot, all of which he considered essential to remaining airborne. The Captain had merely shrugged off this argument and expressed his certainty that his methods were infinitely transferable to all forms of air combat.

Canning had taken particular umbrage to the man's moustache. He had obviously tried to cultivate one of the thin styles that ran low across the top lip, but on the upper part, especially around the nostrils, several rogue hairs had escaped the razor and poked through like wiry shoots. And the more Julian drank, the more he was convinced that these hairs were talking about him behind his back. The real problems began shortly after dinner was served. The Major of 242 Squadron was an old Indian cavalry hand and had a particular fancy for the strong spices that were used in the colonies to disguise the taste of week-old meat that had been left out in the sun. These dishes were known to play havoc with the bowels, and the fighter pilots, who already suffered similar effects from the fumes of burnt castor oil that was used to lubricate the Nieuport's rotary engine, were happily convinced that the combination of the two meant that, by the time the dawn patrol was ready to take off, there was quite simply 'nothing left to worry about.' Unfortunately, several of the BE men, who were unused to this diet, became less than constant as the evening wore on.

The situation came to a head when Canning, who had surpassed even his own normally high standards of inebriation, began to feel decidedly loose. Stomach bubbling, and searching desperately for a latrine, he had been forced to settle for a small, dark, secluded space, taken a general aim, and liberally sprayed the surrounding area. Twenty minutes later, the 'ace' Captain, who had gone to his room to fetch the Iron Cross acquired from the corpse of one of his victims, returned in a state of animation to report that his wardrobe and its contents had been thoroughly befouled. The culprit might have remained anonymous if Canning had not been found passed out ten feet along the corridor, with his trousers round his ankles. Naturally the Captain was less than impressed and was only narrowly persuaded against calling Julian out in a duel. The tale spread from squadron to squadron and Canning had found himself barred from several successive guest nights. Consequently, Shellford quite understood Canning's reticence to venture out to other squadrons. Even when they permitted him to attend, they now always seemed to keep the wine bottles out of his reach on the table. He smiled a sympathetic farewell as Julian shrugged on his coat and lumbered out the door toward his aeroplane.

Half an hour later, as the tender carrying the men bound for dinner with 240 Squadron pulled away, Canning and Two Berts were sat miserably in their cockpits, as the BE's engine refused to start. There was a new and unappreciated chill in the air, and Julian, who had polished off what little was left of his hip flask some time ago, was feeling it through his heavy flying clothes. Sinister, angry clouds had blackened up above them and, in a matter of minutes, it would be too dark for the plates to expose properly. He heaved himself from his seat and leant forwards, about to shout into Two Bert's leather clad ear, when his face was struck by a couple of heavy, wet droplets.

'Well that settles it,' he muttered bitterly, then more loudly, 'Two Berts! Washout! I don't mind the shrapnel but I'm not catching a bloody cold.'

* * *

The snow came fast that evening, not falling, but blown in, dancing and cascading on the wind. Great swirling eddies chased each other in the dusky twilight, hurtling pell mell in a manic dogfight. Innumerable, nameless flakes, each one utterly unique, plunged to earth, a brief, fleeting moment of consciousness that flickered in the evening light, before diving down to disappear into the mud. It settled into the pits and ruts of the airstrip and became dirtied by the ground, and soon the roofs of the huts and hangers, were encrusted in a crunchy layer of slush. It piled up against the mess windows, spattered on the glass panes and dribbled away leaving watery snail-trails. The impression created was one of a painting half-finished, an artist who had tired of creating a winter tableau, and abandoned their canvas mid-stroke.

Canning belched loudly from his tenth whisky and decided to try and orchestrate a snowball fight. The apparent lack of enthusiasm from his fellow officers irked him, and he stormed out of the mess to return spotted with white and carrying two handfuls of slurpy, muddy snow, which he proceeded to heave at the occupants of the room. The first clump hit one of the new replacement officers who, terrified at having any attention drawn to him, pretended that nothing had happened and huddled down further in his chair, icy water dripping into his ear. Two Berts had casually ducked the second, which had splattered harmlessly on the wall behind him. The absence of most of the squadron regulars, and the digestive effects produced by a somewhat pallid dinner of mutton and horribly undercooked potatoes meant that Canning's brief fusillade failed to rouse a reaction, and he marched off to the bar with a grunted, 'Bugger the lot of you then.'

Stuart had briefly peered up from his paperwork to exchange a knowing glance with Two Berts, before returning to hunch over an old school desk, brow furrowed, scratching out the next day's assignments. The flight commander had been too busy doing Major Frost's job to go out drinking that evening, but he was the one, thought Two Berts, who was keeping the squadron running. He greeted the new boys as an older brother, helped them settle in, and then sent them to die. He was a friend to the old hands, drank with them, laughed with them, and then sent them off to die alongside the new men.

But unlike Frost, Stuart climbed into his own machine every day, and faced it all with them.

Right now, the Captain was buried his papers, and Two Berts glanced around the room as he sipped on his whisky. 33B Squadron mess was a sorry affair, shabby and dirty with a rundown feeling. The building was long and low, and had originally been the stable block. The occasional piece of paper, dirty smear or black and white photo (an unusual collection of aerial photographs and scantily clad women) were all that adorned the white-washed stone walls. There were no chunks of defeated enemy aircraft that the fighter squadrons plastered about their messrooms in medieval delight, although the more experienced officers reckoned that the squadron had lost enough aeroplanes to provide wallpaper for half the German Air Force. There was a small bar at the far end that operated by honesty ledger, which sat atop a dirty and ring marked counter, stocked only with whisky and brandy (the whisky being slightly more drinkable). On the rare occasions beer was obtained, it disappeared all too quickly. The rest of the space was taken up by a hotchpotch selection of furniture. Tables of varying heights, that collectively averaged three and a half legs each, and a menagerie of chairs, ranging from the wing backed, leather smoking chair, that Two Berts was currently occupying, to a couple of deckchairs and a floral sofa. Dinner was eaten by pushing the tables together and trying to match their respective heights to a suitable chair.

However, the sheer dilapidation of the place gave it an almost comforting atmosphere that somehow complemented its role as an ante-room to death. A home to the short repose before the final flight, which had seen it host countless drunken evenings, fuelled by forced jollity and desperate denial. Tonight though, with half the squadron absent and the howling of the wind, it took on an atmosphere of gaunt emptiness. In a crowded room death could be sung about and drunk away, but tonight the silence of the mess drowned out any noise they made, and the reality of their situation sat in every empty chair and mocked them.

For Julian, it stopped the alcohol from working its normal spell, and his warm cushion against the world was replaced by an edginess, a skittish feeling that dragged his mind into a multitude of different places at once. He was leaning against a wall wondering whether to take another couple of whiskeys to try and break the feeling or collapse into bed, when the door by the bar opened and Billington entered, followed by Major Frost. Everyone in the room stayed seated, including the replacements, until Billington hissed, 'ten – shun!' and the men began to get wearily to their feet. Julian turned round and tried to fix his eyes upon the two new entrants. Stuart put down his pen, but stayed in his chair.

'Ah...er...good evening, gentlemen,' began Frost haltingly. Behind him Billington was somehow managing to glare at each of the seven officers simultaneously.

'I...er...hope you all enjoyed your dinner.'

A snort from Two Berts provoked a stare of renewed intensity from the adjutant.

'Anyway, as you...ah...may have noticed the weather has... er...taken a turn for the...ah...worse.'

Stuart rolled his eyes.

'As a result of this, we've just received notification that those officers who have travelled to...ah...242 Squadron for the evening are now...ah...unable to make it back. Many of them were detailed for the early show tomorrow so this means that...ah...er...'

Frost trailed off into silence and his eyes dropped to the floor. Stuart's face creased into a sneer as he watched Frost's long fingers twitch at the frayed ends of the stitching in the leather binder he was holding.

Stuart knew that binder only too well, it was old and faded, crossed with scratches from its long use, and had belonged to Frost's predecessor, Major Bartholomew Rope. Rope had been a career soldier, serving with a cavalry regiment when the war broke out. The Army had needed to do something with him once it became apparent that horse mounted infantry was going to be of limited use in this particular conflict, as lots of them kept getting shot. Rope had subsequently been assigned to the Flying Corps on the basis that lots of people seemed to get shot there too.

It had been sitting on Rope's desk in July 1916 when he had given Frost and Stuart an official reprimand for their persistent and vocal criticism of the squadron's tactics and equipment. At the time, the two flight leaders had been piloting the same BE2s that the squadron still operated now.

Rope had carried that same folder for months after, until one of the more choleric staff Majors at Wing Headquarters had died of a coronary whilst trying to tackle two young French prostitutes simultaneously. At the funeral, where the Major was accorded full military honours and an extended eulogy, the Wing's Lieutenant Colonel had offered Rope the newly vacant Headquarters role on the basis that 33B squadron had been losing more men than any of his other units, and so they must have been trying the hardest. And now Frost, who had been excused from active flying duties when he accepted his promotion to Major, cradled the same battered binder in his arms as he failed to deliver the evening's orders.

As the silence swelled, Billington's voice cut harshly across the room, 'What the Major means to say gentlemen is that those of you who are present now will have to cover the operations detailed to be completed by those officers now stranded at 240 squadron. So, the reconnaissance of the German rear positions 19 and 31 at Vimy will now be led by Captain Stuart, one of you…er…new men will act as observer, and two of you in the second aircraft. Sort it out amongst yourselves.

'Lieutenants Canning and Burton,' he paused to pass a caustic eye over Julian who was trying desperately to stop the wall he was hugging from swaying dangerously. 'Will carry out artillery observation over sector 7D, the target is a German field battery known to be operating in the area. Both flights will take off at 0530.'

'Billy,' broke in Stuart, the normally imperceptible Scots accent rising with his anger, 'have ye' looked out the window lately? Its bloody snowing, there's no way we'll get up in the morning. I've already amended the assignments.'

Billington's bright green eyes met Stuart's cool blue gaze across the mess with a crackle of energy. The four replacement officers slunk back against the walls.

'Captain Stuart, I would have thought you were the last person who needed reminding of the importance of our current work to the Allied forces operating in this sector, if there is the slightest chance that these missions are able to be flown tomorrow then you will all be ready to take advantage of it. Now, I believe that is all, Major?'

He turned his face to Frost without actually looking at him.

'Excellent then. Gentlemen dis-' he was cut off by two loud bangs that occurred almost simultaneously. One was Stuart slamming the door at the other end of the mess on his way out. The other was Canning pitching forwards over the legless sofa and landing unconscious at the feet of Frost and Billington.

CHAPTER 5

3rd April 1917

His eyes opened to the gentle purr of voices in the darkness outside the hut. He was still fully clothed and lying on top of the sheets where Two Berts had unceremoniously dumped him last night.

'No, leave Mr Burton and Mr Canning to sleep, we won't be getting off the ground anytime soon, certainly not before midday. Oh, and if you could let the new lads know that they won't be flying either, I think I saw them heading to breakfast. Probably couldn't sleep.'

'Of course, Captain Stuart.'

'Thank you, Rossiter.'

Julian rolled over and smiled. The previous night's whisky was starting to exact its revenge at the back of his brain, but now Stuart had dismissed the steward, he could simply sleep through it. He lolled over the side of his bed and his hand brushed against something cold and hard. His left eye crept open and peered over the side of the mattress in trepidation. A metal tankard filled with water sat near the head of the bed and a couple of headache powders in a paper sachet perched next to it.

'God bless you, Two Berts,' he muttered and poured the powders into the tankard, downed half of it in three huge gulps, then turned back over and went to sleep.

He awoke several hours later to find that the room was empty. Two Berts had left his bed unmade and everyone else was apparently still stranded at 240 squadron. Normally, the seemingly endless cycle of losses and replacements led to ever changing bedfellows, so Julian and his hutmates were relatively unique in being considered old hands. All five of them were in A Flight under Stuart, with Shellford as second in command. Up until recently, his observer, Falconer, had occupied the sixth bed that currently lay unused, but he had succumbed to a bout of dysentery followed by pneumonia, after making too many midnight dashes to the latrine. Whilst the rest of the hut had been sorry to lose him, they were all rather relieved at the marked improvement in air quality. Although Shellford swore that he still caught the occasional whiff of dung hanging around Falconer's cot, as if it were being haunted by a particularly noxious ghost.

Webb and Connolly who occupied the middle two bunks, had joined together as a flying pair at the beginning of January, and had fast become one of the squadron's most effective pilot-observer teams. They were also lovers, although, other than Canning, none of the rest of the squadron had noticed. This was partly because they were very careful about it, being well aware of the regulations and penalties if they were discovered. And partly because such stalwart fighting chaps as Webb and Connelly just didn't fit the official expectations of homosexuals. Canning however, possessing no expectations of himself, assumed nothing of his peers. He simply saw what was there, rather than what others believed should be there. He knew that half of those wearing medal ribbons didn't deserve them, and the half that did were just lucky to have survived, and lucky that their deeds had been noticed. Most of the men who had really earned the right to pin the cheap, mass cut and pressed metal tablets onto their chests were now mere detritus, compost for the fields which were churned into infertility on a daily basis by thousands of artillery pieces. Julian understood all of this and couldn't have given a shit less about any of it. Nor did he care about Webb and Connolly. Whether it was just a marriage of convenience, as so many relationships appeared to be anyway, he did not know. He simply followed the same principles that he applied to any sexual encounters which didn't involve him. Namely that, so long as he wasn't troubled by any rogue fluids, people could do whatever the bloody hell they liked.

Pulling on a fresh pair of someone else's socks, Canning glanced out the window. He thought that the sky didn't look quite as angry as yesterday, but it was still not the kind of sky one would seek to trouble in a pub. It was menacing, frowning at him with stern grey warnings of things to come. But it was the wind that was making flying pretty much impossible, the trees were seemingly clinging to the ground for dear life and the windsock was doing its utmost to break free from the pole to which it was tethered. Having missed breakfast, Julian had decided to head over to the mess to badger one of the stewards into making him an early lunch, when a horrid premonition seized him. He sensed the door to the farmhouse opening a couple of seconds before the wooden planks actually scraped inwards, and Billington emerged, moving quickly down the stone steps. Despite being in his mid-fifties, the adjutant moved with an athleticism that belied his age and the limp from the wound that had seen him pensioned off during the Boer War was barely discernible, as he cut across Julian's path.

'Lieutenant Canning!'

There was no chance of avoiding him this time.

'Morning, Billy! Lovely day, what?' He shouted into the wind.

'No, it isn't. And neither is it morning anymore. What happened to my photos, Canning?'

'*Whose* photos?'

'The ones that you were ordered to take yesterday.'

'My plane broke.'

'Why didn't you borrow someone else's?'

'Because it would have been bloody rude to take one without asking, you know what the others think about my flying...'

'Then I suggest you have another try. Now.'

'Now? Right now?! Have you seen the sky lately? Its right above us as usual, the cloud ceiling can't be more than fifteen-hundred.'

'Then from that height you should be able to provide me with some *excellent* quality photographs.'

The fake, fixed smile fell from Julian's face.

'Bugger that, Billington, you can take a running jump at an airscrew if you think for a second that I'm flying in this shit. Its blowing a bloody gale.'

Slowly and unhurriedly, Billington levelled his gaze directly at Julian.

'Lieutenant Canning, if you are *refusing* to obey orders then there are steps which can be taken...'

'I'm not refusing, the laws of bloody physics are.'

Out the corner of his eye he could see the mechanics struggling to pull his aircraft out of the wind buffeted hangar. Billington smiled.

'Mr. Burton will join you shortly.'

Twenty minute later, Julian was sitting in the cockpit of his BE, distinctly unimpressed. The mechanics had got the engine running and Two Berts had clambered up in front of him. The wind was gusting heavily, singing through the flying wires.

Two Berts turned around to face him, 'This is bloody stupid,' he hollered.

Canning shrugged his heavy, leather-clad shoulders. He hadn't had a drink yet and his nerves were in the pit of his stomach. Without alcohol to censor the sensation of time and place, the thought that in a mere two hours' time he may utterly cease to exist weighed heavily on his mind.

In fact, the sheer strength of the wind meant that he could quite easily be killed just taking off. And it was this initially somewhat dispiriting thought that provoked a tiny flicker in the corner of his brain. True, a pile-up at full take-off speed could well prove nasty, but a gentle four or five-foot drop at zero momentum would be unlikely to harm anything except the aircraft, maybe even keep it out of action for tomorrow... He quickly tried to dismiss the notion from his mind, he had never intentionally crashed an aeroplane before, it was too damned dangerous. Still, the idea would not go away, it would even be fairly safe. Probably.

What happened next Julian, even in his own mind, was never able to completely reconcile. Counsel for the defence would state that the BE was at its designated take-off speed when the pilot instinctively pulled back on the controls only to be caught off guard by the sheer ferocity of the headwind. The prosecution would argue that an officer of Canning's experience should have realised that the extremity of the conditions, coupled with the soft ground, would necessitate a greater velocity in order to facilitate a successful take-off. In truth, he never made a conscious decision to pull back on the control column early, but then again, he never explicitly decided not to either. Regardless, the result was that the BE staggered off the ground only to hit what appeared to be an invisible wall travelling very fast in the opposite direction. Its airspeed died instantly and its nose tipped gently forwards as it flopped to the ground from a height of no more than ten feet and fell forwards onto its nose, tail cocked high. The heavy wooden propeller blades tore great gashes in the moist earth, throwing up a shower of dirt, before snapping and splintering, as Julian hurriedly turned off the engine. Carefully, Canning and Two Berts descended from their cockpits that were now rather higher off the ground than usual. Pursuing his earlier train of thought, Julian considered dropping down in an attempt to break a leg but quickly decided not to, on account that it would probably hurt. The two airmen stood back and eyed the BE critically.

Two Berts placed his hands on his hips, 'I said it was bloody stupid.'

Julian pulled the leather helmet from his head, leaving his hair greasy and tousled. He looked at Two Berts and raised his eyebrows in reply. Tiny snowflakes had begun to fall and the two men started to trudge clumsily back to the hangars, ignoring the mechanics who scurried past to recover the forlorn looking aeroplane.

'Still,' Julian paused to cough as they turned towards their quarters, 'It's probably for the best, it would have been bloody cold up there.'
He turned around to throw a cheerful wave towards the tall, lean figure watching them from the door of the squadron office.

* * *

The tender carrying the stranded members of the squadron finally arrived back at the airfield in the early afternoon to find the squadron grounded for the rest of the day after Canning's midday mishap. The grounding, according to most of the weather reports, would likely remain for the rest of tomorrow, and certainly for the morning. This only served to improve the mood as it meant that, at least for the immediate future, everyone was much less likely to die, and the absence of any dawn action decreed a night out in Lamaincourt.

As senior flight commander, Stuart had readily approved the base leave. Recent operations had been taking an increasingly bloody toll upon the aircrews and in his experience, whilst men were fighting and dying, they were usually quite preoccupied. However, during periods of inaction, they have time to think, and, more often than not, they thought about the fighting and dying they had just done and the fighting and dying that they will have to do. All of which makes them rather tense and, although he never openly expressed this rationale, he had agreed that a night out would allow the squadron to let off some steam in the town's bars and brothels, and avoid another night of mess food.

The intervening hours were spent in grooming and preparation, and whilst ready access to Lamaincourt's prostitutes meant that gratification was all but guaranteed, most of the officers felt that it was a little less sordid if one at least tried to make an effort for them. In Canning's hut, boots were being polished, uniforms brushed, buckles buffed, hair combed, teeth cleaned, fingernails trimmed, blackheads squeezed and smiles practiced. Julian lay on his bed watching all of this in amusement. Shellford was engrossed with attempting to disguise his receding hairline and Two Berts was searching frantically for a clean pair of socks. Webb and Connolly were fussing over each other like a pair of teenage sisters. Julian gave a derisive snort.

'You idiots do realise that as long as you've got some Francs you'll get a shag, regardless of how ridiculous you look.'

Webb turned around, 'Piss off, you scruffy bastard.'

'Aye, the least you could do is have a wash man, I can smell you from here. Hell, I can smell you when I'm in the bloody aeroplane, and I sit upwind!' Chimed in Two Berts.

'Yes, for Christ's sake old boy, you've got to have a shave,' Shellford weighed in, staring in horror at Canning's four days of scrub beard. Julian eyed them all individually, he liked having the whole room against him.

'Fuck that, I have enough money for a decent meal, a couple of bottles of rough wine and enough change left for one of the cleaner whores.'

'Not that she'll be clean after you've finished,' murmured Shellford.

Canning shot him a filthy look and Webb stepped between them, blonde locks flopping.

'Really though, Canning, the least you could do is stand in the rain for ten minutes, you are becoming a touch ripe.'

Julian remained steadfastly on his bed, head propped up on an elbow, daring him to try. Webb looked to Two Berts in desperation. *Soon,* mouthed the Welshman with a wink.

He shook his head in resignation, 'If she's got any sense she'll charge you a surplus for looking like a vagrant.'

Julian grinned at him as Webb returned to fiddling with Connelly's collar.

'Well I'm done.' Announced Shellford, his carefully positioned hair springing back up even as he spoke, 'And if

Canning's not even going to attempt to make himself look even slightly less disgraceful, I suppose we should go for a swift couple before we leave, I'll see you boys in the mess.'
Julian swung his legs to the floor and followed him out while the others continued to preen and polish.

The squadron's communal transport was an aging Crossley tender, which had been found abandoned on the road that lead to the airfield, recovered, repaired and pressed reluctantly back into service. The Crossley was a four-wheeled general purpose vehicle with the engine and driver's cabin up front and a flatbed rear for carrying men and machinery (the optional canvas cover had long since been discarded). Including the driver, it could carry up to ten men. On paper 33B squadron could field fifteen fully crewed BE2s in two flights, which equalled thirty aircrew, although in reality it was lucky if the number of aircraft ever rose above ten, the steady drain on men and machines was compounded by material delays and procrastination over their replacement. However, it was still very rare for less than fifteen squadron members to pile into the Crossley, hanging off the running boards and perched precariously on the bonnet, clinging on desperately to the lurching, rattling vehicle as Stuart hurled it down the French country lanes at breakneck speed. They had once been stopped by the Military Police, who had suggested to them that what they were doing might be considered dangerous. The MPs had been rather brusquely informed what the occupants of the tender normally did for a living, and then kindly asked to mind their own bloody business. Remarkably only one person had ever been injured, when a couple of months ago a rookie pilot had been flung from the roof of the driver's cabin and sent home after suffering multiple breakages to his arm. Since then, there was always a rush to occupy this prized position.

Bottles of disgusting brandy were being passed among the occupants, and above the sound of the misfiring engine and the howls of the wind, sporadic bursts of laughter could be heard as the airmen began what would be a long night of drinking. In the back of the vehicle, Webb cursed loudly as a particularly cavernous pothole sent the neck of the bottle jarring into his mouth, chipping a tooth. To combat the sudden sharp stab of pain, he promptly downed a good half of the remaining liquor, before dry retching with a throaty rasp.

The newest replacement pilot assigned to A Flight, Ripley, sat wedged uncomfortably between Canning and Shellford, horribly awkward and repeatedly passing on the brandy. It was the first time the more experienced crews had really acknowledged the new men in their flight. Webb and Connolly were both talking to his observer, Fuller, who seemed a little more at ease with the attention, whereas Shellford had been delighted to find that Ripley still believed in the goodness of England, the war, and the world in general. With a knowing glance, he grinned at Canning and set about re-educating the young 2nd Lieutenant.

'The trick is to make sure that they're not poxed up,' he shouted over the noise of the tender, 'they need to be wet but if it's greenish at all then let 'em alone. But make sure to take a closer look at any rashes before passing on a looker, sometimes it's just a friction burn, you won't be their first tonight.'

The new pilot looked horrified, his brain struggling to process the multiple outrages as Shellford grinned happily back at him

'But...but you're...married, aren't you?' Ripley stammered, his eyes sliding to Shellford's ring finger.

'Certainly.'

'Well doesn't it, that, I mean to say...does it bother you?'

'No.'

'But, what...your wife...I mean...'

'She's not the one being shot at on a daily basis is she? If she was, then I probably wouldn't object to her seeking out the gamekeeper for the occasional rogering herself. Besides, tupping some cheap French baggage is eternally different to marital relations.'

'I don't see how it's any different whatsoever,' came the haughty reply.

'Well, there's none of that emotional rot, not with a whore. No talking, well not much. No gifts or compliments, just in, out, and rinse it off in the sink. And you must *never* fall asleep with them afterwards, very important that, at best you'll wake up naked and penniless in an alley. Oh, and I would never, ever, acknowledge any children that I may or may not have been responsible for. It is, therefore, entirely different to marriage,' he caught Julian's eye and winked, 'You're not married are you, Rip?

'No...'

'But there is a...er...special someone?' The trace of amusement that laced Shellford's words immediately put Ripley on the defensive.

'No...I mean...what? It's none of your business frankly!'

'Aha! A sweetheart,' Julian took over, 'Childhood affection, I'd guess. So, have you tumbled her yet, Rip? Wet your bayonet?'

'I...'

'Have you served it up to her, dear boy?' Pressed Shellford.

'Oh now really...I ...this is not...'

'You have done it before though?' Broke in Julian with a flash of inspiration, and at the same time recalling with relief that no-one had discovered that he was a virgin when he'd first joined the squadron.

'Of course, yes, definitely.'

A slow smile spread across Shellford's face as the tender rumbled on.

'I do believe that tonight will be a watershed moment for you, Mr. Ripley! Tonight, you shall accompany myself and Mr. Canning to a house of ill repute and there, my boy, you shall fire your first shots of the campaign,' He chuckled, 'Hey Webb, Connolly, tonight will be young Ripley here's coming of age.'

'Looks as if his Lordship has plans for you,' leered Connelly, suggestively and Webb raised the brandy bottle in salute to him.

Ripley shifted uncomfortably, trying not to meet the eyes of the other men grinning back at him, and blushed a deep, heavy red.

By the time the meal had finished, everyone was too drunk to do anything but throw a handful of notes at the restaurant owner and move on to the bars and cafes that lined the main street. Here the group started to fracture, Stuart headed off to a pre-arranged rendezvous with a nurse he was currently courting, whilst Webb and Connelly disappeared on the walk between bars, although nobody noticed them go. Armitage St Clare, the languid aristocrat who commanded B Flight, had made his excuses at dinner, and strolled off to spend the evening with what he viewed as more deserving company, and spend his money on a slightly less world-weary whore. Shellford, on the other hand, felt it far more dignified to turn down the luxuries and pretensions that were easily within his means, and besides, he had found that the cheaper girls were usually more fun.

After being turfed out of the fourth bar, the remaining members of 33B squadron that could still walk, barrelled up to the heavy, ornate door of a large town house with a faded white façade. A shabby sign hung outside, with *Le Flamant Bleu* painted in peeling copperplate, along with a cartoon of the eponymous blue bird, sporting a top hat, an overtly phallic beak and a knowing look. Shellford had his arm around Ripley's shoulders, half dragging him through the doorway. Ripley had the look of a choirboy being led off to hell by the devil. A monstrously fat Madame bustled out from the bar area to greet them. With their lolling, leering tongues, the rolling mall of officers put her in mind of a pack of hyenas, but it had been a quiet night and she was glad of the business.

'Bonsoir, Messieurs les aviateurs,' she beamed, noting the wings on their uniforms, jowls wobbling.

'Bonsoir, Madame,' Shellford replied with a smile that sober, would have been charming, but after two bottles of *vin de table* and eight whiskeys was actually quite threatening, 'Les mademoiselles?'

'Mais naturellement m'sieurs. Thees way pleez.'

The squadron followed her as she waddled through into a large, dimly lit bar room where a grubby, grimy chandelier hung low from the ceiling, large pieces of ornate crystal missing in several places. A motley collection of sofas and chaise-lounges were occupied by a motley collection of servicemen and young women, whose attire ranged between tarnished and ludicrous. The carpet, which must originally have been a rich, deep burgundy, and patterned by a complex Nineteenth Century design, was now just splotched and faded, its pile worn thin by a thousand jack boots. Oil lamps cast a slick, lurid light that threw dancing shadows onto a brown stained ceiling and, mercifully, kept most of the room plunged in purple shadow.

Marshall, who was Stuart's regular observer, was first in and boorishly drunk. He didn't even bother to buy a drink and simply grabbed the nearest mademoiselle by the arm and proceeded to drag her out the room and up the stairs, followed by raucous cheers from the rest of the squadron. Shellford led Ripley gently to the bar, like he was guiding a son, bought him a drink, walked him over to one of the sofas and sat down next to him. Julian slumped down the other side, whisky in hand. Coulter, one of the recent B Flight replacements, paused to neck a swift brandy then followed Marshall's example by grabbing the nearest woman, an older, more motherly figure with red hair, and running out the door with her. Not like Marshall, in a fit of alcohol fuelled braggadocio, but almost as if he were jumping from the high dive for the very first time. Shellford chuckled at the sight of it and cast an expert eye over the remaining women. Marshall, he reckoned, had got lucky with his choice, the remaining options looked far from fresh. A blonde, who was probably only eighteen but already looked at least fifteen years older and whose breasts hung heavily in a patched evening dress, was standing at the bar next to another courtesan, who, even with a skinful of whisky, clearly had one leg shorter than the other (or longer, mused Shellford, it depended upon how one looked at these things).

He saw Stampe, another member of B Flight, seated across the other side of the room, motion towards the blonde girl, nod approvingly and she led him away. Then Shellford noticed a new who put him in mind of a frightened rabbit, with mousy blonde hair who was trying to blend into the wallpaper. She did absolutely nothing for Shellford, who, when all was said and done, liked his companions to be a professional, and not a scared young girl. But he reckoned she was ideally suited to his purpose.

'There's one for you, Rip,' he nudged Ripley who appeared to be frozen in a state of shock, 'Probably as nervous as you are.'
Ripley didn't reply.

'C'mon, Rip,' chimed in Canning on his left, 'time is tail-gap.'
Ripley continued to sit stock-still.

Canning grinned at Shellford, 'Or would you like your Uncle Julian to decide for you?'
He motioned toward the mousy haired girl who approached timidly.

'Now, young Ripley, we have before us an example of the female form, please allow myself and Mr. Shellford to guide you through the process of decision making that leads to a successful purchase.

First of all, note the haunches,' he span the girl around and indicated her thighs and buttocks, 'robust and well made with little discolouration, indicative of good stock and good health.'

'Teeth,' continued Shellford, picking up the baton, turning the bewildered girl around again. 'Observe a nearly full set in good condition, always make sure of good teeth or, failing that, no teeth, trust me, broken or chipped and it's like the devil himself is playing on your pipe.'
The glaze was beginning to slowly lift from Ripley's eyes as he began to realise exactly where he was.

Marshall's lady had reappeared, looking remarkably

unflustered after his attentions. Shellford, surprised to see her back so soon, beckoned her over impressed. He reckoned that with the amount Marshall had drunk it would have taken an age to coax the gunner's gunner to action.

'Mon ami?' he questioned.

'Il dorme,' came the grinned reply.

Shellford smiled and took her hand, 'Well, I reckon I'd better have a crack then, don't you? Would you be so kind as to finalise Mr. Ripley's arrangements?' he asked Canning, and disappeared upstairs.

Julian watched him go then turned back round to see Ripley gazing dreamily at the mousy-haired girl, mouth agape.

'I think you've got a sale there, *Cherie*,' he told the bemused prostitute, who was looking almost embarrassed at Ripley's staring, and giving the young pilot a hearty shove, motioned for the girl to get on with it. Tenderly, she took Ripley's small white hand and led him from the room. Feeling rather pleased with his evening's work, Canning decided to reward himself with some company of his own. He began to survey the room, but other than the girl with the uneven legs, it had been depleted of its female presence.

'A couple of swift ones'll straighten you out,' he muttered and got up from his seat. Russell from B Flight had apparently had the same idea and, approaching from the left, looked as if he might get there first until Julian lent into him with his shoulder, caught him off balance and knocked him stumbling into a French officer who was carrying a round of brimming glasses. Drinks were spilled and angry words exchanged as Canning grabbed the girl by the crook of her arm and swept her off to the bar. A smile spread across her face as her suitor held up two fingers and ordered 'cognac.' It quickly fell away again as the scruffy looking Englishman immediately drained both glasses. She saw him note her disappointment, grin (*batârd*), then order another two drinks.

This time one of them was pressed into her hand and Canning led her back to where he had been sat. Julian was now stinkingly drunk, far too drunk to be able to focus properly on the girl's face, but still sentient enough to realise that this was probably a good thing. He dropped back onto the sofa and pulled the prostitute onto his lap, pleased how much less obviously lop-sided she was sitting down. Fifteen minutes of broken and impenetrable French conversation later however, and Julian was becoming increasingly irritated. The girl was already trying to tease money from him before they had got anywhere near a bedroom and Canning eyed his avaricious partner with distaste. Experience had taught him that money up front was no guarantee of later, greater adventures down below, and he wasn't convinced that his current companion was worth the gamble. And when she continued to slide her chipped fingernails towards a bulge in his trousers that was clearly a roll of Franc notes, he snapped and stood up sharply, casting her off the sofa and onto the floor.

'Mademoiselle, vous et un...,' he scrabbled through a haze of liquor for the right French and gave up, 'vous et un bloody mess,' he finished and turned on his heel, leaving his shocked paramour spread-eagled on the carpet.

He marched back to the bar and pointed at a bottle. The barman looked at him in surprise.

'Vous n'est pas avec Josephine, m'sieur?'

'No, Josephine is a greedy, poxed-up frog-whore,' he smiled back.

The barman poured him a glass of whisky, uncomprehendingly.

'Non, Monsieur, la bottle!' Julian rapped, startling the barman who timidly proffered the bottle in surprise. Canning snatched it from him, swigged heavily, and then threw a handful of paper notes and coinage onto the counter.

He had started to wend his way back to the sofas when, in a flash of inspiration, he realised that he hadn't seen Two Berts since they had come in, and he swerved towards the stairs to look for him, in a rush of drunken loyalty. The barman watched him warily, wondering whether to press the swaying English officer for the underpaid money, but Julian's fierce, red-rimmed eyes convinced him otherwise, as Canning thundered up the staircase bellowing Two Bert's name like a maternal heifer.

He burst into the first room on the landing, interrupting a skinny French officer who was being given head by a rather tired looking prostitute. They both looked up in surprise and the woman mumbled something incomprehensible, but Julian was already gone. The door to the room opposite flew open, where an elderly Major, still dressed in his cap and tunic, trousers round his ankles, was puffing away behind a young, bored looking blonde. The Major glared in red-faced outrage, but his companion seemed rather glad of the interruption, which had broken the tedium of their lovemaking. Again, Julian was gone before either of them could give voice to their indignation. It was only when the third door crashed open, propelled sharply off the toe of his boot, that he found Two Berts. At least, he discovered where Two Berts *was*, because crouched on the bed, on her hands and knees and stark buttock naked, was the Madame. At six-foot in height and at least three-hundred pounds, her body was moving in a pummelling rhythm, heavy folds of pink flesh rippling back and forth in time, creating a rolling motion that put Julian in mind of a stormy sea of blancmange. And underneath, clinging on for dear life, like a newborn gorilla to its mother, was the diminutive figure of Two Berts.

Such was the ferocity of their coupling that neither had noticed Canning's entrance and a combination of the Madame's ecstatic grunts, the tortured protests of the bed, and Two Berts' ears being ensconced between her long, sloppy breasts, meant that they also failed to hear his bellowed exhortations as Julian stood in the doorway, loudly egging them on. In fact, it was only when the mountainous woman threw back her head with a squeal of pleasure that she noticed the bedraggled, leering officer standing inside the room, waving a whisky bottle in encouragement. She instantly screamed and slid off Two Berts before clumsily getting a foot caught in the bed sheets and crashing to the floor.

The brothel shook to its very foundations and Julian doubled up with laughter at the sight of it, before falling to his knees as a now somewhat exposed Two Berts, grabbed desperately at the nearest pair of underwear and clawed them, on only to find that they weren't his and therefore at least seventeen sizes too big. Canning thrashed about on the floor, his sides aching, as Two Berts stood there in a mid-coital flush, with the twenty stone Madame's pants suspended from his erect manhood and, when he turned around to check on his consort, only to display a hairy pair of bare buttocks, the knickers having slipped down to his knees at the back, it all became too much for Julian who vomited onto the ragged carpet.

Two Berts exploded in a flurry of Welsh obscenities and dived over to slam the door. Unfortunately, Canning's face was still in the frame and Julian both felt and heard the cartilage in his nose crunch sideways, accompanied by a flow of hot blood. However, all the alcohol he had drunk had deadened the pain and he lay flat out on the floor, bright red gore mixing with sticky brown vomit. The barman, having heard the Madame fall, appeared at the top of the stairs having come to investigate what, he had assumed to be the accidental detonation of a hand grenade. He looked sadly at Canning's broken face then slid his hand into the pilot's pocket and retrieved just enough francs to cover the cost of the whisky, and left him prostrate on the landing.

Julian awoke with only blackness before his eyes and a cold chill running through his body. He blinked once, twice and then decided that yes, he was dead. Ah! No, the pain in his head made him suddenly think otherwise. His top lip was crusty and he ran his tongue across it to taste salt blood.

'Canning.'

A voice, shit, so there was a God all along, now he was fucked.

'CANNING!'

A large, flesh coloured lump swam in and out of focus above him, calling his name again. He faintly recognised the voice. Shellford. Well if Shellford was God then he might just get away with everything after all…

'Sh-Shellford?' He was surprised at how distant the words sounded.

'Thank Christ for that. Okay, you stupid bugger, this chap with me is an Army sawbones and this is going to hurt. But it may just save your good looks,' A drunken snicker.

Julian tried in vain to muster a protest but two strong hands grabbed his face and pulled hard on his nose. He felt the scraping click with strange detachment. Then the pain hit him.

'Jesus mother-fucking holy CHRIST!'

'Oh shut up, you big girl, I've sawn the bloody legs off men who've made less noise than that,' chided an authoritative voice, which still sounded just as drunk as everybody else. Shellford thanked the RAMC man, hefted Julian up and threw his left arm over his shoulder as Two Berts took the right, with Ripley following them out.

Together they dragged him to where the tender was waiting with Stuart at the wheel.

The Captain, noticing the state of his approaching officers, leaned out the window, 'What the *fuck* has happened now?'

'Oh hullo, Jimmy, no need to worry, old boy,' answered Shellford cheerfully, 'Young Canning here caught a glimpse of that new girl of yours and went a touch weak at the knees, what? Landed on his face the daft bugger. Can't blame him though I must say, you've got a right cracker there…'

'Just throw him in the back.'

'Right-ho.'

The tender rumbled back to the aerodrome with Julian passed out on the wooden floor boards, Shellford and Two Berts sat back with their hands behind their heads, satisfied men. And Ripley staring vacantly into the night, utterly in love.

CHAPTER 6

4th April 1917

A crumpled array of men sat slumped at intervals around the mess, each one suffering through a different stage of his own personal hangover. No one had bothered to switch on any lights and the room was all grey shadow. It was 0530 and the atmosphere was tense and irritable, everything seeming to grate or rub the wrong way. None of the officers had taken up the offer of breakfast, although one or two sipped tentatively from mugs, whose contents of tea or coffee were instantly absorbed into huge, furry tongues.

The 0500 wakeup call had been an intrusion, another cruel invasion of the war upon their lives. They had all been promised the morning for recovery and now it had been stolen from them in a grey-black headache of dawn awakening. The weather outside was grim and shaping up to get worse, but there was still an outside possibility of flying so the squadron had been roused in readiness.

Occasionally one of the newer men would lurch from their seat and bolt for the door to deposit the contents of their stomach into the long grass. Many had drunk several times more than they had ever imbibed before and, helped along by the possibility of a dawn action, their bodies were violently expelling whatever remained. None of the older hands were surprised, the ability to function (or at least appear to function) the morning after a binge was skill that had to be learned through experience.

A few pairs of dark-ringed, bloodshot eyes looked up as Canning staggered through the door, his nose horribly swollen and bloodied. Weaving a meandering path to the bar, he poured himself a breakfast whisky, scribbled an illegible name into the mess ledger, then dropped into a chair opposite Two Berts, who was engrossed in a book about common British houseplants.

'So,' he began, 'last night.'

Two Bert's eyes never stirred from the page, although his left eyebrow lifted almost imperceptibly.

'My nose.'

Again, no reaction.

'Anything to say about what happened?'

Two Berts very slowly and deliberately put his book face down on the open page, as Canning drained his glass.

'Well, if you were to ask me, which you just have, I would suggest that it found itself on the wrong side of an argument with a rather solid door. Drink?'

'Are you buying?'

Two Berts sighed and walked to the bar, 'I suppose I should, but look here, you shouldn't have had your bloody face there in the first place you know.'

'Oh fuck my face, I'm more interested in that er...woman that you were with.'

Two Berts placed another double whisky in front of Canning.

'What about her?'

'Well...you know.'

'No.'

'Weren't you worried?'

'Worried about what?'

'You know.'

'No.'

'That she might have eaten you.'

A hiss of stifled laughter escaped from several spots around the mess.

'No.'

'Oh.' Julian sipped delicately at the whisky then threw the rest of it back, 'Because I was a mite concerned that she was eyeing up taking a bite from my leg when I came in.'

Two Berts tried to assume a pose of complete indifference.

'So, when we went out last night did you think that we were going whoring or mountaineering?' Julian pressed.

A muscle in Two Berts right eye twitched.

'It's just that next time I'll find you some grappling irons in case you fancy a go on top.'

Shellford burst out laughing and Two Berts finally snapped, his accent becoming thick and animated, 'Oh fuck off, Canning. Just because some of us are man enough to need a real woman...'

'She was at least four real women.'

'Well then, I'm obviously four times the man you are, you need to be a real man to handle a woman like that.'

'You need a mining lamp and a bloody canary,' jeered Julian.

Two Berts shook his head, 'Look, if I buy you another drink will you shut up about it?'

'Possibly.'

'Yes or no?'

'Buy me the drink and you'll find out, but you still owe me one for my nose,' Julian grinned.

'I just bought you one for your nose.'

'Well you owe me two then, it hurts like buggery.'

'Oh for Christ's sake,' he muttered as he snatched Canning's glass and got up to refill it.

As the morning wore on, so did tempers, and the atmosphere deteriorated further as bowels rumbled and slurped, bellies struggling to process the night's excesses erupting into flabby, poisonous emissions. A few more joined Canning in a liquid breakfast to try and settle themselves.

'No prizes for guessing whose bloody idea this shit-watch is,' growled Stampe, tipping a large brandy into his mug of coffee. Several tired faces turned in his direction but no one spoke. Everyone knew. Stuart sprung up from his chair, the sudden motion causing the stomachs of several nearby officers to heave.

'Right, I'm sorting this out one way or another,' he announced, just as the door swung open and Billington entered, followed by the Major.

No one stood, except Stuart, who was already standing.

'Going somewhere, Captain Stuart?' Asked Billington icily, his nose wrinkling at the smell.

He stalked across the room, deliberately catching a chair next to Webb and Connolly with his foot, and they flinched painfully at the noise.

'As a matter of fact, I am, 'replied Stuart, coolly, 'I'm taking A Flight up to survey the conditions and ascertain whether they are suitable for operations. When we return, I shall inform the rest of the squadron.'

'That will not be necessary, Captain, Headquarters will provide notification in due course if...'

'On the contrary,' Stuart interrupted, 'as senior flight commander I believe that my judgement will be more than sufficient for *my* men and, as a *former* pilot himself, I'm sure that Major Frost would agree with me?' Stuart turned to the Major with an expectant look.

Frost, utterly shocked he had even been acknowledged, stared about him in astonishment for a few seconds before stuttering, 'Er...yes...o-of...course, James, er...Captain Stuart.'

Stuart then proceeded to ignore both Frost and Billington, and turned to the remainder of the squadron.

'Right, A Flight get ready to take off, Shellford, you're excused since you don't have a full-time observer yet. Ripley, Fuller, you can stand down as well.

'What about my nose?' Piped up Julian, who still hadn't bothered to properly wash the blood from his face. The dry, crusty feeling on the skin around his mouth fascinated him, and he had been picking at it constantly.

'When I see you flying with your nose, Canning I'll let you stay in bed. Look on the bright side lad, at least you can't get any uglier.'

'Scotch wanker.'

'Sorry, Canning?'

'Nothing, Captain.'

'Quite right. Now, the rest of you get back to bed and I'll have you called if I need you.'

Twenty minutes later, three BEs spluttered into the air and flew towards the new day that was doing its feeble best to claw through the clouds to the east. The constant chill of cold air blowing into his face was beginning to make Julian's nose hurt, despite the morning whisky. A deep, pulsing throb as the shattered cartilage began to knit itself back together. The aircraft even appeared to fly as if they were hungover, slowly crabbing across the sky. To his left, Stuart's BE trundled along, with Marshall plainly asleep in the front cockpit. And on his right, Webb and Connolly's machine grumbled through the clouds until, moments later, Webb swung the BE across the front of the formation, and gave the whirled finger and shake of the head to signal engine trouble and turned back toward the aerodrome.

'Wanker,' muttered Julian, annoyed that he hadn't thought to do it first.

The remaining two aircraft were only at the Lines for a matter of minutes before it became clear that there would be no opportunity for effective flying until late afternoon at the very earliest. The cloud ceiling, heavy and grey had dropped to under a thousand feet, and the air was thick with moisture, which was starting to affect the aircraft.

Stuart turned around before they even reached No Man's Land, and they flew back to Pouilly-Yvredon together, one BE touching lightly down, the other thumping heavily across the turf. Stuart, looking towards the squadron office, waved his hand across his throat and shook his head. The tall figure looming in the doorway disappeared and all four men went back to bed.

*　　*　　*

The majority of the squadron emerged at around noon, most of them just about feeling up to lunch. It was clear, however, that there would be no more flying that day. The rain that had been threatening earlier had finally broken and looked thoroughly set in, and the wind was back up to near hurricane speeds. And, since no-one would be flying, this meant that the squadron mess was full of young men with very little to do other than wait around for an opportunity to die tomorrow instead.

The atmosphere in the mess, therefore, was somewhat subdued and the air was thronged with a pale blue haze from a constant chain of cigarettes. Forsyth and Bolinbroke were fleecing their new B Flight comrades Coulter and Elphinstone out of their first month's pay at bridge, and several other officers were dotted about reading, writing, musing, and generally whiling away the remainder of the day. Webb and Connolly had settled into one of their interminable games of chess, gazing into each other's eyes for minutes at a time, wrestling over each lavishly drawn out tactical exchange. Even Shellford seemed unnaturally reflective, his thoughts wandering, lost in quiet contemplation as he lounged in the tattered wingback. Julian sat opposite with Two Berts on the floral suite, that was leaking stuffing from one of the arms. He had a glass in either hand, a cigarette in his mouth, and was puzzling over how to proceed. He grunted in annoyance at Two Berts who had dozed off, slumped against his shoulder, and was in the process of trying to knock back him the other way, when Ripley approached, clutching a tumbler of whisky as if it were a glass of milk. He pulled up a wicker chair that was missing its back leg and sat down with them. The chair's defect meant that he had to us his own legs to keep his balance, planting his feet firmly upon the floor, tensing his muscles for purchase. Tentatively, he sipped his drink.

'Erm, I was just wondering blokes, when we would be heading back to Lamaincourt next?'

Shellford, his reverie broken, caught Canning's eye with a wink.

'Oh, that all depends, young Ripley, what with this thrice damned offensive coming up it could be a while, our day jobs are promising to get a trifle busy in the immediate future. Maybe if there's another dud weather day or maybe when it's all petered out and another hundred-thousand have died.'

'Oh. So nobody's got any plans then?'

'None that I know of.'

'Is it possible for one to go alone?'

'Inadvisable, besides you'd never get Stuart to give you the tender just for yourself.'

'Oh.' The conversation died for a few seconds. Ripley stared at the floor then brightened, 'Today's a dud weather day.'

'Good lord, two nights in a row, you're a bit keen aren't you? We're not all as full of spunk anymore.' He turned to Canning with a look of wistful yearning, 'Oh, to be young again.'

Ripley fell quiet once more, but as Shellford drummed his fingers on the leather arm of the chair, his eyes flashed with amusement.

'Mind you,' he turned to Julian again, 'I think the weather's meant to turn soon, isn't it?'

Canning shrugged, still holding his two drinks, cigarette wagging between his lips.

'And if it does we'll be busy, and there won't be quite as many of us sat here same time tomorrow, I'll warrant. Seems a little like tempting fate to be making future dinner plans.'

He lit a cigarette and blew a neat smoke ring.

'Plus Mr. Canning here isn't actually as old as he looks, he's a veritable fountain of energy…well underneath all of…that.' He gestured towards Canning's morose and battered visage.

Julian glared at him.

'See? He's positively effervescent. So, all things considered, I suppose we might venture out for a couple of quiet drinks this evening,' Shellford grinned. 'I'm sure a few others could be persuaded, there's lots of new places we could show you.'

Ripley's face, which had just begun to light up, fell visibly.

'Oh. I was...erm...hoping that we might frequent the...ah... same establishments as last time.'

'Aha! So you liked the food then?'

'Well ...ah...it wasn't the restaurant that I had in mind...'

'That bar we went to then?'

'I was rather thinking more about the place where we finished the evening, where ah...'

He indicated Julian's nose that was still heavily purpled with a dark red band over the area where the cartilage had split. Canning wanted to tell them all to stop pointing at his fucking face, but the cigarette prevented him from speaking.

'Oh there!' Shellford winked at him, 'There's several places like *that* I could show you! Wonderful, I'll start having a think.'

'No no no!' Ripley, almost lost his balance on the chair, 'I want to see Madeleine again.' He finally confessed in exasperation.

'Madel...? Oh bloody hell Rip, you haven't gone and fallen for a hooker have you?'

'She said she wanted to see me again.'

'That's because you paid her twenty francs!'

'No, this is different, I, we...' He lowered his voice. 'We really got on, you know.'

'Well that's what you paid her for.'

'No, she's...different. I just...I just have to see her again.'

Shellford gave Canning a world-weary glance.

'Look Rip, she's a whore, not your fiancée, and while at times the difference may only be academic, there are certain rules. Well, only one really.' He sat up and fixed his eyes upon the boyish face, 'don't fall in love with prostitutes.'

Ripley blanched, 'I'm not in love...'

Julian was just thinking back to the confusing mix of emotions he had first felt towards the woman that had taken his virginity along with his money, when Two Berts woke up, looked groggily around and asked, 'Are we going back to the Flamingo?'

Julian shook him off his shoulder and looked at him.

'Perhaps...why?' asked Shellford.

'Because I reckon I've got enough back pay saved up to have her up the arse this time.'

Both Shellford and Canning started snickering, the laughter rattling through the room was at odds with the mood of the rest of the squadron. Ripley looked horrified.

'Right,' declared Shellford getting up to find Stuart, 'let me have a quiet word with gallant Hector and see what can be done about procuring our faithful jalopy.'

He loped away as Ripley bounced out the door after him to get ready. Canning spat the finished cigarette onto the floor, and emptied both his glasses in quick succession.

Ripley was dressed and ready to go within ten minutes and spent the remainder of the time before dinner picking through the surrounding woodland in a quest to construct a passable bouquet of flowers. He returned with his shoes, socks and bottom third of his trousers soaked through, sporting a rather pathetic posy of stained snowdrops and broken bluebells, which he dropped into a tankard of water before dashing off to make himself presentable again. Shellford had extended the evening's invite to the rest of the squadron but, anticipating a busy and therefore dangerous tomorrow, most declined, and the only additions were Webb and Connolly.

The tender rumbled down the track leading from the aerodrome, Shellford at the wheel, Ripley by his side and the other four men jolting along in the back. Webb and Connolly pressed unnecessarily close to each other in the relatively empty rear, savouring every rut and bump that brought their bodies closer together.

Once in Lamaincourt, they made a token a visit to a couple of bars but Ripley instantly downed his drinks in an endeavour to hurry them on. Intrigued, Shellford kept buying him more until, by the time they finally set off for *Le Flamant Bleu*, the young pilot was rather boss eyed and hiccoughing like clockwork.

On the walk to the bordello, Webb and Connolly suddenly declared that they had spotted a mutual acquaintance entering a dimly let bar across the street and excused themselves, promising to catch up presently. Canning smiled to himself as they departed. But as they turned the final corner onto the road on which the building was situated, Julian found himself feeling suddenly irritable, the thought of the brothel made him edgy and there was no flush of hormones or anticipatory lengthening of his member. He had also become acutely aware of just how much his shattered nose hurt. And, as he entered through the ornate doorway with the others, he found it even more dark and depressing than before.

Ripley immediately ran off in a frantic search for Madeline, still clutching the flowers that were looking even worse for wear (many now headless) after their journey from the aerodrome and subsequent tour of Lamaincourt's bars. Canning joined Two Berts, who was steeling himself with a double brandy and beginning to go through a routine that resembled a wrestler limbering up for a championship bout. But when his observer left to hunt down the Madame, Julian suddenly decided that he didn't want to be here. The alcohol hadn't cast its usual spell, he was unquestionably drunk but still felt sober, and there was none of the wonderful cloudiness that made the world, however briefly, seem like a barely tolerable place. His nose was beginning to throb again, rhythmically and dully painful, so he turned back towards the exit, swiping a half-full bottle of brandy from a pair of French officers, who were thoroughly engrossed in their respective girls.

The cool night air struck his nose and brought a sharp hiss of pain from between his teeth as he propped his back against the dirty white wall, drinking deeply from the bottle, before setting it on the floor and lighting a cigarette. The throbbing was becoming deeper, the effects of the wind and rain that had battered away at it during the morning's flying had taken a brutal toll, and, unbeknownst to him, it had swollen into a great purple-black tuber. His first match flared then went out. He struck another, sheltering it with his free hand. It flickered, fighting the breeze and then held. The inky black sky was almost hidden by the solid blue-grey overcast and he drew in a lungful of smoke, breathing it slowly out towards the layer of cloud.

'That conk looks rather painful,' said a female voice on his right.

'You must be a bloody nurse or something,' he bit back sarcastically, before turning to see a small figure in the khaki smock of the First Aid Nursing Yeomanry.

'And you must be Sherlock bloody Holmes,' the diminutive figure answered evenly, 'Jesus you flyboys are just razor sharp, aren't you?'

Canning turned away, 'Piss off.'

'Charming, officers and gentleman all I see. Have you been flying with your nose in that state?'

'It's what they pay me for.'

'Have you kept it covered?'

Julian turned back, 'Look, what the bloody hell is it to you anyway?'

The khaki shape shrugged in reply, 'It's what they pay *me* for. It'll only get worse if you don't cover it, haven't you got a scarf?' Julian decided that he couldn't be bothered to explain the surprisingly complex set of circumstances that had led to both his scarf and one of his socks being blown out of the cockpit ten miles over German territory in January, so he just grunted and shrugged his shoulders.

'A pilot without a bloody scarf, Christ, you're either a complete prat or...' she studied him for a moment, 'No, I'm guessing you're just a prat. Got any cigarettes?'

'No.' He lied.

'Last one, eh? Let's have a quick drag, I'm gasping.'

An arm reached out towards his face.

'Look just bugger off will you.' he growled, spinning round irritably and noticing her for the first time.

A young woman in a well-worn FANY uniform looked back at him. He would have placed in her mid-twenties, although everyone over here looked older than their years. She was small, her brown hair was scraped functionally back into a bun. Her features, he thought, were damned average, but her night-black eyes were razor sharp.

Canning swatted away the outstretched hand, 'Christ, just have one of these will you,' he reached into his tunic and proffered the packet.

'Obnoxious, a liar, but generous when finally broken down I will allow. So what's put you in such a foul mood then? Didn't get thrown out by your whore did you?'

She articulated the word 'whore' in such a way, he thought, to convey contempt, sympathy, disapproval, but above all, understanding, not a presumption or arrogance, just an acceptance of the world.

'Seriously though, you didn't get thrown out by a hooker…'

'No.'

'Then why stranded on the dull side of the knocking shop? Give me a light.'

She ignored Canning fumbling for his matches and stepped in, lighting her cigarette from the one that burned between his lips. She smelt of surgical spirit, blood and stale sleep, and took a draw that made Julian's eyes water just watching.

'Maybe I didn't fancy getting poxed up…' He stumbled his words in reply.

'Unlikely, if you go in armoured…' She grimaced at Canning's blank expression, 'God, and they thought the shell shortage was a worry.'

Julian ignored her and took another pull from the bottle of brandy, then offered it without thinking. She took a hearty swig.

'So what bunch are you with?'

'Eh?'

'What's your unit, where are you based?'

Julian sighed heavily and gave in, 'A few miles up the road at Pull-the-other-one, with 33B.'

'Pull the…Oh, I see. I'm at the field hospital near Le Hameau, if you ever get shot they'll probably send you to us.'

'Wonderful,' he muttered caustically.

'I'd be a little nicer to the person who may end up tending to your wounds and changing your bedpan…'

'I wouldn't let you anywhere bloody near me.'

'Ha!' She eyed him up and down, leaning back on the wall next to him and noticed his DSO ribbon, 'I see they gave you a medal.'

Julian grunted again.

'What was it for?'

'I don't know, I was drunk when they gave it to me. Surviving for more than a month, I presume.'

She cocked an eyebrow, testing his words for false modesty.

'33B Squadron…' she continued, 'I think we had one of your chaps in a while back…Caldwell, or something like that? Couple of bullets in the stomach?'

Julian shrugged. She stared at him and for the tiniest moment her eyes, shrouded in darkness, flashed understanding. Then she ploughed on.

'He didn't last long though, went during the night, as deaths go it was a relatively good 'un,' she paused to draw on the cigarette, 'We had a man in a couple of weeks ago, Canadian Sergeant, got caught by one of the Germans' new fire launchers. He lasted almost three days, screaming, with his skin falling off his bones. His eyes had melted. There was nothing we could do for him, every time we so much as touched him a piece of his flesh would fall off. He'd been… cooked.'

Again, Canning passed across the bottle without thinking, 'Why are you telling me this?'

'Because it's the kind of thing you have to tell someone and, believe it or not, it's a damn sight easier to tell someone who obviously doesn't care. Most people either don't understand or make some great show of sympathy, and that's even worse. Usually the men put an arm round my shoulder then try and slip a hand down my blouse.'

'Yeah? Well, don't worry yourself on that front.'

She snorted in mock outrage, 'Bloody hell, don't you know just how to make a girl feel on top form.'

Her head pricked up as she noticed a couple walking up the cobbled street, a tall, blonde, Canadian infantry Captain, accompanied by a shorter, red-headed young woman, dressed similarly dressed to herself.

'Aha, looks as if my ward for the evening has returned, I'm her chaperone, charged with protecting her honour tonight, see. Only, well, I don't think Frances really *wanted* to be protected from Jack. Quite the opposite actually. Looks like this is goodnight then, Lieutenant...?'

'Canning.'

'Canning.' She spoke the name with a hint of mirth. 'I hope you go on to win a whole chestful of medals, Lieutenant Canning, and I promise not to laugh if I ever have to give you a sponge bath.'

And with that, she threw down her cigarette and made her way towards the strolling couple, before becoming lost in the darkness. Julian shook his head, drained the contents of his bottle, and sat down against the wall to wait for the others.

CHAPTER 7

5th April 1917

The dark monotony of the night sky was broken by a subtle flush of pale pink in the east, rising like smoke along the horizon, almost immediately changing into a subdued yellow. The single, deep blue-black that had been the night sky was rolled back and took on a myriad of new tones that mixed into a liquid turquoise where it met the sunrise. The underside of several large puffs of cumulus clouds burned a deep orange just as the sun flared proper, bursting all the colours of flame across the landscape. A firm but unhurried breeze accompanied it and the first birds took flight. They revelled in the distant warmth of the early sunlight and allowed the wind to carry them, soaring above the shortening shadow. It was good flying weather. Which meant that today, men would die.

Billington was stood near the bar, in front of the Major, who was peeking out from behind him. A spark of sadistic pleasure was dancing in his bitter green eyes and his lips twitched in an attempt to suppress a smile.

'Everybody here?' The adjutant asked crisply, and, upon receiving no reply, continued, 'Good. Today's orders, gentlemen. Headquarters has reinforced that all squadron activity is to be concentrated in support of the upcoming offensive. Artillery observation is to be our main priority and we can expect a delivery of new radios this evening. However, in their absence, the squadron has been detailed for a bombing raid.'

Several groans came from the more experienced men.

'The target will be the railway junction at Don.'

The groans disappeared into shocked silence.

'Escort will be provided by 43 Squadron with their Sopwith 1½ Strutters. All planes will be fully loaded with two 112lb bombs and observers will be left behind to ensure aircraft performance is maintained...'

'No, they won't,' broke in Stuart, 'Don is only seven miles short of Lille and I'm not leading the squadron into that wasps' nest without observers for protection.'

'As I already specified, Captain, there will be an escort...'

'And th' day a bluddy escort turns up,' he paused and composed himself, 'I still won't fly over enemy lines unarmed. All aircraft will carry two crew members and be equipped with six 20lb Cooper bombs.'

'But the orders...' Billington trailed off. The sheer ferocity of Stuarts eyes forced him to drop his own.

His fun spoiled somewhat, Billington continued, 'Very well...primary targets will be the tracks and buildings at the junctions and any locomotives en situ. These are crucial in disrupting the German reinforcement of men and equipment. Take off will be at 0700, rendezvous with escort over Neuve Chapelle at 0730. That is all, gentlemen.'

'Jesus Christ.' Stuart shook his head sadly.

Marshall turned to him and spoke softly, 'You do realise that twenty-pounders will just bounce off anything they hit?'

'Yes,' he breathed heavily, 'I know. But it would be bloody suicide to go over unarmed, and I'm not getting in a BE with two hundred pounds of bombs tacked on in addition to *your* fat arse. It's just HQ trying to find us something useful to do until the radios arrive, they should have re-equipped us months ago. Art obs is where we earn our pay. Besides,' he smiled, 'We never bloody hit anything anyway.' He got up and clapped his observer cheerfully on the shoulder.

'Okay blokes, let's get some breakfast, it's going to be a long one, assemble at the hangars at 0630 for pre-flight briefing.'

'Right,' Stuart began, 'we're going over in two V formations, I'll take A Flight in the first, St. Clare will lead B Flight behind and above.' Armitage St. Clare shifted irritably at the truncation of his surname.

'I'll take us straight to the rendezvous where we'll climb for height while we wait, I'm not going over below ten-thousand feet. Do NOT rely on our escort even if they turn up, for those of you who have never seen a Strutter fight let inform you now that they can't.

'Keep your eyes open and if we're attacked, for Christ's sake stay in formation, it's the only way we can cover each other. If you find yourself separated for any reason, go home. If you have engine problems, go home. Keep the formations loose, no parade ground flying, I don't want anyone crashing into anyone else.'

His gaze paused on Canning for an extra fraction of a second. Canning didn't notice.

'We go there, lay our eggs, and get the hell out, sharpish. Clear?' There was a round of nods. 'These are for you new men,' he finished, starting to unwrap a bulky brown paper parcel that he had been carrying under his arm. From it, he produced four new Webley service revolvers that he passed to Ripley, Fuller, Coulter and Elphinstone in turn.

'I've loaded them so be careful.'

Ripley examined his pistol, weighing it in his hand, frowning, 'What are these for?'

'You'll have noticed no-one's given you a parachute, so if your plane catches fire you have three choices,' Armitage St. Clare said nastily, 'You can stick it out and broil, you can jump and have time to say your prayers before you hit the ground or…' he shrugged, 'The quick option.'

The four new airmen turned a touch greener, it was their first 'big show.'

'Personally, I'd jump every time,' offered Julian, 'Burning's unpleasant and blowing your brains out is guaranteed to do the trick.'

'Except you'd probably miss.' Muttered Shellford.

Julian ignored him, 'If you jump, then there's a million to

one chance you might just not die. You hear stories of chaps who have done it, one of the buggers in the first Zeppelin that Warneford shot down landed on a bed in a nunnery. Better odds than *that* thing offers,' he nodded at the gun.

Ripley considered this, then aimed the revolver along the runway, holding it at arm's length and looking down the sights.

'I suppose,' he mused, 'that one could always use it to fight their way out of Hunland.'

Julian sniggered. 'Yeah, I carry this for the same reason,' he said, producing a large, white handkerchief with several unpleasant stains on it. 'If I end up over the other side I'm going to wave it at the first Germans I see then order the bratwurst for dinner.'

At 0645 propellers were swung and pilots and observers began to clamber into their unwieldy mounts. Pitiably small, grey-green bombs hung under wings. Men smoked their final cigarettes before revving up their engines and testing their control surfaces. At 0659 Stuart's BE waddled forwards to the main airstrip and accelerated into the air. One by one, the other eight aircraft followed. He led them in a straggled group to Neuve Chappelle, climbing a few thousand feet of on the way and, once there, broke formation as each aeroplane circled for height individually. German scouts rarely, if ever, operated over the British side of the lines so the squadron was more preoccupied with searching for their escort than for the enemy.

Large, billowy cumulus and cumulonimbus clouds were scattered across an otherwise clear sky, and overall visibility was good. But the only other aircraft they saw were a group of four FE2s, a 'pusher' type aeroplane with the engine mounted so the propeller pointed backwards, set in the middle of a fuselage constructed entirely of thin wooden struts, while pilot and observer sat in an exposed nacelle at the front. Canning had always thought they looked like crane-flies, horribly fragile, and barely superior in performance to the BE2s.

The sun was working hard, taking only the occasional respite behind a cloud and this unsettled Stuart, because the danger would come from the sun, it always came from the sun. He eyed it continually, but all that emerged was, what from a distance appeared to be a German two-seater, that passed them far away to the west and shortly afterwards a group of five British Sopwith Pup fighters tore after it in a pursuit that they had already lost.

Julian noticed very little of this, he was experiencing the uncomfortable sensation of going to war sober. His flask was empty and he hadn't had the chance to refill it, or himself, before breakfast, and he considered this an unforgivable oversight on his part. He thought he had seen Armitage St. Clare swigging from a bottle on his way to the sheds, but Canning didn't reckon he would have shared, and the catch was, being sober, he didn't have the absence of inhibition that he needed to demand it. Instead, and partly in an attempt take his mind off the pain in his face, he was trying to light a cigarette, holding the control column between his knees and burying his head deep in the cockpit to avoid the slipstream, with one glove removed. He was managing to strike the matches okay but the back draft from the propeller still found its way into the cockpit and kept blowing them out, and he was becoming increasingly frustrated.

The process was also occupying all of his attention, with the result that he almost collided with Coulter and Elphinstone who had been allocated the freshly repaired Number 8, with its radio removed. Two Berts had been too busy adjusting his Lewis gun to notice, and had only been able to gape in horror as a pair of wheels very nearly struck him on the head, as the aircraft passed within inches of each other. Julian remained stubbornly buried in his cockpit and Two Berts continued to stare curiously until Canning suddenly surfaced with a lit cigarette between his lips, grinning triumphantly. The wind promptly whipped it from his mouth and carried it aft, to begin a long decent to the ground. Julian sat in his cockpit looking like a child who had dropped his ice-cream.

At 0750 the squadron had managed to climb to ten-thousand feet, but still there was no sign of any escort and Stuart decided to wait another ten minutes then head off without them. It would be no great loss, he mused, thinking how ridiculous it was to assign them 43 Squadron as an escort. The 1½ Strutter aircraft that they flew was a two-seater made by the Sopwith company, with one Lewis gun in the back for the observer and a single Vickers machine gun for the pilot, synchronised to fire through the propeller. It was the addition of this forwards firing weapon that had led to some bright spark at Headquarters thinking that 1½ Strutters qualified for scout roles. They couldn't. And really, really shouldn't. They were underpowered and sluggish and the only real protection they could offer, would be to fly in a formation similar to the BEs and let their observers, who were at least seated in the rear of the aircraft, put up a field of defensive fire. If it did come to a fight, it would be like a one-armed man attempting to protect a paraplegic. It was almost farcical. The small clock mounted in his instrument board ticked around to 0757 and, now thoroughly fed-up, Stuart decided to turn for the lines. The wind was following at this stage and would assist them in their journey towards Don. The return flight however, would be a painfully slow crawl, and the Huns would doubtless be a touch peeved at the allied planes that had been lobbing explosives at them, and calling up the closest fighter squadrons to seek revenge. Their best chance, he decided, would be a shallow dive back, trying to cross the lines at about four-thousand feet, that way they would at least maintain a semi-respectable speed.

He straightened out of the climbing curve and rummaged in one of the canvas pockets sewn to the inside of his cockpit, until his hand clasped on the bulky handle of his Very pistol.

Clumsily, impeded by his gauntlets, he loaded a red flare which would be the signal to rally and fired up and over the side of the BE. Slowly, the rest of the squadron began a cumbersome shuffle into formation around him, and he steered them towards German territory.

The nine aircraft trundled over No-Man's Land in two roughly formed chevrons, one behind the other. Above them, the sky was a clean, clear blue interspersed with puffy mountains of white-grey cloud, reflecting the blindingly sharp yellow of the sun. Below them was brown. Just brown. A huge brown weal that gruesomely carved the landscape in two. Looking down, the trenches were mere pencil lines, etched upon an indistinguishable brown canvas, an ugly scar across the face of France. Then the war on the ground intruded upon the relative peace in the air as the first anti-aircraft shells exploded around them. They were black puffballs that appeared suddenly and then lazily drifted apart on the wind before disappearing. From a distance, they seemed innocuous and most airmen regarded them with disinterest, although if they ever got close, close to enough to hear the shrapnel whine, then stomachs began to turn. Today however, the German gunners were apparently content to send up a token salvo of shells in their general direction and then let them be.

A combination of the wind and the fact that the squadron was flying in the opposite direction to safety meant that the outward journey went quickly, although not for one second did pilots and observers let up on their incessant scanning of the sky. Necks became sore from stretching and turning, eyes watered from continually peering into the searing sun. Still they continued to search.

Stuart had picked up the railway line, and presently, creeping over the horizon, he saw the scatter of buildings and locomotives along with the tangle of tracks that made up the junction. Gently, he pressed his right foot on the rudder bar to bring the squadron into line. Stuart had no faith in aerial bombing whatsoever, there was no scientific approach and no real acknowledged technique, he would simply fly a course over the target and drop his bombs when he reckoned they would hit, and the rest of the squadron would follow his lead. From this height, he would be lucky if the free-falling projectiles landed in a mile radius of where he intended, and any notion of picking out selected targets was ridiculous.

As such, it was with an air of inconsequence that he pulled the bomb toggle when he was still some way from the target, in order to roughly compensate for the forward distance they would travel after release. The small, metal lever low down on the right under his seat, clicked upwards and the six tiny Cooper bombs were released from the aeroplane. The rest of the squadron, seeing that their leader had effected a release, dropped their bombs seconds later. Everyone except Canning, who had decided that it was such a nice day for flying that he simply had to have a cigarette to complement the experience and had once again buried himself back into his cockpit.

A loud 'Hi!' from Two Berts, carried to him on the wind snapped him back to reality. He jerked his head up and was met with the sight of his observer miming a pulling motion while desperately jabbing his finger downwards.

'Oh shit,' he muttered and fumbled for the bomb release.

Freed of a hundred and twenty pounds of extra weight, the BE's engine immediately took on a slightly more cheerful note and it actually rose a few feet in the air. Stuart, staring fixedly downwards to see the result of the bombs, had not noticed Canning's late release and his face wrinkled in disgust as most of the small explosions fell short of the train yard. Then, just as he was about to turn away in exasperation, a final small group of 'crumps' blossomed on the roof of a large, flat building that a split-second later, erupted into a colossal fiery explosion. Flames billowed upwards and outwards, whilst tendrils of smoke spiralled in all directions as the roof and walls disintegrated.

The nine aircraft bumped on the uneven air from the sheer

scale of the blast, whilst Stuart remained mesmerised by the extent of the destruction. At least two trains had been blown clear from the tracks, their carriages scattered throughout the junction like discarded toys. The fire had quickly spread to the neighbouring buildings and a third train was desperately trying to pull away whilst beginning to burn. The whole scene was rapidly becoming obscured by a huge pall of black smoke rising from the ruin. He twisted in his seat to ascertain who had dropped those final six bombs and his eyes instantly fell on Canning in the BE next to his, sitting in the cockpit with his arms raised above his head, dancing in celebration. Very softly he smiled to himself and began the long turn towards home. The smile disappeared when he saw Canning's aircraft lose its place in the formation and almost career wildly into Ripley and Fuller, the pilot's head lowered deep within his cockpit.

As soon as the squadron completed its about turn, the wind began to noticeably impact the BEs' airspeed, and at this altitude, it posed a serious obstacle to their safe return. With one eye fixed nervously on the sun, Stuart fired a violet flare as the signal that the squadron should close up and then pushed the stick forwards into a dive that was slightly steeper than he was comfortable with so far from the front. The speed they gained from the dive couldn't quite cancel out what that the wind was taking out of them though, and he reckoned it would take them as long as the outward journey and then half again before they reached the aerodrome.

Marshall was waving at him to get his attention, pointing over his shoulder, and Stuart turned to see one of the aircraft in Armitage St. Clare's chevron lagging a way behind the rest of B Flight, trailed by a small stream of blue smoke. He gritted his teeth, well aware that he could not countenance endangering the rest of the squadron by slowing them down to allow the stricken aeroplane to keep pace. The other BE was much too far away for Stuart to make out who was flying it but Armitage St. Clare, leading B flight, could see that the only aircraft in the squadron marked with a large, faded black eight, was missing from his formation. Which meant that the new boys, Coulter and Elphinstone, were being left behind. Like Stuart, he had no intention of slowing down, they would just have to take their chances.

As they had cleared the edge of a large wood, the squadron was greeted by a few desultory bursts of anti-aircraft fire that started far above them but soon marked a smoky black trail towards the formation as the gunners corrected their aim. Once the shells had reached the BEs however, they stopped abruptly and the hairs on the back of Stuart's neck prickled. He forced himself to stare into the sun, burning his eyes and leaving a scorched red circle in the middle of his vision, but still he saw nothing. Then high up on the opposite side to the sun, six small spots appeared and began to descend, growing rapidly, moving through the trail of black shell bursts that he now realised had been laid out for them by the German gunners.

They appeared to have misjudged their dive however, and finished up some way behind the BEs, which told Stuart that these pilots were inexperienced, the mere fact that the squadron had not been massacred already was testament to that. If the Huns had been seasoned campaigners then they wouldn't have needed a gunnery trail to spot them, and would have merely dropped like hawks from the sun, picking off their selected man in a matter of seconds, using their speed to sprint out of the range of the observers. The Germans were still much faster though, and very soon they had caught up with Coulter and Elphinstone in Number 8 and after a brief flurry of dark tracer bullets, a small lick of flame appeared and began to eat hungrily along the fuselage and onto the top wing. Against six Albatros scouts the lone BE hadn't a chance, it had been more of a murder than a battle and Stuart watched sickened as the flames grew rapidly, until all that was left was a horrific airborne fireball that fell towards the ground, shedding charred black lumps as it went. He was suddenly glad that he had handed out the revolvers before take-off . The six fighters now turned their attention to catching the rest of the squadron, and the miserable top speed of the BEs, meant that they would soon have a fight on their hands.

By the time they caught up with B Flight, the Albatroses had split into two groups, and each trio went after one of the remaining BEs either side of Armitage St. Clare. Their attacks were uncoordinated though, coming in from all angles and getting in each other's way. Armitage St. Clare spotted this and dropped his BE down a couple of hundred feet so his observer, Fish, would always have a shot firing upwards, over his shoulders. Fish didn't cause any significant damage, but managed to frighten off one the fighters that had been drawing a bead on Forsyth and Bolinbroke, sending a stream of tracer between its wings.

More dark pencil lines flashed past, as the A Flight gunners added some long range shots to the melee, more in an attempt to put the Germans off their stroke than in the hope of actually hitting anything. But the weight of numbers was beginning to tell and it wasn't long before one of the Albatroses firing at Russell and Stampe managed to send a burst of fire along and through the fuselage. Three bullets tore through the pilot's wicker chair, striking Russell in the small of the back, shattering his spinal column and exploding out through his stomach, spraying the instruments in front of him with blood and chunks of his gut. The stricken BE shuddered sideways as his feet lolled helplessly on the rudder bar. Desperately, fighting through a red sheet of blinding pain, he struggled to steady the aeroplane with the flight stick alone, but his useless legs kept disturbing the rudder, and the BE lost too much speed and stalled. Its nose dropped and the aircraft began to spin as it fell towards the ground. Mercifully, Russell passed out after the first few revolutions, but Stampe remained conscious for the entire eight-thousand foot drop, jammed against the side of his cockpit by the sheer force of the spinning aeroplane.

Stuart, seeing one of B Flight's aircraft stagger and then fall from the formation, decided that he had to act, and pushed the nose of his BE down into a steep dive. This served a dual purpose, it increased the squadron's speed and brought them nearer to the Lines and it made them harder to attack since the German scouts had to follow them in the dive and would struggle to get underneath the BEs to target their blind spots. The trade-off was that they would end up very low over enemy territory, still some distance from the safety of the Lines, but Stuart felt he had to do something or risk losing the entirety of B Flight. He glanced nervously at his altimeter as the wind whistled through the flying wires and the aircraft groaned and rattled in protest. The needle crept round very slowly and deliberately, six-thousand feet, five-thousand, four thousand... A crackle of gunfire sounded close to him and he cursed bitterly at the appearance of this new foe before thanking God seconds later as a swarm of RFC Nieuport fighters swept overhead, machine guns chattering at the pursuing Albatroses.

They quickly found the measure of the inexperienced German pilots, and as the little silver scouts whizzed past, one of the black-crossed machines rolled onto its back and burst into flames. Not for one second did Stuart throttle back or ease up on the dive, just in case the British fighters had only been making a hit and run pass, but his fears were quickly allayed as the formation of Nieuports split and swung round to engage the German scouts in the fantastic chaos of an aerial dogfight. Stuart pulled up a touch but kept the throttle wide open. Over his shoulder the dancing aeroplanes were rapidly diminishing in size. A long streak of black smoke scrawled across the sky as another aircraft tumbled to the ground, but whether it was too far away to tell from which side. The squadron crossed the lines at two-thousand feet, pursued by an angry flurry of ground fire, and Stuart muttered a quiet prayer of thanks. Canning cursed as the wind blew out his last match.

Back at the aerodrome, pilots and observers were clambering

stiffly to the ground, exaggerated black beards around their mouths and noses, where the engine fumes had stained the exposed parts of their faces. The areas protected by goggles and caps were, in contrast, eerily pale. Armitage St. Clare strode up to Stuart, a cigarette twitching between his oily lips.

'Russell and Stampe, Coulter and Elphinstone.' He spoke briskly, and clipped the names in a flat monotone.

Stuart nodded, patting him gently on the shoulder as he turned away. Ripley and Fuller stood looking about them, they had joined the squadron with Coulter and Elphinstone only a few days before, and now no-one seemed to even remember them. Webb, walked across to them, releasing a cascade of blonde hair on the way as he removed his cap. There were no words that would help, and he just took them both by their arms, steering them towards the bar with the rest of the squadron.

Stuart jogged to catch up with Julian as the aircrews trudged heavily towards the mess, 'That was a bloody lucky bomb, Canning, you must have hit their ammo dump.'

Julian looked hurt, 'Luck be damned, I saw you dropping too soon and felt that I needed to correct your cock-eyed Scottish aim.' He drew a cigarette from his coat, 'You don't happen to have match do you?'

Stuart glared at him, 'You had better not try and write that in your combat report.'

'About the matches...? Oh, you mean the wonderful and intentional accuracy of my bomb aiming, I *was* aiming for that ammo dump by the way. Tell you what, if I admit that it was a fluke will you buy me a drink?'

'No.'

'Then I have no choice but to mention my deliberate correction to Captain Stuart's rather below par bomb release in my report. They'll probably give me the MC for it.'

'Bollocks will they.'

'Hell, I deserve something for that bomb and if I can't get a whisky then I'll have a medal instead,' Canning replied and rushed off to the mess to write his report and hand it in before Stuart could censor it.

Combat report of Captain James Stuart 5/4/17

Took off at 0700 on bombing raid. Target Don railway junction. Escort absent at rendezvous. Outward journey uneventful. Released bombs over target, scoring hits on enemy ammunition dump resulting in significant damage. On return journey attacked by six EA. Two aircraft lost.

Signed J. P. M. Stuart

Combat report of 1st Lieutenant Julian Canning 5/4/17

Took off at 0700 on bombing raid. Target Don railway junction. Escort absent at rendezvous. Outward journey uneventful. Over the target I noticed that Captain Stuart had dropped his bombs rather early. Realising this and wanting to inflict maximum damage on our nefarious German foe, I deliberately waited, and succeeded in scoring a direct hit on the ammunition dump, at which I was definitely aiming. By doing this, I succeeded in destroying most of the junction, including several locomotives single-handedly and severely inconveniencing the German war effort. Top notch stuff on my part really. On return journey attacked by several EA. Two aircraft lost.

Signed J. H. Canning

The squadron had returned to the airfield at 1010, by 1025 the fifth bottle of whisky was being emptied at the bar. When Billington entered the mess shortly after, his nostrils twitched at the smell of the alcohol.

'33B squadron, 'ten – shun!'

A couple of officers put down their glasses.

Billington's top lip curled in an unpleasant sneer, 'Orders for the rest of the day gentlemen, squadron is stood down to allow radio equipment to be fitted and calibrated for the commencement of artillery liaison operations in earnest tomorrow.' A collective sigh was breathed around the mess.

'Except…' Nerves twanged, 'Lieutenant Canning…' all but two men relaxed, 'I believe you still owe me some photographs.'

'Oh for Christ's sake, Billy…'

'*Your* aircraft has been fitted with a camera and refuelled.' Billington turned sharply on his heel.

Canning drained his glass and spoke quietly to Two Berts so no-one else would hear, 'Look, this mess is my bloody fault, you stay here and I'll go and get those photos, just make sure there's a whisky waiting when I get back.'

Two Berts eyed him coolly and with a slight smile, 'You do realise you can fuck right off, don't you?' He replied.

Thirty minutes later and Julian was back above the earth, with Two Berts sat resolutely in front of him. His engine, in protest at being in use for almost five hours straight, was vibrating unsettlingly, the needle of the tachometer jumping around erratically. The air had become more crowded as the day had gone on, and as he approached the Lines, it was seemingly brimming with aeroplanes, operating both alone and in formations, bustling to and fro. The sky above the Front Lines appeared to be permanently stained with smoke from anti-aircraft fire, white on the British side, black on the German. Julian climbed for height as he approached the front, he was hoping to simply fly over, take the photographs and make a sweeping dive back to the aerodrome. But as he crossed the lines he was alarmed by the intensity of the anti-aircraft barrage that the Germans put up. He took it rather personally, since there were so many other aircraft in the sky, and yet they had apparently singled him out for a real pasting. The BE bucked and rocked on the blasts of uneven air produced by the shells and his progress across the heavens was marked by a splattered smoke trail of black shell bursts. Two Berts was busy searching for enemy scouts, although he was quite aware that none would dare approach them through the hail of gunfire, it would be a cessation in the maelstrom that would signify danger. Well, danger of a different kind at least. A shell exploded unnervingly close on his right-hand side, shards of metal rattling through fabric, whining and pinging off the metal cowling of the engine. Julian was infinitely grateful for the four double whiskeys that he had managed to down in between flights and he slipped off a gauntlet to take a pull from his now freshly filled flask. He swilled its contents around his mouth, relishing the musty, comforting liquor that made the world just that little bit further away, as another airburst under his left wing lifted the BE bodily. Fortunately, the target was just over the Lines and still amid a thunderstorm of anti-aircraft fire, he exposed three plates and then swung back towards home in a shallow dive, his features slowly becoming less and less tense as the shellfire trailed away behind him, and he only remembered the pain of his nose as Pouilly-Yvredon swam into view. He bounced across the airfield minutes later, almost overshooting the landing strip, ending up quite near the sheds. He had just climbed down and was walking away when a strangled cry from the photographic Sergeant brought him spinning back round on his heel.

'Sir! You'd better 'ave a look at this.'

'This' was a large, twisted gash that had been torn in the metal body of the camera, wrecking the inside workings.

'Shit,' he muttered, 'Double shit. Develop the bloody plates, Sergeant, and hope it happened after I took 'em,' he ordered, gesturing at the shapeless mass of metal despairingly.

The new wirelesses arrived shortly after lunch and the mechanics spent the afternoon fitting them to the BEs whilst the aircrews calibrated them to the correct frequencies. Billington appeared briefly and tried to force Canning to retake the photographs, as the damage to the camera had apparently happened on the way to the target, which meant that the plates he had exposed had been completely spoiled. Julian started to put up an animated protest, which Stuart overheard and intervened, overruling Billington, and telling him that preparing the radios was far more important than an out of date reconnaissance.

'I will have my photographs, Lieutenant,' hissed the adjutant, his mouth close to Julian's ear, head bent forwards, 'There is a gap in my records, which is... unacceptable.'

As he walked away, Canning gave the V-sign to his back, then hid his face in a panic and pretended to busy himself with a transmitter, as the green eyes flicked back over the pristine khaki shoulder. He kept his head buried until Billington disappeared from the corner of his eye, and exhaled the breath he had been holding, returning to the task of calibrating his radio. And since this was fairly gentle work that could be accomplished whilst drinking, most of the squadron were pleasantly lubricated by the time it came to dinner. The fact that four men were dead was forgotten, because it had to be. One less table was added onto the hodgepodge furniture that formed the dining arrangements, and it was almost as if they had never existed. Or, more accurately, as if nobody had died. The conversation carefully avoided almost the entirety of the morning's events, with one exception, the damage that Canning's final bomb had inflicted.

'You do realise that you're an unconscionably lucky bastard, don't you?' Webb said to Julian through a mouthful of tepid corned beef, 'I mean that was an utterly outrageous fluke.'

'Bollocks,' grunted Canning in response, 'No such thing as luck.' He caught a glimpse of his freshly equipped BE being wheeled into a hangar through the mess window, 'And I'm not lucky.'

'Piffle.' Broke in Shellford, sitting back and blowing a smoke ring, with the air of a man about to impart monumental wisdom, 'Of course there's such a thing as luck, and some people *are* just lucky,' he said definitively, 'It's a mathematical inevitability overlaid with an interpretive lens.'

He paused, waiting for someone to bite. No-one did, although a few of the newer faces turned towards him, curious.

'Think about it,' the tall pilot decided to persevere regardless, and Canning felt his brain begin to drift away in protest at being subjected to another of Shellford's sermons.

'Things happen to us, events or outcomes, that have a probability of occurring, the most basic example would be rolling a die, each number has a one in six chance of appearing. So, the die falls, and "stuff" happens. And then when this "stuff" is viewed through a societal lens, or applied to our own personal circumstances, we imbue it with positive or negative connotations. Again, to simplify things, it's like tossing a coin, heads or tails, good or bad. For instance, whilst we happy few around this table would view Canning's bomb as a jolly good show, I'd wager the poor old Huns on the receiving end feel somewhat differently. But the fact that a bomb dropped from ten-thousand feet landed smack bang in the middle of an ammo dump is simply a singular, factual event.

So, to summarise, we can all agree that the occurrence of each event is objective and probability based. And its subsequent perception is based on an individual circumstances which are constantly in flux, and let us say therefore, also randomly determined.

'Oh God,' muttered Two Berts, as Shellford swirled his cigarette imperiously.

'But the laws of probability dictate that some people will experience more events of low probability, which they view to be positive. Basic mathematics. If an infinite number of people are all rolling dice and tossing coins then someone is going keep rolling sixes, and landing heads, and someone will keep rolling ones, and getting tails. And of course, it could all change with every roll, but for some folks it doesn't.

'And those are the people fated to move through their lives either almost entirely lucky, or unlucky. They are fated, ironically enough, by the laws of chance.' He exhaled and his prominent Adam's apple oscillated as he drained his glass, 'So you see Canning? You're an outlier, you don't belong in the bell curve with the rest of us. You're a mathematical freak.'

He turned triumphantly to Julian who whose mind was currently back in the cleavage of a prostitute he had hired in Amiens back in December.

'You're a bell curve,' muttered Two Berts and Shellford was about to throw the salt cellar at him when Billington and the Major intruded to allocate the following day's assignments. The majority of targets were enemy batteries that threatened to disrupt the advance if left unmolested, although Shellford and Armitage St. Clare both received forward supply dumps for their morning objectives, which were a little more interesting, as they promised big fireworks if they could get their shots ranged accurately. Julian was given a small field battery for his morning target and a communication headquarters embedded in the trench system, which would almost certainly be impossible to hit, for the afternoon.

After orders had been issued, the post was distributed, and dining arrangements dispersed as men dragged whatever chair they had claimed for the evening, to squirrel away in their own corner of the room, and hungrily consume the thoughts and words of loved ones. Canning received a short note from his mother bemoaning the lack of growth from her latest geranium crop and detailing his father's ever worsening ingrown toenail. He crumpled it up in exasperation and tossed it at Webb, who was sat across an armchair, smoking, his legs still in their sheepskin boots, dangling languidly. The blonde pilot looked up in mild surprise as the paper missile landed gently in his lap, then shook his head at Julian.

'It's that sort of behaviour that just goes to prove him right, you know.' He said reprovingly, waving his own four-page missive at Canning.

'Proves who what?'

'My father, thinks us flyboys are all cavalier, workshy

malingerers. Says so in his latest treatise.'
Canning's expression asked why he should care.

'Sent me a newspaper cutting about the latest Zepplin raid. Says people are dying back home in England and none of us are lifting a finger to defend them.'

'That's 'cause we're in France,' chipped in Shellford laconically, who was sharing a sofa with Ripley.

'How many people were killed?' Asked Ripley, with genuine interest.

'Eight in London. Plus thirteen wounded.' Webb studied his fingernails. 'A veritable bloodbath.'
Canning snorted.

'Perspective was never his strong suit. But apparently that's where we should be, defending the people, not buggering about over here.'

'Sign me up,' declared Shellford, 'I'll gladly spend the rest of the war arseing about, chasing balloons over Surrey. Nice little local in the evening, leave the flying jacket on, hair uncombed and the barmaid'll be bouncing around on top of you in a matter of minutes.'

Webb was shaking his head, still reading his letter, 'Thousands dying out here daily, and they'd pull back the one group of people stopping it being triple that number, just for a handful of civilians.' He ground out his cigarette in the bottom of the tumbler, 'I mean, do you think they really know how bad it is out here, back home?'
Stuart, sitting in a corner chair with a brandy, looked up from his newspaper with a frown. He had found that discussions that took this tack were very rarely constructive.

'I mean, how can they?' Webb continued, answering his own question, 'With all the censorship, and just look at the bloody papers.' He waved the black and white clipping that showed an artist's impression of a great, cigar shaped monolith emerging menacingly from a cloud bank.

'And look at all the rubbish written about the Huns when all this started,' he continued, 'Raping babies and bayonetting nuns. Do people really believe that crap?'

Julian got up walked to the bar and poured himself another drink, scratching it into the mess book.

'People are idiots,' he offered with a shrug.

'That's your in-depth, considered opinion?'

He nodded sincerely in reply, sitting back down, 'Apparently, they believe it. Therefore, they're idiots.'

'It's why they hanged a monkey in Hartlepool,' declared Two Berts, jumping in with a flash of inspiration.

Several pairs of bemused eyes turned to him.

'Seriously, they found a monkey in Hartlepool and thought it was a Frenchman, so they hanged it.'

'When was this? I didn't read about it,' asked Shellford, frowning.

'No, no, it was years ago, Napoleon and all that.'

Julian looked confused, 'Was the monkey French?'

'Wha...I don't know, that's not the point. The point is that all the papers and proclamations, or whatever it was they had back then. They all showed the French as evil, vicious, ape-men. And people took it literally.'

'Yes, but Hartlepool's in the North,' explained Shellford patiently, 'you can't expect too much from them up there, they've only just discovered fire.'

He grinned at the observer, 'And one day, when you've proved yourselves ready, we'll ask them to share its secrets with the Welsh too...'

Two Berts threw his cigarette butt at him, 'The Prime Minister of bloody England is bloody Welsh.'

'True enough,' Shellford conceded, 'somehow, we've now got one of you sheep-shagging luddites running the show,' he got ready to duck behind Ripley, as Two Berts looked like he was about to throw his glass at him, 'It's the bloody papers again, he's got them in his back pocket and made himself a hero. Sort of goes to Mr. Canning's point, people are idiots.'

'He did a bloody good job with the shell shortage,' protested Ripley, his faced flushed from his third whisky.

Shellford turned to him and put a long arm around his shoulders.

'Ripley,' he said, in a fatherly tone, 'If you think that any politician or figure of power has ever done anything for the greater good at their own expense, for any sustained period, then you're an idiot too.

'They may make an occasional gesture based upon a sudden flash of social conscience or a need for publicity but they are, to a man, self-serving, self-aggrandising, vain, evil creatures, more interested in their own wealth, power and control than the welfare of any one of us.'

He lit another cigarette and it wobbled between his lips as he spoke, 'I know them, my father sits in the Lords. Well, he has a seat in the Lords, he never bloody bothers to turn up. But you have to be one of them to get into those positions, if you don't play the game, you can't join in. It's all designed specifically to keep everyone else out.

'Which is probably for the best, we can't have the damned peasants running the show, they'd start eating each other. But don't ever let that blind you to what they really are. Not one of them would ever take the bullet for you that you will end up taking for them.'

Webb dropped back into his armchair after refilling his glass, 'So you don't think there's any chance of the Old Goat stopping all this?' He asked Shellford.

Maybe, if it suited him, but imagine if we were to go on and win it now though, *the man who won the war.*'

'Jesus fuck, no man can win this war, a million bloody men can't,' broke in Connelly, who up to this point had been listening silently.

'Be happy for a few more of 'em to die trying, just in case,' replied Shellford.

'Maybe if we made him put on some whites and help with some mustard gas cases he might take a different view,' mused Webb, 'then again he'd probably just pose for the cameras while he was doing it. Still,' he waved his letter again, 'Dear old Papa thinks he's the man to sort us all out.'

'It's like I said,' broke in Julian, with an imperious waft of his cigarette hand, 'people are idiots. Most are happy to believe anything in order to avoid thinking for themselves. It's why religions have done so well.'

'So you don't believe…' started Ripley, shocked.

'It's horseshit,' Canning interrupted, 'Believing in magic like a bunch of bloody children.'

'But isn't there…'

'Horseshit.' He repeated decisively. Killing the discussion before it could be resurrected

Over the next few hours, the mess steadily emptied, as the aircrews reached the limits of their capacity for whisky, and went to collapse on their cots. But Two Berts, Shellford, Webb and Connelly all stayed up, and doggedly spent the remainder of the evening plying Canning with an inordinate amount of alcohol. Julian had learnt two things during his time in the Flying Corps, the first was never volunteer for anything. Ever. And the second was never to pass up a free drink. Heroically, he stuck to this principle as he became increasingly insensible and finally succumbed when, attempting to launch into song, he opened his mouth, emitted a mighty belch and keeled over. Immediately, the four men dragged the unconscious Canning back to their hut where they stripped him and went to work. Shellford was whistling cheerfully as he set about giving him a full shave and haircut, whilst Webb was flinching as he hacked at the yellow toenails. 'Shit,' he yelped, as one struck him in the eye and he reached for his flying goggles for protection.

'Right,' said Connolly as he finished sponging the armpits with a bucket of water and threw a liberal coating of talcum powder across Canning's midriff. 'Turn him over.'

They had drawn lots to divide up the various tasks and Two Berts, who had drawn the short straw and consequently Julian's bottom half, turned an odd shade of puce.

Half an hour later and they dumped a freshly scrubbed

Canning back onto his bed in his underwear.

'Oh bollocks, I forgot his fingernails,' grumbled Webb and set to work with a pair of scissors.

Slowly, all four men stood back to admire their handiwork. It had been a unifying experience, one that binds men together but also leaves scars that they never talk about. Two Berts looked particularly shaken. It was worth it though, they were all in agreement about that. For the price of a few drinks and forty-five minutes best forgotten, they had guaranteed themselves a couple of weeks' sanitation in the hut. And, best of all, right now was the longest amount of time before they'd have to do it again and, if they were lucky, thought Shellford, they might all be dead by then.

CHAPTER 8

6th April 1917

Julian awoke to the immediate realisation that something was different. His head hurt, which was normal and he was cold, which was also normal. He was colder than usual though, because apparently he hadn't slept in his uniform, which was odd. And he felt strangely...clean? Delicately, he stroked his face with his fingertips and noticed two things. The first was the absence of the comforting roughness of his stubble, the second was that his fingernails no longer made contact before his fingertips.

Tentatively, he edged out of his bed, seeking reassurance in his hangover. He watched the sunrise from the hut doorstep, realised what it meant and, in the absence of any alcohol, lit a cigarette, smoked it, lit another and still felt scared. He really, really didn't want to die, the whole idea of it terrified him. Not being religious, he could only imagine the black nothingness, and since it was impossible for a human being to really grasp the concept of that black nothingness, he remained very scared. And the most galling thing was that he was in completely the wrong place for people who didn't want to die. The notion that in a few hours' time he might actually cease to exist seemed unreal, and yet his insides seemed to grasp it perfectly and were squirming in protest. Quickly he lit another cigarette and searched for something to distract him from his thoughts. He was quite pleased that his head hurt though, it would have been such a waste to die in good mood, far better to go down with a hangover.

Grumbling softly to himself, he crossed to the single mirror at the far end of the hut and, striking a match, he examined himself. In the pathetic, flickering half-light he caught sight of what, if one discounted the swollen black and purple nose, would have passed for a respectable young 1st Lieutenant in the RFC. He was clean-shaven and his hair, apart from a few strands disturbed by sleep was shorter, oiled and combed over in a neat side parting.

'YOU BASTARDS!' he exploded and Shellford in the nearest cot fell out of bed with a yell, and sprawled on the floor.

'What the fuck have you done to me?' The entire hut was still recovering from the shock of being woken up so violently, and no one answered. After a couple of seconds Two Berts hurled a cake of soap that missed Canning's head by a foot.

'You've done it *again*! You utter bastards.'

'Oh stop whining, you might be able to get a whore now,' Shellford muttered as he struggled to get back into bed.
Julian promptly dragged him back out by his leg and the two of them grappled clumsily on the floor. Webb and Connolly looked at each other enviously and then the hut door opened and their steward was greeted by the relatively common sight of officers brawling, and the utterly unheard of sight of Lieutenant Canning clean shaven and wide awake.

He paused for a moment to gather himself then announced, 'Major Frost's compliments gentlemen, would all officers please assemble in the mess at 0530, prior to take-off.'
He ducked neatly as Julian flung the bar of soap at him.

'Thank you, Rossiter,' called Shellford, digging his elbow sharply into Canning's ribcage.

Julian found himself the recipient of several surprised glances as he entered the mess and he scowled back at each one in turn. The squadron had been detailed to take-off at 0600, but a sudden influx of cloud and rain had caused a delay, provoking a brief flaring of hope that the day might be abandoned to dud weather. Headquarters however, had decided that this was very definitely not to be the case, and at

0615 a call came through to that effect. The result of all of this was that Stuart took off at 0630 through a fine mezz of water droplets. A replacement pilot and observer crew had arrived early that morning, and the new observer was immediately detailed to fly with Shellford. He had introduced himself, but due to a combination of the noise of the engines and his muffling, fur-lined flying helmet, Shellford couldn't quite make out his name, so had just given him a broad smile and clapped him on the shoulder encouragingly, as the young man quickly donned his flying gear.

Canning's mechanics swung the big, four bladed propeller and the engine coughed into life. The wind whipped the rain into his face at a speed that made his nose hurt and he winced at the solid draft of air as he opened the throttle, clambering into the sky to rendezvous with his battery over Le Tilleuls. Half an hour saw the remainder of the squadron airborne, apart from Cross, the replacement pilot whose observer had been assigned to Shellford, who had been left standing uselessly on the steps of the squadron office without an aeroplane, next to Billington and Major Frost, watching the BEs depart. Without a word, Frost turned and walked slowly back into his office and sat behind his desk. He would stay there, doing nothing, just sitting and listening for the first spluttering throb that would signify a safe return. Billington glanced over, gave a satisfied little smile and strode to his office. Cross remained alone on the steps, getting wet.

The first pair to return were B Flight's Forsyth and Bolinbroke, a mere twenty minutes later, trailing a line of dark smoke from an engine that was misfiring horribly. Forsyth, hoping it was terminal, went back to bed. Bolinbroke sat in the mess reading a week-old French newspaper. He didn't notice Cross sitting quietly in the corner.

Several thousand feet above them, Canning was having a far less relaxing time. He had made it to the target area, wound down the aerial and contacted the battery, all without getting lost. But now, a disconcerting lump of dark cloud had parked itself directly on top of him. In addition to gently pissing down on him as he flew the shambling figure-eights, it provided the perfect hiding spot for any predatory German fighters. Two Berts shared his misgivings and both men watched it suspiciously.

As the shoot wore on the pile of cloud grew more and more menacing, deep, craggy crevices lining its ugly, evil face. Its figures shifted, transfigured to become a decrepit old man with a heavy, protruding brow fixed in a frown, and a huge curved proboscis of a nose. The face glared down upon them, the two airmen watched and judged by some great celestial visage, and it was no great surprise to either of them when a dark speck emerged from the left nostril and fell upon them, rapidly taking the form of an Albatros scout. The Hun aircraft dropped, rolled and then seemed to scythe across the sky in a flashing, arcing curve, which made shooting at it near impossible, and it fired a vicious machine gun burst that passed between the BE's starboard wings. Two Berts had not been idle and had snatched off a couple of long-range warning shots over Canning's shoulder, but such was the German's angle of attack, they had gone embarrassingly wide. The Albatros shot past, rocketed below the BE and then soared upward again in an attempt to rip into the two-seater's blind spot. Julian, who had been engrossed in a desperate endeavour to wind in the aerial, so he could manoeuvre without it tearing the aircraft apart, saw this and booted his right foot hard against the rudder bar, with the result that the BE lurched sickeningly and fell into a jerky sideslip that threw a helpless Two Berts against the side of his cockpit, winding him slightly.

The move succeeded in throwing the German scout pilot off his aim though, and the stream of bullets that would have carved up through the fuselage directly under them both, instead burst through the wings with the sound of tearing fabric. The Albatros soared over the starboard side of the BE in a half roll. It was painted a dull green and brown all over with the exception of the nose, which was blue, and a large white 'G' on the fuselage next to the menacing iron crosses. The German fighter continued on past the British two-seater then made as if to loop but, halfway through while it was upside down, rolled out level in a perfect Immelmann turn and swooped back down on the BE again, guns sparking and black tracer streaking from the engine cowling. More bullets tore through the wings and shots pinged and sparked off the metal of the engine as Two Berts desperately tried to find a clear path to return the fire, from amongst the tangled cage of struts and wires.

As the German flew back overhead, guns rattling, Julian realised that he was hopelessly outmatched. His aircraft was already riddled with bullet holes and it was only a matter of time before one found a critical spot in either him or the engine. Then, in a flash of inspiration, he realised that the same cloud which, moments earlier, had spat out the German fighter like an avenging angel, could also be his sanctuary. The BE had lost a lot of height during the hobbling dance that Canning had forced it through, but it was now his only chance and he streaked flat out, climbing for the base of it. The Hun pilot, discerning his intention, attacked again but this time Two Berts managed to put a burst of fire through the drab fuselage, sending up shivers of plywood, as the Albatros banked away.

The BE was so nearly there, Julian could almost reach up and touch the thick grey vapour but the Albatros came back for one final attempt before its quarry could escape. The Hun came in from the right, guns blazing and bullets buzzed like wasps, some of the shots tore through the struts that bordered Two Berts' cockpit and the Welshman went down amongst a hail of splinters. The guns on the German scout kept up their staccato death chant, and in a desperate panic, Canning grabbed furiously for his flare gun and launched a fiery green ball in the general direction of the Albatros.

It passed harmlessly wide but for a split second the German

pilot's experience counted against him. Reconnaissance aircraft often used flares to signal to their escort and bring them down upon attacking enemy fighters, the German knew this and although he had not seen any British scouts on his approach, he now shared the same reservations about the brutish mound of cloud in which he had previously hidden. The pale blue eyes that peered through the crosshairs mounted over the twin machine guns, eyes that had seen the observer in the BE collapse into his cockpit under a storm of gunfire and that had now lined up the begoggled pilot for the same treatment, began a rapid search of the sky as the green fireball dropped to earth underneath him.

Those few seconds gave Julian just enough time to heave the nose of the BE up into the solid mass above it. He felt the cold damp of the heavy mist as it smeared his face, along with the lurching of his stomach as he caught sight of the empty cockpit in front of him that quickly subsided to relief as a rather shaken looking Two Berts emerged, blood flowing freely from a head wound. He pushed up his goggles and grinned sheepishly at Julian. Canning leaned forward and proffered his hipflask. The observer reached back and took it, drank deeply, then glanced at his compass and pointed towards home. Canning obligingly turned and followed the outstretched finger.

He stayed in the cloud for as long as possible and whilst, in any other aeroplane keeping on even keel whilst flying blind would have been a challenge, the BE stayed rigidly on course. Eventually they ran out of cloud and emerged out the other side into a world only slightly less grey and damp, with the trenches passing below them. It was Two Berts who saw it first, the same Albatros diving down from the top of the cloud formation. It had been waiting for them. He waved at Canning, pointed, then much to the consternation of his pilot, disappeared into his cockpit. Julian took a couple of seconds to realise that his observer, possibly as a result of blood loss, was intent on setting up a trap for the approaching German. The Albatros thought that the gunner of the BE was dead, had seen Two Berts fall, and therefore thought the lumbering two-seater utterly helpless. He would come in, close, and make sure of his kill. All it needed was for Canning to hold his nerve... and he lost it when the German was still well over five hundred yards away.

'Get up you Welsh bastard!' he hollered above the noise of the engine. 'Shoot the fucker!'

Panicking, he seized his Very pistol, stood up and hurled it into the cockpit in front of him but failed to provoke a reaction. The Albatros was now only a hundred yards away and Julian's head was very neatly centred in the crosshairs of the twin Maxim guns. Desperately, he heaved at the control column but the BE seemed to take an age to react. Eighty yards away now, the sinews of a pair of neatly manicured hands that were ensconced in fine Bavarian leather pulled tight, fingers seeking the firing button on the control column of the blue nosed fighter. Suddenly Two Berts erupted from his cockpit, seized the dormant Lewis gun and sent a murderous stream of bullets over Julian's shoulder, directly into the complacent Albatros. Canning watched as shards of blue cowling splintered off and the German rolled desperately to escape the withering hail of fire that was tearing chunks from his machine, and fell away below. Two Berts stood up and grinned triumphantly, dried blood crusting on his forehead and a feral look in his eyes that blazed through the goggles. Slowly, he reached into his cockpit and retrieved Canning's flare pistol, waving it at him with a grin that was all teeth. Beneath them, the Albatros continued to spin towards the ground.

Two hours after they had taken off, Canning and Two Burts bumped across the aerodrome, their aircraft trailing shreds of fabric from the wings and fuselage. The initial concern of their mechanics subsided as both pilot and observer climbed stiffly down. They were the third crew to return. Stuart and Marshall had destroyed their target and Webb and Connolly had been chased home by an entire *Staffel* of Albatroses and both were smiling about it now, if only somewhat wanly. As the sound of the engine died away, the surrounding squadron members heard Canning's voice rise up.

'You stupid arse, what the hell were you playing at? You nearly got me killed!'

Two Berts smiled wolfishly, 'Not a chance, Canning boy. I had that Boche all sewn up and I owed it to him…'

'Owed what to him?'

'Have you seen my head? The bastard shot a chunk of strut into it, bloody hell but I thought I was a goner.'

'Not a chance. You could put a fucking field shell through your empty pissing head and you'd still be bloody grinning.'

'Bloody 'ell, Sir, you took a pastin' didn't you?' Julian's Flight Sergeant interrupted, admiring the bullet-riddled fuselage.

'Oh, how very fucking observant of you, Flight Sergeant.' Canning snapped, turning his ire on the mechanic.

'Oh, shut up you miserable bugger and let's go and claim my kill,' broke in Two Berts and shepherded Canning off to the squadron office.

A half hour investigation failed to produce any reports of a crashed Albatros over Le Tilleuls though, and Two Berts was becoming increasingly agitated.

'He went down, straight down spinning, you saw him didn't you, Canning?' he pleaded desperately as Billington replaced the receiver on yet another call to a forward observation post.

'Sorry Burton, no confirmation, no kill. You know the rules.'

'Bugger the rules, I saw him go down.'

'But you didn't see him crash?'

'No,' Two Berts conceded, 'but he was going down sharpish.'

Billington shook his head dismissively, 'He could quite easily have been shamming, especially if he was as good as you claim.'

Two Berts was about to argue back when the sound of an aero engine became faintly apparent. The only BE yet to return was Shellford's and the distant growl, growing ever louder, suggested that the squadron had made it through the morning unscathed. However, when the BE failed to complete the usual circuit of the airfield prior to landing, instead making its approach directly, hitting the ground clumsily and taxiing at speed towards the hangars, the onlookers sensed that something was amiss and began to sprint towards the aeroplane. By the time they reached it, Shellford was standing on the grass next to the aircraft, ashen faced. A group of mechanics were clustered around the front cockpit, trying carefully to remove the limp form of his observer from the front cockpit. Finally, they managed to extricate the leather-clad figure, feet first, and as Ripley rushed in to help support the head, he reeled away and vomited.

The entire top left quarter of the boy's head had been shot away, and in its place was a ragged red gash that was pitted with shattered scraps of skull, like broken eggshell. The shards of bone nestled among the mashed brain and stuck to the trailing tendrils of jelly that dribbled into the turf, as the body was laid prostrate on the ground. Shellford walked over in carefully measured steps and stood over his observer, staring. A single, remaining eye peered back through shattered goggles, blood beginning to congeal in the creases around the nose. He pulled off his own helmet to reveal the jumbled wisps of fair hair, with the faintest trace of grey. The airfield was oddly quiet, the only noise the distant crackle of a Lewis gun being tested in the pits. Then he noticed that Two Berts and Julian were standing at his shoulders.

'Albatros,' he paused. 'Came out of the sun just as we were coming back, got the poor little bugger with his first burst.'

He gestured with a dismissive flick of the arm to the front cockpit. The struts had been stained a deep burgundy with dried blood and chunks of tissue. More globules of brain matter had splattered on the underside of the top wing.

'Never even found out his name,' he muttered huskily and then suddenly seemed to realise where he was and who he was and, like a man shrugging on a coat, he became Shellford again.

'Flight Sergeant?'

'Yes, Sir?' The mechanic's voice was softly reverent.

'Make sure someone takes some soap a scrubbing brush to that,' he pointed at the blood spatter, 'I'll need her brain free and ready for 1400 this afternoon.'

He turned away and then stopped by the small group of mechanics who were still staring at the shredded red hole, which oozed a sickly pink gel that seeped into the earth.

'Alright take it away now, it's making the bloody place untidy,' he ordered in a voice that quavered mid-sentence but finished firm and sure, before turning to walk back to his quarters.

Five minutes later, Julian and Two Berts entered the hut. Shellford was laid on his bed, an open book in front of him, although he wasn't turning the pages. Without a word, the two men quickly dumped their flying gear on their respective mattresses and made to leave. As he turned, Canning's boot appeared to clumsily catch a third full bottle of scotch that was standing next to his bed and sent it spinning the length of the hut, to finish just short of Shellford, who didn't even look up from his book. As the door clicked shut behind Canning and Two Berts, a hand reached down. A hand, whose trembling subsided as is grasped the cool green glass.

Walking back towards the mess they were accosted by Billington, who informed Canning that a despatch rider had dropped a packet off for him.

'I've almost copped a packet already this morning,' muttered Julian, but Billington was already striding back across the turf. His curiosity was piqued however, by the thought that someone might have been decent enough to send him a crate of whisky for all his hard work in the war so far, so he trotted after Billington, into the squadron office, where the adjutant tossed across a brown paper parcel, tied with string. Julian caught it, surprised and disappointed at how light it was, and tore open the paper. Out fell a long, thick, rusty claret coloured length of knitted cord that unravelled to hit the floor. Extended to its full length, it was well in excess of seven feet. A small square of card was tied to the end that Canning was holding and in neat, spidery handwriting was written:

Dear Lt. Canning. This is to keep your extremities warm.

There was no signature but Canning glared at it, an unwelcome intrusion into his otherwise simple life. Noticing that Billington was watching him quizzically, he balled up the scarf and walked out, sniffing the wool as he went. It smelt of surgical spirit. He screwed up the paper along with the note and tossed it away, looked at the scarf irritably, then remembered how the chill of the wind hurt his nose and wrapped it four times around his neck

The afternoon passed far less eventfully, and for Julian, with his nose now buried deep within the woollen folds of his new scarf, far less painfully too. The communications bunker he had been assigned to destroy was so embedded in the brown mess of the trenches that Canning couldn't even make out where it was, and instead occupied himself by directing his battery to scatter its shots throughout the coordinate square marked on his map, in which the bunker allegedly lay. It was a process that utterly perplexed the gunners who had no idea quite where their pilot was trying to direct them. After a couple of hours of potholing what used to be the French countryside, Julian turned for home to report his mission accomplished. This time he overshot the aerodrome and finished up landing in an adjacent field but, having caused his aeroplane no apparent damage, dismounted cheerfully enough and left the BE for the mechanics to recover. About half the squadron had returned already and, mercifully, over the next hour the remaining aircrews all returned safely, with no worse damage than a punctured tyre sustained on landing.

As the light faded, Julian was happily pouring himself a rather large whisky at the mess bar when Stuart appeared on his left shoulder, announcing his presence by clearing his throat.

'Canning,' he began, rather formally, 'I have a, er request.'

Julian looked up from his glass sharply, 'Oh for God's sake, Jimmy, I've nearly been shot down once already today, get someone else to do it.'

'No, Canning, this is something a little…different.'

Julian frowned at him, noticing the Captain appeared to be rather smartly dressed.

'I have just taken a call and it would appear that the young lady I am currently courting is part of the same medical unit as another young lady, one you met the other night, the one who gave you that scarf, actually. And they have realised that you and I are part of the same outfit too.'

Canning's furrows deepened.

'She has requested a meeting with you, and Clare, that is my, er, friend, has agreed to go to dinner with her, and us, tonight.'

'Fuck off.'

'Look, Canning, I've already tried to kybosh the idea, I told her what you were like, but it seems her friend was quite set on it.'

'We only spoke for a couple of minutes outside the whorehouse, I don't even know her bloody name!'

'It's Lucy,' replied Stuart, looking at him curiously, 'and you obviously made enough of an impression on her in that short space of time to be sent knitwear.'

Canning threw back his glass, 'Don't care, I'm not going.'

The Captain sighed, 'And I'm not giving you a choice.'

'You're ordering me out to dinner?'

'Yes.'

'Or else what?'

Stuart levelled his gaze at him, 'Or else you'll find yourself taking a series of low-level photographs over Douai tomorrow, where I happen to know the Red Baron has just moved in with his mob of multi-coloured killers.'

'Fuck off, you can't do that.'

'Try me. I don't want you there any more than you want to be there. But Lucy must be insistent, because Clare was insistent. Therefore, *I* am insistent.'

'Jesus, if you're that worried about getting your pecker wet just come to the knocking shop with the rest of us tonight.' Canning, along with Two Berts, had managed to orchestrate another trip to the Lamaincourt brothel that evening, mainly in an endeavour to revive Shellford, who was had been hollow eyed since the morning sortie. Stuart's right hand tapped on the bar in agitation. He closed his eyes and breathed slowly to restrain himself.

'Go and get changed, Canning.'

Two hours later and Stuart's face creased in anger as Canning trudged through the mess door, still dressed in his flying gear.

'Take that bloody coat off, you're not wearing that.'

Julian stubbornly tried to stare him down until Stuart took a pace forwards, menacingly.

'Take it off, or I'll take it off you myself, laddie.'

Petulantly, and fixing Stuart with a sullen glare, he dropped his flying jacket onto the floor of the mess and remained standing in his scarf and sheepskin boots. Stuart thought about ordering Julian to take those off as well but decided not to push him too far, and instead led them all out to the tender.

The atmosphere that evening was strained, grating and un-oiled, as if something wasn't quite right. Even Shellford's usual verbosity and carefully projected boorishness lacked its normal hearty carnality. It felt forced and empty, like Shellford was trying too hard to be Shellford. His rigger had done his best to remove the stains that had speckled the wings of his aircraft but traces had remained, no more than a darkening of the canvas in places, but Shellford had still spent most of the afternoon staring at them, his eyes fixed on the constellation of blood spots. The armoury Corporal, serving as a temporary gunner in the front seat, had been blissfully unaware of his pilot's preoccupation. As the Crossley ploughed on, bottles of whisky circulated, Shellford's, gulps lasting that bit longer than usual. So much so, that by the time they arrived in town, he was already reeling and struggling to maintain his balance. Canning watched solemnly as Two Berts hefted Shellford's left arm over his shoulder and steered him towards the nearest bar.

'I'll be leaving for home at half-past midnight, anyone not back here by then will need to procure a bicycle.' Stuart hollered at the rapidly diminishing backs of the squadron as he pulled Julian away from them and towards the restaurant.

CHAPTER 9

6th April 1917

Stuart contemplated the two young women opposite him, although other than their age, nothing else about them was actually young, he thought. There was creasing and bagging around their eyes, their mouths were tightly drawn, and their faces were dulled by a pallid grey caste. He had the same look himself, and so did Canning beside him. It told of the death that their voices never would. Nothing could come to this place and keep its youth, the new boys were either killed or became old too. There was no escape. And someday, when they could all finally go home, he was sure their comfortably middle aged parents would still look at them as the youths that they remembered the day they left. That they could never be again. They had killed youth.

The Captain grimaced, embarrassed at the melodrama of his own thoughts, then swigged his wine and grimaced again. Plenty of youth in that, he mused. And besides, not everyone assumed this cadence, he had met several fighter pilots whose gaze was blank and who only saw the scorebook and a game. He wasn't sure if they were natural born killers or just idiots, unable to make the connection between canvas and flesh. Others immersed themselves in hatred, but that was often just a way to find the parts of themselves capable of ignoring pleading eyes and driving a bayonet into a soft gut. Then there were those that thrived on the war, enjoyed it, who revelled in the violence. They were the real sadists, the ones who took their sick pleasure in debasing others, breaking them down, examining their pain and feeding off it. They had always found their niche in the world, but war was their element, their cruelty going unnoticed or even celebrated.

His eyes fell to Canning's hands. They looked large and clumsy, and yet even these hands had worked the Morse-tapper, had directed the shells and gas that would have killed... hundreds? Thousands? Maybe. And he had done exactly the same from his own aircraft. The only difference between himself and the sadists was that he took no pleasure, felt no thrill from the killing. Did that make him different or better? Whatever the real answer was, he thought, the answer was yes.

Suddenly aware of his reverie, he snapped back to reality and glared at Canning, who was staring blatantly at Clare's ample chest. He gave his shin a hard kick under the table, drawing a sharp intake of breath and a dirty look, before Canning's eyes fell back to his plate. The man had hardly said a word since they had sat down and Stuart realised that he was still sulking. He shook his head, exasperated, and looked apologetically at Clare and Lucy. Clare just motioned at him with her head to hurry up and eat so they could leave. Lucy looked on, apparently unflustered by Canning's peevishness.

Stuart motored through the rest of the meal, making perfunctory small talk, but Julian's contribution never extended beyond a cursory grunt. Eventually the Scotsman gave up and quickly finished his desert, dropping a handful of Francs onto the table as he and Clare went to find somewhere that would rent them a room for an hour or two. He distinctly heard Clare's whispered apology to Lucy as they made to leave and saw Lucy's slight shrug of her slim shoulders in reply. Canning sucked on his wine glass, eyeing his Captain evilly from below a darkened brow as he left, before realising that he was now alone with Lucy, and he accidentally met her gaze. They looked at each other and in the brighter light of the restaurant he considered his initial assessment of her, and thought he had been right. She looked damned average.

She smiled at him, 'Nice to see that you've made an effort, you look a lot healthier than you did the other night.'

Canning scowled at her but said nothing, she continued unabashed.

'And you must like the scarf then?' She inclined her head towards him and Julian cursed inwardly, as he realised that he hadn't taken it off when he had discarded his flying jacket in the mess.

'You knit bloody quickly.' He grunted.

She smiled again, and something flickered for a second inside of him, mirrored by the candle that sat between them as the shadows danced and played in the small wrinkles around her mouth.

'Actually, I took it from a fighter pilot who died on the table.' Julian looked at her with distaste.

'Don't worry, I disinfected it. And it's red, so the blood stains don't show.'

She sipped her wine, the liquor staining her lips slightly purple. The notes of *Poor Butterfly* wafted over them from a battered gramophone in the corner. Cigarette smoke cast a veil between them.

Neither of them said anything and Julian began to look around irritably. The music stopped and was replaced by the crackle-snap of the needle, repetitive and grating on his nerves. Despite normally being eminently comfortable with social awkwardness, he cracked first.

'What?' He snapped, tersely.

'What do you mean, "what?"'

'What do you want? Why are you here?'

'Well I thought you were interesting when I met you the other night and when I found out you were in the same squadron as Clare's regular shag, I thought it might be interesting to see you again.'

'What do you mean "interesting,"' frowned Canning, taking a swig of wine.

'Well, there's an awful lot of smartly dressed chaps walking around with their chests puffed out, saluting each other and dying horribly as a result. You, on the other hand, appear to be

such an unapologetic disaster, and so at odds with everything and everyone else around here, that I find you interesting. Similar to the way the chimps in London Zoo are interesting.'
Unconsciously, Julian scratched his head. Someone reset the gramophone and *Poor Butterfly* started up again.

'So why are *you* here?' She asked him.

'Because Stuart ordered me to be.'

'Oh,' she looked a little hurt.

In the ensuing silence, Canning filled their glasses from what remained of the wine, drained his, then grabbed a waiter by the arm and ordered another two bottles of house red.

She raised her eyebrows at him, 'Two bottles?'

He shrugged, 'Saves asking him twice.'

More silence followed. The wine arrived, placed on the table with a soft but satisfying *thunk*. Julian refilled his glass. Lucy's was still full. He looked up to find her studying his face intently.

'So how exactly did you manage to bust your nose? It looks rather fresh?'

'Hit by a pigeon,' he replied, deadly serious.

She sniggered despite herself and Julian found that he had to stop himself from smiling back. Instead he drained another glass. She sipped from hers.

'What's it like, up there?'

'Shit.'

'Really?'

'Yep. It's cold, wet and there are lots of people trying to kill me.'

'So why do you do it.'

Canning filled and drained another glass, he was two thirds through the first bottle already. He made a sweeping gesture across the restaurant, whose clientele were almost exclusively service personnel.

'Why the hell do any of us do it?'

Several heads turned towards him.

Lucy placed a gentle hand on his and leaned in to quieten

him, 'I mean why did you choose to fly?' She said softly.

'Because it's better than the bloody infantry. At least I thought it was.' He sighed and topped up their glasses again, finishing the bottle and lit another cigarette.

'When all this rubbish started I didn't rush to join up. A lot of the boys did though. Football, rugby, cricket teams, all desperate to do their bit. What could be more fun than a rugby game where you get to kill the other team? Not playing, I thought. But then I was never any good.'

Another swig.

'Then all the top rated chaps got themselves killed and they decided to throw the rest of us into it. So, I thought fuck that, I don't like running, and I like running whilst being shot at even less. And I can't swim, so there went the Navy. Aeroplanes seemed interesting though, peaceful even. Birds and butterflies and all that.'

He stabbed out his cigarette ferociously and lit another.

'I scraped through training, they pass you as long as you can get the bloody machine off the ground, on the basis that everyone gets better once they get out here and into it properly. Except I didn't. And it's not peaceful, it's fucking dangerous. And if I decide I don't want to do it anymore they'll take me away and shoot me.'

His face was starting to flush as he started on the second bottle, his voice beginning to rise again.

'So here I am, a choice between certain death or almost certain death. And all because a bunch of gutless old shits decide to spend their lives playing power games they don't understand. Then they put their old mates in charge of us, and here we all are, dying for the whims of decrepit old men, who tell us we can never be real men ourselves until we've watched the chap next to us having his bowels shot out and screaming like a child as he bleeds to death in a fucking puddle.

'But they keep rolling in, every day a few more kids desperate to earn a respect they don't need. I've met the most vicious killers in the sky and lived, I must've killed hundreds of men through a simple tap of my fingers. I've done more to fuck up the German war effort than pathetic old shits like him will ever do.'

He jabbed his cigarette viciously towards a bespectacled Colonel seated a couple of tables over, who pretended not to notice.

'But if I ever said no, that's enough, no more, they'd brand me a coward and kill me. So I carry on, shit scared. But I was still more of a man than any of 'em the day I pissed myself over Arras'

He was almost shouting now and several patrons were starting to look over. A couple of larger tables were trying to make more noise themselves to drown him out. Lucy watched on, fascinated. Eventually Julian noticed that he was being stared at with particular intensity by a blond youth in a clean RFC uniform, whose chest was bare except for some newly stitched wings. Canning rounded on him.

'What the fuck are you looking at me like that for? I'll tell you now you'll do more than just piss your pants when Jerry gets you. You'll shit yourself as well, then beg for your mother to save you as you burn up in some goddamned corner of French sky.'

The lad spun back round quickly and Julian fell to silence for a good ten seconds, then looked up and met Lucy's eye and shrugged.

'Well, you asked. I'm not apologising.'

'I wouldn't expect you to.'

Through the morass of alcohol, Lucy was beginning to look increasingly attractive, and in a sudden surge of hormones, Canning decided that he would very much like to have sex with her. Or, more accurately, he very much wanted to have sex and Lucy was geographically convenient. He realised that on this occasion however, he couldn't just throw across some money and get what he wanted and that he would need to seduce her instead. He tried to give her what he thought was a charming smile and winked.

Lucy visibly shuddered, 'What the hell was that?' She demanded.

'What?' Canning looked taken aback.

'That.' She repeated, gesturing at his face.

'Look,' he said earnestly, trying to gaze deeply into her eyes, 'I could be dead tomorrow.'

'Oh God, we're at that stage of the evening, are we? Christ, the number of times I've heard that one. Do they issue you all with a phrase book or something when you enlist?'

She downed the rest of her wine in a single swallow and stood up, making to leave.

'Oh don't sit there looking at me like a kicked puppy. I'd like to see you again. Sober though. Because, whilst I have to admit this has been something of a singular experience, you do seem to become a bit of a boor when you're drunk. Not that I've ever seen you in any other state, mind.'

She unfurled a roll of Francs and dropped more than enough to cover her share on the table.

'So, come by and look me up, you know where to find me, field hospital at Le Hameau. I'll be there, Christ knows they let us out rarely enough.'

Something was telling him that he ought to offer to walk her back, or at least object to her walking by herself. But then he thought that might come across as threatening, given what she had just said, so he decided that he was far too drunk to deal with any of this, ordered himself another bottle of wine, and sat back in his chair to wait.

By the time Stuart arrived back, Canning had managed to finish his bottle and was halfway through another, and looking decidedly unsteady, he leaned heavily on his Captain as they left the restaurant. Stuart carefully disentangled his arm as they walked and despite the occasional stumble, once he'd built up a head of steam, Julian seemed capable of making his way back to the tender under his own momentum. Then, as they rounded a corner onto the main square, he projectile vomited a dark, red stream across the street without breaking stride. Stuart quickly stepped out of its path in disgust as it splattered across the flagstones.

They reached the tender as the early hours of the morning threatened and found the rest of the squadron already returned from the brothel, congregated in and around the Crossley. Julian arrived to find Two Berts, looking utterly exhausted but entirely satisfied, sitting slumped against one of the wheels. Webb and Connolly had only just made it back themselves, walking arm in arm. Ripley, his eyes not focused on this world, was meandering gently around the vehicle and finally Shellford, staggering, weaving but looking like a man exorcised.

He stumbled up to Canning, caught his shoulder and, giggling slurrily, stage whispered into his ear, 'I'm broke Canning, flat broke you ugly bastard,' he laughed, then spinning to the group announced with pride, 'Two of 'em! Cost me a fucking fortune but I've just had two of 'em! At the same time! Bloody marvellous…four tits!' And with that he toppled sideways and sprawled on the floor.

CHAPTER 10

7th April 1917

It started as a whisper between Marshall and Shellford in the mess and by 0600 everyone knew, the date of the attack on Vimy had been set for two days' time. This was obviously classified information, so most of the squadron naturally assumed it had been received via the Germans rather than their own intelligence services, who seemed so wonderfully adept at keeping their Teuton equivalents up to date on Allied battle plans, and yet so utterly incompetent at passing on information to their own forces.

Billington stood in front of the assembled officers, clustered higgledy-piggledy in the jumble of chairs about to begin their breakfasts, and allocated them targets. Fresnoy, Arleux, Willerval were all areas designated for shelling, as it was felt they would contain a notable German presence. Canning and Webb were given the task of hammering the town of Farbus, which the British forces were hoping to gain in the offensive. Each BE would work with a single heavy battery of 60-pounders and try to range its guns on the most built up areas, in an attempt to reduce their functionality as defensive positions. Headquarters, announced Billington, had taken a special interest in Farbus, and would be sending them out on a follow up reconnaissance mission the next day to monitor the results.

'Due to the importance of this target,' Billington continued, you will have the entire day to cause as much damage as possible. But, if there is any time remaining Lieutenant Canning, you will provide those photographs that you *still* owe me.'

'Bloody big place Farbus,' grunted Julian with a cigarette hanging from the corner of his mouth, 'take all day to properly fuck it up.'

Billington's teeth clicked at his profanity.

'And one more thing gentlemen, you may be pleased to know that as of yesterday the United States of America has joined the Allied nations, and announced its entry into the war.'

The declaration was met with a distinctly unimpressed silence.

'Silly bastards.' someone muttered and a fart came from the end of the line of tables.

'They will provide much needed men and equipment,' Billington persevered, 'including a large number of trained pilots and the latest combat aircraft.'

'When?' Asked Marshall laconically.

'Soon enough, Lieutenant Marshall.' Billington snapped irritably.

'It won't be soon enough if I bump into the bloody Baron today,' muttered Marshall.

He and Stuart had been ordered to target a battery near Bailleul, where the red-painted Albatroses of Manfed von Richtofen's Jasta 11 had reportedly been hunting. A significant increase in the amount of charred wreckage in the area was testament to their presence.

Billington closed the briefing by announcing that all available fighter squadrons were being directed to destroy the observation balloons that hung just behind the Front Lines, in an attempt to blind the Germans as men and equipment was moved up, meaning that escorts for the observation planes would be limited. Again, this announcement was met with a terse silence.

'A few words, Captain Stuart?' Invited Billington finally, expecting Stuart to take a few minutes to try and impress upon the squadron how crucial their efforts could be to the thousands of troops, huddled in preparation.

Stuart was well aware of how important the work done with

the batteries would be and that, if the German heavy guns and strategic emplacements could be knocked out of action for the next twenty-four hours then maybe, just maybe, the poor bastards below might not have to suffer another Somme. He was often asked to utter little speechettes like this and usually managed a few sentences of encouragement

Today he took a moment to look around at his men and simply said, 'Keep your eyes on the sun.'

Fifteen minutes prior to take off, Webb caught up with Canning at the hangars.

'Hi! Julian!'

Canning turned.

'Round of drinks says I can knock the top off the bloody church off before you.'

Julian grinned, 'You're on!'

The destruction of the already battered town afforded Canning little in the way of a moral quandary. At this point, any civilian with an ounce of sense would have fled the place, meaning that the only inhabitants would be Germans. And it was almost unanimously agreed by everyone he knew that it was absolutely fine to kill, maim and terrify them to whatever extent he was prepared to go.

One by one, the squadron took off and made their way across Northern France towards their targets. Canning and Webb flew side by side before peeling away at the Lines to make contact with their respective batteries. Julian began to fly the figure-eights that enabled him to keep both the guns and the town in view and signalled for the first howitzer to fire. He watched dispassionately as it landed amongst the houses in the outskirts, reducing one of them to dust and broken masonry. A few more shots and he had begun to take a perverse satisfaction in the damage he was able to inflict with apparent impunity. The thumping explosions and crumbling brickwork made him feel like a child again, scattering his building blocks in an orgy of noise and destruction. Not that there was any great noise at seven thousand feet, save the rhythmic buzz of the engine.

The detachment gave him a sense of power that he felt slightly ashamed of, and yet exhilarated by, as an eighteenth-century maisonette was completely shattered by another high explosive shell. There was no need to try and range the guns on a precise target, it was more about keeping the shell bursts within the boundaries of the town, although Julian did his best to try and direct the shots towards the church, whose steeple rose prominently, topped with a large crucifix. Webb, whose BE he could see plotting its own figure-eights in the distance, was doing the same and Canning kept a close eye on his comrade's shots, as both men tried to zero their batteries in on the structure. Irritatingly, the steeple stayed defiant above the smoke and dust from the destruction that raged around it. Julian was annoyed to think that this might in any way be attributed to divine intervention when it was the same thing seemed to happen with all of his art obs targets.

The morning wore on, and the town of Farbus was slowly and systematically pounded to dust and rubble by the British heavy guns firing from just over five miles away. Above, the two slow, plodding BEs swam their ponderous, repetitive paths, orchestrating the destruction. After a couple of hours, they returned to the aerodrome, refuelled, and took some lunch before returning. The German infantrymen, who had begun to emerge after their morning of punishment, now sought desperate refuge again in cellars and makeshift shelters. They could just about discern the faint buzz of aero engines, barely audible in between the whizzing of the shells, the thumping, grinding, ear bursting explosions, which flung the broken masonry that crushed and dismembered, and the dust, which choked and blinded.

The two British pilots were working methodically now, directing the guns into one sector square at a time. The German Colonel who commanded in the town was hunkered helpless under his desk, in the empty wine cellar that served as his command bunker. He had led his men into battle since the war's beginning, planned and executed attacks, and won victories that had claimed the lives of thousands of allied troops. But now he was rendered impotent by the two slow, droning aeroplanes that lumbered above and directed the shells that hammered his men, his *Junge*, into the debris of the French town. Every shell that thundered home shook free a pall of dust from the ceiling, liberally coating his uniform, burying him by fractions. His aide, a one-armed Captain from Hamburg, was curled up in the corner, his single hand balled white, praying that God would eviscerate the English fliers above and end their torment.

God, in this instance, was currently a couple of miles away at twelve-thousand feet with his back to the sun, watching the two BEs, noting the brief flashes of sunlight that reflected off the doped wings as they banked into yet another figure-eight circuit. His chariot was an Albatros scout, painted red from nose to tail, washed in blood, with two large, black Maltese crosses atop brown and green wings. Beside him, above him and behind him, were eight of his avenging angels, also daubed red. One of them, propeller spinner and rudder painted yellow against the scarlet fuselage, roared alongside him and the figure in the cockpit raised his goggles enquiringly. The Red Baron waved to his brother and nodded, pointed at another red machine, this one with a white nose and elevators, and jabbed a fur-lined, gloved finger downwards. Moving in perfect unison, Manfred von Richtofen, his brother Lothar von Richtofen and Karl Allmenroder, three of Germany's best and deadliest pilots, began a steep dive down towards the BE2 of Julian Canning.

Julian, who was engrossed with demolishing Farbus, initially failed to register Two Berts' panicked exertions as the observer watched the three Albatroses materialise out of the weak sun and lunged for his Lewis gun. His first burst of fire brought Canning round with a start, the harsh staccato crackle alerting him to the imminent presence of death, and he twisted in his seat to see the three, shark-like shapes bearing down upon him. Two Berts' initial shots had been at range and were merely intended to let the Germans know that he had seen them, but they at least had the effect of splitting up the neat V-formation as one fighter looped high, one low and the third came in close from the left. Having only the one gun against three foes meant that the BE was doomed by simple mathematics and Julian watched two of the Huns move in for the kill, even as Two Berts' tracer caused the Albatros that had gone high to veer off from the attack. Closer and closer they came and still they didn't fire. He could see the whirling propeller arcs, the bracing wires that held the German scouts together, as they moved in, closer still, until in a panic, he booted the rudder bar left and threw the stick hard over. The BE creaked and groaned, staggering sideways in a drunken lurch that lost it both speed and height, and a fraction of a second later, the Baron's bullets passed where Julian's head would have been, and Canning was rewarded with the sight of two Albatroses screaming past as they overshot the BE. He saw them only as two streaks of red, but at that point he realised who his attackers were, and the fear hit him. For a second his eyes met Two Berts' and then the third Albatros, which had initially been driven off, came diving down again and sent a burst of gunfire through his fuselage that ripped and tore the canvas. Two Berts moved, fired again, then ducked instinctively as a pair of red wheels skimmed over the top of him.

Glancing round, Canning saw that Webb and Connelly appeared to have somehow slipped away from another group of Albatroses, and managed to gain a head start in the chase back to the Lines and safety. He felt a pang of angry jealousy, but his attention was quickly drawn back to his own problems, watching in slow horror as the two dispersed Germans who had overshot, now regrouped and came back towards him. He was suddenly overtaken by a desire to scream at them to stop, to say that he was sorry he had smashed up the town and that he didn't want to die. The fear coursed through him as the Albatroses came nearer, and he was able to make out the red markings again. He was terrified, he was fighting not just a man but a legend, the myth of *le Chevalier Rouge* had permeated the allied squadrons ever since the Baron had started to paint his aircraft red back in January. To the scout squadrons it was almost a figure of fun, the current in-joke was that the red Albatros was flown by a woman, in a parody of Jean d'Arc. For the two-seaters, the red aeroplanes signalled cold, efficient death, and tears welled in Julian's eyes behind his goggles, as it began to dawn on him just how highly skilled and better equipped his opponents were.

Bullets pinged and sparked off the metal of his cowling and the engine suddenly revved high and loose, screaming in protest, and Canning braced for the flames or for it to cut out altogether, but miraculously, it returned to its normal spluttering throb. Julian once again kicked desperately at the rudder, throwing off one of his pursuers but not the other two, who now closed in as the BE wallowed helpless from the resulting loss of speed. Two Berts had his gun in the wrong position and Julian realised he would not have time to redeploy before the Huns opened fire. As if in slow motion, he watched the Welshman wrench the Lewis gun from its mounting on the right and desperately haul it across. He was deliberately ignoring the two red Albatroses that were about to kill him, hiding from them, hoping that they wouldn't fire and just leave him alone. The controls of the BE were still sloppy and unresponsive and suddenly, the need to look death in the face before the end took him and he turned, trembling, to see the two spinners, one red, one yellow, appallingly close, and the black dots on top of their engines that would imminently come to life and fire the shots that would kill him.

Then suddenly, inexplicably, they swerved, careering across the sky and almost colliding with each other as they went. Arcing round in a clumsy circle, having come close to ramming the two Germans was Webb and Connelly's BE, Connelly crouched over his gun, spraying bullets wildly in all directions. They came about, this time the black tracer lines spitting at the Albatros with the all red fuselage. The consternation that the unexpected reappearance of the second BE had caused the Huns was almost comical, but Canning's urge to laugh was soon tempered as a further two Albatroses that had been watching from above, came hurtling down to join the fight. Another withering burst of fire hit Canning's machine, a flying wire was cut loose and slapped on the fabric, a strut splintered and his altimeter flew to pieces in a shower of glass. Out of instinct, he thrust the stick forward in an attempt to escape the stream of bullets that was dissecting his aeroplane. A few hundred yards away Webb had done the same, his BE now trailing a plume of pale blue smoke. The wind began to whine in the wires as the two BEs gathered speed and the ground started to rush towards them, Julian glanced at the altimeter to gauge his height, realised that it was broken and heaved back on the stick in a panic. His stomach dropped as there was no reaction from the damaged aircraft but then he felt the resistance and the BE began to flatten out. He levelled the machine at not more than five-hundred feet and saw that Webb and Connolly had pulled out only slightly higher, engine still smoking. Whilst the manoeuvre had provided them a momentary respite from the machine gun fire, the problem of the ravenous red Albatroses remained unsolved, as they had come hurtling after them, falling on them again as the BEs struck out for the Lines.

The German garrison in Farbus, having spent most of the morning being tormented by the two British aircraft, now saw their opportunity for revenge as the BEs flew low over the town and every man with a working machine gun or rifle raised it skywards and fired at their persecutors. After their dive however, Canning's and Webb's aircraft were now travelling at speed and in order to hit their targets the Germans on the ground would have needed to aim way out in front of the BEs to give the bullets time to travel. But, like the majority of infantrymen, the troops in Farbus were unaware of the extremity of these mechanics and simply took a quick aim at where the aeroplane currently was, and fired. The result of this was that the BEs made their way through untouched, but the pursuing Albatroses diving onto them were met with a devastating hail of small arms fire from the ground, which forced the German pilots to sheer off hurriedly, disgusted as the two British machines fled across the Front Lines.

The Red Baron watched the two BEs disappear to specks and allowed a slight frown to crease his forehead. As a practised hunter, he was well aware of the angles of deflection that aerial shooting required and he sighed at the ignorance of the soldiers below him. His eye fell upon a single hole where a bullet had perforated his bottom right wing, a neat, round puncture of the fabric, and he thought what a tiny and insignificant thing a single bullet was unless applied properly. He had fired a few hundred rounds at his Englishman today, who had seemed, through an odd mixture of skill and luck, to have led a charmed life in the face of his Maxim machine guns. Ultimately though, it had been the courage of his comrades that had saved him, and the Baron admired that courage. His brother Lothar flew alongside him and pulled a face. The purple Albatros of his friend Kurt Wolff, who had uncharacteristically let the other BE slip away, circled overhead. He must speak to Wolff about that. And about the colour of his Albatros, purple was a ridiculous colour to paint an aeroplane…

Julian was two miles over the British lines when his engine stopped but he was able to glide for a short distance and fortunately found a suitably large field, surprisingly unmarked by shell holes, and proceeded to stick the BE into the hedge at the end of it. He clambered out and found that he was shaking and, looking across at Two Berts, saw that his observer was suffering the same symptoms. Their eyes met and suddenly both of them broke out into uncontrolled, hysterical laughter. Their shoulders heaved and trembled and they gripped each other for support.

The Sergeant who led the squad of British Tommies from the nearby infantry regiment over to the crashed aircraft eyed them with concern, 'Poor bastards,' he muttered.

Three hours later and a motorcycle spluttered its two-stroke way across the aerodrome and the two officers packed into the sidecar tumbled out, one sprawling in the dust as the other propelled him with a bodily shove in order to make his own exit. Julian picked himself up, still wielding the bottle that they had been sharing on the journey and proffered it to the driver who took a swig and passed it back.

'Thank you, Sir.'

'Much obliged, Perkins.'

'It's Peters, Sir.'

'Excellent.'

Leaning heavily on each other, Canning and Two Berts crashed through the door of the mess with a cheer. Julian grabbed a couple of dirty glasses from a table and staggered over to where Webb and Connolly were sitting across the chessboard. He thumped the bottle down, scattering pawns, and poured until their glasses were brimming with the potent, ruddy liquid. The four men exchanged glances.

'You two,' began Julian, lighting a cigarette, 'are fucking idiots.'

And all of them proceeded to drink themselves into a stupor.

CHAPTER 11

8th April 1917

With Julian's BE still stranded in the field where he had left it the previous evening, and Webb and Connolly's machine in need of such repair as to render it unflyable, the squadron was down to only five operational aircraft. But another four BEs were delivered overnight, accompanied by two replacement crews, who arrived early in the morning. The aircraft were all repairs and reconstructions since the Royal Aircraft Factory no longer produced the obsolete machines. Connelly circled the BE that he and Webb had been temporarily assigned, eyeing it with professional disdain. The aircraft was the normal, drab green-brown colour, except for the bottom right wing, which had been left a pale, undyed linen.

He shook his head, 'They could at least paint the bloody things the right colour before they send them back here,' he grumbled.

The replacement officers looked equally as patchy. They were comprised of a tall South African named Poulton and his observer, a frail, pale boy called Davies, whose wispy fair hair was already thinning at just seventeen. They were allocated another of the newly delivered BEs, whose fuselage was mottled with a patchwork of the fabric squares used to repair bullet holes. The other pilot was an ex-cavalry man named Lannock, who, with his shaggy mane of dark brown hair and long, jutted-jaw face, resembled the horses he was used to riding. With him came an overweight, ruddy faced Captain called Metcalfe, who had transferred from a Staff position after an appeal had gone out from the Observer Corps for volunteers. The red tabs still adorned his uniform.

'Come to join the suicide club,' he announced, grinning irritatingly.
Billington regarded him icily and assigned him to fly with Shellford.

Canning and Webb were ordered to give the unfortunate town of Farbus one final morning of shelling, before conducting a photo reconnaissance of their handiwork in the afternoon. As they circled the aerodrome for height, it appeared as if the entire earth below them was crawling over itself in a hive of activity, as huge numbers of men and equipment moved in preparation for the following day's offensive. Some of the airfields based on the main roads had columns of men marching across them, accompanied by lorries and horse drawn artillery, and amongst them, strange metal boxes that lumbered clumsily, screeching and smoking, gouging deep ruts in the turf, leaving behind them a churned wake of parallel lines.

As the BEs reached the trenches, the usual desultory burst of anti-aircraft fire greeted them, but they appeared half-hearted, at best a token gesture of resistance from the gunners. The replacement BE that Julian had been allocated seemed to pull constantly to the left and this irritated him, as it meant he actually had to fly the aircraft rather than being able to sit back, drink from his flask and let the BE plough a straight and steady course of its own accord. Once over the target, Canning and Webb began their figure-eights, a thousand feet of height between them in order to prevent the gunners on the ground from being able to target them both without having to make adjustments. The British guns flashed and the shell bursts flowered in the remains of Farbus. Dust and debris flew again, but this time the practice was tedious, the town had been mostly reduced to rubble, and all that the shelling seeming to accomplish was to refine its consistency, and it was with great relief that the two aircraft turned back at 1000, their petrol gauges sitting low.

The squadron was operating most of its aircraft independently again, and BEs continued to drift in and out as morning turned to midday, the crews trampling a path from the sheds to the mess to take coffee and whisky in equal measure. Julian, after giving Webb a minor heart attack by almost landing on top of him, immediately spent some time trying to persuade his rigger to sort out the trim on his aircraft. But the man refused to see any problems, so Canning snatched his tools from him and proceeded to tighten and slacken a series of wires without the faintest idea of what he was doing, supporting his endeavours with regular pulls from his flask and a solid chain of cigarettes. His rigger stood patiently by, quietly noting what was being altered, and waited until his pilot had left for his quarters before systematically undoing all of Julian's adjustments to ensure that the BE did not fall apart in mid-air.

Both aircraft took off again at 1110 and puttered back towards the same broken town, which was now a depressingly familiar sight to them. The obdurate church, which had survived the barrage, still rose above the ruins. Julian had been allocated reconnaissance for the northern half of Farbus and Webb the south. They worked systematically, taking photographs at regular intervals in order to produce a set of mosaics. Julian assumed that these would then be pieced together back at headquarters to create a giant picture of the town, which elderly, moustachioed staff officers would then plan and plot over, and send their sons to die in. Two Berts and Connolly both became rather animated when four blobs appeared at a distance and began to grow progressively larger. Lewis guns were readied and pre-emptive shots fired to warm them when, to the surprise of all concerned, the four aircraft proved to be their escort. The drab coloured, Sopwith Strutter biplanes flew in close and one of them came up alongside Canning's BE, the pilot waving. Julian answered with a waft of his flask before taking a gulp and then cursing as he realised he'd missed his spot to take the picture. The Sopwiths climbed and circled above the BEs, screening them from German fighters as they continued their reconnaissance, exposing plate after plate in a rhythm until Julian had become almost pleasantly immersed on his task.

The rattle of gunfire brought him about with a start and he turned to see four Albatroses falling out of the sun, tracer spitting viciously. The same Sopwith dived down beside him, this time the pilot, looking panicked, gesturing furiously for the BEs to make a break for home. A split second later Julian understood just why the pilot appeared so desperate, as an Albatros with its fuselage painted all red rocketed past him, Two Berts sending a burst of fire after it, before turning with a manic grin on his face.

'Would you look at that, it's the bloody Baron again!' He hollered, before being thrown against the side of the cockpit as Canning hauled the BE around to race for the Lines, with Webb and Connelly flying a parallel course on his left.

The Sopwith Strutter pilot who had given them the orders to leave, had quickly cocked and warmed his gun before haring after the red Albatros and putting a burst of fire through its tail plane. The Baron, irked by this, rose to the fight and pulled his machine around in a sharp, climbing turn. The Sopwith could not hope to follow the nimble German scout and instead banked clumsily as the rear gunner fired wildly, his shots cutting the sky at all angles. The rest of the Strutters were putting up a valiant defence, and any time an Albatros tried to break out and attack the BEs in an attempt to destroy the precious photographs, one of the large brown two-seaters chased after it and forced it to break off the attack. Canning was aware of none of this though, he was fixated on the fight between the Sopwith and the Baron. The Strutter was totally outclassed by the Albatros as a fighting aeroplane, and as the red machine began to climb above it, a horrible certainty settled over the conflict. Julian began to feel a touch ill. It was, he thought, like watching an execution, the imminent guarantee of death as the Baron briefly swapped shots with the Sopwith's gunner. Then it was over. The black tracer emanating from the British aircraft's rear cockpit stopped abruptly and the Strutter began to dive steeply, the Albatros following all the way, still shooting at the doomed aircraft so it started to break up in the air. And for Canning, a little light was shone on the mentality of the Baron, some understanding as to why he was such a force. It was not just a will to win, to dominate other men but there was also a fierce desire to kill, to see his enemy splinter apart, to see him hitting the ground and die, a need to destroy allied machines, and this made him very good. What made him great was the cold, calculating manner in which he went about it. Once his attentions had been turned on the Sopwith that had attacked him the outcome was a certainty, and it was carried out with such calm, brutal inevitability, almost as if he were following an instruction manual on how to kill. He was the consummate hunter and Julian's mind boggled at how he had escaped from him for the second day in a row.

Canning and Webb found Billington stood waiting for them when they landed.

'Get those photos developed and dispatched immediately, Headquarters wanted anything to do with Farbus in by midday,' he snapped and turned to walk briskly back into his office.

'Wanker,' muttered Webb.

Julian and Two Berts supervised the removal of the camera, before turning to watch as a BE flew low overhead. It completed a long drawn out circuit of the airfield before dropping in to land by the hangars. Julian recognised it as Shellford's machine and it had a conspicuously empty front cockpit. Automatically, he made his way over to the now stationary aircraft, Two Berts by his side. They exchanged a look, nervous at how their friend would react to the loss of another observer. Shellford, it seemed, was already acting strangely, standing on his seat and craning over the front cockpit like a giraffe, and he appeared to be particularly animated. As they got closer they could hear him shouting.

'Hi! Get out of that, I said! You useless fat prick, get your fat, fucking arse out of my bloody aeroplane damn you!'

Intrigued, Two Berts and Canning walked up to him, pushing through the circle of amused mechanics and aircrew that had formed.

'Everything alright?' called Two Berts taking the cigarette that Canning had just passed him.

Shellford evidently didn't hear him and continued to harangue the empty space, only noticing them when they were standing next to the fuselage. He turned to them, pointing an angry finger at the vacant gunner's cockpit.

'He looked bloody green when we got down this morning but I thought it was just air sickness.' He turned back to the cockpit, 'Should've turned bloody yellow, you useless fuck!'

'Is he alright?' Asked Ripley, timidly from behind them.

'Alright? Alright?! Of course he's not bloody alright,' shouted Shellford, 'He's in a blue bloody funk!'

'What happened?'

'What, you mean before he shit his breeches and burrowed into my aeroplane like a tick? Well he was jumping like a cricket as soon as we crossed the lines and archie started shooting, and it wasn't as if it was good shooting either. Then a couple of Albatros two-seaters turned up and the gunners had a pop from distance. Fuck knows where the bullets went but this sorry bastard turned white and hid on the floor of the cockpit and hasn't moved since.'

'Are you sure he hasn't been hit?' Ripley persevered.

'Of course I'm bloody sure, nothing went close to us. Plus, I can see the yellow bastard moving.'

He pulled off a leather gauntlet and hurled it into the cockpit in front to illustrate his point before sinking back to sit perched on the fuselage, his rage exhausted.

'Well we can't just leave him there.'

'Might as well,' sighed Shellford, calmer now, 'he'll be more use as ballast than a bloody observer.'

'What was the bugger's name?' Asked Julian suddenly, throwing away his spent cigarette.

'Metcalfe, I think.' Shellford replied.

'Right then…METCALFE!' Julian hollered loudly and, drawing his revolver, sent a bullet through the fabric near the top of the cockpit. Everyone around jumped back instinctively.

'Bloody hell, Canning!' Yelled Shellford.

'Julian,' Two Berts began, in a rather more measured tone, 'I'm not sure that shooting at a man hiding from gunfire is really going to…'

Another shot cracked.

'Right,' Canning shouted, 'The next one is going to be lower and the next one lower still and eventually I'll put one in your fat hide.'

Another shot echoed around the hangars. The three bullet holes made a neat vertical line downwards and Julian took aim even further down. The onlookers, half torn between a desire to prevent a murder and a fascination over how far Canning would go, stood watching. Two Berts, having seen his pilot empty his hip flask a couple of times already this morning, knew exactly how far he would go and was about to intervene when a brown leather dome crowned above the lip of the cockpit and a pair of wide, begoggled eyes followed, whites showing behind the glass. Shellford immediately flipped again and went to grab Julian's gun off him.

'What in the hell is going on here?' A voice, barely raised but fraught with danger cut across the scene and everyone fell silent.

Billington, in full belted, crisp khaki uniform, paced across to the BE in measured steps. His eyes fell on the revolver in Canning's hand and his green eyes burned.

'You have,' he breathed, 'Thirty seconds to explain to me what is going on.'

Julian had opened his mouth to speak when Shellford

suddenly leapt in, and in spite of Billington's frown, proceeded to narrate the events of his morning.

'So you see, Lieutenant Billington' he finished, 'Lieutenant Canning was merely encouraging Captain Metcalfe to extricate himself from the aeroplane.'

Billington stood glowering, torn between incredulity at Julian's actions and utter contempt at Metcalfe's round, red face that still hovered over the edge of the cockpit. It seemed as if the twin outrages were too big for him to cope with simultaneously and his features twisted in a black rictus, a vein popped out above his greying left temple and began to throb, as the two conflicting furies fought it out inside of him. Finally, his disgust at Metcalfe seemingly won out and he turned on the plump face in a righteous fury.

'Captain Metcalfe, you will remove yourself from the King's property and accompany me to my office.'

The words were ridiculously magniloquent, but none of the onlookers dared to do anything other than look on silently as Metacalfe's large rump, tightly clad in cream britches, descended clumsily from the BE. He followed Billington like a naughty schoolboy, the shreds of courage that had kept him on the floor of the cockpit now completely broken down by a combination of the wild Lieutenant with the horribly bruised face, and the green eyed demon who was now leading him to whatever fate awaited. Billington turned back to address Canning but Two Berts had already pulled Julian very firmly back towards the mess as soon as the adjutant had begun to walk away. No one saw Metcalfe again.

The afternoon saw the entire squadron in action once again, all machines assigned to zone call duty. It was a prelude to what they would be tasked with for the next few days during the offensive, and was effectively a patrol mission for the ground forces. Each BE would work independently, covering a section of the Lines and, should any evidence of a German artillery battery be identified, immediately call in its location on the radio. Any allied battery in range would then open fire on the entire sector square, obliterating anything that lay within it. It was an expensive business, using hundreds of shells at a time but could often tip the balance for the troops fighting below. However, in the event, only Stuart and Ripley had cause to make a zone call, although Ripley unfortunately made his against a couple of fallen telegraph poles that, from a height, loosely resembled howitzer barrels. Neither he nor the gunners were aware of this though and, as the telegraph poles were utterly wiped out by the shelling, the action was reported as the successful destruction of another German battery.

As the squadron began to filter back to the aerodrome, Canning was surprised to find the landing strip crawling with ants, which, upon closer investigation and descending a few thousand feet, proved to be a battalion of infantry. Curious, he flew low over them, startling a team of horses that proceeded to bolt across the airstrip towards Ripley's BE as he was taxiing to the hangars. Shocked by the sudden equine intrusion, Ripley kicked at his rudder bar to avoid the leading horse and his undercarriage groaned, creaked and snapped under the strain, his aircraft sliding to a halt as Julian made an uncharacteristically neat landing beside him. Ripley grimaced as Canning descended from his machine, shot him a condescending look and went over to investigate the presence of the ground troops, a group of artillery men sprinting past him in a desperate endeavour to secure the horses.

Most of the squadron were making their way over to talk with the officers, whose men stood, sat and sprawled about in obvious impatience. They turned out to be a Canadian unit attached to the 1st Brigade, but accompanied by a full Colonel, and on the way to their front line jumping off point for the offensive. The Colonel, it appeared, had led them onto the airfield by mistake and was now with Billington and the Major, trying to sort out directions. As Julian approached he could see Shellford surrounded by a small group of Canadian

Lieutenants who he was earnestly trying to recruit as a replacement observer. They were eying him sceptically.

'Come on chaps, it's a wonderful way to go to war, wind in your hair and all that,' he was becoming visibly desperate, 'All you need to know is how to fire a Lewis gun, and those wings on your breast work wonders with women.'

'What happened to your last guy?' A stocky subaltern queried him suspiciously, eyes narrowed.

'Oh, they died, well apart from the last one whose nerves went,' he answered candidly, as the group quickly dispersed.

Julian walked through the khaki masses, most of the soldiers, men and officers, were young, fresh faced and even enthusiastic at the prospect of taking part in the upcoming offensive, although the atmosphere was tense. But as he passed a huge, bearded Corporal carrying a baseball bat and smoking a cigar, who grinned at him, he realised that there was also a genuine gratitude towards the airmen who had been working to eliminate the hated artillery. He joined Webb and Connolly who were talking with a tall, lean Captain with a scar across his chin and whose face seemed a little older than the rest of his countrymen. He seemed to take a more measured view of the next few days.

'It'll be shit hard,' he stated frankly, 'Jerry will be dug in deep and it's a messy job getting' 'em out.' His voice carried an air of experience and authority. 'But that's our job.'

He patted a large bowie knife, which was in no way standard issue equipment, attached to his Sam Browne belt and grinned. The smile twisting and pulling at the scar, giving his features a nasty edge.

'So where are you chaps heading for?' Asked Connelly.

'Farbus,' Came the laconic reply, 'We take that place tomorrow and HQ will be pleased as hell.'

He paused to light a cigarette. Julian, overtaken by a sudden desire to impress the Captain, relayed how they had spent the last two days shelling the town.

The Captain grimaced, 'Well sure we appreciate the effort,' he said, 'but all it really means is that we'll be fighting Jerry in rubble rather than houses.'

The three airmen felt oddly deflated by this.

'Where you guys earn your pay,' he continued, 'is keeping those bloody guns off us, do that and we'll all bloody drink to you. Aha, shit for brains has recalibrated his compass.'

The Colonel emerged from the farmhouse, talking with Billington, with Frost in close attendance.

'Well, wish me luck boys.' he called, turning to follow his Colonel, 'he won't be leading us though, thank Christ! Fucker will stay in his dugout.'

'Yeah, lot of that going about,' muttered Connelly.

The airmen stood watching as the infantry formed up and marched away towards the line. The reality of the next day had been suddenly brought home by meeting the men who would actually slog through the mud below them and face the bullets and bayonets. These were the men that relied on them and, for a brief moment, the squadron understood its role in the great machine.

'Cowardly shits,' grumbled Shellford in quiet outrage as he walked up to join Canning, Webb and Connolly.

'Eh?' Julian grunted.

'Not a single volunteer to sit in my front seat, not one! Buggers would rather sit in a bloody mud-hole than my BE.'

'Not entirely sure I blame them,' muttered Webb ruefully, eyeing the stricken aircraft that Ripley had broken on landing. Very faintly, they heard the sound of singing from the marching troops, carried back to them on the wind.

Good Old General Haig, had fifty thousand men
He marched 'em up onto Vimy Ridge and he marched 'em down again
And when they were up they were up, and when they were down they were down
And the rest of the time they were stuck in the mud with their balls flat to the ground...

The departure of the Canadian troops was accompanied by the announcement that the squadron was to wash out for the day. All officers were to remain on the airbase for the night, as they would be in the air at 0500 the next day in readiness to support the ground attack. The nervous tension that the infantry had brought with them seemed to have infected the aircrews as well, and the atmosphere in the mess was subdued with drink and cigarettes taken abnormally slowly as they sat about, watching the sun begin to sink.

CHAPTER 12

8th April 1917

'Listen to me, you cannot, CAN NOT, expect me to ask my men to do this, it is utterly out of their remit, they are not equipped or trained to conduct such an operation…Yes sir, I understand that but I must also consider the lives of…but damn it, Sir...!' Frost's voice rose in impotent rage at the telephone, then continued more abashed, 'No, Sir...no I do not mean to be insubordinate, Sir, but you must see…very well, Sir.'

He dropped the receiver into the cradle and placed his head in his hands. A couple of seconds later Billington's door opened timidly after a brief knock.

'Err…Billington…could you ah, that is would you kindly ask Captain Stuart to attend me in my office please…'

Three minutes later and a strong brown hand rapped heavily on the wooden door.

'Ah come in James, I've…erm…got…erm…something to… ah…ask of you.'

Stuart sat down without being invited.

'I've just been on the phone to Headquarters and it seems that there is a…a unit, the Canadian…ah…49th, they need to move up to the Lines adjacent to us.'

Stuart remained silent, staring at the Major.

'The only issue is that…ah…it seems the Germans have a…er…kite balloon just opposite and the troops can't move without being spotted by it.'

Stuart continued to sit, impassive, his brow furrowing ever so slightly.

'Now usually they would…ah…wait until dark but it…er…

seems that they have a lot of specialist equipment that has to be moved in daylight, and there is only an…er…hour or so of that left tonight…'

The pale blue eyes never once left the Majors face.

'So obviously this…ah…balloon needs to be brought down, quick-sharp, and it seems that the surrounding scout squadrons are…er…either occupied on missions or too far away to…ah…bring it down in time and, since this balloon is in our…er…own back garden as it were…'

His voice trailed off and his mouth twisted into a limp smile. He wanted to tell Stuart about the time he had spent arguing with the Colonel, about the insubordination charge he had been threatened with, but whatever he said or did would be nothing compared to climbing into the aeroplane next to him, so he sat with his hands clasped, Stuart's eyes boring into him.

'Time is…er…of the essence of course…'

Stuart never blinked as he stood up, 'Right.'

The mess door flew open and Stuart's figure filled the frame, a black silhouette, ringed by the gold of the setting sun, casting a long, shapeless spectre across the floor.

'A Flight get your kit and meet me at the hangars in five minutes.'

'Why…' Julian started, his lips wet with whisky.

'Because I fucking told you to, Canning, that's why.'

Julian fell silent and drained his glass with a sullen glare.

'Not you Ripley, Fuller,' Stuart commanded as the two men rose from their chairs.

'B…but…sir?' Stammered Ripley.

'You're in B Flight.'

'Since when?'

'Since I decided not to take a couple of green kids to go after a bloody balloon.'

Looks of horror crossed the faces of the rest of his flight. Stuart smiled icily.

'I've ordered incendiaries loaded into the machines, balloon

strafing papers also. I trust none of you had any particular desire to see tomorrow?'
Shellford finished his drink and stalked past, 'Too right Jimmy, this living malarkey is overrated if you ask me. I'm going to find some poor sod to fire my gun.'

Outside, the sun hung dull and bloody, washing the land in a dying light as Stuart relayed the orders to the gaggle of officers standing about him, the darkness dancing on them every time they moved. It made it difficult to see their faces and eyes and Stuart was glad of this. Drums of incendiary ammunition, daubed with red paint to denote their flammable contents, were stacked in the racks next to the gunners' cockpits. The mechanics exchanged silent glances as they worked to ready the BEs, as stupefied at the situation as their crews, none of them expecting to see either men or machines again.

Stuart spoke, quick and clipped, 'I'm going to bring us in from behind, we've no time to climb for height so we'll go round the back and make one pass while we're pointing in the right direction, then sprint for home. Hammer that bastard hard as we pass because we won't be turning back for another go. Fuck knows what'll be chasing us.' He paused, eyes resting on each of them individually, 'Good luck boys.'

Kite balloons performed the same job as artillery observation aircraft, watching the ground and directing the guns. They were filled with hydrogen gas, which meant they were incredibly vulnerable to the incendiary ammunition that burnt on contact with whatever it hit. As such, they were heavily surrounded by anti-aircraft guns on the ground and protected by fighters patrolling above. Destroying them was exclusively a scout pilot's job, the faster, more manoeuvrable aeroplanes being able to dive down onto the balloon at a speed that would enable them to avoid the gunners and outpace any enemy fighters. Sending the lumbering BEs to plod past the gasbag, whilst the gunners had to shoot at the balloon rather than defend their own aircraft was, thought Stuart, akin to asking the eight men to walk into their own whirling propellers. The everyday dangers that they faced were usually met with grumbling and sarcasm. This was new and the threat so extreme that it had resulted in shocked silence, no smart quips or flippancy. They had simply got into their aeroplanes, and prepared to die.

The replacement pilot, Cross, who had yet to fly a mission, had agreed to take on gunnery duty for Shellford, and as he clambered into the cockpit and clamped a red ammunition drum onto the Lewis gun, he looked as if he was thoroughly regretting his decision. Canning wrapped his scarf tight around his face as his engine was started, deeply breathing in the fabric's surgical tang, searching for some comfort as the smell of petrol fumes permeated the material and overpowered it. The rest of the squadron watched from the hangars as the BEs trundled across the airstrip and wobbled into the sky.

They flew directly towards their objective, climbing for height on the way. Julian's hands shook as they gripped the control column. Rays of light cast by an expiring sun reached out to him from behind, trying to bring him back to their warmth and safety. The engine droned on pulling him forwards, a coarse, inexorable rattle that mocked him even as it propelled him towards whatever awaited. In front of him, Two Berts seemed small and diminished, buried in the black hole of his cockpit. He turned to give his pilot what was intended to be a reassuring smile, but came across as a mirthless show of teeth. Canning huddled further into his scarf, the air around him was cooling and his nose hurt as the chills found their way through the weave.

The BEs continued to swim through the milky pool of evening light, the sun, huge and red at their backs, the horizon in front beginning to darken. Long tendrils of cloud crossed the sky edged with orange sparks like smouldering scraps of paper. Then a dot appeared on the pale purple canvas of sky in front of them and seemed to grow like an ink spot until the silhouette of the German balloon was plain against the evening sky. Julian strained his eyes to search for the fighters that must be above but could make nothing out. Stuart gave a brief wave of his hand then swung away to take the formation on a roundabout course that would see the BEs approaching from the East and let them dive straight for home. They plotted a route carefully around the balloon, staying out of range of the guns and its still invisible escort. Canning was taking small, regular sips from his flask and the world was beginning to blur and swim. It couldn't quell the fear though, and his throat felt burnt and sickly. He coughed and pulled down his scarf to spit over the side of the cockpit. Stuart was turning now, curving them back round towards the balloon, waving his hands again, ordering them to stagger their height to confuse the gunners. Julian duly dropped a couple of hundred feet, all trust and attention focused on his Captain. The balloon loomed ahead, a grotesque tumour leering at them and Canning felt a sudden urge to see it burn, if he had to die, it only seemed right that something should be on fire alongside him.

It came on like a hailstorm, a few isolated, seemingly random puffs of smoke and then hell came to their tiny box of sky. The deep, thumping *whoofs* of the exploding shells that blackened the air around them, interspersed by the screaming whine of flying metal as the shrapnel sliced wickedly through the air. They pressed on, torn between a desire to twist and evade and the need to keep their speed up. A shell burst under Webb's left wing tearing a gaping hole in the fabric and knocking him off course. The BE lurched drunkenly before righting itself and turning back towards the balloon. Stuart could hear the dull flak of shrapnel tearing through his machine and a flying wire snapped with a twang, then sprang back, striking the metal of the engine cowling with an unusually pure note. He ducked instinctively as another lump of metal whizzed over his head. Cross gripped the sides of his cockpit, frozen in mute terror as Shellford sat behind him singing loudly. He had no idea what the song was but his brain pulled some words and a tune from somewhere and he bellowed an unknown chorus as the world around him erupted into a maelstrom of smoke and fire. Propellers churned through black airbursts, throwing the acrid fumes aft to blind and choke. They were still seven hundred yards from the balloon. Julian watched horrified as Two Berts fell suddenly, but he emerged seconds later to point at a ragged shard of black metal embedded in the wooden handle of his gun. Five hundred yards now and the observers began to line up their sights on the balloon, forced into aiming between the wings by the illogically placed gun mounts. The noise was terrific, it was ceaseless, insistent, deafening, any attempt at thought instantly shattered by another jarring explosion. They found themselves wanting to shout out loud just to replace the crushing reports with their own cries. Shellford had now moved onto singing 'I Don't Want to Join the Army' and Cross could just about hear him over the noise of the engine and the shellfire. The sheer incredulity of the situation mixing with the fear and adrenalin that was coursing through his veins provoked him to sudden a fit of laughter, before a large chunk of shrapnel took his head quite cleanly off at the shoulders and sent it spinning into the air. The blood fountained upwards from his severed jugular and was thrown backwards into Shellford's face by the backdraft of the propeller. He was still singing and the sticky, viscous gore choked him as it caught him in his open mouth and blacked out his goggles. He tore them off, screaming and spluttering as the headless body slumped onto the floor of the cockpit.

All of the BEs had suffered badly in the approach, holes had been torn through fuselages and wings, scraps of fabric trailed and flapped in the wind and bracing wires hung loose. Stuart's machine was leaving a plume of black smoke in its wake and one of the elevators was hanging uselessly by a thread. Cross's blood had splattered all down the side of Shellford's aircraft and the other crews eyed it fearfully. It would be said afterwards that the pilots had held their nerve brilliantly, flying a steady course in spite of the shelling. In reality, they were all in a state of shock and flying straight was all their battered brains could cope with. All three observers had almost emptied their drums of ammunition when the first lick of flame crept up the side of the balloon, casting a lurid glow as they took hold and the flimsy fabric was engulfed in a ball of orange fire. The German observers in the basket underneath were equipped with parachutes and had jumped out when the firing had started, but now the blazing remnants of their craft dropped onto them, and they joined it in burning plummet.

As the balloon fell, the anti-air gunners appeared to redouble their efforts to avenge themselves upon the British aircraft before stopping abruptly. The drone of the aero engines seemed eerily quiet. A crisp staccato rattle and a flash of dark tracer lines cut across the formation and the first Albatros hurtled past, wings flashing in the last of the day's light. Another followed, sending a stream of bullets through Stuart's top wing. Three of the BEs moved in closer together to provide mutual protection but Shellford carried on alone, transfixed, flying a dead straight course with a dead observer in a bloodstained aircraft, and the German scouts moved in to pick off the lone machine. Stuart cursed, grimaced, then led the other two aircraft in a dive towards Shellford's BE. Two Berts was firing at a drab painted Albatros through the descent, his shots flying perilously close his own propeller but they had the effect of sending the Hun fighter spinning away and the three British machines took up station around their lone comrade. The wisdom of Stuart's decision to attack from behind was realised as they were almost at the Front Lines already and they pushed on into the last red segment of sun that boiled above the horizon. Clinical defensive bursts from the three remaining observers seemed to be keeping the Albatroses at bay and the incendiary bullets glowed brightly against the ever darkening sky. As they crossed the trenches they steepened their dive, increasing their speed but also forcing the German scouts low over hostile territory and they broke off, the leader firing one last long range burst at Webb and Connolly with no discernible effect before turning back to their lines. Shaking, sweating, but flooded with relief, the surviving aircraft flew a low, straight course back to the aerodrome.

They landed alongside each other without ceremony, their shadows stretched and distorted to the last extremes before they would finally be eaten up by the night. The ecstatic shock of the waiting squadron at seeing all four aeroplanes return was tempered by the sight of the empty front cockpit of Shellford's BE and the dark red stains that were plastered over both pilot and machine. He had just climbed out and Julian and Two Berts were quickly making their way over to him when his legs gave way and he fell to his knees and vomited into the bare earth. Red streaks ran through yellow mucus where he had swallowed Cross's blood, his face was coated in a thick brown crust. Then a howl of agony caused them all to turn is shock. A small crowd had formed around one of the other BEs, it was Webb and Connolly's machine. A couple of silhouettes rushed into help the lone figure that was bent over the cockpit, sobbing, and together they lowered Connolly's shattered form to the ground. His left leg was all tattered rags and ruined flesh, while just under his left collarbone, a jagged red gash about half the size of a saucer spilled dark blood down the front of his flying jacket. The worn brown leather mingled with the deep red pools that formed in the cracks and crevices of the material. Slowly, Connolly raised his right hand, still in its fur lined flying glove, up to cover the wound. He gasped for air, face pale, dark brown eyes wide, then started to laugh, a harsh guttural hiss that trailed off into a hacking cough.

'You know,' he rasped, staring into Webb's blue eyes as his pilot knelt at his feet, 'it doesn't hurt as much as I thought it would.'

He choked on another laugh and spat a gout of blood out the

side of his mouth that dribbled down to join the wound in his chest.

'Hold on, Michael, the d-doctors coming.' Webb stammered.

'No need, old chap, reckon he got me through the lung,' he pushed another gob of bloody phlegm from his lips.

The surrounding group of officers and mechanics seemed to slide into the background of the evening. Only the two of them remained in the spotlight of the last rays of a setting sun. Connolly groped for his partner's hand with his other arm and Webb limply held out his own as his observer grasped it tightly.

'No one I'd rather have flown with, Andrew.'

Webb hiccoughed, 'Same here, old boy.'

Quietly and gently, very gently, Connolly began to choke, his body convulsed as blood began to fill his lungs. More blood bubbled from between his lips, bright red this time. His eyes remained locked on Webb's until they slid upwards and only the whites remained. His body fell still. Webb pulled his leather flying cap from his head and slumped forwards, his long blond hair dipped into the blood on his observer's chest. A curled lock soaked up a small puddle that had formed in one of the folds next to the RFC wings, now dyed forever red. For minutes he remained face down on Connolly's chest and then slowly he rose up, face and hair coated with blood. Suddenly he fell back to his knees, unable to utter a sound. As a team of mechanics appeared with a stretcher, Stuart walked up behind Webb, placed his hands firmly under his armpits and carefully lifted him up without a word. His face was a mass of tears that carved paths through the dirt and part-dried blood, drawing great weals down his cheeks. Julian pulled his hip flask from his jacket and handed it to Webb who drained it, then with agonising deliberation, turned and began to walk towards his quarters. His fading shadow hardly seemed to move at all as darkness slowly swallowed the airfield.

CHAPTER 13

9th April 1917

As the night set in the rains came, driving hard into the ground and churning the earth into a thick, muddy paste. Behind the Allied trenches, thousands of men were moving through the darkness, those who would form the vanguard of the attack making their final journey to the front lines, whilst the secondary waves were taking up position in the network of communication trenches behind them. It was anything but quiet, the night air alive with the cacophony of clattering equipment, the noise of nervous horses, the stifled grunts and curses as men struggled, stumbled and slipped in the mire. The thumping of the British artillery, throwing innumerable gas shells into the German positions provided the percussion, as the rain lashed angrily against the world below it. No matter where the troops huddled for shelter, it found them and soaked them. Occasionally a German flare or star shell would light up their surroundings in an eerie, green glow, twisting the shapes on the horizon and the faces of their comrades. Mercifully though, they were mostly untroubled by the enemy artillery, and although they moaned and grumbled at the weather, the majority were silently grateful that water was the only thing falling on them from the sky. Few slept, and those that did slept fitfully.

Dawn came slowly, fighting through the cloud and managing only a pale, pallid light that still left much in shadow. By 0430, just about every square foot of allied territory behind the Arras Front Lines was a hive of activity. In the foremost areas, equipment, weapons, and lucky charms were checked then checked again. Tea, coffee, water and rum were all eagerly imbibed and a hedge of smoke appeared above the frontline trenches, as thousands of packets of cigarettes were worked steadily through.

Further back, the squadrons of the Royal Flying Corps were tearing themselves from their beds in a sleep stained daze, cramming toast into dry throats, washed down with tea and whisky. Further back still, the staff officers were finishing their morning ablutions and sitting down to eggs and bacon, waiting for the first results of the day like eager stockbrokers. Later, they would compare their profit against their loss and decide whether the day had been a success and how to subsequently balance their numbers. And as zero hour inexorably approached, those numbers tossed away their final cigarette butts, drained their flasks and at 0530 the allied batteries opened fire, as tens of thousands of shells were flung through the sky to batter into the German lines. They had been accurately ranged the day before by the two-seater squadrons and hurled hundreds of tonnes of metal across the dull brown of No Mans' Land and the white streaked mound of Vimy Ridge, whose chalk deposits had been disturbed and dissolved by the night's rain. The noise was terrific and the Allied troops could only offer thanks that the thunderous fusillade was not directed at them.

Two colossal thumps were heard above the deluge of metal casing, as two huge mines were detonated beneath the German lines by the allied sappers, throwing mud, men, and barbed wire high into the air. This was the real signal to begin the advance, the accompanying shrill of whistles lost in the hammer blows of the barrage, and thousands of British and Canadian troops clambered clumsily out of their trenches and began to pace slowly towards the German lines.

The RFC were already in the air, fighting through the soup of low cloud, peering desperately through the muck and mist in an endeavour to spot any sign of active German artillery and radio its location to the British batteries. As the huge opening barrage began, the aircraft kicked and bucked as the shells passed close below them. The rocking made Canning feel sick. He had been awake at 0430 and had starting drinking as soon as he had opened his eyes. Everyone who had been on yesterday's balloon run had. A replacement for the decapitated Cross had turned up late that evening and had immediately been assigned to Shellford, who had spent the night in the corner of the mess with a bottle of brandy. He had been steaming drunk when he clambered into his aircraft at 0450 and the new observer, whose name was Pinches, had tried to ignore the state of his pilot, as his eyes fell on the BE's blood-stained wings and fuselage.

'Don't worry sir,' the flight sergeant offered helpfully, 'it didn't all come from the same chap.'

Pinches turned whiter still as he climbed trembling into the front cockpit, his nostrils twitched at a sweet and cloying charnel smell, but whether it was real or imagined he couldn't tell.

Each aircraft was ordered to operate independently in order to maximise the coverage of the battlefield, although Canning and Two Berts, tried to stay close to Shellford, who had barely spoken since yesterday and Webb, whose eyes were red-ringed and vacant. They carefully kept them both in sight, looking on intently as the BEs circled over the trenches, wobbling and sliding in the wind.

All across the front, the observation crews were patrolling, fingers poised to tap out a zone call for the batteries. Below them, the advancing troops could not hear the aircraft on account of the shelling but occasionally they caught glimpses of them hovering overhead, watching over them as they walked onwards, slowly and deliberately.

They walked because of the mud and because ahead of them hundreds of heavy guns were laying down a creeping barrage, slowly moving their shells forwards to obliterate all that lay in the path of the infantrymen. It had been the plan at the

Somme on 1st July last year and sixty-thousand allied infantry had died. But this time it worked. Weeks of preparation, of shelling, gassing and targeting key German positions had paid off. As the British and Canadian forces advanced, instead of a determined German resistance, they met clusters of reeling, stunned and shell-shocked young men. Occasionally, small pockets of enemy troops who had escaped the artillery, would gather around machine guns or in dugouts and wipe out a few Tommies, before being mopped up with hand grenades and bayonets. The Canadians tasked with taking Vimy Ridge advanced behind a barrage and a smokescreen, and by the time they reached the German lines they couldn't find any trenches, only craters and body parts. The hill was taken almost instantly, the white of the chalk sluiced with red, as the allied forces regrouped, and prepared to sweep down onto the German garrisons at Farbus, Vimy and la Chaudiere.

High above it all, the RFC could see little to tell them how the offensive was progressing, they were half-blinded, buffeted by the wind and soaked by the sleet and rain, patrolling and protecting from the clouds, periodically calling down the wrath of the British artillery. The German Air Force was active too, the occasional orange flicker of a burning aeroplane, reflecting on the cloud as it dropped to the ground, was proof of that. 33B Squadron spent an unusually untroubled morning in spite of the weather and the *Jadgstaffeln*, and were all back and refuelling at the aerodrome by 0830. Some flyers were trying to force a second, more substantial breakfast on top of the morning's liquor. Most just knocked back another couple of glasses of whisky. Ripley was busy trying to organise another run into Lamaincourt that evening and there was a general consensus that this would be much needed come the end of the day. Even Shellford managed a lugubrious nod after looking slowly up from his glass. On his way back to his aircraft, he tripped over a stool and grabbing onto his new observer for support, sent them both sprawling onto a table that instantly broke under their combined weight.

'Don't worry, boy,' Two Berts grinned as he hauled Pinches up, brushing off a liberal coating of splinters, 'you've still got a better pilot than I have.'

The squadron was airborne again by 1000, their duty the same. As they looked down there was nothing to signify the brutal hand to hand struggles that were taking place, men inflicting their basest killing instincts on each other. They couldn't see the dismembered and dying, the gassed and the gangrenous. They couldn't here the screams, the cries and the soft pathetic mewing calls for mothers, who were hundreds of miles away. They just watched the earth for the tell-tale flashes, utterly removed, and yet so vital to the success of the operation.

The weather worsened and almost every man in the air was suffering from motion sickness as wind, rain and shells threw their aeroplanes across the sky, vomit was carried aft by the propellers' backwash, to splatter down fuselages and across tailplanes. Julian just pulled his scarf down in time as a massive howitzer shell sent the BE rocking like a piece of tissue paper and his toast and whisky breakfast was hurled into the morning air. He had made three zone calls so far, which seemed low, but what the significance of that was he didn't know. He was cold and sick and wanted to go back to bed, but he understood the importance of the work and doggedly stayed in the air.

The day wore on, the flying constant. Returning aircraft were quickly readied to go out again, their crews only pausing to relieve themselves onto the airfield grass, smoke a couple of quick cigarettes and swig from mugs of scalding coffee whilst their machines were refuelled. Shellford had been sick at least three times upon landing, but Canning thought he was starting to look a little more human for it.

By mid-afternoon, Julian was on his fifth sortie and looking down he could see the pink stains marbling the white chalk of Vimy ridge. He hoped that it was German blood, then instantly found himself jarring at the thought, no matter whose guts were running rivulets down the hillside, it was still a fucking travesty. Four-thousand feet below him, hundreds of envious eyes stared upwards, eyes that stood dark against faces smeared with the white of the chalk deposits. The 2nd Canadian brigade lay prone at the top of the ridge, the town of Farbus strung out before them seemed to sag like an ancient ruin, all broken houses and piles of brick. Here and there crooked sprigs of tree rose defiantly, branches cropped and splintered by shrapnel, lining a narrow road that wound its way into the town, curving behind the church. An invitation to the men on the ridge to step forwards into the jaws of death. The Canadians were using their upturned helmets as bowls to balance their rifles on, preventing the soggy clumps of clay from jamming the mechanisms, letting the chalk into their hair, greying it prematurely.

The heavy allied shelling had all but swept the German forces away. The attackers, having endured a sleepless, fearful night, had made their trudging assault up the ridge to find its defenders either shell-shocked, dismembered or dead. The silver wedding band around a grubby, curled fingers on a chalk-smeared severed hand, distracted a newly married Lieutenant, who shifted uncomfortably, his eyes flicking between the greying flesh and the gold on his own ring-finger. The blast of a whistle and a volley of shouts brought him back to reality as the waiting men prepared to charge into the town.

'Steady lads,' a voice bellowed, then a second whistle shrilled, and suddenly it was all breathless running down the other side, feet struggling to keep up, lungs gasping for air.

And the first shots hitting home, gouts of blood sluicing upwards as machine guns blew chunks of flesh from bodies which tumbled forwards to trail a red wake in the clay.

Canning could see the tiny figures starting to trickle black and ant-like against the white of the ridge, down towards the broken buildings. He could just about make out machine gun tracers spitting from the windows of the ruined houses but the Canadian troops were too close now to call in artillery.

The sky was darkening and the weather becoming progressively worse. A solid cloud ceiling was pressing down on them, forcing them lower and lower when a sudden gust took the BE briefly out of his control and hurled it towards Farbus Wood. He wrestled desperately with the controls but the aircraft fell onto its right wing and slipped into a spin. It made four full revolutions before Julian was finally able to catch it and as he hauled back on the stick, he heard the wingtips scratching the tops of the tallest trees. He looked down, watching the leaves skim by, and then jumped as a bullet tore through the bottom of the cockpit, through the wicker chair and between his legs to buzz past his face. Another pinged off the engine cowling and a patchwork of holes appeared in the fabric of the lower wing. Searching desperately around him for the danger, he saw a myriad of tiny, twinkling sparks amongst the trees and swiftly steered the BE away from the woodland, as the first grey coated figures emerged from its borders. The German infantry had been lying in ambush, waiting for the opportune moment to hit the Canadian troops, but having now broken cover and given away their position, their officers were urging them into the attack, driving them down towards the flank of the Allied forces assaulting the town.

Canning watched them pour from the trees, took a quick grid reference, rapped out the zone call on the wireless, and waited for the artillery to erupt and eviscerate the running grey specks. But nothing happened. He keyed it again, repeated three times, but still the tide of troops continued to surge towards the unsuspecting Canadians who were now fighting through the first buildings on the outskirts. Opening the throttle, he climbed for height to make sure the signal wasn't being interrupted, then saw the smoking remnants of shellfire several hundred yards distant and realised that the attack had progressed past the range of the British field guns. Two Berts was waving at him, miming a writing motion with his hands before jabbing a gauntlet downwards at the allied soldiers. Canning, understanding his intent, swung the aircraft around towards the edge of the town, when the unwelcome shape of an Albatros dropped out of the clouds, between the BE and the Canadians. He groaned, and made to turn and run, but the German had the height of him, so instead he shoved the nose of the BE down to get as low as possible and make himself a tougher target for the Hun pilot. To his chagrin, Two Berts was still writing his note, and he bawled at the Welshman to grab his gun. But the observer continued to calmly scribble on a page from his notepad, before stuffing it into one of his flying boots, tying his scarf around the ankle as a makeshift streamer, and then heaving it towards a clump of khaki figures as they shot over them. A couple of the Canadians mistook the gesture for an attack and fired back in response but the shots went safely wide even as the Albatros sent a more murderous stream of bullets across the nose of the BE in a diving pass.

Julian was in a full panic now, low over enemy territory and with no clear escape route, he zig-zagged wildly over the town, engine chattering above the noise of the battle below. He made a clumsy turn that caused the BE to lose speed and gave the Albatros the chance to cut across him. The German pilot, seeing his advantage made a lightning change of direction and came at the two-seater's broadside but Two Berts had seen the threat as well and sent a burst of fire between the BEs wings, that startled the Albatros, causing it to bank sharply in evasion. The observer clucked his tongue in irritation as his shots flew wide then broke into a grin of relief as, too eager to make its turn, the enemy fighter's wing caught the church spire that the previous day's shelling had failed to destroy. Both layers crumpled as they hit the masonry and the Albatros span into a wild cartwheel, spreading itself across the ruined town.

Gazing out across the battlefield, Two Berts could see the flow of German troops had reversed and they were now streaming back towards the woods, the improvised air mail had seemingly given the Canadian soldiers time to orchestrate an effective defence. As the BE soared over them, the Tommies waved their thanks and Two Berts cheerfully returned the greeting. Canning looked pissed off behind his scarf and goggles, but then he always looked pissed off, so Two Berts paid him no mind and settled back down into his cockpit as they turned for home. The church steeple, crooked and bent but still standing, faded into the distance.

The last useful light of the day faded behind the solid cloud screen as the final BEs drifted home, their crews cold and hungry from the days' exertions. The squadron had lost two aircraft, the first was one of the replacement crews, who had failed to return earlier in the day. The second was only confirmed late on, when Billington reported that a BE had been spotted falling in flames by a forward observation post after what had been reported as an apparently deliberate move to ram the Albatros that had been attacking it. The only machine that hadn't arrived back at Pouilly-Yvredon by that time, was Webb's.

CHAPTER 14

9th April 1917

Despite the weather, the need to continue supporting the offensive promised more of the same tomorrow. No one wanted to spend an evening contemplating that, so all of the day's survivors piled into and onto the tender for the drive into Lamaincourt. They would drink and whore, whilst their mechanics would toil through the night, patching holes and tuning engines to have the aircraft operational for the morrow. But then their mechanics didn't have to fight and die in the patched up stringbags, so there were no feelings of guilt as the rickety flatbed pulled away from the airstrip. Ripley had volunteered to drive, but took the winding lanes at such a terrifying speed in order to hasten their journey that Stuart had to order him to pull over so he could take the wheel himself.

With so many British and Canadian troops committed to the assault, the town seemed more subdued and it made the contingent of French troops more prominent. In the confines of the bars and brothels, relations between the two Allied nations could become somewhat strained, and as the wine and whisky flowed the atmosphere became increasingly fractious. To the extent that, as the church bell tolled eleven, the squadron entered *Le Flamant Bleu* to find it chock full of French officers, who glared at them threateningly, muttering in a Gallic fashion, and they decided to find somewhere more welcoming to end the evening. Except for Ripley, who insisted on staying and in a flash of drunken altruism, Shellford, Two Berts and Canning agreed to chaperone him, feeling partly responsible for his *affair de Coeur*. They were greeted by a warped and crackling version of *Poor Butterfly*, croaked by an ancient gramophone.

With the house so busy, a disappointed Ripley was informed that Madeleine was currently 'engaged' and he would need to wait. His disappointment turned to anguish when a huge French infantryman with an unpleasant face barged past him, closely followed by a half-naked Madeleine, face streaked with tears and a fresh bruise purpling on her cheek. She ran over to the Madame, sobbing and Ripley rushed over to join them, but as he didn't speak any French, the Madame began to shoo him away. Shellford, noticing the disturbance, signalled Canning and Two Berts and went over to investigate. He spoke briefly to the two women in his very English French, whilst an agitated Ripley tried to listen in.

'Wha...what's happened?' gabbled Ripley breathlessly as Shellford broke away

'Oh it er, seems like the young lady is a little upset at that rather large French chappie who just left. Apparently he gave her a bit of a slap and then er...' he pulled a rueful expression, '...dropped his payload on her face, so to speak.'

Ripley looked blank and then his face reddened and his shallow brow creased.

'I mean it's pretty standard stuff,' said Shellford hurriedly, 'normally you just have to pay a bit more, I think your girl's just a bit new to it all. Not that that sort of thing is my bag of course...' he added hastily.

'The fiend,' Ripley breathed, no longer listening.

Canning appeared at his shoulder, 'I'd go after him, Rip,' he suggested helpfully, 'give him what for, chance to be her knight in shining and all that.'

Ripley nodded slowly, and the without another word, turned and shot out the front door.

'Oh Lor,' grumbled an exasperated Two Berts as he joined them. 'Let's go and get the silly little sod before we lose another pilot.'

They emerged to find Ripley prostrate on his back, with the

French officer on top of him thumping at his face. Ripley had initially caught him by surprise but the Frenchman was a big man, a vicious trench brawler whose muscles bulged against the coarse blue fabric of his uniform, and he had turned the contest in an instant, fists now pummelling his would-be assailant. Shellford took a second to absorb the scene then muttered a brisk 'bloody hell,' grabbed an empty wine bottle from one of the vacant outside tables and hammered it over the grizzled head of the Frenchman. Glass fell in a glistening shower, tinkling on the cobbles. In Shellford's experience, the standard response to being struck stoutly about the head with a heavy bottle was to sprawl unconscious, or at the very least show a diminished enthusiasm for one's prior endeavours. The large Frenchman on the other hand emitted a great, bellowing roar and twisted sharply to drive meaty fist upwards into Shellford's groin. At which point, Shellford promptly collapsed whimpering to the floor. With another mighty yell, the Frenchman made to get up and finish off this new aggressor before Two Berts clouted him with another well aimed wine bottle and this time he went down unconscious, to collapse on top of Ripley.

'Jesus fuck, Two Berts, you've killed the bastard!' Spluttered Canning, gazing in horror at the thick red splashes that were seeping into the gaps between the cobblestones and running in rivulets down the street.

'Bollocks have I, the bottle was half full when I hit him.'

'Mmmmph.' Added Shellford.

Then a fourth, airy voice piped up from under the blue mound of French uniform, 'You know chaps, there *really* are an awful lot of starts up there, I mean when you start to look, really there are. It's quite beautiful you know…'

'Shut up, Rip.' Snapped Canning, 'Oh Jesus fucking Christ, look here Two Berts, we've only gone and clobbered a bloody Major.'

'Shit. Fuck. I haven't killed him have I?'

'Don't think so, but a court martial may not extend us the

same courtesy.'

'Oh, pissing hell, what are we going to do with him?'

'Urrrrgghhh,' gurgled Shellford.

'Let's just fuck off and leave him,' suggested Canning, 'he didn't see us.'

'He saw Ripley though.'

'Fuck Ripley, he bloody started it.'

'You bloody egged him on!'

'You know chaps, I believe I'm starting to get something of a headache.'

'Shut up, Ripley! Fuck. Right. Fuck. Oh fuck. Okay, let's get them off the ground before anyone gets too interested in us.' The sight of inebriated soldiers splayed out on the ground was not uncommon and so long as they were tidied away quickly by their comrades, the MPs normally looked the other way. But left lying around, they were likely to end up in the drunk tank and on charges. The street had been empty during the scuffle, which had only lasted a matter of seconds, but now small groups of men were making their way home and some of them had noticed the three prone figures and were starting to titter. Canning and Two Berts manged to heft the French Major off the floor and carry him to the low wall on the opposite side of the road. As the weight was lifted from him, Ripley began to complain about his head again until Canning, the Frenchman's limp right arm draped around his shoulders, fetched the young pilot a sharp kick in the ribs and told him to get up. Gingerly, Ripley scraped himself off the floor. He was swaying slightly and his face was covered in cuts and lumpy with bruises. Shellford was still rolling around in a ball, crying softly to himself but, Ripley somehow managed to drag him across the street by an arm and prop him up against the wall next to Two Berts and Canning, who sat with the Frenchman supported between them. For ten minutes or so they remained there, acknowledging the jovial jeers and greetings from the occasional groups of passers-by. Then they began to panic about what to do next.

At this point Shellford had recovered enough to utter his first coherent words which, whispered weakly, were, 'My God I think he's burst one.'

It had also become apparent that Ripley was suffering from a rather severe concussion, happily narrating the details of his last family holiday to Margate seafront. Canning and Two Berts were in urgent conversation, desperately wracking their scotch addled brains for a way out.

'We could kill him?'

'Genius, Julian, make sure the noose is nice and tight, what?'

'Well I've said, just leave him here then.'

'When he wakes up, he's bound to go to the nearest French unit and we'll all be up for assaulting a senior officer, Ripley's face is a bit of a giveaway...'

'Why should I care? I didn't bloody do anything!'

'Guilty by association,' warned Two Berts menacingly, stoking Julian's drunken paranoia, 'But we do have to get rid of him somehow.'

'How? You said we can't kill him.'

'You're a pilot, we have aeroplanes...'

'What, you want me to fly the bastard to Africa or something?'

'How about,' interposed Shellford breathlessly, 'if he was taken prisoner...'

Two Berts watched as the furrows of Julian's already pronounced frown deepened until they resembled the Front Lines.

'That is, the Germans would report that he had been taken prisoner and no-one would be any the wiser.'

'What, you're proposing a little night time sojourn sausage side?' sneered Canning

'In a manner of speaking, yes.'

'And what happens when people start asking questions about how he got there?'

'As long as no-one sees us it doesn't matter does it? It'll be weeks before anything gets reported by the Boche and filters through, if it ever does. And then what would they actually be able to say?

‘It’s a fucking stupid idea,’ said Julian, although his voice wavered when he caught sight of Two Berts’ face.

‘Actually…’ began the Welshman.

‘Fine, if you want to go pissing about over Hunland in the dead of night that’s none of my business.’

‘Oh, there’s no way I could fly,’ protested Shellford, ‘I’m going to have to see the MO after what that dirty bastard did to me. The thought of even tapping the rudder bar is making my eyes water.’

‘Well Ripley can go then, it’s his bloody problem.’

‘Ripley can’t fly, he’s not even sure what is name is at the moment. I’m afraid you’re the only one, Canning.’

‘Fuck off.’

Three hours later and the limp body of a large French Major was being unceremoniously dumped into the front cockpit of a BE2, on top of Two Berts’ lap. The stolen motorcycle and sidecar, which had provided their terrifying ride back to the airfield, had been driven into the trees a half mile away and abandoned. Julian was standing by the wing, wrestling clumsily with his flying jacket as Ripley meandered over to him.

‘Dashed decent of you to do this, Canning. I’d be in a devil of a mess otherwise.’

‘Piss off Ripley, it should be you going out on this bloody shambles.’

‘Well to be perfectly honest, I’m not convinced my head is quite there, I’m talking to the one of you on the right at the moment.’

‘Right,’ Shellford came loping over awkwardly, ‘*Le Majeur* is all tucked in nice and snug, all you have to do is drop down in a field a couple of miles over, Albert will heave him out and then pootle on home, simple. Oh, and we doused him in half a bottle of whisky so the Huns won’t know what to believe even if he does talk.'

'What do we do if he wakes up?'

'He's still out cold, but should that transpire, I've found something that young Albert can to put him back to sleep with.'

He pointed to the front cockpit where Two Berts was happily waving a monstrous wrench.

'And when Stuart asks why you were flying, we'll just say you were pissed and went for a night flight, you won't be the first person to go joyriding after a skinful.'

As Canning clambered into the rear cockpit, Ripley swung the propeller and the engine stuttered reluctantly into life, shattering the silence and, Julian assumed, waking the rest of the aerodrome. He quickly opened the throttle before anyone could stop him, and the BE rolled out to take off. Despite Two Berts leaving his gun behind, the extra weight up front meant that it took an age to lift off, and his heart skipped wildly in the darkness until he heard the wheels brush the treetops at the far end of the airstrip.

Julian yawned heavily as they approached the Lines, alcohol and lack of sleep catching up with him, and he was just beginning to doze when he was shaken back to life by the sight, or rather the sense, of something huge and heavy hurtling past him, missing his face by inches. As he opened his eyes, it took a moment for him to fully comprehend the scene in front of him, but it seemed their captive had woken up and as Two Berts had made to swing his bludgeon, the slipstream must have torn the wrench from his hand and swept it aft. His weapon lost, he was now grappling with the Frenchman and the BE bucked and swayed wildly as their weight shifted. Canning watched stupefied, unsure quite what to do other than keep flying. In the darkness, it was difficult to see what was actually going on but he got the impression from the silhouettes that the Frenchman had somehow got behind Two Berts, and was slowly throttling him, with an arm wrapped around his neck. In a panic, he kicked the rudder bar and the resulting lurch took both combatants by surprise. In the sudden pause, Two Berts managed to butt the Frenchman's chin with the back of his head, catching him off balance throwing him backwards onto the fuselage. Canning, seeing his chance, leaned forwards and seized a hunk of the Major's hair in his leather gauntlet and bodily hauled him backwards, over the side of the cockpit. For a second he clung to the fuselage, pleading with eyes that bulged wide in fear and confusion, before disappearing into the darkness with a yelp that Julian heard over the noise of the engine. He looked up to see Two Berts staring at him, the whites of his eyes visible behind his goggles. Canning shrugged at him, holding his arms wide, and turned the BE back around towards the airfield.

'What the fuck did you do that for, you daft English prick?' Two Berts hissed at him as the noise of the engine died away.

'No need to thank me, you ungrateful Welsh cum stain.'

'Thank you, for what? You killed the bastard!'

'He was kicking the shit out of you.'

'Oh, so that's a good reason to commit fucking murder?'

'Murder be damned, how many thousands of people out there were killed today.'

'Yes, but that was by the Huns.'

'Well what bloody difference does it make?'

'To a court martial? Quite a bit.'

Julian caught some movement over Two Berts' shoulder and his eyes widened.

'Oh shit, shut up will you, it's Stuart.'

The Captain had been waiting for them as the BE had landed and bounced towards the sheds, and was now marching towards them at a pace.

'With me. Now,' he ordered, as Two Berts and Canning dismounted clumsily and staggered, still reeling from the night's drinking.

They followed Stuart into the empty mess, where he stood and stared at them in silence. Julian, whilst perturbed by the glare, began to drift off to sleep despite himself.

'Well?' Stuart's bark brought him back into the room.

'Well, Jimmy.'

Stuart's hands balled into fists, 'Well, *Sir*.'

'Well, Sir...' Canning paused to choke down some bile that had been rising in his throat.

He had drunk wine on whisky on more wine and his late night flip was now causing his stomach to do the same. He wanted to say something eloquent in their defence but only managed a belch of 'joyriding.'

Stuart's blue eyes cut through him.

'No one Canning, not even you, can claim that your relationship with flying has ever come close to being joyful.' He spoke icily. 'So I ask again. What in the bastard hell were you doing swanning about in a fucking aeroplane at three in the fucking morning?'

Julian struggled for a response, the night had been a drunken blur with very little thought given to explanations. He looked to Two Berts for help but his observer was staring mutely at the opposite wall.

'We were...disposing...of...something...' Shit. He shouldn't have said that. Out the corner of his eye he saw Two Berts wince.

'Disposing of what, Canning?' asked Stuart, menacingly.

Julian didn't reply and the three of them stood there in silence. Then Stuart reached out and slapped him round the face with a resounding crack. Canning staggered a little then righted himself and felt ridiculously like bursting into tears.

'What the fuck was it, boy?' Hissed Stuart.

'A French Major.'

'A Fre...a what?!'

'French Major, Sir.' Put in Two Berts helpfully

'Yes I fucking heard him. Jesus...why?'

'Two Berts hit him with a wine bottle.'

'Oh Christ, did you kill him?'

Two Berts shook his head.

'Good…no…what, so he's still alive?'

Canning grimaced. 'Possibly not.'

'Froggy didn't like flying,' Two Berts put in hurriedly, 'he woke up and was a little bit too keen to get out, so to speak, and jumped into the nearest cloud.'

Stuart slumped into the nearest chair with his head in his hands, still half pissed himself.

'The most crucial offensive in months and you two cretins decide to help by throwing a French officer out of your fucking aeroplane in the middle of the bloody night.' He breathed heavily. 'Did anyone see?'

Julian had fallen asleep on his feet again.

'Canning!'

'Aah!'

'Did anyone see?'

'Who…what…no, don't think so.'

Two Berts nodded in agreement.

'Right.' Stuart sighed, 'I should just report the whole sodding affair and let things run their course. However, twenty miles away and up to their necks in shit and shellfire are several thousand Canadians, Scots and probably even some bloody English, whose lives we are largely responsible for. And we are running out of trained aircrews. So I might as well leave it up to the Huns to deal with you as well as a court martial, in the slim hope that you might just help some of those poor bastards in the meantime.'

He rose from his chair and stood close, face to face with them, breathing whisky and tobacco.

'But let us get one thing eminently fucking clear. This conversation did not happen. I have no knowledge of this. If anyone ever comes asking what a French officer is doing on top of the Red Baron's fucking wine cellar, you two will take your chances.' He shook his head and sighed, 'Although shit to a shilling says we'll all be dead by then anyway. Now go the fuck to bed, you're on the dawn show in an hour's time.'

CHAPTER 15

10th April 1917

The Colonel clambered from his car wearing a heavy great coat and a cap pulled down low against the cold and wet, and marched briskly up to Frost and Stuart who snapped to attention, saluting smartly. Having received notification of the visit earlier in the morning, both were in full dress uniform.
The Colonel nodded in reply, 'At ease, gentlemen.'

'Major Thomas Frost and Captain James Stuart at your service, Sir.'

'Filthy weather, what?'

'Ah…yes, frightful, Sir.'

'First order of play, got a request of you, Frost. One of our top fighter fellows, chap called Bannister of the 242nd, you may have heard of him, bagged twenty or so Huns, father's a close friend of Brigadier Hume.'

Frost and Stuart looked nonplussed.

'Anyway, he knocked down a Jerry kite over Monchy-le-Proux yesterday but the damnable thing is he was hunting alone over Hunland, so there was no one to confirm it.' He shivered at a chill gust of wind. 'Need one of your chaps to pop over to Monchy and grab a photo of the crash so he can add the notch to his saddle, so to speak.'

'You want one of us to "*pop over to Monchy-le-Proux…*"' began Stuart threateningly.

'Yes, Captain Stuart,' Frost broke in, 'I'm sure that will be fine, Lieutenant Shellford hasn't been up this morning, perhaps he would be good enough to er…oblige?'

'Capital,' declared the Colonel.

Stuart shot Frost a terrifying glare and strode off, returning minutes later with Shellford in tow, still limping from his bruised testicles.

'Thought you may want to confirm the orders yourself Sir, be sure they were perfectly clear,' said Stuart, pointedly.

Frost pulled a sardonic smile back at him.

'Lieutenant Shellford, the Colonel has…ah…requested that you fly across to Monchy-le-Proux with a camera and secure a photograph of a downed German aircraft in the sector.'

'Might I ask why, Sir?'

'To enable Captain Bannister of the 242nd to confirm his twenty-first victory, Shellford,' broke in Stuart, his voice dripping with irony, 'a most worthy cause.'

Shellford, eyes wide, turned back to Frost and inclined his head.

'Of course, Sir. It would be an honour.'

Frost kept his eyes locked on Shellford's forehead.

'Good man!' Beamed the Colonel, oblivious. 'Oh yes, Captain Bannister asked me to pass these on to the men who accommodated him, with his compliments.'

He passed across two large photo prints of a superior looking officer with a thin pencil moustache, posing in front of a fighter plane in full military regalia. Both had been autographed:

With very best regards,
Captain F.V.B. Bannister

Shellford looked from Stuart to Frost incredulously.

'Right, let's get out of this blasted cold, shall we?' barked the Colonel, clapping his hands together and Frost led him away.

Shellford and Stuart were left standing alone as the wind and sleet whipped round them. Then Canning emerged from the latrine and walked up to them, 'Fucking cold,' he grumbled, 'what's up?'

'My time, I think.' Answered Shellford with a sad smile, then a shock of recognition took him. 'Hey Canning, didn't you take a shit in this fellow's wardrobe?' He held out the photograph. Canning peered at it for a minute then nodded sagely, 'Yep, I reckon that's him. Why the fuck have you got his picture?'

'He's my new bit on the side.' Shellford replied. 'Oh, do me a favour, if I don't come back, find him, and this time shit in his bloody bed for me will you?'

The Colonel was a portly man, whose thinning grey hair was complemented by a regulation handlebar moustache that, in Frost's experience of Colonels, seemed to come as standard issue with the uniform. A uniform that in this case had been immaculately tailored to give the rolling, misshapen flesh beneath a veneer of dignity and authority. It stretched taught as he sunk into Frost's own chair, pointed the Major to the one opposite the desk, and crossed his legs. As the sound of Shellford taking off echoed in the background he struck a match, lit a large mahogany pipe and said portentously, 'Well, Frost, I suppose you've been wondering how it's all been going, eh?'

'Yes, Sir.' Frost nodded politely.

'Remarkably well, dear boy,' he smiled like a self-satisfied walrus, sending up a gout of smoke, 'remarkably well. Damn guns fairly blew Jerry off his ridge and our boys just strolled up there and took it. Same approach we used at the Somme you know, but this time proved that it works.'

'Harder for the Germans to properly fortify a ridge I'd have thought though, Sir...'

'Pshaw! Boche could be on the bally moon and he still couldn't take that kind of pasting, it works. Heavy guns and cold steel.'

Frost shifted uncomfortably, 'The thing is...ah...Sir, some of my chaps reported the infantry advancing beyond the range of our guns...'

'Yes, dashed nuisance that, means that Jerry slowed us up in places.'

'Is he reinforcing?'

'Oh probably, probably, but we'll roll up some more guns, and we still have the real heavies of course.'

'Not in the same concentration as before though…?'

'No.' The Colonel frowned, puffed smoke through his nose and pointed at the Major with the stem of his pipe. 'You're sounding a bit damned defeatist, Frost.'

'Just trying to understand how to…er…best help our lads on the ground, Sir.'

'Yes well, it's true enough that this blasted weather will hold us up and we need to get the 3rd moving again. All about momentum, Frost, how many times have you seen the team with momentum blow the other buggers clean off the pitch?' He paused, then jabbed a gloved finger onto the desk. 'Gough's 5th are going to be looping round in a diversionary attack at Bullecourt to allow the 3rd to press on.'

'Against the Hindenburg Line, Sir?'

'Yes.'

'But they won't have any artillery?'

'No.'

'*Christ.*' Frost breathed, but the Colonel didn't hear.

'No guns unfortunately but we'll be sending in some of those new tank contraptions with them to clear the way.'

'Straight into the German guns.' Frost said in a deadpan tone. The Colonel shifted uncomfortably and a seam on his britches creaked.

'Yes well, a tactical defeat in this instance would be acceptable to draw attention away from the 3rd, we need to do *something* Frost.'

'Will the…ah…tanks work, Sir?' Frost had heard tales of them not even being bullet proof, let alone able to withstand cannon fire.

The Colonel ran a liver spotted hand through what was left of his hair.

'We're not sure, Frost. We hope so. The thing is it's…it's all moved on so quickly. It's not like it was when we were like you. We're still trying to understand how to fight this sort of war.'

Through the haze of smoke, Frost actually saw tears well up in the old man's crinkled eyes and it tipped him over the edge.

'That's it? That's your explanation, your excuse for the hundred thousand dead? The world's moved on around you? You pathetic shower of cunts. It's your job, your fucking job to understand these new developments, to direct them, push for them…to help us, protect us. Not to sit back and scratch your heads because things are happening that are beyond you. And even if they are, put your fucking hand up and step away. At least let somebody who understands make the decisions. Have the basic fucking decency to crawl back to your armchairs, your beds, and watch from a distance. Because not to understand and still take the reins and stand behind us is fucking criminal. And when we do the fighting and dying at your word, and you just watch the scores roll in and sit around confused at why it's all gone wrong again, that's murder. Truly it is. You are murdering us.'

Except Frost didn't say that. He didn't say anything. He just gave the Colonel an encouraging smile as his pipe expired and his mind slipped back to the present from the memories of Waterloo and Balaclava that he didn't have.

'The thin red line will hold, Frost, it always does.' The Colonel announced standing, 'I'd better get on with this inspection. Can't sit about all day gossiping like a fishwife.' He banged out his pipe into the ashtray on the desk, chipping the glass and scattering cinders.

'Er, yes, of course, Sir. Um, I must ask you to bear in mind though, Sir, that the squadron is in a period of intense activity and operational pressures will inevitably take their toll on some of the normal spit and polish…'

'Nonsense, Frost, I'm sure you're running a damned tight ship. Standards on parade reflected in the field and all that, and your boys have got a good reputation.'

Out the corner of his eye, Frost could see Canning trudging between the hangers in that abominable coat, an absurdly long scarf trailing in the mud behind him. 'Oh Jesus Christ,' he thought, I'm going to be court martialled.'

'So, what machines are these, Frost?' The Colonel, having toured the rest of the base, was now inspecting the hangars.

'BE2s, Sir. The squadron operates a mixture of the c, e and f variants, I think we may have some g's as well, sometimes all within the same aeroplane. They are rather dated, Sir, and most are repairs or rebuilds.'

'Mmmh? Yes, capital, capital.' The Colonel had become distracted by his reflection in the engine cowling of one of the aircraft and wasn't listening, 'glad to hear you're well equipped. Could do with keeping them a bit cleaner though Frost, some are looking a bit shabby.'

Frost didn't reply. He had caught the unmistakable note of an engine on the wind, and a very sick engine at that. He turned towards the noise. Shelford's BE appeared over the trees at the far end of the field. It was trailing thick black smoke and one of the wings was drooping alarmingly. The buzz of the engine was high and erratic, cutting out every couple of seconds. In the cockpit, Shellford was being simultaneously blinded and choked as he staggered onto his final approach. The sickly, burnt, oily fumes were being belched into his face and he was using all of his 6 feet and 4 inches to try and peer over the top of the stream of exhaust. A small crowd had gathered in front of the hangers and, when it became evident that he had misjudged his speed and was coming in too fast, they scattered out of his path. The BE arced towards the sheds where Frost and the Colonel had been inspecting the aircraft and Frost, seeing the danger, sprinted for the group that had reformed a safe distance away, whilst the Colonel stood still, mesmerised by the stricken aeroplane. Shellford's BE overshot the landing strip then buried its nose in the turf, the undercarriage giving way as the pilot desperately tried to ground his machine. The shattered aircraft ploughed a furrow through the grass as it barrelled inevitably towards the Colonel. The rest of the squadron watched in fascination as the tubby figure, finally realising his peril, tried to frantically waddle out of its path. He failed, and his overweight body burst open like a overripe fruit as the BE smeared him across the muddy turf.

The tattered hulk slid to a halt and Shellford miraculously managed to extricate himself from the tangled mess of wood and wire, with nothing more than a couple of scratches. He turned to look at the wreck in dismay.

'I've lost another.' He gestured hopelessly to the remains of the bullet riddled observer's cockpit.

Then he noticed the long bloody streak dotted with fleshy lumps that marked the trail of what was left of his BE. He pointed at it in confusion. Frost ran up to him, pale and panting.

'You...you just hit the Colonel!'

'Really?' Shellford's mood brightened instantly. 'Is that him?' He asked, indicating the meaty gobbets.

Two Berts nodded encouragingly.

'Well, every cloud as they say. Do you think we could scrape up enough of him to hang on the wall as trophy?'

'Lieutenant Shellford!' Frost shouted in outrage, 'A man has just died.'

'Yes, I know,' replied Shellford evenly, 'Poor little sod put up a good fight until some Hun bastard got him through the neck. Be careful with him boys,' he told the medical crew that had started to lift Pinches' corpse from the wreckage then gestured at the bloody trail 'and someone clean the rest of this mess up.'

CHAPTER 16

10th April 1917

Despite the weather, operations continued throughout the day and between the refuelling and re-arming, the ruin of Shellford's BE was cleared away. Frost reported the incident to headquarters and later that evening a pair of Staff officers, a Major and a Captain, arrived to collect the Colonel's remains, whereupon they found that the squadron's mechanics had helpfully collected whatever pieces they had been able to find in a sack. Being presented with their commanding officer in such a fashion unnerved them somewhat, and Stuart had to escort them to the mess for a stiff drink.

Shellford was sat in the leather wingback with a large scotch, still in his flying kit, drunkenly holding court with a small group of officers. He had somehow managed to find the Colonel's mahogany pipe amongst the debris of the crash, rinsed it off, and was now smoking it cheerfully

'It's all about numbers,' he asserted, with the air of a man who knew about such things, 'Simple numbers. Think about it, what were the ground losses that we took at Ypres and the Somme, twenty, thirty thousand? And three times as many wounded. Now think of how many that would have been if our guns hadn't blown Jerry to buggery beforehand.'

He paused for effect. Canning belched quietly.

'Now how many squadrons do we have at the front, fifty odd? With about thirty of 'em doing art obs. Average of twenty blokes per unit and that gives you something like six-hundred of us sighting for the guns. Bloody hell, the brass would sacrifice us all five times over if it means getting our heavies on target. Because no matter how many of us succeed in getting shot down, it cannot possibly compare to the number of foot sloggers that would end up dining on Flanders mud if we didn't do our jobs. It is therefore, eminently more economical to scatter a few of us over large areas of France than lose sizeable chunks of the trench-wallahs underneath. Q-E-D. And that, my friends, is the reason why several more of us will die tomorrow, and damn me if you can think of a decent reason against it!'

Two Berts rose to him.

'Well, the thing is, boy,' he began thoughtfully, 'that I don't really know any of the chaps that you seem to think are so dependent on me and my little old BE but, and this is the devil of it all, I do know *me* and, whilst I know this flies in the face of popular opinion, I happen to rather like *me* and would like to return home with my soft pink balls still attached.'

'No can do I'm afraid Mr. Burton, my deepest sympathies to your nearest and dearest, and your tiny Welsh bollocks, but you are, after all, the sainted protector of one Mr. T. Atkins and, as such, it is your duty, nay, your privilege to lay down your life for him and his chums.

'What a charming way of saying that we're all going to die tomorrow,' broke in Canning, 'you do talk some arse, Shellford.'

'Numbers, Canning, numbers and money. Seven hundred years ago a few hundred peasants would have thrown themselves under the hooves for my ancestors, I suppose it's only fair, that I should now do the same. And as the biggest fucking peasant of them all, you should be grateful.'

'Except that I'm in the next aeroplane.'

'Except for that, yes.'

Shellford's right eye twitched as he noticed the red tabs on the two staff officers standing at the bar with Stuart. He beckoned Two Berts and Julian closer as the other officers drifted away.

'So what happened last night?' He asked conspiratorially

Two Berts briefly recounted the events of their night flight and Shellford whistled softly.

'Bloody hell chaps, that's a bit heavy, what did you say when you got back?'

'Stuart found out,' said Canning

'Well, you told him,' corrected Two Berts

'Piss off, you were no help. Anyway, he decided that we'd be more use here than in the Bastille so concluded that he hadn't seen anything and told Billington he'd disciplined us for joyriding.'

'Damned decent of him,' nodded Shellford approvingly, 'You know, you can say a lot against this war, but with hundreds of men dying each day it does mean that a fellow can steal a bike or kill a Frenchmen, and folks don't get half as excited about it as they would back home.'

Two Berts leant in.

'How are you after...well...the other day with the balloon...'

'Eh? Well its put me off tomato soup for a bit I must confess, I'm no vampire I can tell you that.'

The darkness behind his eyes belied the levity.

'And that poor little bugger Pinches didn't go quickly either,' he shook his head, 'still, the rest of us are still casting shadows at the end of another day which I suppose we should be grateful for,' he waved his empty glass at them, 'another?'

As Shellford reached across the bar to pour three whiskeys and scratch them into the mess ledger against his name, he overheard the Staff officers talking with Stuart.

'Of course, there will have to be an inquest...' the Staff Major was saying.

'I'm sorry,' interrupted Shellford, ignoring Stuart's warning glare, 'An inquest into what?'

'The events surrounding the Colonel's death,' the Major replied, frowning at the intrusion.

'I landed on him. There, that's your inquest done.'

The other red tabbed officer, the Captain, looked outraged.

'I didn't do it on purpose,' protested Shellford, 'I'm not that good a pilot.'

'Captain Stuart, who is this officer?' Asked the Staff Major icily.

'Lieutenant Shellford, Sir, and he's clearly been very affected by what happened today. I apologise on his behalf.'

Shellford met Stuart's eyes.

'Oh fuck off with the shitty looks, Jimmy, these red tabbed desk jockeys roll up and expect us to scrape and grovel because they've abused their privilege and asked Daddy to pull some strings to get 'em a cushy number out of harm's way...'

'I am your superior officer, Lieutenant, and as such, you will show me due deference. Now, apologise,' the Staff Major broke in.

Stuart, standing behind the man's shoulder, saw the look on Shellford's face and buried his face in his hand.

'Apologise?' Shellford repeated dangerously, 'You walk into our mess and stand there throwing your weight around, then demand that *I* apologise? Fuck off.'

'I am an officer in His Majesty's Army, same as you Lieutenant, a senior officer, and your superior officer. I have a right to stand anywhere I want in this godforsaken hovel. I was also my college boxing champion...'

The Staff Major, a tall and thickly built man, had squared up to Shellford, but fell to silence and took a quick step back as the pilot drew his revolver from his jacket, then broke it open and emptied out the bullets. As they clattered about the counter, he picked one up, dropped it back into the cylinder, spun it and slammed the pistol onto the bar, gouging the wood and sending the glasses rattling.

'You want to stand among us, drink with us? Pick that up. Put it to your head and pull the trigger. Do it every morning when you get up, do it again after you finish your lunch, and again before you go to bed. Do that and then you can join us.' Silence ensued, 'Thought not. Now fuck off back to your paperwork.' He swept up the gun and walked out the mess.

As the murmur of conversation resumed, Canning heaved himself from his chair, walked up to the Staff Major, took the red-tabbed officer's glass of scotch from in front of him, raised it in mock salute and followed Shellford out. Emerging into the chill air, Julian blinked, his nose had been feeling a touch better but the cold air always made it ache. He looked around him through the mist of his breath, then over by the hangars he caught a glimpse of movement as the moonlight flickered over the pale skin of his friend, sat in the front seat of one of the BEs. Canning walked slowly over. Shellford saw him coming, smiled slowly and raised his gun to his temple. He pulled the trigger and the hammer clicked onto an empty chamber.

'Took the bullet out.' he waved the empty pistol as Julian came to stand beside him. 'Damned dangerous thing to do otherwise.'

Julian put his hand on the leather lined edge of the cockpit.

'Got a bit carried away back there,' Shellford admitted.

Canning shrugged, 'I'm sure you'll receive a less than favourable mention in their report.'

'I can live with that. Turns out you can live with quite a bit if it means you get to keep on living. I've lost three of the lads who sat in this seat over the last two weeks.' His voice was deadpan, 'I'm just glad it was them and not me.'

Canning lit a cigarette then offered one to Shellford who declined with a slow shake of his head and instead sucked thoughtfully on the now empty pipe.

'I just wish there was some good reason for it, that's all.'

'Like you were saying, it's the numbers.'

'Numbers.' Shellford echoed, 'Except, these numbers have faces, families, friends.

I do wonder whether our elders and betters would be quite so relentless in their insistence on an offensive spirit if they had to break the news themselves. Make 'em scrape up the bits and pieces, then taken 'em to the wives and mothers. We'd see how much they really believed then.'

Julian nodded and exhaled a stream of smoke towards the cloud covered stars. Shellford started to stand.

'Here, give me a hand out, old chap.'

Canning took his arm as he clambered unsteadily from the

aircraft.

'The thing is,' he continued as they walked back towards the hut, 'I don't really mind dying in principle, I just think the cause needs to be a damn good one, being that there are so many good reasons to live.'

Canning frowned at him sceptically.

'Tits?' Offered Shellford

Julian nodded, giving him that one.

'Good whisky'

'Not sure I've ever tried it.' Canning replied, tasting the burnt sickly bile at the back of his throat.

'Well, between bad women and good whisky I'd choose the women, and at least you've tried them.'

'I'm not sure they're that *bad*,' replied Julian, 'they seem just as tired as we are.'

'Maybe, but they'll be able to retire on their earnings when it's all over. What are we going to do? You think you could just go back home and work in a bank for the next thirty years like nothing ever happened?'

Canning paused and looked around him for moment.

'I think that I'd rather get up every day and work in a bank than do this.'

Shellford considered that, 'Fair point. But the bastards in red tabs will still run the bank though.'

Julian gave him a sideways look.

'Less chance of them getting me killed in a bank.'

'Another sound point.'

They entered the hut and noticed three bodies occupying the previously empty beds.

'Tell you what though,' said Shellford as he climbed into his cot and tucked the Colonel's pipe under his pillow, 'These new lads have got the right idea. Good to get a solid eight hours in before having your bollocks shot away.'

The three young men, all lying awake under their bedsheets, shivered at his words.

CHAPTER 17

11th April 1917

The day began badly, Canning had awoken to greet his traditional daily hangover that, today, had decided not only to thump through his sinuses but also migrate south and rumble cyclonic through his gut. An explosive twenty-minute trip to the latrine settled the problem, temporarily at least, and he then went and sat in the mess, staring down a boiled egg and tugging at his flask in a vain attempt to quell the gurgling in his bowels. He had half frozen during his dawn egestion, his bare arse numbed by the morning air and a wind that was particularly sharp and cutting. Lavatory paper consisted of old canvas squares, cut from discarded aircraft fabric, that rubbed his buttocks raw in the cold, and as he had scampered painfully back from the tent towards his breakfast, he had noticed heavy black clouds in the distance that looked as if they might promise something more than rain as they moved in.

The ground crews were having a torrid time as they tried to get the BEs operational by de-icing wings and control surfaces and encouraging the seized up engines to turn over. One of the fitters hatched the idea of lighting a fire in an empty oil drum and standing it underneath the nose of the aircraft. This met with some success and within ten minutes, two of the BEs had sprung into life, casting a film of blue exhaust over the rock-hard ground. Then Stuart appeared and shouted at them to put the fucking thing out before any embers landed on an aircraft, and the mechanics sullenly doused the flames and pulled the barrel away, returning to their previous methods of arduous scraping and pre-warmed blankets.

Orders hadn't arrived until the early morning and once

they did, they were to simply patrol a section of the front and call down the wrath of the artillery on anything wearing Feldgrau. Billington informed them that the ground offensive, which had been temporarily halted, was now being renewed and their aim was to subdue any German artillery or counter attacks. They would work on a zone call basis as many of the batteries were now out of range, so all aircraft would be dialled into a central artillery control unit, that would coordinate the heavier pieces that could still throw the high explosive shells the requisite distance.

Julian felt himself feeling a bit sorry for the Huns, they'd be miserable enough as it was in the cold, without him making it worse by lobbing shrapnel at the poor bastards. His skin tightened in the chill air, pulling tight over his bruised nose in an incessant throbbing that worsened every time a blast of wind struck it. The wicker chair in the BE creaked and cracked as he lowered himself into it, clumsy under the double layer of jumpers he had donned beneath his coat. Two Berts was wrapping a greasy sheet around the firing mechanism of his Lewis, in an attempt to prevent it from locking up. Starting the engines without the fire barrel was proving a laborious process and Stuart ordered a round of coffees brought out to the flying crews as they sat shivering in their cockpits, which they swigged from steaming mugs as their mechanics looked on enviously. Canning tipped half his flask into his and sat back slurping it happily as he fiddled with his goggles, tying to make them sit comfortably above the bridge of his nose. Then his bowels gave an almighty lurch and he leapt from the cockpit, throwing the dregs of his coffee to the ground and sprinted to the latrine, moving with more urgency than anyone had ever seen before. He spent a good ten minutes gripping his knees in agony as his anus burned and his stomach cramped until he pleaded silently with the God of stool that he had nothing more to give, and finally it subsided. Pathetically grateful, he hitched up his breeches.

The engine was still dormant when he clambered back into

his aircraft, but eventually it spluttered into life and the BE reluctantly dragged itself into the raw sky. Canning snuggled down into this coat and scarf and steered his way over to the section of front he had been assigned to patrol. The wind got up and knocked them about a bit but they persevered, hovering beneath the low cloud ceiling, Julian watching the ground for sign of activity, Two Berts the sky for danger.

Eventually they returned to Pouilly-Yvredon, having made only one zone call, a convoy that Two Berts had spotted deep behind the German reserve trenches, but most of the shells had been fired from near frozen gun barrels and fallen frustratingly short. Back at the airfield, they found that a second breakfast had been arranged to replenish the energy that the morning sortie had sapped from them. Billington, the cold causing shooting pains in his thigh, was trying to argue with Stuart that the extra meal would throw his ration ledgers out. Stuart, who had already survived a half-hearted attack by an Albatros, whose pilot must have been as miserable as his allied counterparts, clearly couldn't have cared less and walked away from the adjutant, even as he was jabbing an irate finger at a table of figures.

Standing space around the mess room fire was at a premium and in an endeavour to maximise its impact, Two Berts threw a double whisky onto the flames and one of the replacement observers who was standing closest, reeled away with singed eyebrows. But just as soon as their blood had melted and circulation had been restored, it was time to go out again. The ground crews had kept the engines idling, so there were no issues with starting up, and within minutes Julian was in the air again, back patrolling the lines, and after a couple more hours he found himself looking back longingly to a time when he could still feel his balls.

Two Berts appeared to be thoroughly fed-up in front of him too and he was finally about to consider heading back when his vision was engulfed in a white blur as a sudden snowstorm struck the aeroplane and he was left grappling with the controls to keep the machine airborne. Cold, wet flakes flew in his face, clouding his goggles and his windscreen, ice started to build on the wings and he instinctively pushed the stick forward, leaving both his and Two Berts' stomachs behind. Whilst Julian could only dry retch, the Welshman in front heaved up both his breakfasts past Canning's left shoulder and into the cascading snow. Julian pushed up his goggles, eyed a couple of chunks of carrot that had splattered his jacket in disgust, and desperately began to search for the ground. The aircraft was still descending and he decided to pull up to be safe but, just as he levelled out a dark object flashed past him on the right that he recognised as what was left of a tree and, panicking, he dragged the stick back to force the BE into a climb. The aeroplane shot up far too quickly, lost speed into the headwind, stalled and dropped. Its left wing and tail hit the ground simultaneously before falling forwards onto its undercarriage to stand there, motionless but apparently unharmed, apart from a slightly crumpled wingtip and elevator. Two Berts looked round incredulously. Canning shrugged, switched off the engine and fished for his flask, the snow still falling around them.

'Where the fuck are we?' he shouted, the clamour of his voice against the silence startled him.

'Not sure,' replied Two Berts, 'I thought we had made it back over our side but I can't be sure.'

'Yeah, that's what I thought, wanna go for a look?'

Two Berts shrugged in reply and clambered down only to sink surprised into three or four inches of snow.

'Christ but it's come down thick,' he muttered, looking about him, only able to see a few feet as his field of vision was absorbed in the whirling white flurries.

All around was a blanket of crisp white, hiding the detritus of war that lay beneath. It made the world seem unnaturally bright, an eeriness compounded by the claustrophobic, muffling effect of the snowfall.

'Nice,' Two Berts commented sardonically, eying the BE, 'one of your better ones.'

'It's in one piece,' Julian answered irritably, 'and so are you.' He glanced up nervously, they could hear reports of gunfire that sounded unsettlingly close, a rattling, thumping mixture of rifle, shell and machine gun. The mists were starting to lift and as their range of vision increased, they could make out moving shapes in the distance. Julian instinctively stripped off his gauntlets and drew his revolver.

'Put that away you ass!' Hissed Two Berts, 'We're in the middle of a bloody battlefield, you'll get us shot if you go waving that about.'

'If we're in the middle of a bloody battlefield then we're bloody likely to get shot anyway...'

Crack! A strut three inches from Two Bert's face flew to pieces and both men threw themselves flat and sprawled in the snow.

'Oo goes there?' A voice with a sharp southern twang called out.

'Pilots, airmen! British airmen!' Two Berts shouted back, the snow seeping through his flying coat to wet his chest.

'Password?'

'What?'

'Password!' Insisted the voice, 'If yer British, whassa password?'

'How the fuck would I know? We've just crashed here!' Two Berts called back.

'Sounds like some sort of 'Un buggery to me,' came the muttered reply, then "Ere Jack, toss me that 'and grenade.'

'No wait!' Two Bert's yelled and then much to Canning's horror got to his feet and in a piercing tenor let rip into a rousing rendition of 'Men of Harlech.'

A long silence greeted his grand finish.

'What the fuck was that?' the voice asked incredulously.

'Welsh!' Two Berts replied.

Another shot banged and whistled overhead and the observer threw himself back to the ground,

'Hi!' He called angrily.

'Bloody Welsh.' The voice grumbled.

Two Berts clambered to his feet and started scrambling for his own pistol, before Canning launched himself at his ankles and tackled him into the snow.

'Alright,' the voice came again, 'In you come. Slowly mind, an' if you try any jiggery pokery, I'll blow yer fuckin' 'eads off.

They crawled forwards to find a begrimed balaclava-ed head, topped with a Tommy's tin hat, poking out of a shell hole. The eyes, white slits in the grey-black face peered at them curiously.

'What did you blokes want to go an' land 'ere for?' The head asked, as they both scrambled into the shell hole with him.

Julian peeled himself from the wet and muddy ground and glared at the Tommy.

'We didn't bloody want to,' he replied brusquely, 'Where the hell are we?'

'Bully-court, we turfed Jerry out of 'is trenches about 'alf an hour ago, lucky for you. Then this shit came down and not 'aving anythin' better to do we decided to stay 'ere.' The CO's back in the trench over there with the rest of us and a couple of tame 'Uns.' Two Berts and Canning nodded and clambered out of the shell hole and set off in the direction that had been indicated.

'Two comin' in!' The Tommy hollered over their heads as they made their way towards a lip in the snow.

'Alt!' Another voice with a similar southern growl challenged them from up ahead.

'If you start singing again I'll shoot you myself.' Julian muttered vehemently.

'We're airmen,' Two Berts called back, 'We were told to head this way by the chap in the hole.'

'Alright then, come forward, slowly though!'

Two Berts and Canning walked carefully up to the edge of the trench and were ushered in by two soldiers dressed identically to their previous acquaintance, with heavy woollen balaclavas over dirt covered faces.

'Jesus Christ you blokes are a bit jumpy aren't you?' Canning grumbled to one of the Tommys.

'Buggers tryin' to kill us round 'ere don't tend to paint themselves red, Sir.' Came the sarcastic reply. 'Anyway, what'd you want to go and land 'ere for?'

'For the fucking company, *Private*. Where's your CO?'

The dirty, lined face creased into a frown, 'Back there...*Sir*,' he replied, gesturing to a side passage off the wall of the trench.

Julian nodded curtly and he and Two Berts squelched off through the zig-zag walls of the connecting trench. What little snow had made it to the bottom of the earthworks was rapidly melting and every time they put out an arm to steady themselves, the grey-brown mud stained them, until they took on the same appearance as the infantrymen, who eyed them curiously but made no comment. They stepped over several bodies, which were caked in mud and curled up like sleeping children on the floor of the trench, but whether they were friend or foe they couldn't tell. In one portion, the wooden parapet was torn and splintered from a hand grenade, and spattered with gore, an arm, cut off at the elbow, lay discarded nearby.

They came out into a slightly widened section where two of the ubiquitous brown and khaki figures stood as a rough guard outside the black hole of a dugout entrance. They eyed the two newcomers suspiciously.

'Here to see your CO.' Two Berts told them.

Appeased by his accent, one of them nodded towards the roughly hewn doorway and they stepped inside.

They were immediately hit by a wall of dark, dank air. A thick stink of stale body odour, shit, rank food and damp caused them to baulk a little, before they walked across to a tall, lanky officer with tousled brown hair who was craned over a battered table that was erratically lit by a flickering gas lamp, hanging from the ceiling. A tin mug was clasped in one hand, its contents steaming in the chill of the air. He looked up in surprise, taking in their flying leathers and mud splattered appearance. As he turned to face them, Canning and Two Berts could make out a long face, young looking skin with a liberal coating of acne, and a bumfluff moustache.

'Welcome to the Bullecourt Ritz, gentlemen. Christ knows why you decided to land in this trench, 'cause the rest of us sure as hell don't want to be here. Lucky for you we are though eh?'

His voice was surprisingly deep and sonorous.

'Lucky for us,' agreed Two Berts, 'when did you boys get here?'

The commander raised the mug, vapour still rising from it, 'This belonged to the previous occupants of this little corner of paradise, damn good chocolate and still warm. If you'd have been here ten minutes earlier you'd be chatting to its original owner instead.'

Canning and Two Berts exchanged glances.

'It was the only mug otherwise I'd offer you both some, looks like Jerry bothered to take the rest of it with him when he scarpered, sensible chap. Stuff must be like gold dust.'

He drained the contents of the mug, froth settling in the fur on his top lip that he wiped onto the sleeve of his tunic, 'I suppose you boys'll want to be getting back to your outfit?'

Canning and Two Berts went to nod their agreement but something whizzed low overhead outside the dugout and the two airmen ducked instinctively. The young officer seemed unperturbed.

He sighed, 'You'll have to make your own way I'm afraid, I can't spare anyone to escort you. The attack has pretty much ground to a halt and two thirds of us went down just getting here. But I need to hold as a rear guard for a Division of mad Australian bastards who have pressed on to Riencourt, in case they get thrown back again.'

He shook his head in admiration.

'Look here,' He beckoned them over and pointed at his map, 'we've just taken this line from Jerry and are holding here.' He stabbed the map with a dirty blue pencil. 'You'll need to head back towards our line at Croisilles, there's a field surgeon there where you should be able to grab a ride.'

Aware of his own incompetence with directions, Canning let Two Berts study the map and his eyes wandered over the dugout, the shoddy wooden bunks and personal effects of the recently evicted German officers. He noticed a dark hunk of sausage next to a coalscuttle helmet and licked his crusted lips.

'So it's out of this trench and back across No-Man's land. Don't worry, we've chased the Boche away and our guns cut up the wire so it's easy going. Just follow the bodies, no-one will have cleared 'em away yet, they'll make a nice line of breadcrumbs for you. Imagine you're pretty parched, speak to one of the boys outside and they'll fix you up with some water.'

'Thank you, Sir.'

'Oh, you don't need to sir me, I'm just a lowly 2nd Lieutenant, only reason I'm giving the orders is because the rest of the officers copped it as we came through.'

One of the sentries poked his head into the dugout, 'Sir? Bradford's back.'

'Right, thank you Parker.' The young Lieutenant pushed roughly past Canning and Two Berts and the two airmen followed him out into the trench to find him talking to a mud and blood grimed Sergeant, who was still panting for breath.

'They're dug in hard sir and their wire's still intact. It'll be hell to try and get through 'em. I've already lost Boyle and Tanner.'

The tall Lieutenant grunted thoughtfully, 'Are the Boche showing any signs of moving themselves?'

The Sergeant shook his head, 'Jerry seemed pretty 'appy where 'e was, sir.'

'Right. Set a picket to watch them, Sergeant. Tell our lads to keep their heads down but if the Huns show any signs of movement they're to get word to us at any cost.'

'Yessir.' The Sergeant trotted off and the young man turned

to Canning and Two Berts.

'Jerry's still got trenches south of here. If he decides to come after us before we can sure up our defences we'll be in trouble,' he explained. 'I'm not sure if we'd be able to stop him.'

There was a scuffle of activity as a group of five or six Tommies prepared to move out and set up the pickets.

'Covering fire!' Someone bellowed and there was a crackle of gunfire as the tin-hatted figures scrambled up and out of the trench. The rattling continued for a few more seconds and then died away, but a low, desperate moaning remained, carried on the wind above the whine and thump of distant shells. Then a sharp crack, closely followed by a terrible, wailing shriek that trailed away into quavering sobs.

Two Berts looked across at the Lieutenant.

'One of our lads, got caught up on the wire most likely' he replied flatly, 'Boche will torture him for an hour or two, use him for target practice. Legs, arms, balls. Sometimes you can hear them laughing.'

The Welsh observer looked horrified, the young man shrugged his narrow shoulders.

'There'll be a couple of snipers trained on us, waiting for anyone who sticks their head up to try help. Or put him out of his misery. The really nasty fuckers leave them alive overnight and that's when the rats come out looking for breakfast. Try sleeping listening to that.'

He clapped his hands together, matter-of-factly, 'Anyway, you chaps will want to be getting off, Parker! Get these men a couple of canteens and help them out towards our lines'

'Sir. Follow me please.' A large, lugubrious Corporal approached them.

'Good luck.' Two Berts held his hand out to the Lieutenant, who took it briskly.

'Oh I wouldn't be too keen to give that stuff away, you may need it,' he looked about him with a frown, 'I may not envy you blokes your jobs but I am damned jealous of where you'll bed down tonight.'

As the distant sobbing receded to a whimper, Canning and Two Berts were handed two heavy metal water canteens with long leather straps that they swigged gratefully from, then looped over their heads and under their arms. The young Lieutenant snapped a couple of orders and the shout for covering fire went up again as the big Corporal bent down to give them a boost over the side of the trench.

'Straight through the gap in the wire, Sirs, then back across No-Man's land. Easy 'nuff,' he grunted, before propelling Canning and Two Berts out of the trench in swift succession. They scrambled up and over the lip then fell into a brisk dog trot that was all the soft ground would allow as the rattle of gunfire echoed behind them. Almost immediately, they came to the first remnants of the attack as they approached the gaps in the German wire. A twenty-metre deep field where great rolls of the stuff, covered in millions of jagged barbs, were tossed pell-mell in a silver black jumble, like a cruel industrial parody of rose field. In places, the wooden holding posts were splintered but the wire was still intact, where the explosive shells had lifted it up, but failed in cutting it or breaking it up, and it had fallen back to the ground in an even more impenetrable morass than before.

Bodies hung at intervals like abandoned rag dolls, suspended above the earth. Heads and limbs limp, drooping at irregular angles in a sinister puppet show. But the real carnage lay where the gaps had been created by the incessant shelling. Huge craters had carved a path through the tangled mesh, and stacks of bodies were piled atop one another where the attacking troops had tried to break through in the face of the German machine guns. Streams of blood stood stark against the pale, paper white of exposed flesh, running down to mix with the dark earth, becoming indistinguishable against the mud. There was a desperation to how the dead had fallen, a panicked funnel where they had been cut down like cattle, and Julian and Two Berts realised they were going to have to climb across one of the mounds to get back. Despite the proximity of the firing behind them and the occasional angry hornet buzz of stray shots overhead, there was no urgency in their steps as they approached the nearest gap with trepidation.

Exchanging a look of mutual revulsion, Two Berts put a boot onto the nearest khaki covered back and tried to haul himself over, cursing as he slipped and dislodged a freckled, red-headed teenager whose body toppled backwards to fall on top of him.

'Fucking hell, get this ginger cunt off me, will you?' He yelled, a shrill note to his voice.

Julian grabbed a stiffening arm and hauled the thin, cold bag of meat off of his observer. A marked intensity to the gunfire behind them meant that they both attacked the pile with renewed ferocity, occasionally hearing or feeling the snap of bones as their heavy boots encountered fragile, wrists and fingers. Canning instinctively reached out to grab a hand that had risen from the top, using it to haul himself up, shocked by the cold skin that greeted him. Eventually they made it up and over, struggling in their heavy leathers, descending the far side carefully so as not to dislodge any more of the corpses, before falling to sit panting at the base.

As they gathered their breath, they looked up to see the open expanse of No Man's Land which the advance had crossed and an even more horrific sight greeted them. A German battery, not quelled by the art obs work had seemingly zeroed in on the attack and bloody hunks were strewn across a smouldering, cratered wasteland. Ragged shreds of torn skin hung over clotted red stumps among the discarded limbs and the occasionally discernible human carcass. A shallow mist had descended over the scene and for a second, Julian was terrified that the sector had been gassed as well, but no burning fumes rose to bite his lungs and he began to mentally plot a route across the charnel house. As he pushed himself up off the pile of bodies, he disturbed a couple, and his foot got stuck in someone's belt. He shook his leg hard in frustration then fell over backwards as it suddenly came free. Something small and round rolled away with him and finished up next to his face. He picked it up as he got back to his feet and recognised the square-patterned metal casing of a Mills Bomb hand grenade. There was no pin. Stupefied, he held it out to Two Berts whose eyes bulged for a split second before he threw himself to the ground. Canning was then seized by a moment of horrible realisation and he hurled it away in a blind panic as it detonated, the blast throwing him to the ground, he tremendous bang bursting through his ears and a red shaft of pain.

Two Berts picked himself up and anxiously looked around for Canning, before yelping in disgust as he realised his boot had become entangled in a length of purple intestine. He quickly unwound the offal and threw it into a shell hole. A brown lump emerged from the floor a few yards away and Julian staggered towards him, clutching his shoulder.

'What the fuck was that?' Yelled the Welshman, 'Don't you know what a hand grenade looks like?'

'It's bloody dangerous leaving those things lying around!' He shouted over the ringing in his ears, then started laughing hysterically before stumbling over a bare leg, cut off at the knee, that rolled horribly under his boot. Two Berts caught him and Canning cried out as his observer gripped his shoulder where a large rent had been torn in the leather coat and white flesh and red blood were showing through.

'You hit bad, boy?' Two Berts asked, concerned.

Caning was inspecting the wound and didn't hear him, and Two Berts had to yell the question in his face.

'It's a scratch,' Julian replied loudly, 'let's keep moving.' He pushed past his observer and started to pick his way back.

Together they embarked on a hideous trek though the gore strewn patch of ground, shellfire echoing in the background. They weaved a path between the scattered remains, which seemed to alternate between recognisable human body parts and indeterminate lumps of flesh, until they almost became inured to the horror. Canning found himself almost dispassionately trying to identify what the pieces of people had originally been until he was shocked from his trance as gaze met a pair of green eyes that were looking straight at him from the floor, encased in a segment of head that had been carved out like a chunk of apple, teeth protruding from where mouth and chin had been torn away.

They had just about become accustomed to the desolate stillness when the flicker of a silhouette in the distance made them both start as it rose up from a crater and sprinted away from them. Two Berts drew his revolver and jogged over to where the figure had materialised. An almost intact body lay at the bottom of a shell hole, missing a foot and with a deep purple stain on a caved in chest. The ring finger of the left hand was missing and the wound looked fresh and bloody.

Two Berts shook his head, 'fucking vultures,' he muttered scathingly.

Another hundred yards saw them back through the Allied frontlines, shouting loudly at the reserve troops that they were British airmen on their way through. As Julian's hearing slowly started to return, they paused briefly for a rancid mug of lukewarm tea and directions towards the field surgery that the young Lieutenant had referenced, before trudging on again, back through the maze of communication trenches that fed the Front Lines. They smelt the forward aid station before they saw it. A noxious broth of blood, shit, piss and sweat, that hit them at the same time as the noise. A twisted, jarring symphony of wailing, moaning, whimpering, pleading, and crying, set on top of the gurgling death rattles and squelching of voided bowels, as men and boys met their individual ends, alone, in a welter of pain and fear. It came from the wounded who were beyond hope, a corridor of khaki, grey and crimson, soldiers laid out in ranks to die, no distinction given to rank or nationality, German Corporals lay next to British Captains, lining the way to the hastily erected canvas tents. The broken, shattered forms writhing in an orgy of death. Bodies that had been rent and torn, cut and butchered in ways that, even after all they had seen so far, brought the bile to their throats.

They marched on through the cavalcade of agony, Canning slowing to a halt as his eyes fell on the stomach of a young boy that had been ripped open, and whose guts were boiling forth from his pale, unblemished skin, stinking of meat and shit in the open air. Julian blinked as a narrow black arrowhead began to force itself out of the frothing mass of intestines, growing in size. Then a red slit opened up at the point of it, growing wider and wider, an expanding pink maw set with pointed yellow teeth and a pair of tiny red eyes squinted as they struggled out into the light.

The young lad was still half-alive and, sobbing quietly to himself, moved a hand to his open bowels and the gaping mouth seized his finger and little fleshy feet kicked and pushed on the purple innards as the rat hauled itself from the tangled ropes of intestine. The long, dark body came sliding and slopping out, rank black fur slick with blood, dropping to the floor as the boy that had birthed the creature screamed, his guts tumbling into the mud alongside it. It was too much for Julian, whose own stomach convulsed and he vomited, splattering the mass of intestine and empty stomach cavity with a sickly brown spew as the rat scuttled off beneath the corpses.

They staggered into the heart of the aid station, which was buzzing with aid workers working feverishly to stem severed blood vessels, stitch parted flesh and desperately keep alive as many of the mutilated men as they could. Canning and Two Berts stood hopelessly in the middle of it all, getting in the way of the mud and blood stained medics, who roughly pushed them aside cursing. Slowly, stepping with care over the prone bodies, they made their way out of the chaos and perched on a mud bank at the edge of the encampment. They sat opposite an open fronted tent where a grey-haired and grizzled surgeon was performing a seemingly endless stream of battlefield amputations with a huge, curved pipe clamped between his teeth. The two airmen looked on, almost in fascination, as within a matter of minutes he had pared away skin and muscle, sawed quickly through bone, discarded the useless limb, which he tossed onto a pile of ruined flesh outside the front of the tent, fingers, toes, knees and elbows sticking out at all kinds of conflicting angles. He then cauterised the wound and took the left over flaps of skin and sewed them up over the stump. It was the ghastliest form of master craftsmanship they had ever seen.

Unsure what to do next and not wanting to interrupt any of the medical staff, they lit cigarettes and sat, mesmerised by the sheer pace and efficiency of the activity going on around them. After an hour or so, Two Berts exhaled a great cloud of smoke and gestured towards the mound of discarded limbs with his cigarette.

'You know,' he began slowly, as Julian turned to him, 'I reckon that pile's grown by at least a couple of feet since we got here…'

Canning closed his eyes in despair and was about to belt him round the head with his gauntlets when a motorcycle courier with a sidecar pulled up, the tired two stroke engine chattering and the Welshman jumped up and flagged it down. The driver was delivering casualty reports from the aid stations back to the commanding Generals, and agreed to make the short detour on his return journey and drop them off at the Pouilly-Yvredon.

* * *

When Canning and Two Berts finally arrived back at the airfield two hours later, covered in mud and shit and utterly exhausted, they walked into the mess to be greeted by a delighted Shellford, who promptly stood them a bottle of whisky. Stuart entered the room half an hour later, his day's paper work complete, to find the two errant officers that he had just reported as missing in action along with another four aircrew, getting drunk in the corner. He stalked over, asked them why the fuck they hadn't reported to him, then welcomed them back. As he reached over to take a dram of whisky, the gash in Julian's arm dripped blood onto his boot.

'What happened to your arm Canning?'

Julian shrugged, unwilling to recount his escapade with the hand grenade, and promptly winced at the shaft of pain.

'You need to get that seen to.'

'It's fine.'

'No Canning, it's not fine, you have a bloody great hole in your arm. It's covered in crap, the MO's not back until Sunday, and you need it sewn up. Get yourself down to the field hospital tonight before it goes septic.'

Julian looked appalled, 'But I'm drinking…drunk. Not safe to drive the tender.'

'Piss off, you're more sober than when you get in your aeroplane.'

'But I can't drive with just one arm.'

Stuart sighed, 'Very well, let me get a coat and I'll take you.'

Canning opened his mouth to protest but Stuart had already turned and was walking away. Then he suddenly remembered Stuart's nurse 'friend,' who worked nearby and wondered if his Captain's apparent magnanimity wasn't part of some wider plan, not necessarily rooted in concern for his own welfare. However, he decided this was only more likely to increase the Scotsman's resolve, so he grabbed the rest of the bottle from the table and bolted for the door, shouts of protest from Shellford and Two Berts following him out.

Given what he had seen earlier in the day, Julian was surprised to find the field hospital relatively quiet and he was ushered into a small, dark operating tent that stank of blood. It contained a battered and stained wooden table with a few horribly surgical looking implements jutting from steel kidney dish that sat upon it. The young orderly had politely offered to take his coat and 'dispose of it,' but Canning had scowled him, then dropped his jacket on the floor. He had finished the whisky on the drive in and, perching on the edge of the table, he started to doze, his head lolling onto his chest.

He was woken by a bolt of pain lancing through his right bicep as a small, khaki and white nurse drove a needle into the flaps of torn flesh.

'Aaaah! Jesus Shit! Stop that!'

The khaki-white figure tutted at the profanity and dragged through another stitch. Julian pulled away.

'I said stop it, damn you!'

'Oh pipe down, you wimp. You didn't even notice me cleaning it,' chided a strangely familiar voice.

He looked up confused and recognised Lucy's face ensconced within a dirty white hood, covering her hair.

'What...who...? Ow!'

Another stitch.

'Me. First aid. It's what I do. Stop winging. You smell like you've drunk enough to numb an elephant anyway.'

Another searing shot of pain as she drew the needle again and he reached for the surgical alcohol she had used to swab his wound.

She slapped his hand away, 'Don't be a dick, that stuff will kill you if you drink it. Well, maybe it would just sedate *you*.'

He glared at her with a pained expression. She shook her head.

'And thanks for looking me up after the other night.'

Julian looked at her taken aback, 'I didn't...you wanted to see me again?'

'I said so didn't I?'

'Well I suppose, but, I mean, you were pretty sharp about it.'

She sighed 'You really don't know many women do you?'

Canning's mouth hung open, struggling for words.

'Any women?'

'I've been...busy,' he protested

'Whores?'

'Flying!'

'In this weather? Pull the other one.'

'We fly anyway, why do you think I'm sitting here? We came

down in the middle of the attack today.'

She looked at him long and hard, something new in her eyes, 'Did you see it?'

'We saw what was left of it.'

She pulled a pack of cigarettes from behind her tabard took one, offered him the packet then lit them both, 'Poor bastards.'

He nodded, 'You're quiet here, you know, considering.'

'We processed most of them during the day, its mainly triage here. Bandage, bed or bury. Most of the serious cases have already been sent back to real hospitals, and the no-hopers sent somewhere else to help the flowers grow. The chaps left here will be patched up and sent back to it.' She paused for a moment, 'How did you get your latest decoration?'

Canning sniggered drunkenly to himself, 'Some silliness with a hand grenade.'

'Silliness?'

Julian couldn't think of a better word, 'Forgot to throw it.'

'Oh. Were you fighting?'

'No.'

She frowned and finished off the final stitch more delicately, snipping the thread.

'Has it been bad for your lot too?'

'Bad?'

'Have you lost many?'

He shrugged. It didn't hurt as much now, despite the stitching, 'Lots. An awful lot. Not nearly as many as on the ground though.'

'How are you?'

'My arm hurts.'

'You know what I mean. Some chaps say it carves them up inside, watching the others go.'

'They're lying.'

She stared at him. He shrugged again,

'You know most of 'em for a few weeks, couple of months maybe. That's all. Not long enough to start to care.' He snorted, 'I've heard that brotherhood of war rot, it's crap, you're just a bunch of unfortunate bastards thrown into the same fucked up circumstances and sometimes you need each other to stay alive. But most of the time you die anyway. You eat, shit and live together, you watch each other die, but they're not your friends.'

She took a step back, still holding the bloodied needle. He studied her expression.

'What about the girls you work with?'

She paused to think, 'Well, we work closely together and you get on with some more than others but are they properly close friends? No, no I suppose you're right.'

'And would you die nobly for them?'

'Probably not.'

'There you are, then.'

He stopped as an image of Webb and Connelly in an antiquated BE, returning to the fight and tearing a path through the most vicious killers in the Hun airforce flashed through his mind. The follicles on his arms started to prickle and he tried to dismiss the thought.

Lucy went to drop the needle in the kidney dish and almost tripped over Julian's jacket that still lay on the ground.

'What the hell is that?'

'My coat.'

'Jesus, you wear that?'

Canning nodded.

'Good Lord, I'm surprised you haven't caught the bloody plague.'

She let out a surprisingly loud, shrill whistle and the young orderly appeared.

'Get this cleaned for me will you, Whelan?' She gestured towards Canning's coat

'Yes Ma'am.' He replied, scooping it up distastefully and darted back out.

The metal needle rattled in the dish as she tidied it away and then made to swab the puckered skin, and neat stitching.

'Did you really almost blow yourself up with a grenade?'

Julian nodded again, clenching his teeth as the spirit bit into the weal in his flesh.

'I've heard of soldiers shooting themselves in the foot to get themselves out of it, but there must be a safer way than a live grenade if you wanted a ticket home.'

She joshed him playfully but something in his drunken mind snapped at the inference and he flared up at her, jerking his arm away viciously.

'I'm not some damned coward!'

She backed away hurriedly and he saw her shock at the ferocity of his response, as she stammered, 'I'm sorry, I didn't...'

'No, no I'm sorry.' His head dropped into his hand, the look on her face extinguishing the anger as quickly as it had risen, 'It's just that's something that gets thrown about too much here. That's why they don't give us parachutes, they're worried that it might encourage cowardice.'

He looked back up at her.

'How may cowards do you know who would jump out of an aeroplane at ten thousand feet with just a bit of silk tied to them?'

She placed her hand gently on his forearm. He started to shake.

'You know the infantry call us pilots 'thuds?' It's because when a dogfight is going on above them it's not uncommon for someone who's had to jump from a burning aircraft to land among them.' He buried his face in his hands again. 'Christ, what we saw today though, I just...is it always like that?'

She nodded, eyes sombre.

'It's just...why? What's being achieved by turning all those poor bastards into...meat?' He wasn't expecting an answer, and he sat there, still shaking as she held his arm. Then her grip tightened and she turned to him suddenly.

'He's a great believer in Great Britain, my father. Never done a thing to make it that way, though that doesn't bother him. He's lived a happy, cushioned life. A comfortable man prone to comfortable belligerence, when he's in his armchair or the pub. Kind of chap that takes an inordinate amount of pride in the sacrifices and achievements of better men. His pride and ignorance are more important than our futures. And there's so many of them like that, back home, and that's why we're all here. It's why you're here getting lumps shot out of you and its why I'm here patching you up again. Tell me this, at any point did you want to be out here?'

'No.' Canning replied softly, taken aback by the ferocity of her words.

'Then, why are we here? Because of them, because they think of nothing but themselves. Because they are simple enough to think that the bloody landmass you were born on makes you great. Because they treat the tiniest compromise made on their behalf as a death blow. So they sent us here, waved us off to preserve their greatness. But they've never fought and died, never even come close. They're still comfortable and they're happy wallowing in their outrage, in believing our generation doesn't match their standards. But they've set no standards, done nothing of note in their tawdry little lives, and they'll burn us all because of it.'

She seemed calm but her eyes blazed and as Canning looked into them, he thought he saw something twisted and ancient, lifetimes of pain concentrated in a single soul. He felt tiny in the face of her rage. Her scourging, scouring contempt. Her shallow chest was heaving and her skin radiated heat.

'Have you noticed how quick they are to appropriate the acts of others? This war, it's all "we" and "us." Even the accomplishments of their fathers and grandfathers become their own personal accolades. But it's not "we" or "us," it's *you* and *me*. And they have no right to it, they can never know, and they can never claim otherwise.'

She had let go of him now, and was pacing in front of him.

'It makes me sick, a nation fat on the blood of its children, a fetid, bloated pride. An unjustified, unearned self-righteousness. We're going to bury a generation for the sake of old men's tales.'

She swept the dish and its contents onto the floor with a flash of her arm, in clatter of metal and stood before him, disgusted, even as she played her part in the great machine. Julian wasn't entirely sure what to do, so he did nothing. Normally he would offer his flask, but he had left it in his coat.

Then Lucy started to laugh bitterly, 'I really am sorry,' she said, shaking her head, 'if this were a play the scene would end here, but it's not, and we're still here, so whatever happens next will be horribly anti-climactic.'

Julian thought that was a pretty fair summary of whatever he had to offer her. So he just took her hand and she sat on the table beside him and smiled a sad smile.

'So why the hell are you here?' He asked her bluntly, 'You're right, of course, everything you said, but why join in?'

Her narrow shoulders fell and her head dropped to her chest.

'I don't know, something just felt...wrong. So much pride and glory when it all began. So much ghoulish joy at the prospect of death. It didn't feel right. I needed to do something but how can one person, a woman, stand against such raw bloodlust? So I decided to come over here to help, and I needed to see for myself. But this is worse than anyone could ever have imagined, I didn't know people could do this to each other.'

She gestured helplessly to the tents where the wounded slept.

'I come from a good background. Not too good, but enough to make life more than bearable. Probably similar to yourself.'

Canning thought back to a modest house in Hertfordshire, clean and orderly.

'And now it doesn't matter, breeding, society and all that. We care for all of them the same. The girls that came here with visions of swabbing the brows of regatta heroes, bravely grimacing at flesh wounds, pack the guts of some guttersnipe back into his belly with the same care and devotion. We all adapt to it and that's the sad thing, there's no outrage any more. Maybe I just needed to know I still felt *something*.'

They sat together in silent, then Canning turned to her, looking intently into her eyes said, 'I love you.'

She burst out laughing, properly this time, 'No you don't, you

daft bastard, you just met me. You'd love a shag, maybe.'
He grinned back.

'Not a chance. Do you know how many blokes have told me they love me?'

'Thirty-two?'

She gave him a look of withering mock contempt, 'Seven.'

'Including me?'

'One chap lay in his bed, coughing up chunks of his lungs and then, just before he died, he told me he loved me. How the fuck is that love?'

'That's probably the closest you'll ever get to real love.'

'What the bloody hell does that mean?'

'Think about it, I just told you I loved you because I wanted to ferret about under your skirts and I'm guessing the others wanted something similar. But the chap who was dying, what did you have that he could possibly want? What could he ask from you? He was dying, he knew it and he loved you simply because somehow you made those last few seconds the tiniest iota less terrifying. He loved you for no other reason than because of who you were right then and there, and he wanted nothing from you in return.'

Something in Lucy's eyes softened, ever so slightly and she moved to lay her head against his shoulder.

'You're a strange fish, Canning.' She murmured as she reached for his cigarette packet.

Their quiet, smoke filled solace was interrupted by the orderly returning Julian's coat, the shoulder tear neatly stitched in homage to his arm. Shortly afterwards, Stuart came in, red faced and looking a bit blown, to drive them back. As the two pilots stepped out into the chill night air, Canning suddenly turned and darted back inside the tent.

'Dinner tomorrow. I'll pay.'

'Christ I didn't even give you any morphine!'

He smiled expectantly.

'Jesus, okay, I'll sort something, I'll need to swap a shift, just promise to stop smiling at me. Pick me up from here at eight.'

He grinned again and swiftly withdrew, ignoring Stuart's open mouthed stare as they walked briskly back to the tender.

CHAPTER 18

12th April 1917

The sharp trill of the telephone cut through the darkness and shook Frost from his dreams. He sat up shivering in a cold sweat and gasping, as his brain slowly processed that the burning wood and canvas surrounding him was just the walls of his sleeping alcove. There were no dark fumes that had been suffocating him, just the curtain that had drifted onto his face. The tang of smoke rescinded from his mouth and nostrils, and his palate was left dry and sticky.

The telephone's shrill ring bit into the night again. He swung his legs over the side of the bed and his bare feet hit the cold stone floor. He pattered across to his desk on his tiptoes to protect himself from the chill, and groped in the dark for the receiver. His hand knocked the gilt framed picture of his fiancée and it fell to the floor with a tinkling crash as the glass shattered.

'Shit,' he croaked, then picked up the receiver, 'Hello?'

'Is that Major Frost?' An unfamiliar voice, soft and susurrating, not the usual peremptory, clipped, public school bark of the red tabbed Staff officers who normally dictated his orders.

'Yes, speaking.'

'Major Frost, I understand that a senior officer of the Wing high command was killed en situ at your squadron on,' there was a brief pause and a rustle of paper, 'the 10th April, at approximately oh-nine fifteen hours.'

'Yes, although well, I think he was just a Colonel.' Frost's sleep addled mind hadn't slipped into its usual military proprietary and he cursed inwardly at his words.

There was a pause on the other end of the line but the Major could feel the look.

'That's senior enough, Frost,' it hissed icily, 'there is to be an investigation, an inquest. And since you hold responsibility for the area of operations where a senior officer was permitted to be killed, your fitness to command has been compromised and you are to be held under close arrest until the inquest is completed.

'B…b…but, it was just a…crash landing…accident…' The Major stammered.

'The inquest will make that decision Frost,' the voice sliced across him, 'an escort will arrive for you shortly.'

'But…Sir!' Frost protested, but the line had clicked dead.

The Major stared about him in desperation, the telephone still clamped to his ear, but his panic was cut short by a sharp rap on the door, which flew open a second later and two burly, red-capped military policemen strode in, boots crunching on the broken glass.

'Major Frost?' One of the MPs enquired in a deadpan voice. Frost nodded meekly, placing the receiver slowly back onto the desk.

'Come with us please, Sir,' he said formally, politely almost, as he took an iron grip on one of Frost's arms and began to lead him from the room.

'But my things…'

'Your small kit will be collected and sent on to you shortly, Sir.'

His shoulders slumped as the other MP fell in behind him and they escorted Major Thomas Frost, still barefooted and dressed only in striped pyjamas, through the door and out to the waiting car. Frost cast a final despairing look back over his shoulder and saw a lithe, lean figure watching him from the doorway of the squadron office. Despite the darkness, he thought he could see the smirk on Billington's face.

Stuart awoke to the thump and rattle of someone banging on

the door to his room. Groggily, he reached out for his watch on the table next to him, the luminous hands told him it had just gone 0500 hours. He hadn't expected to be woken for another half hour. Every part of him wanted to roll back over and sink back into a blissful, black unconsciousness, but the banging persisted. Cursing softly to himself, he levered his legs out of bed and walked over to the door in his vest and trunks, to find Billington, in full dress uniform, papers in hand.

'What is it, Billy?'

'I have to report, Captain Stuart, that Major Frost was relieved of command of the squadron earlier this morning...'

'What? Where is he?' Stuart interrupted.

Billington's eyes gleamed, 'Gone.'

Stuarts brain struggled to process what was being said, 'Gone? Gone where?'

'He was escorted back to General Headquarters in Amiens under close arrest, they came for him twenty minutes ago.'

'And you just let them take him? Why for fuck's sake?'

'An inquest into the death of the Colonel who was killed here a couple of days ago.'

'Jesus Christ.' Stuart whispered.

'In his absence, Captain Stuart,' Billington continued officiously, 'you are the ranking officer and therefore in command of the squadron until we receive any notification to the contrary.'

The Scotsman's mind was spinning.

'I have taken the liberty of speaking with Wing Headquarters to ascertain the day's orders for you, I have also prepared the assignments in support of these...'

Stuart snatched the papers from Billington's hands and studied them, then looked up at the adjutant incredulously.

'Who gave you these orders?'

'Wing Headquarters.'

'I'll call them back myself to confirm, I want to hear it from them. And I'll make the assignments.'

Billington opened his mouth to protest but Stuart cut him off.

'And get Tom's,' he checked himself, 'get Major Frost's office ready for me, I'll be moving into his quarters later today.' Then he turned his back and slammed the door in the adjutant's face.

Hearts sank amongst the assembled aircrew at the look of disgust on Stuart's face as he walked into the mess two hours later with a sheaf of papers in his hand. The scattered group of brown and khaki figures fell quiet, waiting for him to speak.

'First off, Frost's gone,' he said briskly, 'so I'm in command until they send someone else.'

The news was greeted with silence. Stuart had been in command for months.

'Secondly, today. Shit weather, shit job,' he continued, and proceeded to narrate from the orders sheet how Headquarters had noted that the increased intensity of operations over the last two weeks had seen the German Air Force take a fearful toll on the RFC observation aircraft. And since the ground attack had stalled and artillery observation was now limited by the weather and the range of the guns, in an effort to hit back at the Albatroses, the squadron had been assigned to conduct a bombing raid against a German fighter airfield.

Canning and Two Berts looked at each other, neither particularly sure why the paperclip aces at Wing Headquarters thought that throwing a few fire crackers at the Albatros squadrons on the ground would discourage them from continuing the butchery in the air. In fact, it seemed fundamentally stupid to actually visit the lair of the very beasts they spent their days desperately trying to avoid in what amounted to a token gesture to piss them off.

'And finally,' finished Stuart and though the attendant squadron wouldn't have thought it possible, his face seemed even more annoyed at this final announcement, 'someone, somewhere has decided to award Lieutenant Canning the Military Cross.'

'Why? Ouch! Fuck off Ripley' Snapped Julian, as Ripley gave

him a hearty, congratulatory clap on the shoulder.

'Something to do with that bombing raid on the Don railway junction,' Stuart glowered at him, reading on, 'what the hell did you write in your report? There's a note here criticising my bomb aiming.'

Several of the other officers sniggered, Canning looked up at his Captain, 'Does it come with a cash award?' he asked with genuine interest.

'Does it come with a ca...no it bloody doesn't!'

Julian looked put out, 'Well what's the bloody point of it then?'

Stuart didn't have an answer to that so instead he dismissed the squadron, ordering them to be ready for take-off in the next hour.

For once, Julian thought, this probably wasn't his fault. The squadron hadn't been able to get airborne until well past midday and when they had finally taken off, a dense fog had descended suddenly on the straggling line of two-seaters and now he could barely see Two Berts sat in front of him, let alone the rest of the flight. He did his best to hold a steady course in the hope that he would emerge from the cloying grey paste, still in formation but the murk persisted, drenching both himself and the BE in a heavy vapour.

After five minutes of blind flying he began to become disorientated and he carefully dropped a few thousand feet below the cloud layer and into the murky half-light that shrouded the earth. He looked from his pasteboard map to the ground, searching desperately for something recognisable but nothing seemed to fit. He was just beginning to despair when he saw a dark purple patch of forest that sort of matched one on the map, fairly close to where he thought he ought to be, and he struck off on a course that he calculated would take him over the enemy airfield. Two Berts turned and gave him a querying look but Canning gave him a thumbs up and grinned triumphantly as a line of hangars set along the boundary of a large grass field materialised from the gloom.

He swung round in a long, climbing turn then, as he reached the edge of the airfield, he levelled the BE and ploughed a course across the line of hangars and began to drop his bombs at regular intervals, pleased at the apparent lack of anti-aircraft fire. Banking away as the final bomb fell, Julian twisted in his seat expectantly only for his face to crease in disgust as he saw that he had only managed to churn a neat trail of potholes across the runway. He cursed into his scarf and, in a surge of belligerence, was tempted to swoop in low so Two Berts could pepper the antlike specs that were now milling about in consternation on the ground with his machine gun. Then a squall of rain rattled against the BE, causing it to wobble alarmingly, and he decided better of it and struck a bearing for home.

The same errant cloud bank that had engulfed Two Berts and Canning had also swallowed the rest of the squadron. When it came down, Shellford had immediately dropped his aircraft and banked away to minimise the risk of collision with the other machines, when a gust of wind had blown him in the opposite direction and he had lost control of the BE in a flat spin for few heart pounding seconds, before managing to recover. But his relief was short lived as a pocket snowstorm crashed into the side of his machine and flung it wildly across the sky like a ship in a storm, terrifying his new observer, Houghton, who clung on desperately with both hands gripping the sides of his cockpit.

The snow was blinding, great sheets of it were hurled backwards by the whirling propeller and both pilot and observer choked and spluttered as it forced its way down their throats, despite their scarves and coats. Another great blast rocked the BE, snapping a flying wire and making the struts and airframe creak so loudly in protest that Shellford decided he had no choice but to try and get the machine down. He was struggling to make out the ground, let alone any kind of landmark and he was forced to fly lower and lower, fighting the controls all the way to keep the aircraft level. Then he felt his wheels bounce with a jarring thump before settling into a steady rumble and he quickly switched off the engine and let the BE run, saying a quiet prayer that it wouldn't encounter anything solid before it stopped. The noise of the engine was replaced by the whistling of the wind and trundling of the wheels as he drew his long legs up to brace behind his knees against any impact. But both noises died away and he breathed again, thankfully, as the BE rolled gently to a halt. Houghton turned round to him, his face was pale but he was grinning and Shellford decided the lad would do okay.

'We'll have to wait it out.' He hollered, shouting unnecessarily into the silence where he was still half deafened by the engine. Houghton nodded and huddled down into his shiny new leather flying jacket, that still squeaked when he moved. Shellford extracted the battered book on houseplants, which Two Berts had lent him, from the inside pocket of the BE and craned over it, to protect it from the snow, periodically brushing off the errant flakes before they could soak into the paper. He lost himself in the pages for a good thirty minutes before a pronounced cough from Houghton took him away from the best way to propagate an aspidistra and back to the present.

The flurries had stopped and all around him the world had been carpeted in a rough covering of white. Snow had piled up on the wings and control surfaces and even his own jacket and helmet had a light dusting that shook free as he clambered out of the aircraft, grumbling to himself. Shellford wasn't sure what side of the lines they had ended up on, he thought it was Allied territory but he couldn't be sure and he didn't intend to be stuck on the ground when he finally found out. Delicately, so as not to damage the fabric, he started to brush the snow deposits from the BE and, jumping from the front cockpit,

Houghton followed his lead.

'Let's swing her round and take off back the way we came,' instructed Shellford, 'We know the ground's clear that way and the wind's swirling all over the shop so it makes no odds.'

They each grabbed a wingtip and slowly started to rotate the big machine. Houghton, still a bit heavy handed in his gauntlets, accidently punched his finger through the canvas.

'Right, you pop round and give her a swing,' ordered Shellford, 'She'll have got cold so start turning the prop with the drive to get her run up. About twenty revolutions or so, then three spins counter-clockwise to suck-in. Then fling back it the other way and stand back.'

Houghton nodded and squelched round towards the front of the aeroplane through the snow that was rapidly melting to slush. Moving stiffly from a combination of the cold and his bulky leathers, Shellford climbed back into his cockpit and made sure the ignition was off as the young observer began to slowly rotate the big, four bladed propeller.

'Switches off, suck in!' he shouted, watching as it started to turn in the opposite direction.

'Right, that should do it. Contact!' Shellford flicked the ignition switch and Houghton gripped the slippery wooden paddle and put his shoulder through a hefty clockwise swing. It span twice, then came up against the compression and fell back limply. Frowning, Houghton grabbed the propeller again and this time hurled it round with a swing of his leg. His boots slipped on the muddy turf and he fell forwards onto his knees, planting both hands deep into the sodden earth. Above him, the engine clattered into life and without thinking, he pushed himself up to get out of its way. The heavy wooden blades hacked into his head and shoulders with a wet, slapping noise and threw a shower of blood, bone and brain into the air, to patter over the aircraft and surrounding ground, splashing red across the snow.

His view obscured by the engine bulkhead, Shellford had only seen a red spray thrown up, but deduced what had happened and switched the engine off again, sinking back into his seat with a deep sigh. Another one gone. Slowly, fearful at what he would find, he extricated himself from the cockpit and walked to the front of the machine. A great, red slash had been drawn in the snow next to the prone figure that was missing a head and half its left shoulder and bleeding profusely into the snow. Chunks of skull and meat were scattered liberally around. Shellford wasn't entirely sure what to do. It didn't seem right just to leave what was left of Houghton lying in a field, but he couldn't bring himself to try and lift the shattered remains back into the cockpit, and he had no time or tools to bury him. He had heard of scout pilots collecting the cap and goggles of defeated foes and dropping them back over their home airfields as a sign of respect, but Houghton's flying helmet had been shredded along with the rest of his head. Thinking hard through the shock, Shellford decided that he would take back a boot instead and bent down to pull one of the fleece lined flying boots off of Houghton's leg and carefully placed it beneath the seat in his cockpit. He then proceeded to grab the grey-socked foot and drag the observer's corpse out of the way of the aircraft, leaving a deep crimson trail that the BE dispersed in a rush of air as he restarted the engine and took off to find his way back to the airfield, buffeted by the swirling winds.

Canning was having an equally miserable time with the weather on his return journey, twice he was blown off course by severe gusts of wind and once, much to both his and Two Berts' chagrin, they were swallowed up by a thunder cloud, the lighting forks and booming crashes terrifyingly close. Julian had never seen what happened when an aeroplane was struck by lightning, but he couldn't imagine its effects being pleasant, and it was with great relief that they finally emerged out the other side. Another twenty minutes and the aerodrome loomed up ahead, and Canning grinned again as they saw it definitely was Pouilly-Yvredon. He burst a tyre landing too heavily and the subsequent run across the turf rattled through their joints, but both he and Two Berts still dismounted grinning, buffing their arms to restore circulation to their cramped limbs.

'Where the bloody hell have you been?' Stuart bellowed, walking over to meet them. 'I washed out ninety minutes ago.'

Canning lit a smug cigarette, 'Successfully conducting a bombing raid, Captain.'

Stuart frowned sceptically at him, 'What you actually made it through?' He asked disbelievingly.

Two Berts nodded with equal surprise.

'What did you hit?'

'Well the weather made it difficult to see for certain,' Canning replied evasively.

'Canning…' Stuart hissed threateningly.

'Well we definitely made some holes in their runway.'

'Fucking hell, you really are useless.'

'Now hang on a minute, Jimmy,' Julian wagged his finger, flaring up, 'We've done a damn sight more than rest of you.'

'No,' replied Stuart evenly, 'the rest of us ditched our bombs over the countryside and made some holes in a French field, which I think, and do correct me if I'm wrong, is exactly the same as what you managed to achieve.'

Canning was about to argue the toss when the rasp of an unfamiliar engine made them all look skywards. A Nieuport scout, painted silver with red, white and blue RFC roundels, emerged from the heavy grey cloud and circled low, before landing neatly and taxiing up to the hangars. A tall, leather clad figure descended as the engine died away, roughly shoving away a mechanic who had come forwards to help him. A small group, had emerged from the mess and clustered by the hangars to investigate the newcomer, who now strode up to them.

'Which one of you cretins just bombed my airfield?'

Silence.

Stuart gave Canning, whose stomach had already started to

sink, a withering look then turned to greet the scout pilot.

'And you are, Sir?'

'Captain Bannister of the 242nd. Who the bloody hell are you?'

'Captain Stuart...'

'Did you just bomb my bloody airfield, Stuart?' The scout pilot interrupted, pulling off his cap and goggles

Canning's stomach took another, queasier lurch as he recognised the face from Shellford's autographed photo and, more worryingly, from his own untimely wardrobe evacuation just over a month ago. Panicking he pulled up his scarf in an attempt to hide as much of his face as possible and tried to slowly slope away. He had just made it across to the main group of officers and was trying to blend in, when Shellford's BE appeared over the trees at the end of the aerodrome and circled once to make as perfunctory landing. As the empty front cockpit became painfully apparent, the squadron lost interest in the irate Nieuport pilot and migrated across to meet the newly returned pilot.

Stuart walked up to the aircraft as the engine died, the final cough of blue fumes drifting away on the chill air. As he got closer, he could see the specks of red that were dotted all over the aeroplane and dyed into the fabric. He peered nervously into the front cockpit, wary of what new horror he might find, but it was clean and empty. He turned to the pilot who was still sat in his chair, face blackened and eyes tired. He had pulled off his flying cap and his hair looked wispy and delicate.

'Where's Houghton, Shellford? He asked quietly.

In reply, Shellford reached down into his cockpit and proffered him a boot, dark leather with light fur. Stuart stared at it, finding himself at a complete loss as what to do or say next, when a sudden commotion broke out behind him. It seemed that the fighter pilot had recognised Canning amongst the cluster of aircrew and now had him firmly by the lapels of his coat. Several squadron members were attempting to intervene on their comrade's behalf and Julian himself was squealing in protest that he was a decorated war hero.

'What the hell is going on?!' Stuart bawled as the two men were pulled apart and he marched in between them. 'Drop that, Burton.' He snapped at Two Berts, who had found what appeared to be a broken length of interplane strut, and was creeping up behind Bannister, with the apparent intention of braining him with it.

The Welshman let the lump of wood fall to the ground and looked disappointed.

'Take him away for Christ's sake and lose him in a bottle,' Stuart growled, gesturing at Canning and Two Berts caught his pilot's arm and quickly led him away towards the mess.

Stuart then turned to Bannister, 'Right, that man is a dick. I won't dispute that. But what the hell was that about?'

The scout pilot shook himself free from several pairs of restraining hands and squared up to Stuart.

'He's the one that soiled my room and now he's bombed my bloody airfield!' He jabbed a gloved finger viciously towards the mess where Canning had disappeared.

Stuart closed his eyes for a moment, inwardly suppressing a laugh despite himself, then drew a deep breath.

'Look, whatever happened between the two of you before is in the past. Leave it there. What happened today was an accident, genuinely. We were ordered to attack a Jerry airstrip and the squadron got lost. Lieutenant Canning was just following through on the mission.

'By bombing the first bloody airfield he came across?'

Stuart had to concede that it didn't sound great, but he could feel himself becoming defensive. His usual ire for Canning had been tempered by the fact that the man had actually been trying to do his job on this occasion, however incompetently. Also Bannister was starting to irritate him. He couldn't forget that this was a man who gave out autograph cards to the aircrews who died confirming his kills.

'We all got separated and he didn't realise he was still on our side of the lines.' He ran his hand across his face, exasperated,

'Did anyone actually die in this attack?'

'Well, no.'

'Was anything damaged?'

'Other than the runway…no.'

'So what's the bloody problem? I've explained it was an accident, we're sorry but no harm was done. At worst a couple of your blokes might have some holes to fill in.

'Well your man can come and fill them in himself.'

Stuart snorted at the thought of trying to persuade Canning to pick up a spade and head over to the scout squadron, 'Yeah. Good luck with that.'

'Well you can bloody well order him!'

Stuart levelled his gaze, 'No I can't. We're at war. Stupid shit happens in wars. And compared to some of the stupid shit that has happened to date, this is actually pretty mild.'

'Well you lot need to be more bloody careful…'

The conversation continued in this vein for another fifteen minutes or so, with the squadron watching on. Stuart had just about convinced Bannister to leave when a now thoroughly inebriated Julian managed to escape Two Berts and emerged from the mess, called the fighter ace a cunt and threw one of his flying boots at him. At that point the Captain broke free of the restraining pilots and mechanics and went for Canning, who promptly turned and ran away, and the squadron watched in bewilderment as two grown men chased each other around the airstrip. After a couple of minutes, Bannister finally gave up and stood in the middle of the airfield looking lost until Shellford wandered over and helpfully offered the fighter pilot his revolver. Bannister took it gleefully and took aim at Julian, who dived behind some oil cans with a yelp. The Captain pulled the trigger only to find out in disgust that it was empty where Shellford hadn't bothered to reload it after the previous night. He hurled the pistol at Canning with a roar of frustration, missed, and then strode up to Stuart.

'Captain Stuart, this situation is utterly unacceptable. I demand that you take some kind of action.'

Stuart eyed him in disdain, 'You've just spent five minutes looking like a complete ball-bag, chasing him around the airfield, tried your damnedest to shoot him, and now you want me to court martial him? Don't be a prick. Go the fuck home and bother some Germans instead.'

'I'll have you know I have connections, Brigadier Hume will hear about this.'

'Good, we'd be glad to receive him. We've already killed a Colonel this week so we can take a step up and off a Brigadier next. Now fuck off.'

The Captain looked like he was about to burst into tears. Then he spun on his heel, got into his Nieuport and took off without a look back. Stuart permitted himself the faintest of smiles as he turned his back on the rapidly diminishing fighter plane.

Canning emerged sheepishly from behind the barrels to retrieve his boot, furtively making sure that Bannister had really gone then turned on Shellford.

'What the fuck was that?'

'Oh, I knew it was empty,' chortled the tall pilot, recovering his pistol, 'I just wanted to see how angry he really was. You do have an impressive capacity for pissing people off. Something to do with your unique ability to be both stubbornly obtuse and utterly apathetic, I wouldn't wonder.'

'No, he's just a dick.' Offered Stuart, walking past them as the murmur of the scout aircraft's rotary engine echoed above them.

A distant hum that turned into a whistle and then a full blooded wailing shriek as the Nieuport hurtled back down towards the straggling line of officers like an avenging angel. From his cockpit, Bannister couldn't make out his nemesis in the line of brown and khaki bodies and his fingers left the firing button on his control column in disappointment. He could still give the bastards a fright though, and with commensurate skill, he pulled up mere feet from the ground and screamed across the airstrip, wheels skimming the turf, laughing as pilots, observers and mechanics alike threw themselves flat against the muddy ground to escape the winged demon. He shot up in a superb climbing zoom, rolling out into level flight, and departed for his own airfield, waggling his wings as he went.

Canning hauled himself up from the ground, face flushed, and sprinted towards he BE, yelling orders at his ground crew. Shellford caught him by the arm as he ran past and dragged him back.

'What the hell are you doing?

'I'm going to drop another bomb on the fucker.'

'Canning!' Shellford snapped at him, then continued in a milder tone, 'You took a shit in the man's wardrobe and you bombed his airfield. All he made you do was lie on the floor. I think you're still up on him.'

Canning glared at the departing Nieuport and his eyes flickered towards his own BE. Then he shrugged, lit a cigarette, gave the whole thing up as a massive fucking write-off and went to find another drink.

He materialised in Stuart's doorway two hours later. The squadron commander was engrossed in a pile of equipment requisitions and didn't notice as Canning walked up to his desk.

'I need the tender,' Julian said loudly, without announcing himself.

'Jesus fuck!' Cried Stuart, almost leaping out his chair, 'Will ye knock or cough or something, ye cannae just creep up on me like that, ye bastard.'

Julian looked at him serenely, secretly pleased with himself.

'I need the tender.' He repeated.

'What the fuck have you done to yourself?' Stuart asked, composing himself, pointing at Canning's hair, which was neatly combed and even the shoulders of his uniform had had the worst of the skin flakes and dandruff brushed off.

'I'm going out. I need it.'

'Where?'

'You know where.'

A vicious grin crept over Stuart's face.

'And why the bloody hell should I let you have it? Just so you can get your nasty little leg over?'

'Because if you don't, I'll make damn sure Clare finds out which sadistic Scotch bastard stopped me meeting with her friend...'

'Okay, okay. Touché, you conniving English sod. But you're back here by oh-five-hundred for morning orders, weather's meant to pick up.'

Canning nodded and walked out. Stuart shook his head, and went back to trying to convince Headquarters to replenish the squadron's dwindling stock of engine magnetos from the masses held in stock at the main pool.

As Julian strolled smugly down the corridor, Billington emerged from the door opposite, blocking his path. Canning stopped in his tracks and looked around for an escape route.

'Canning,' the adjutant breathed.

Julian could have sworn he saw Billington's tongue flicker from between his teeth, tasting the air.

'I still have an open entry in my records, Lieutenant, those photographs you were detailed to take on April 1st remain outstanding.'

Canning looked at him incredulously, 'It's a bit bloody late to be playing Fool's Day jokes, Billington.' His voice trailed away at the look in the recording officer's eyes.

'You still need to provide photographic reconnaissance of the ground around St. Laurent, Lieutenant.'

'St. Laurent?' Spluttered Canning, 'We took St. Laurent in the bloody offensive! You want me to go up in this shit and take pictures of our own bloody troops?'

'I want you to execute your orders, Lieutenant.'

'You mad bastard, I'm speaking to Stuart.'

Canning made to turn away but Billington caught his shoulder in a vice like fist and spun him back round, pressing his face close. He smelt very faintly of cologne.

'Before you take a step through that door, Canning, I'll be on the telephone to Headquarters, informing them that we have a pilot refusing to obey orders. Captain Stuart is squadron leader in an acting capacity only and his tenure is in its infancy, to say the very least. His reputation as a commander is...unestablished. And if Headquarters were to look further into aspects of your own behaviour, perpetual drunkenness, unsanctioned late-night joy-rides, and a propensity for women of ill-repute to name but a few, along with Captain Stuart's subsequent failure to invoke the proper discipline, then life may become rather unpleasant for the both of you.'

Julian's hand twitched by his side, longing to strike the man.

'So, why don't you follow orders like a proper soldier for once. Go and get your kit, then go and get me those photographs.'

Canning shook his head in disbelief and opened his mouth to protest.

'Just try me, Canning,' hissed Billington.

Julian's teeth snapped without a word and pushed roughly past the adjutant and out towards the hangars.

Canning sat in the cockpit, instantly regretting his decision as the wind roared around him, and he wished that he had dared to defy Billington. He hadn't told Two Berts what he was doing and was silently cursing the mechanics as they struggled to get the engine to turn over. Eventually, it coughed into life and Julian eased at the throttle, running the motor through its full range of revolutions to warm it up before preparing to open it completely and launch across the airfield when something cannoned into the fuselage next to him with an almighty bang. He span in his seat to find Two Berts' face, red and puffing, inches from his own, black hair askew in the wind.

'Don't you dare try and go up without me again!' The Welshman shouted over the clatter of the engine, appearing to

be genuinely angry for a second before a grin broke across his features, 'You'll get yourself lost and end up ditching in the sea and drowning, or something equally bloody stupid.'
He swung a leg over the edge of his cockpit and clambered in, jamming his flying helmet onto his head and checking his gun, 'And then they'll assign me to fly with Shellford, and we all know how that ends...'

A rogue gust of crosswind caught the BE as they were taking off and Julian nearly lost the aircraft into the trees at the end of the airstrip, clearing them by a matter of feet, and Two Berts raised his eyebrows at him, cheeks pale, before settling down to his usual routine of searching the sky for danger. The fact they would not be crossing the Lines apparently doing nothing to diminish his tireless concentration. Julian was more concerned about the danger of simply being in the air. It was a constant battle to keep the BE on anything like an even keel as gusts of wind and blasts of sleet flung it across the sky like flotsam. If any Huns wanted to venture over the British Lines in this muck, he thought, then good luck to them.

The constant buffeting rattled him against the sides of the cockpit and the newly stitched wound in his shoulder sent jarring, shooting pains down his arm as it crunched repeatedly against the leather lined edges of the compartment. By the time they reached St Laurent, they had been pressed down to under a thousand feet by the clouds and wind, and Canning somehow kept the BE flying straight with the control stick clamped between his knees as he used both hands to work the camera. Then an almighty squall hit the aircraft from below, lifted it up and flipped it over almost completely onto its back. All the photographic plates that Julian had been exposing fell out the cockpit and swirled away on the wind as he instinctively clutched wildly for them, cursing viciously, even as his knees hit the wooden instrument board as gravity dragged him from his seat. His legs kept him jammed into the cockpit as he wrestled with the stick to try and roll the BE back over, but Two Berts had been standing and Canning watched in horror as his observer slid from the aircraft and dropped into the open space below the top wing, arms outstretched, grasping desperately.

Somehow he caught hold of the rim of the cockpit in one hand and the handle of his Lewis gun with the other and clung on wide eyed as Julian slowly tried to recover the BE, crashing into the side of the fuselage as the aircraft finally righted itself and hauling himself back in to safety, head first. Canning's heart was racing, blood thumping in his ears as he watched his observer shakily turn to him, give a limp thumbs up, and take a firm grip on one of the interplane struts. With Two Berts safe, Julian's attention turned to getting them home as quickly as bloody possible, when the memory of the photographic plates scattering to the wind came back to him, and he was beginning to despair when he noticed one final plate, still in the camera and, thank Christ, still unexposed. He swung the aircraft back round towards the target area, ignoring a concerned look from Two Berts, made sure that the picture would capture what were clearly British tanks, just to make a point, and tucked the finished plate into his jacket, taking great care to press it safely to his chest.

CHAPTER 19

12th April 1917

The unexpected afternoon sortie meant that by the time they had returned, Julian was running rather late to make his rendezvous with Lucy, and the conditions had undone a lot of the careful work he had put in to make himself, at least what he considered to be, mildly presentable. He leapt from the cockpit as soon as the BE's wheels had stopped turning, carefully passed the precious photograph to Two Berts and dashed off, forgetting to ask if his observer was okay after hanging out of the aircraft for a good twenty seconds.

Despite his appearance and his tardiness, Lucy seemed pleased enough to see him, as she said bade farewell to her token chaperone, and climbed up beside him. On the drive in, Canning found himself unusually talkative as he recounted the day's events with Bannister, much to Lucy's amusement. He decided he liked the crinkles at the side of her eyes when she smiled, but he also noticed that the lines remained even when the smile faded.

When they reached Lamaincourt, he rolled the tender into the kerb at the side of the main street, and they walked together down the cobbled road. The town was still quiet and they picked out a half empty restaurant, where they were ushered to a small corner table with the ubiquitous bottle mounted candle. To Canning's irritation, the strains of *Poor Butterfly* were being piped into the room from somewhere. That bloody song seemed to haunt him wherever he went. He grabbed the waitress as she passed and ordered, 'duh buttils van rouge.'

Lucy smiled, 'Saves asking her twice.'

Julian tried desperately to think of something interesting to say, failed, and sat staring at his cutlery with a particularly gormless look on his face as his brain stalled.

Lucy leaned her head forwards and tried to peer up at him from under her lashes, 'I'm sorry about last night.'

Canning, who had drifted into something of a trance, looked up, slightly startled, 'Sorry for what?'

'How I was, what I said. I just...needed to vent.'

He topped up her wine glass, 'This helps.'

She drank, long and deep, and let out a satisfied sigh, her cheeks flushing slightly, 'I read in the despatches today that you got awarded another medal.' She turned to look at him bemused. 'What on earth did you do?'

Canning thought back.

'I mistimed a bomb and scored a lucky hit on an ammo dump.'

'But you just said you bombed one of our airfields...'

'Oh no, this was a week ago. That time I bombed some Germans.'

She looked at him again, 'So are you actually any good? You keep saying you're not and James told Claire you were a bloody liability.'

'Christ no, I hate flying, it's bloody dangerous.'

'But they keep giving you medals?'

Julian sighed, 'It's the Army,' he tried to explain, 'They just... give people medals sometimes. It's sort of what they do.'

She eyed him sceptically.

'It doesn't mean anything!' he protested, 'I just wrote in my report they should give me a medal and they did.'

'Which one did you get.'

'MC'

'Well,' she paused to lift her glass in mock salute, 'here's to your MC, Lieutenant Canning. A more gallant and deserving officer there never was.'

'Piss off.'

Someone had flipped the record and the piano notes of *Alice in Wonderland* now wafted across the room. The restaurant was running a set menu due to shortages and their first course, a watery fish and potato soup, was brought out to them. Canning had never liked soup and particularly not in a restaurant. When he was paying someone to cook for him, it seemed like a complete con to then present him with liquid food. He spooned it grumpily into his mouth and washed it down liberally with wine, beckoning for another bottle. Lucy watched him, mildly amused. Canning, aware he was being studied, scowled at her.

'I have to say you make stunning dinner company,' she said lightly as Julian spilt spots of soup into his lap. He took another swig of wine.

'Although to give you your due, you might be a drunk, not too great at conversation, or coping with the world generally. Oh, and your nose makes you looked damned ugly too. But you don't have any pretensions. You just, sort of...are, I suppose. It makes you very easy to talk to.'

Julian rolled his eyes.

'Even amongst all of this, people still play politics. It's very refreshing to spend time with someone so...apathetic.'

Canning couldn't work out if he was being insulted or complimented. Or both. Eventually he decided he didn't care and returned to emptying his wine glass.

The main course of chicken arrived, a chicken, he thought, that looked as if it must have led a very depressing life, and some tired looking vegetables. Julian decided he had been very much misled about French cookery. But as the wine flowed, they started to talk. Or more accurately, Lucy talked and Canning did his best to join in. He had never quite mastered conversation. Sometimes, when he had a particularly strong opinion on something he could talk at people, but mostly he just nodded or grunted. But Lucy seemed pleased enough with his attempts to participate, and they stoically avoided the war as a topic.

Desert arrived, some yellow cream thing that made Julian

long for proper custard, and after the dregs of the fifth bottle of wine had been shaken into Canning's glass, they both threw down a handful of Francs and weaved a path to the door. Julian suggested another bar but Lucy decided she had drunk enough and as they walked back towards the tender, she linked her arm through his. The gesture surprised and pleased him, and his pace slowed.

A gaggle of RFC pilots and VAD nurses walked past them, laughter rippling in their wake. Lucy's grip on his arm tightened. Julian looked at her. A handful of stars had broken through the cloud cover and their pale, waning light reflected off a tear that was rolling down her cheek. Canning stopped and turned her towards him.

'Sorry,' she said, briskly brushing it away, 'It's the wine.'

He looked at her, sceptically.

'It's just. Well, I mean, just look around you, at all of this. All the lives that won't be lived, all the loves never consummated, children never born. And for what? So a bunch of comfortable, fat, complacent jingoists, whose best years passed them by the womb, can hang up the bunting and sing God Save the King.'

She was right. And Canning couldn't think of anything to say in reply so he just took her arm and carried on walking. They reached the tender and Julian offered her a hand up into the cabin of the Crossley but instead she turned and kissed him and their teeth clicked together. Then she pulled away and took a step backwards, fixing him deep brown eyes that danced with life.

'I just need to be close to someone, to feel something for a few hours before I have to wake up and sew men back together again. Are you okay with that?'

Canning nodded. He felt awkward and nervous, not quite sure what to do with his hands.

'We'll find a place that lets out its rooms for the night. You can run us back early morning. Before we both have to do it all over again.'

She grabbed his shoulder and turned him towards her.

'This isn't a free pass by the way, this is one night and I need someone.'

'I don't think anyone has ever needed me.'

She smiled mischievously, 'I don't need you. I need someone and you're here. Now stop being so pathetically self-pitying or I'll chase one of those proper pilots down, with one of those daft moustaches.'

He snorted in amusement.

'Have they issued you with rubbers?'

Julian shook his head, feeling suddenly very young.

Lucy rolled her eyes. 'Great, well we're not doing this without one, not if you've been at the jump houses. Where's the nearest brothel? We hand them out there but the bloody tarts never use 'em. They'll be sure to have some knocking about.'

For form's sake, Canning started to plead ignorance but quickly gave up under her gaze and steered them towards *Le Flamant Bleu*, where Lucy quickly ducked in and emerged shortly afterwards with a small cardboard box and an enticing grin.

'We could just borrow one of their rooms...' offered Canning helpfully, his voice tailing away at the look of open disgust on her face.

Thirty minutes later, and he found himself alone with her, in a room they had rented for four hours at a small, cheap hotel. He barely noticed the surroundings, except that the lighting was soft and it seemed clean and then she was standing opposite, close against him and he felt horribly awkward again, almost as if he wanted to sheer away. But she kissed him, lifting herself onto her tiptoes and he responded, gently wrapping his arms around her. Then she pushed him away and stepped back, sliding out of her clothing. It was somehow so naturally elegant, so perfect and he tried to do the same but his fingers fumbled with the buttons of his uniform tunic and he couldn't think of a way of dropping his trousers that wouldn't seem comical. She stepped in to help him, hands flicking open the brass buttons embossed with the RFC wings, stripping it from him and tossing the rough khaki cloth across the room. He sat on the end of the bed, thinking it the most dignified way to remove his breeches and then realised he had left his socks on and, exasperated, abandoned any attempt at sensuality and tore off the rest of his undergarments. She grinned salaciously and jumped him, knocking them both backwards onto the mattress, springs creaking in protest.

His hand slid between her thighs and he felt the warm wetness of her, and suddenly he was scared. He had only known prostitutes and he wasn't sure if there was something else he should be doing. Automatically, he rolled her over and pushed her legs apart to clamber between them and she slapped his face, firmly but without spite. He looked at her, shocked, but there was a smile in her eyes and she took his hands and showed him and when she finally let him in, their bodies clashed together, moving in short, sharp jerks, reaching for the shafts of pleasure. But it was more than just physical gratification, it was about not being alone. Their eyes stayed locked, hands, arms and legs moving without thought, just desperate to stay pressed close to one another. And when they finished, they lay naked beneath the sheets, holding each other, clinging to the heat of another breathing, beating human form, as the darkness enveloped them and they started to doze.

When Canning finally crept back into the hut, the time was well past 0300. As the door clicked behind him, Shellford's voice rose from the swell of darkness at the far end, 'Mission accomplished, brave aviator?'

'Yes, I think so,' Replied Canning, sheepishly. The fact that Shellford was still wide awake in the small hours of the morning didn't register.

Shellford chuckled and a light flared, briefly silhouetting his profile before receding to a deep red glow that rose and fell as he puffed on the pipe he had appropriated from the dead Colonel, 'Always more fun when both sides are into it,' he observed with an air of sagacity, 'Bit of a dark horse you are, Canning, old trout.'

Julian was tempted to say that he thought 'horse' was a little generous but he was feeling somewhat tired, and Shellford seemed in a talkative mood and was standing between him and his bed, so he remained silent, not wanting to encourage the conversation.

'Always a bit detached with a whore,' the tall pilot persisted, 'sometimes you want something a bit more than bored submission behind the eyes. So just who is this latest piece?'

Canning was saved by Two Berts, who stirred in his cot and grunted something, interrupting them.

'What was that?' Asked Shellford.

'I think he called us a pair of women and told us to shut up,' replied Julian.

'Wankers,' slurred the Welshman, 'Goffuckterbed.'

'He has a point,' said Canning, 'I've rather done myself in.'

Shellford gave another empty chuckle, 'Good man, get yourself some beauty sleep, Christ knows you need it.'

Julian rolled into his bed and curled the cheap, Army issue blanket around himself as the dull light from the embers of Shellford's pipe burned gently at the other end of the hut.

CHAPTER 20

13th April 1917

A tremendous crash shook the hut and Canning cried out as he woke. For a second he was back in the cockpit, petrol fumes and gunfire all around him. Another echoing bang and one of the new men in the hut fell out of his bed in shock. The smell of cordite drifted across the room. Gasping, sweating, Julian peered through the gloom to see Shellford's normally languid frame tense and alert, poised at the window. A wisp of smoke curved from the muzzle of a revolver held tightly at the end of a long arm.

'What the fuck, Shellford?' Called Two Berts, angrily.

'Rats,' Shellford snapped a terse response, 'Big as fucking donkeys. Must be following the corpses back from the Front.' He took a deliberate aim and loosed off another round, the noise bouncing off the curved walls. Canning and Two Berts exchange a worried look as the tall pilot fired again and Two Berts had taken a tentative step forward to disarm him, when Shellford let out a triumphant yell and sprinted out the door. Tentatively, they followed him out into the brush-scrub. In the distance, more figures, disturbed by the commotion, were starting to materialise in the early morning mist and make their way across the airstrip.

Shellford had stopped now and was parting the long grass with the barrel of his pistol, craning over to peer down at something.

'Holy fuck,' breathed Two Berts, as he came to stand beside him.

A long, fat, bloated black lump, if not quite as big as a donkey then at least the size of a morbidly obese cat, lay curled in the grass. Dirty brown blood leaked from it.

'Told you,' muttered Shellford, 'Makes better sport than grouse, I'll give 'em that.'

Suddenly the sleek, dark shape twitched and unfurled with a dreadful hiss, and turned a pointed, malevolent face with evil red eyes and long yellow teeth onto them, snapping at Shellford's legs. He jumped briskly backwards and fired two shots into the swollen black head, which shuddered, before falling still. Watching it carefully, he reached down to grab the foot long, fat pink tail and hauled the creature off the ground. A corpulent mass of matted fur dangled in the air, rotating slowly, its stubby little feet protruding stiffly. They all stared at it in muted horror.

'Didn't realise the mother-in-law had made it over here,' Shellford murmured, before swinging his arm backwards and hurling the giant rat into the undergrowth. It cracked into a tree trunk with a wet thud before falling to the floor. He pocketed the revolver and wiped his hands down his tunic.

'Breakfast?' he asked brightly.

A wan sun had broken through the thin layer of grey cloud and it bathed the airfield in a milky light. As Julian walked towards the mess, his eye was caught by a sudden flicker, a bright, sulphur yellow butterfly was flitting between the wildflowers in the surrounding woodland. Brimstone. He recognised it easily from its colour and flight, his mind drawn back to a childhood fascination. A spring butterfly, it had always signified the turn of the seasons for him and he smiled for a moment, before remembering where he was and what he was doing, and the smile left his face as he groped for his flask.

Stuart and Billington arrived to deliver the day's briefing as the squadron was sitting down to eat, the muted conversation quickly died away as their new commanding officer entered the room.

'Orders,' he growled, his forehead deeply furrowed, 'Weather's improved so we're back on infantry support and art obs for the poor bastards dug in past Arras. We'll be working with the mobile field batteries that have been moved up over the last few days, but they won't have wireless so we'll be using flares to communicate.'

A soft, collective groan signified the airmen's thoughts about that. It was hard enough work trying to direct the guns with direct radio contact, let alone trying to correct their aim through a series of Very lights. Not to mention that it often ended up with them putting on a veritable firework display that attracted German fighters like moths.

Stuart cut across the noise, 'I know it's not ideal but it's what it is. So get on with it. Armitage St. Clare will lead B Flight on the morning assignments and I'll take A Flight in the afternoon. We'll head over the Lines in a group for safety then break off to our induvial objectives.'

Billington started distributing sheets of typed foolscap to each of the pilots.

'The day's flare codes are being handed out now, as ever, if you're forced down over Hunland, make sure they are destroyed along with any maps or notes before you are taken prisoner.'

As Julian was passed his code sheet, he mind drifted longingly to a cold, dank, and heavily secured German prison cell.

'Right,' Stuart continued, 'The individual targets for the day...'

CHAPTER 21

13th April 1917

Stuart paced across his office, boots thumping on the bare floorboards. He stopped, listened intently for a few seconds, then retraced his steps for the hundredth time. None of B Flight had returned yet and they were at least an hour overdue. In the office across the hallway, Billington could hear the steady thud of the Captain's footsteps. Strange, he thought, it had been the same with Frost every time an aeroplane was late to return. He found the noise comfortingly metronomic.

Earlier that morning, Armitage St. Clare had led the group of five aircraft out together as planned, but on their way across the Front Lines they had been caught by a group of eight Albatroses, that had fallen on them from out of the sun. Armitage St. Clare had gone first, the aristocratic flight commander had been offered up to the German squadron's newest recruit as his first kill, like a pride of lions blooding a cub. The leading Albatros directed him towards the Captain's lumbering two-seater, as the others watched over him for protection. An eighteen-year-old minor noble from Saxony, he turned out to be a rotten shot and expended most of his ammunition at Armitage St. Clare, who twisted like an eel, using all his long experience to evade the flood of bullets. But the BE was just too slow, and his observer wasn't able to put up a proper defensive fire ensconced between the wings, and eventually he fell into an uncontrollable spin, control surfaces shot away. The rest of the flight fell in quick succession soon afterwards, clinically dispatched by the experienced German fighter pilots with bursts of fire into either the aircrew or the engines, meat or metal. And less than an hour after they had taken off, all that was left of B Flight were a couple of oily smudges that drifted away on the spring breeze.

The rest of 33B squadron didn't know this though, there was just an ominous silence that extended throughout the morning and into the early afternoon, causing Stuart to hurl his tumbler of whisky into the defunct fireplace in the corner of his office, as A Flight prepared for their afternoon sortie.

Canning and Two Berts had been ordered to target a nest of pillboxes that were preventing the advance of a British regiment east of Wancourt. It would be a tricky task as the concrete bunkers would only succumb to direct hits, and even then the lighter calibre field artillery would still be relying on an element of luck to crack open the reinforced structures. Canning's mind boggled as he walked with Two Berts over to their aircraft, cigarette in hand, trying desperately to make out from his sheet of paper the combination of coloured flares that would denote direction and distance to the gunners. When they reached the hangars, they found Shellford in a heated debate with Stuart, who was holding his hands up, helplessly.

'There's no one left lad, all the other observers are paired up and I've just lost the whole of bloody B Flight. We'll be getting some more replacements tonight.'

'What about the gunnery chap I took up last time?'

'He's an armoury specialist, not a trained observer, we can't keep using him. Besides, he's none too keen to go back up either, given your...reputation.'

'What reputation?'

'Folks don't tend to last long in your front seat.'

'Oh for fuck's sake, tell them to grow up and grow a pair.'

'Look, your target is close to Canning and Two Bert's, just stay within sight of each other and they can give you a hand if you get into trouble.'

'That's your solution, ask a BE to escort a BE?' Shellford asked, outraged.

'What else can we do? There are a hundred and fifty

thousand men stuck in the shit down there and we need to help get 'em out. No-one's going to care if you're a bit pissed off that you have to make a solo flight. And yes, that's an order.'

Shellford spat viciously at the Squadron Commander's feet, 'Right.'

Stuart, taken aback, made to respond but Shellford was already stalking towards his aircraft. Two Berts scurried after him.

'Stay close boy, and we'll keep an eye on you,' he tried to reassure Shellford who was shaking his head in anger.

As the mechanics went through the engine start up routines, coaxing life into the tired machinery, Stuart walked over to Canning and Two Berts as they were preparing to climb into their aircraft. Julian had wound his scarf six-times around him and was shrugging on his coat.

'You two are my old hands now, God help me. And we need to hit those targets today, I have to assume B Flight made no impact. Get 'em and make sure you get back here.'

Two Berts nodded silently in reply as Julian continued to belt up his jacket. Stuart grabbed him by the shoulder.

'Canning, I need you to concentrate and I need you to do your job. No fucking about.'

Julian also gave him a nodded response and dragged on his cap and goggles. As Stuart turned to walk away, he fished out his flask and took a defiant pull. Burnt exhaust fumes drifted across the turf as the BEs spluttered into life.

The five aircraft stood with engines idling, waiting for Stuart to lead them into the air, when one of the orderlies ran down the flight line, shouting in the ears of each pair of crewmen.

'Hold taking off,' Canning heard him yell, the man's voice hoarse as he moved down the line, 'Orders might be changing!'

Julian shook his head in frustration and sat back in his chair, the wicker creaking. God, war could be so...boring. If he was going to die today he'd rather just get the bloody hell on with it. Sitting on the ground in what could very shortly become his death box for twenty minutes with sod all to do just rubbed harder on his already raw nerves. He began to take rhythmic sips from his flask and the numbers on the dials of his instruments started to blend into one another. In front of him, the engine was getting progressively hotter. Even ticking over at low revolutions, it wasn't getting the airflow it needed to keep itself cool.

Finally, the runner returned, handing some of the pilots pieces of paper, and he stopped next to Julian's cockpit and handed him a sheet of foolscap.

'Front's shifted,' he hollered into Canning's ear through a cupped hand, 'Jerry's made some inroads so the targets have changed.'

Julian stared at the paper, but the blocky, hastily typed letters all swam together through the haze of drink and he passed it up to Two Berts. The observer read it, nodded, then turned and jabbed a finger at Shellford's aircraft next to them, with the empty front cockpit.

'What about him?' He called over the rumble of the engine.

Canning shrugged, unsure. The orderly had stopped by Shellford's BE and handed him a different target too. Two Berts turned to look around him anxiously, then leant over to Julian, 'Follow him!' He shouted and instead of memorising and destroying the paper orders as protocol demanded, he tucked it into an inside pocket of his flying jacket.

As the BEs started to drag themselves into the sky, Julian hit a pocket of uneven air taking off and the aircraft rocked and bumped horribly, threatening to fall over onto one of its wings if it lost any more speed and Canning thrust the nose down to desperately try and keep it aloft. His pulse slowed as the machine stabilised and he started to search for Shellford. The other BE was drifting towards the lines, and Canning set off after it. He could see Two Berts' hand tapping nervously on the spade grip of his Lewis gun but the observer gave no indication they should change course and he continued to follow Shellford. Then, decisively, the Welshman stood up, extracted the paper orders, screwed them up in his gloved fist, and tossed them over the side of the cockpit. He turned to Canning, holding his arms outward, palms upturned in and expression of cluelessness. Julian, deprived of his navigator, nodded in understanding and opened the throttle to chase after Shellford's BE. They were still being buffeted by the wind and, despite the increase in airspeed, he was struggling to make up the distance they had lost to the other machine during take-off. It hung in the air ahead of them, silhouetted against the scattered white of the clouds, alone, fragile, and hugely vulnerable.

Two Berts saw it first, the briefest flash of light, the sun catching the wings of a banking aircraft high above Shellford's BE. He jumped up from his seat and started waving desperately at Canning, jabbing a gloved hand towards the threat. Julian, understanding immediately, was surprised at how willingly he followed his observer's instructions and turned towards the danger. He supposed that Shellford's talent for sourcing hookers made him worth a little extra effort to save. The BE's lack of speed meant that the Hun had already made a pass at the other aircraft before they arrived on the scene. But Shellford had dealt with it well, slipping inside the arc of the Albatros's dive, forcing it to pull up and turn away to line up another attack. Two Berts started firing from a distance in an effort to throw the German off his aim, but the Hun pilot ploughed on regardless and Shellford had to throw his aircraft wildly across the sky to get out of the way of the murderous stream of gunfire being poured at him, his BE now trailing a line of pale vapour.

The Albatros swooped up and over to come hurtling back down on the helpless British aircraft. Canning and Two Berts were closer this time though, and the Welsh observer managed to send a stream of Lewis fire across the German's flight path. He expected it to sheer away but, as before, it carried straight on, the Hun pilot apparently intent on the destruction of Shellford's aircraft, even at the expense of his own life. Two Berts' tracer passed straight through the green painted fuselage and the Albatros's engine threw out a great gout of black smoke that tailed away in an oily wake. Slowly, the German aircraft rolled onto its back and span downwards in a whorl of exhaust fumes. The Welshman turned to Canning, thumbs up, but their joy turned to agony as they saw that the vapour trail Shellford's BE had been venting had erupted into orange fire that was consuming the front of his machine. Canning felt sick but couldn't turn away as he flew in closer to the second aircraft to see Shellford in the cockpit, arm raised to protect his face from the flames. Two Berts was gripping the handle of his Lewis gun to steady himself and Julian felt the bile rise and tears prick at his eyes behind his goggles.

As the fire billowed back from the engine it started to engulf the pilot's cockpit, and Shellford's spindly figure awkwardly began to extricate itself, and clambered out onto the wing. One was hand still reaching down to the control column as he stood there trying to keep his machine level, the flames growing, eating the fabric of the wings and fuselage, turning it to burnt scraps and charred wooden spars. The blaze grew, licking at Shellford, charring and blackening his leather flying gear. Two Berts and Canning watched helpless as their friend, edged along the wing spars, away from the fire, then looked up at them, gave a brief, sad wave, and then stepped out into nothing. The rapidly diminishing brown doll turned over and over as it fell, disappearing beneath the cloud layer. The burning BE crumpled into itself and followed it down.

CHAPTER 22

13th April 1917

As soon as they had landed, Canning and Two Berts marched straight to the bar and started to silently knock back tumblers of whisky in quick succession. The mess room around them was quiet. The young lives that had given it breath and energy in the morning now extinguished. Ripley walked slowly up to them with a solemn nod and accepted a glass, raising it in wordless salute. He downed it, no longer blanching when the spirit hit the back of his throat, before leaving to join the handful of remaining squadron members at the card table. Two Berts and Canning were left alone. There was nothing to say, so neither of them said anything but as they drank, they gradually became aware that the patter of voices around them had risen, and the room was now filled with bodies, freshly clad in spotless khaki. Replacements. Bright eyes and excited faces that shot them nervous glances when they thought the two more experienced men weren't looking. Canning and Two Berts didn't recognise a single face. Ripley, still green enough to blend in with the crowd, was lost amongst them. Stuart was absent, removed to his position of authority..

The jollity and chumminess of the new men grated on them. One of the new observers, evidently the troubadour of the group, had brought a guitar and proceeded to lead a rendition of a song they didn't recognise but must have been popular at the training schools. Like so many others, it spoke of death with levity. They didn't attempt to join in. Stuart would look to them to lead these men now and they wanted nothing to do with it. They could all find their own deaths easily enough without Canning and Two Berts showing them the way. It dawned on them both that they couldn't stay there that night. It didn't feel like their squadron any more. They could try, of course, stand with Ripley and introduce themselves, welcome the new faces, but what was the point? They would all just burn up as the rest of them had. Sacrificed on the altar of the greater good. Although that greater good was a more heinous aberration of death and mutilation than either of them could ever have conceived. Without saying a word, they exchanged a look, set down their glasses and left the mess, unaware of the sense of relief that accompanied their exit, and walked towards the Crossley tender. Canning made to get in the driver's seat but Two Berts hauled him back by the shoulder.

'It's bad enough having to fly with you,' he muttered as he scrambled in and started the engine.

Julian leapt out the way as the vehicle shot backwards in reverse then sprinted to grab hold of the passenger side of the cabin, hauling himself over and in, as the Welshman barrelled away from the aerodrome and down the lane towards Lamaincourt.

They rolled drunkenly through the town, moving from bar to bar, quickly knocking back their drinks, then moving on. As they came to the fourth establishment on their tour, they encountered a group of FE2 two-seater crews, who, it transpired, had managed to force down an Albatros fighter over the allied side of the lines, resulting in the capture of both man and machine. Consequently, they were in a particularly buoyant mood and moreover, they had managed to secure the unfortunate German pilot before he could be taken prisoner and brought him back to their aerodrome to give him a proper send-off, prior to his impending incarceration. Somehow, they had subsequently managed to smuggle him off the airfield and into town, where his field grey uniform and iron cross medals were drawing considerable attention and appeared to be a source of some tension between the British aircrews and a group of French fighter pilots on an adjacent table. Recognising fellow RFC comrades, the Captain of the FE squadron beckoned Julian and Two Berts over and poured them each a drink. Pulling up a pair of wooden stools, they settled over their whiskies and watched the interaction between the two groups of airmen with interest. The Frenchmen, as far as Canning could see, were just doing what fighter pilots did, namely getting drunk and trying to shag anything in sight whilst making exaggerated claims about their achievements and telling overblown tales of derring-do. They also appeared to have obtained some beer, which was a source of great envy, and the FE squadron were now baiting the French airmen by flaunting their German trophy. One of the FE2 observers also seemed to speak passable French and was barracking the fighter pilots with poorly pronounced invective. None of the British aircrews understood what was being said, but it seemed to be provoking a reaction, and if he hadn't been so thoroughly inebriated, the young German might have been a little nervous about some of the looks he was getting.

He was the first Hun that Canning had seen up close, who had not been behind a pair of Maxim machine guns, trying to kill him. He was young, fair and clean shaven, with bright blue eyes that were currently pointing in different directions. Put him in a khaki uniform and he could easily have been a cousin to Ripley, Julian thought. The German noticed him looking, turned to him, picked up a glass of whisky that belonged to the man sitting next to him and gave a stiff, exaggerated jerk of his head in a mock Prussian bow, before throwing back the liquor. Canning slowly raised his own glass, returning the salute.

A renewed burst of shouting made him look round where, to his consternation, he saw Two Berts leading the observer who had previously been in charge of international relations and two of the FE pilots in a loud rendition of Le Marseilles, standing on chairs. Except none of them knew the words so they were just shouting incoherently to what appeared to be a very liberal interpretation of the melody, but from their expressions, clearly close enough for the Frenchmen to recognise. As they brought their act to a rousing finale, each one of them turned and dropped their trousers, baring their arses towards the fighter pilots. This proved to be the limit of what they were prepared to tolerate and the first beer bottles started to sail towards the chorus line, who quickly dispersed, scrambling to avoid the missiles. One of them caught a large, bearded FE pilot a glancing blow, grazing his temple, and he rose from his seat with a roar and hurled one of the vacant chairs into the group of Frenchmen, scattering bodies and smashing glasses. The scene rapidly descended into a drunken melee, which Canning quickly backed away from to watch from a safe distance. Two Berts appeared at his shoulder with the same wild grin on his face he sometimes wore when he was firing his Lewis gun. Clapping Julian cheerfully on the shoulder, he picked up a chair and placed it between himself and the group of brawling airmen. Then, like a golfer lining up a putt, he took several paces backwards, carefully measuring the distance, before sprinting forwards, up onto the chair, and leaping from it, propelling himself high into the air, landing slap in the middle of the tussle, skittling French and British officers alike.

A large proportion of the barroom furniture had been wrecked, and was being variously used as bludgeons or projectiles as the fight became increasingly vicious. Three Frenchmen had made to rush the German prisoner, but were being fended off gallantly by the bearded FE pilot. He was slowly being overwhelmed when the MPs arrived. Fifteen tall, burly British Royal Military Policemen burst in armed with heavy wooden truncheons, and began hauling the combatants into the street, fetching sharp blows to elbows and kneecaps to quell their belligerence. Then one of them, a simple looking lump of a youth, noticed the protagonist he was dragging away was dressed in a German uniform and proceeded to lay into the young pilot with boot and truncheon, with a couple of his squad mates joining him.

Canning, who had pressed himself against the wall to avoid the attention of the MPs, now slipped out one of the side entrances and started searching for Two Berts. He saw the Welshman, face bloodied, black hair tousled, squirming in the grip of an RMP Sergeant. Julian was at a complete loss for what to do next, when a shout went up and he saw that the MPs beating the German pilot had managed to crack open his skull, and the wet paste of his brains was spreading across the cobbles. The provosts who had killed him were now standing around in a panic, talking rapidly, trying to work out a story. Then the bearded FE pilot emerged from the main entrance, saw what had happened, and with a howl of anger, went for the group of MPs with a broken whisky bottle. The Sergeant holding Two Berts dropped his prisoner and rushed to aid his comrades and Julian, seeing his chance, seized his observer by the wrist and dragged him swiftly away down the street, ducking through a couple of side alleys to break their trail.

They came panting to a halt, leaning against the window of a boulangerie and Julian saw that the Welshman was laughing even as he gasped for air.

'Jesus, that was a rare old scrap,' he choked.

'You're a fucking idiot.' Canning told him breathlessly, offering his handkerchief to help stem the blood.

Two Berts waved it away, terrified that he'd catch an infection if it went anywhere near an open wound, and pointed to a bar opposite that was showing signs of starting to shut up for the night.

'Reckon we can get one more in there?'

'Reckon we can try.'

They each lit a cigarette and started to weave their way drunkenly across the street towards an alarmed looking owner, who was carrying in his outdoor seating. As the two airmen reached the doorway, the elderly proprietor looked them up and down disapprovingly, in a manner Julian could only think of as being very French. And when he noticed Two Bert's bloodied face, his consternation turned to panic.

'Non!' he shouted at them as they tottered towards him, then darted inside the building when he realised they weren't turning away, emerged with a hefty looking broom, which he jabbed towards them, menacingly.

'Whisky M'sieur.' Shouted Julian cheerfully.

'Non!' came the reply, 'Il ferme.'

At this stage of the evening, Canning was prepared to admit defeat, but Two Berts was apparently still up for a fight and made to rush at the old man, who deftly hit him on the crown with the heavy, bristled head of the broom. The Welshman slipped and fell and Julian, struck by the sudden irony that his observer, who had fought off some of the deadliest killers in the sky, was about to meet an untimely end at the hands of a septuagenarian's cleaning apparatus, burst out laughing.

Two Berts, who had staggered to his feet and looked as if he was going to murder the old bar owner, was taken aback by his pilot's reaction, giving Canning the couple of seconds he needed to drag him away, the Welshman petulantly kicking over a table as he went.

'Bastard!' he shouted over his shoulder, then instantly forgot the episode as he noticed the street name, daubed on a brick wall in faded paint and turned to Julian with a grin.

'You know the Flamingo's only a couple of blocks from here...'

Canning thought for a moment, then nodded and they both set off with renewed vigour.

The corpulent Madame recognised Two Berts as they entered and Julian marvelled at the expression of excitement and trepidation that his observer provoked when he winked at her. He picked out a girl for himself, a tall brunette who still seemed to have a spark of life about her. Even though it felt better without one of those bloody sheaths, it was all a bit quick and perfunctory, and he ended up waiting for another tedious hour in the lounge for Two Berts. Slumped in a faded, floral patterned easy chair he fell into a doze as one of the house's girls prodded him with her foot from an adjacent chair, in a futile attempt to entice him into further exertions.

When they finally left the building, Two Berts put a sweaty arm around him, 'Shit day,' he slurred, 'But at least with us, we'll go together. It can't get any bloody lonelier.'

Canning shook his head, 'You really should find yourself a better pilot.'

'Probably,' agreed his observer, 'You're not getting any better.' They reached the tender and he clambered up to start then engine.

'But then again,' he said with a deep yawn, 'I'm not sure how I'd cope with a competent driver. I'd probably get bored. And besides, some unlucky bugger's got to keep an eye on you. Might as well be me. Oh shit!' The exclamation came as he backed the tender into a royal blue Shelby tourer parked behind him with a horrible crunch and, he slammed his foot down and bolted before anyone around could intervene.

CHAPTER 23

14th April 1917

Stuart intercepted them as they walked across the airstrip towards the hangars, where the fragile BEs were being dragged out onto the damp turf to be fuelled. The tart tang of petrol carried on the heavy morning air made his nostrils twitch. Canning's face was buried deep in the folds of his scarf and Two Berts was fiddling with his flying helmet that was sitting uncomfortably on one of his bruises from last night.

'Looks shit,' said Stuart by way of greeting, gazing at the distant mass of darkening cloud. He handed Julian a pack of papers.

'Day's assignments,' he told them brusquely, turning his glare on them, 'Busy one.' He paused, 'You two were AWOL last night. You missed the orders and left the aerodrome without permission.'

'And you sent him up without a gunner,' snapped Two Berts and pushed past the Captain towards the waiting aircraft.

'Don't tell them that when you write the letter to his family though, Jimmy,' Canning advised, 'Tell them he died quick and clean, not jumping from a burning box kite because you left him defenceless.'

He jammed his flying cap onto his head and followed Two Berts, leaving Stuart standing alone.

Two Berts tore the top off the packet as the mechanics readied their machine.

'Jesus,' he breathed, reading down the sheet of foolscap.

Canning heard him and closed his eyes, then opened them quickly as without a reference point to focus on, a wave of nausea swept over him and the world started to rock. Christ, he felt like shit.

'What is it?' He asked, belching a little.

'Photos. A fucking lot of photos. And not nice ones. Arleux, Drecourt, Oppy.

'Jesus. Do you think he's done it deliberately?'

Two Berts looked down the flight line of BEs, which stood just in front of the deep ruts carved into the grass where he had slewed the tender across the airstrip trying to park it last night. All of the recent replacements were mustered by their aircraft, preparing to take off. One of the pilots had his flying cap on back to front and was struggling with his goggles as his comrades tittered at him in the background.

'Nah, we're all up and at it this morning, even the fledglings,' he replied, striking a match and touching it to the paper orders, letting the black embers scatter in the wind.

As if to prove his point, mechanics emerged from the sheds carrying the heavy cameras and began bolting them to the aircraft that weren't fitted with radios. He watched silently as the young pilot, who had since managed to right his helmet, succeeded in putting his boot through the fabric of the wing as he tried to climb into his machine. A patching square and tin of dope was being rushed out to try and get him airborne in time.

After the disaster that had befallen B Flight yesterday, group formations were disbanded as it seemed that, regardless of the numbers they were in, if the BEs met with the German *Jastas*, it always ended in tragedy, so splitting the flights up to operate individually lessened the odds of another massacre. Canning and Two Berts were sweating in their heavy leathers as they clambered into the BE, but they knew it would be cold enough once they got up there. The horizon had taken on a sickly yellow tinge that they both eyed critically. The engine misfired on the first and second swing, catching on the third with a harsh, hacking cough. Julian let it run for a bit in case it was carrying a problem but it soon settled into a familiar hum and he waved away the chocks, allowing the aircraft to wander forwards towards its take-off run. The stifling, muggy atmosphere made the pulse in his temples thud painfully to the rhythm of the engine. His groin has started to itch again, but he struggled to scratch at it through the leather of his coat.

They flew out with the mountain of cloud building ominously behind them, but the first sortie to Arleux proved uneventful, the most serious incident occurring when Two Berts swallowed a rather large beetle whilst they were over the objective, turning bright red, and he spent the return journey choking up pieces of wing and carapace.

Mid-morning saw them return to Pouilly-Yvredon, where the BE was refuelled and the camera restocked with fresh plates as Julian swigged from a cup of coffee and Two Berts extracted a long, segmented leg from between his teeth. A couple of hopeful spots of warm rain tapped on the wings as they mounted up for the flight to Drecourt, but they faded away to nothing, neither breaking the oppressiveness of the day or washing out operations. Canning nursed his headache with a double brandy, which he dropped into his second coffee, then had to leap from the cockpit as the engine was being started, to piss fiercely behind the hangers as the liquid ballooned in his bladder.

This time the BE sprang an oil leak when it finally coughed into life, covering both Julian and Two Berts in a fine mist of grease as the exhaust spat up an evil looking cloud of brown smoke. Ten minutes under the practiced spanner of the fitter and a length of emergency tubing had it up and running, but it seemed a worryingly quick fix, and Canning did his best to try and break it again as he gunned the engine at full revs to test it, but it held irritatingly firm.

The ever-growing storm clouds cast a frustrating half-light over the landscape, making it hard to pick out the details on the ground. It took Julian twenty minutes to find the forward supply dump he was meant to be photographing and partway through the search, Two Berts became uncomfortably aware of a shadow flickering amongst the cloud layer, silhouetted above them. As Canning exposed the sixth and final plate and circled back for home, Two Berts watched the darting shape turn with them and signalled his pilot to climb into the grey mists himself, in an attempt to lose whatever was stalking them. Julian lifted the BE so it was absorbed into the thin film of grey that extended out from the large black monolith that they were now heading back towards. He tracked the heading off his compass, for once thankful of the BE's inherent lack of manoeuvrability as it held its course.

Then, almost as if they had hit the edge of a cliff, they emerged into open sky as the cloud layer ended abruptly, with the next bank several thousand feet above them. Almost immediately, an Albatros popped out of the murk besides them, the pilot looking as surprised as they were, before swooping away to line up an attacking pass. Canning reckoned the Hun pilot had been smiling at the prospect of an easy score against the antiquated BE. He watched the Albatros enviously as it turned and climbed away from him effortlessly, noticing a grinning skull and bones motif etched on the fuselage, forward of the iron crosses. The device irritated Julian, who felt that sort of thing to be unnecessarily aggressive. It was pretty obvious from the rattle of machine guns and thud of bullets hitting his wings that the German was intent on killing him, without needing to paint that sort of thing on his aeroplane. Another stream of lead hammered past and something plucked at his shoulder, leaving a score in the leather, even as Two Berts stood up to the flurry of black tracer to return fire and send the Albatros scuttling away. They were still well over the enemy Lines though, and the German had the luxury of time and territory as he made to line up another pass. He was flying a clever line that made the British observer's shooting difficult, but he was still mildly surprised when the Tommy, standing upright and alive in his cockpit, stopped firing at him altogether, especially after the old crate had put up such a spirited defence so far. It was almost as if he had given up trying to defend his aeroplane, and for a moment it baffled the German pilot. He still hadn't puzzled it out when his brains were dashed across his windscreen by the two Sopwiths that had dropped in unseen behind him. Two Berts had spotted them though, they were the new triplane versions, their high wing stacks looking rather unwieldy, but they moved quick enough and the Welshman had ceased fire so his shots wouldn't endanger the British fighters. The triplanes were decent enough to escort them back to the Lines, at which point they departed north, with a cheerful wave.

Canning could almost feel the hairs on his arms standing with the static of the storm as they refuelled again, and took on a brisk, if unappetising lunch of beef and biscuits, forced down with a mix of tea, whisky, and water. Of the ten BEs that had flown out in the morning, two of the replacement crews had failed to return and Stuart was already on the phone to request more men and machines for the following day, as the remainder of the squadron took to the air once more. The throbbing of the pregnant clouds, aching to break, was palpable, but all that transpired was a slight shift in the wind speed as they started out for their final run to Oppy in the early afternoon. The gusts carried them swiftly towards the transport depot that was their objective, and Julian took his final set of photographs, flying a zig-zag course to throw off the anti-aircraft fire, and turned, with a mixture of relief and anticipation, back towards Pouilly-Yvredon, and into the impending storm.

The clouds in front of them boiled black and sinister, blotting out the light. Canning huddled a little lower into his cockpit, trying to lose himself deep in his flying gear. He shivered, the wind that was slowing them down was also taking the dark mass towards them. As they inched agonisingly towards the lines, Two Berts spent most of his time searching over Canning's shoulder for signs of pursuit behind them, but as he turned to survey the rest of the sky he suddenly stiffened, then stood up on his wicker chair to better peer forwards through the struts and sheen of the propeller.

He remained frozen for a good ten seconds before turning to Julian and pointing. Following his observer's outstretched gauntlet, he could see a handful of twinkling white dots ahead of them, stark against the black of the cloud. He puzzled at them for a moment before realising that they were British anti-aircraft shells being fired at a German aircraft that was still too far away to make out. British shell bursts were predominantly white and German black, a distinction reinforced by the first jagged airbursts from the enemy guns that greeted them as they drew nearer to the front.

Two Berts pushed up his goggles, turned to give Julian a reassuring smile, and then started to prepare his Lewis gun. The aircraft shuddered as he fired a couple of short bursts towards the ground to warm it in the cold air, before taking up a position that would enable him to fire forwards towards the approaching German. His eyes were fixed relentlessly on the white specks, waiting for the first sign of danger to emerge, only relaxing his vigil to quickly scan the rest of the sky to make sure they weren't caught unawares by anything dropping in behind them.

Slowly, inevitably, they saw a dull speck materialise in the midst of the white shellfire and steadily begin to grow as the two aircraft crept nearer to each other. Behind it loomed the rolling cloudbank, almost if it were being pulled along in the wake of the enemy machine. Julian altered his course slightly in an attempt to skirt the approaching foe, but it had no effect and the speck had now transformed into the shape of an aeroplane as they ploughed inexorably towards each other. The confrontation now a forgone conclusion, Canning began to climb for height to give himself some options once the fight started but the German, who had evidently now seen them too, did the same and then slewed his machine round at an angle to cut across them. Very deliberately, Two Berts pulled down his goggles and adjusted his aim. As the Hun pilot turned, Julian could make out the profile of the aircraft and recognised it as an Albatros C-type two-seater. Produced by the same works responsible for the effective and ubiquitous D-type fighter, the C-type shared similar responsibilities to the British two-seaters, mainly reconnaissance, art obs and bombing, and was only marginally superior in performance to the BEs and FEs that the RFC operated. Canning racked his memory, he was pretty sure that the C-type had a fixed forward firing gun for the pilot and a mobile Parabellum machine gun for the observer in the rear seat. He examined the approaching aircraft, wondering how the German would choose to attack and the fear started to creep up on him. He was close enough now to see the black Maltese crosses, stark with their white outlines that always seemed so alien and threatening, and the brown and green mottling of his adversary's camouflage.

Julian was scared, but he was also mightily pissed off. He just about understood the Albatros fighters, hated them with a passion, but knew that it was their job to find and kill people like him. In the same way, the British Nieuports and Sopwiths were tasked with hunting his German two-seater equivalents. Destroying other machines was a fighter pilot's responsibility, whilst his was to stay alive and do his job, and consequently he silently cursed the approaching Hun. They shared enough perils as it was, without starting to shoot at each other as well. The enemy aircraft was swinging across his nose now and he hauled the BE round to the left to follow it, so the two machines would finish broadside and Two Berts would at least have an equal chance with the German observer. The heavy, brooding thunder cloud hung over them and he heard a low rumble carried on the air. As the two lumbering biplanes fell alongside each other he closed his eyes and ducked down into the cockpit, bracing himself against the death rattle, the tearing of canvas, splintering of wood, and searing hot pain of the bullets.

He waited, waited, Christ he wanted to piss himself, still more waiting, still no gunfire and then he realised that neither was Two Berts firing back. Slowly, he lifted his head to see the Welshman with his goggles raised, waving a cheerful greeting to the observer in the C-type who was returning the gesture with a broad smile. Feeling suddenly limp, and cold from sweat, Julian raised a half-hearted glove towards the pilot of the black crossed machine who grinned at him, white teeth beneath an enormous black moustache. Well, he thought to himself, it would have been a bloody pointless way to die and the Huns, reasonable fellows that they were, had evidently felt the same. They flew beside each other for a couple of minutes, too close to each other to be troubled by ground fire from either side, before his moustachioed new friend threw him a mock salute and peeled away for home. Canning exchanged a look of relief with Two Berts and turned towards Pouilly-Yvredon himself. A few desultory bursts of German anti-aircraft fire had started up again but the clouds ahead of him had begun to disperse. Then there was an almighty bang and his world went black.

His ears were ringing and his stomach lurched as the BE bucked wildly and he guessed that the engine had let itself go again. Desperately he clawed at his blinded eyes, succeeded in tearing off his goggles, he could fell something wet and cloying covering his face and he scooped what felt like a sticky, viscous oil from his eyes, just about clearing enough vision to make out that the BE was still airborne and flying level. He mopped at his face with his scarf and as the cockpit swam into focus, he noticed that Two Berts was no longer in the front cockpit. He was all over it.

Canning's world turned to red as he looked around him to see tendrils of gore hanging from the wings, struts and wires. It was everywhere. His gloves, his chest, his face and the wash from the propeller kept blowing jelly like chunks of head and brain back at him. It tasted sickly and salty as it found its way into his mouth. He sat, stupefied, thinking that he should shout, scream, panic, but nothing happened. He just sat there, thousands of feet above the earth, covered in pieces of his observer, his friend. Then his breathing started to quicken until he was panting. He had to get out, get away. But he couldn't. He was stuck in this fucking charnel house of an aeroplane, trapped in a cradle of gore. Sitting there, covered in Two Berts, whose blood was starting to dry and crust on his face. Red slashes were painted all across the wings and fuselage where the shrapnel had blown his head apart.

Then he looked down and saw it. Sitting on his lap, staring at him accusingly, was a single eye, seemingly unscathed and bright white against the red and brown of blood and leather. The green iris glared back up at him. He remained transfixed by it, the red spider veins that ran across the smooth blue-white of the eyeball, the length of nerve, like an unravelled strand of wool tailing from the back of it. The life, light, and humanity gone from it as it watched him in an unblinking death stare. He couldn't bring himself to touch it, so it remained there, fixated on him throughout the entirety of the flight back, rocking slightly whenever he pressed on the rudder bar or moved the control column. He tried to look away, but every few seconds his gaze flickered back to it, as all around him the strands of blood and tissue swayed in the wind.

Julian landed automatically and the BE's momentum meant that it ran right up to sheds, narrowly missing several parked machines, causing a buzz of activity. As men milled around him, he stayed seated in the aircraft unmoving, paralysed. The blood dripping from the tip of his nose tickled. The green and white eye still looked up at him.

'Sir?' one of the mechanics climbed onto a wing then fell away with a curse, choking on his vomit.

'What's going on?' Stuart's strong voice cut through the bustle and he strode up in his flying gear. 'Oh God,' he breathed taking in the scene then clambered up next to Julian and saw the eye on his lap. 'Oh Jesus, alright lad.'

He reached down and swept it into the well of the cockpit with a gloved hand. Julian looked up and wanted to punch him for doing it, for brutally casting away the last part of Two

Berts. Instead he pushed him away then scrambled from the cockpit, head and torso coated in gore. Stuart gripped him by the shoulders and stared hard at him.

'Canning, listen to me Canning.' He reached into Julian's jacket and pulled out his flask, unscrewing it and jamming it into his hand. 'I've got you lad, come on, drink that now.'

Julian swayed and then his eyes seemed to swim back into focus on Stuart's face, the lids flared and he shoved him away with both hands dropping the flask. Stuart staggered.

'What the fuck did you say to me?!'

'I...I said I've got you...'

'Get the hell away from me!' Canning yelled, 'You're the one that fuels this fucking slaughterhouse. Daddy fucking Stuart, our grim and stoic Captain with a friendly arm. You're the worst one of all. Because you know what this is and still you play the game. How many have you burnt Jimmy? How many are scattered over the French fucking countryside because of you? Christ I hope you see their faces when you sleep.'

Stuart took a pace forwards but Canning continued

'They get here and they're boys, boys! Not even men. And you put one arm round them so they can't see the fucking knife in the other, and you send them up to die. And you know what you're doing and you still fucking do it, you murderous cunt...'

Stuart's right hand crashed into Canning's face and sent him sprawling into the dirt. Julian reached for his flask then dragged himself up without a word, spat a bloody gob at Stuart's feet and walked off the airfield.

CHAPTER 24

14th April 1917

Canning stood outside the field hospital for three hours, his jaw throbbing, the dried blood crusting on his face and in his hair. No-one paid him any mind, he was just another of the War's blood stained, tattered leavings. He watched a steady stream of mutilated men drift past him, then eventually Lucy emerged among a cluster of young nurses. They were laughing in spite of everything but, far from seeming inappropriate, the lightness in their voices lifted those around them. Lucy's smile faded when she saw Canning, and she detached herself from the group, hurrying over to him. She was dressed in stained white coveralls over her khaki uniform, and her hair was scraped back tightly.

'Jesus,' she breathed as she walked up to him, clutching his wrist, 'Are you okay?'

'I need you,' his voice quavered and he fell forwards onto her.

'Okay, love, okay,' she cradled the back of his head as his body shook against hers, 'What happened?' she asked gently.

Julian shook his head, unable to put it into words, 'Two Berts is dead.' He finally blurted out.

'Who's Two Berts?'

Canning stumbled, 'My, my...' Friend? Partner? Protector? Guardian bloody Angel?

'My observer.'

'Oh God, is that...was that...him?' She touched his blood matted face.

Julian nodded, his eyes wide and white.

She took both his hands and fixed him with her eyes, 'We're going inside now and we're going to fix it, okay?'

He nodded again, and she led him back into the hospital and through a winding maze of tents to a rough wooden bench, where he sat trembling, as she sponged off the dried gore with warm, soapy water from a chipped metal bowl. It turned quickly red when she dipped the cloth back in, the blood clouds billowing in the clear liquid. He cradled a pint of rum in his hands that he sipped from, as she mopped down his temples and scraped the remains of Two Berts from beneath his collar.

Lucy could see the dead look behind his eyes, she had seen it a thousand times before in a thousand other men, and said nothing as she worked, just letting the rum take effect as she unbuttoned his shirt and picked a fragment of white skull from his chest hair, flicking it away before he could notice. She moved quickly and clinically, a process known by heart. A fresh bowl of water to finish, but even as she wrung out the cloth, the final drips still turned the water pink. She ran a hand over his bare shoulders but he recoiled from the touch and shrugged his tunic back on.

'What are you going to do now?' She asked him

His glazed eyes spoke of helplessness and his head lolled.

'You will need to go back you know,' she said more firmly, 'or they'll report you AWOL. And despite all your medals, even you can only get away with so much…'

He looked blankly back at her, any hint of playfulness lost on him.

Lucy sighed, 'Come on, old lad,' she said decisively, hauling him up by an arm, 'let's get you somewhere that isn't here for bit. I know a chap in the motor pool who'll let us borrow one of the jalopies, I rather enjoy driving.'

The hotel room was small, shabby and smelt of damp, a picture of a cow in a tarnished gold frame, staring outwards wide-eyed, hung slightly askew against greying, patterned wallpaper. An oil lamp flickered meekly, screwed to the wall in a glass case, turning everything to yellow shadow. But it was clean, or at least not noticeably dirty, and a handful of Francs had bought them a few hours and no questions asked. A few more had obtained a bottle of cheap brandy, now half emptied between them. They sat next to each other on the side of the bed. Canning had hardly spoken since the hospital and Lucy was starting to quietly panic, she had seen it before, too many times. Normally, after something particularly horrific, the afflicted were given a few stiff drinks and a few hours to catch their breath, but unless they were physically injured, they were expected to be back and fighting without delay. If Julian wasn't back in his aircraft the next morning, it would be AWOL or LMF or whatever bloody trappings of process they wanted to invoke to brand him a coward and take his fate for their own.

She had tried to console, to coax him, to bring him back to her with gentle words and reassurance and now, hating herself for it, her palm cracked hard across his face, the force of the blow twisting his head. He turned to her, blinking with eyes full of shock and hurt.

'People die Canning,' she forced the steel into her voice from somewhere, 'It's a war. It's shit and he's dead and you're not. But that just means you need to go back and do it all over again. Because if you don't, they will take everything from you.'

The look on his face tore at her but she pressed on, 'You're still alive,' she clamped a hand to his breastbone, 'and this is still beating, which is more than can be said for a whole bunch of other sorry bastards. So pick yourself up and go back, and do the whole thing all over again.'

'I'll die…'

'That's the bloody hand you've been dealt. So play it. What else are you going to do? What else can you do? You poor sod.'

His hand grabbed the neck of the bottle from where she had clamped it between her legs, and his Adam's apple bobbed as he tipped back his head. The light danced across their faces, diving into the lines and creases, and at that moment, no one could have told for certain whether they were eighteen or fifty. The liquor burned deep in his belly. A fog was lifting, but something worse was lurking, waiting to take its place. Lucy's voice chased it back.

'You two were friends?'

It took Julian a moment to work out who she was referring to, and he opened his mouth to reply but stopped. Was he a friend? They had never really spoken intimately as friends might, about their past secrets, their hopes and fears for the future. But they had shared every life-tearing, soul-shredding moment of the last five months. A presence, a constancy, every bit as scared as he was, but always there with him. Canning didn't know if that was friendship or not. Two Berts was just some daft Welsh boy, and they had gotten each other through the most terrifying parts of their young lives. And now Julian had to do it all again tomorrow, alone.

'You said before that you didn't get too close to the men you flew with.'

The replacements? No. The others? He didn't know now. And had he actually known Two Berts? He didn't know what town he had grown up in, anything about his family, his friends. He knew the wild looks of terror though. And they had seen into each other's souls through shit caked goggles at ten thousand feet. Had slept within yards of each other every night, seen each other in appalling states of drunkenness, fear and horrendous acts of sexual congress. Canning didn't say anything in reply. He just started crying. As his body heaved and racked, she curled around him, her arms a soft white cocoon as he shook and sobbed and shook, then stood bolt upright and staggered over to the small window, threw open the grimy panes and heaved a stomach full of whisky, rum, brandy and blood out onto the cobbles below. Lucy followed him and threaded her arms around his waist and suddenly Julian was acutely aware of the points of her breasts in his back and felt a flush of conflicting emotions and hormones surge through his aching body and exhausted mind. And a burning need to feel alive again. He span to kiss her.

'Fuck off!' She pushed him away, 'At least wash your bloody mouth out first,' she grinned and proffered him the brandy that had fallen to the floor.

He swilled a rough, fiery mouthful around his cheeks and teeth, gathering up any lingering chunks that had risen from his gut and sluiced it out the same open window. Then they crashed together in a sickly meeting of alcohol and saliva in the oil light, grinding against each other as they tore at layers of clothing. Lucy shrugged off her smock, threw it across the room and then wriggled from her pants, dropping them but failing to step out of them entirely and they stayed looped around her ankle. Canning felt for her, clumsy and grasping, his fingers slipped inside and she moaned softly. He struggled to undo her bra with his left hand and, cursing to himself, withdrew his right to help out. That was when he saw the blood. A thin, brown, glistening film on the first and second fingers of his right hand. Lucy noticed and carried on tugging at his tunic with a muttered, 'Doesn't matter, I must've just started.'

But Julian was already back in the cockpit, the blood and gore dripping from him. The smell. The strands of flesh hanging from the winds and wires and he shoved her away instinctively, rushing to wipe his hand on the bedsheet then sliding to the floor as the room span around him. Lucy, overcoming her shock at being treated in such a fashion guessed what had happened and sunk down to sit beside him.

'I'm sorry,' he said as the tears rolled hopelessly down his cheeks, 'I can't.'

'I know. And It's okay,' she hitched up her knickers then put her arms round him, hugging him tightly.

His shoulders shook gently as even now the rumble of the field guns was carried in on the wind through the open window. She shifted gently to lay her head against his bare shoulder, her arm still grasped across him, 'I understand.'

CHAPTER 25

14th April 1917

Stuart was tired. He was twenty-two years old and men relied on him. They followed him because they had no-one else to follow. They trusted him and yet all he could offer them in return was death. He showed them how to die properly though, how to leave the world in an organised, manly, military manner. He kept the machine running with the lives of the boys that were sent to him. But deep down he knew that the war, the military, the squadron was a hollow bureaucracy, a thin film of skin over the ludicrous endless death. It processed and repressed the emotion, made the outrage, the burning, screaming outrage of mothers, fathers, wives, and families selfish and unacceptable, insisted they were replaced with pride. Pride that a loved, warm and walking human being, a unique package of blood and spirit had marched with blind faith into the meat grinder, not wept or whimpered but stood upright and died with their hair combed and their collar done up. Somewhere at the back of his mind there was an awareness that, whilst he stood at the door ushering men through, the embodiment, the bait, he was always moving inexorably closer to the pit himself. A crude, cruel joke. Laughing at him from beneath the years of conditioning at the hands of society. Not that many years admittedly, but enough, and at such a stage in his journey towards adulthood that it had embedded itself deep, deep inside. Until he almost believed. Almost really believed. But that other side gnawed at him, pried at the edges, seeping into him during the quiet of night. So he had drank it away, battered it into a stupor and played the game methodically and mechanically, like a savant whose fingers knew the keys but who no longer heard the music. And it made him tired, so very tired, that sickly hint of betrayal, grinning behind the denial, behind the myths and stories, behind everything he so nearly believed. Sometime around the eighth whisky it normally dulled, quietened to a distant whisper, a flickering shadow. But Julian Canning had blown it all open that afternoon. Had stood in front of him and opened him up to the core, then shown him the blackness and decay within himself with a mere handful of words. *You know what you're doing and you still fucking do it.* He couldn't event blame the man, standing there covered in pieces of his friend, having to fly home with the gore crusting on him, his soul stripped back to nerve and bone. Of course he had cracked. And all he had done was speak truth, given voice to something he had always known himself, but carved through his heart all the same. He had always been able to justify the squadron's devastating losses in terms of the bigger picture, their work saving the lives of thousands who would otherwise have been butchered, but he could never look that bigger picture in the face. It could never stand the scrutiny, a vile stew of political ambitions, rabid national pride and breakfast table belligerence from armchair warriors who would never feel the hot shrapnel or cold bayonets.

And now here they all were, trapped, feeding the great maw that they had cracked open across the face of France to swallow young lives and shit them into the Flanders mud. He threw back the rest of his whisky and it dribbled out the corner of his mouth, dripping a brown, spreading stain onto the purple-white ribbon of his MC. Another joke. Children in and out of uniform eyed it enviously as the mark of bravery, coveting one for themselves. A meaningless cotton weave. His service revolver lay on the desk in front of him. He had never fired it in anger and its most likely victim would always be himself. As he eyed the relentless grey metal, he wondered if he would be able to press the barrel sharp into his temple and pull the trigger when it came to it. Possibly not he thought, but then it probably became a different question when the fire was flensing the flesh from your skull. And now, it was a question he may never need to answer. Like Frost, the command of the squadron offered him his ticket out, a chance to take one step away from the devastation, to never have to get into a fucking BE again, to command instead of lead. Christ, he had earned it. Maybe he would even get to grow old, have a family, become fat and certain. He understood now what it was like for his once friend, how it must have torn him apart. Having stood beside them, fought next to them, watched them as they burned, to then sit back and watch them go up and wait in a lonely office for the silence that meant they weren't coming back. The price for his life, letting it all happen and knowing what it was. Really, he thought, pouring another drink, it was no different to what he had been doing himself. Except maybe now he'd get to see his children.

He picked up his pencil, and took the eraser end to the sheet of foolscap with the next day's assignments. Slowly, he rubbed away one of the names against a 1045 reconnaissance, then scratched his own in its place.

* * *

He awoke from his dozing in the small hours with a start, and his eyes searched frantically around him for a couple seconds until he felt the warmth of her thighs curled around him and he remembered where he was. Then he truly remembered and felt instantly sick at the thought of having to clamber back into that dirty, dope and petrol soaked cockpit. The pathetic splutter of the engine, the smell of exhaust fumes and thump of anti-aircraft fire, the crackle of machine guns as someone else tried to kill him. He dry retched, his hand gripping her calf sharply as he sat up and woke her too. His breath was fast and his heart frantic. She gently laid her soft, hot hand on his shoulder. His breathing slowed and she reached up, turning his face to hers.

'They're all gone,' he told her, shaking his head.

'I'm still here.'

And Canning wondered what in the bloody hell he had ever done to deserve her. For this tiny spark of the divine, this shard of utter goodness in a world gone to shit, this...angel, to ever show the slightest interest in him, to sit beside him and take his side. To want to save him. But even as his heart soared, his stomach lurched and beneath it all, his soul crumpled. Her fingers had begun to stray into his hair as he turned to her suddenly.

'I can't see you anymore.'

Her face fell, visibly stung, a rare and genuine show of hurt, 'Why?'

He looked at her, saying nothing, as if he was weighing something up, then after an age, 'Because I want to.'

'What kind of dickhead logic is that?'

He smiled despite himself, 'It means I'm starting to care, no, don't worry, I'm not going to say I love you or any kind of shit like that, just that I do care if I see you again.'

Her eyes, gentle green and questioning, pressed him silently.

'I...I can't do this...' he threw out an arm to gesture at the world, 'If I care. The only way I can get into those stinking crates every day is by killing any meaning, any hope. As soon as I want to come back, as soon as there is something to live for, it'll bury me. I'll...I'll fold.'

She clasped him tightly, small and warm, 'I can help you. I'll get you through it.'

He smiled again, sadly. 'I'm not strong enough and, up there, there's nothing anyone can do to help me.'

He made to stand but she held him firm.

'I don't know how the ones with families, with wives, children, who have people they are desperate to see again, I don't know how they do it.' He shrugged. 'I can go to war and die Lucy. And if by some miracle my balls are still attached to my body at the end of it all, maybe then I'll think about living. I can't do both.'

She slid her hand from him, leaving him naked and cold, 'It was nice to finally meet you, Julian Canning.'
As she got up and pulled the rest of her clothes on, he reached out for his tunic, pulled it across his shoulders and lit a cigarette then offered her the packet. She took one and smiled, the most genuine gesture he had seen all his life. Very gently, she kissed him on the cheek, chapped lips scraping stubble, then said softly, 'I'll meet you at the car.'
As the door clicked shut behind her, the part smoked cigarette slipped from Canning's fingers, burning his thigh as his hand started to shake.

Lucy pulled up at the end of the poplar lined track that led up to the airfield. Canning reached down, opened the door and swung his legs out, levered himself to his feet, and reached into the back for his jacket. He shuffled round to the other side of the cabin and his eyes met with hers. They both opened their mouths as if to say something but the metallic rattle of an aero engine being started interrupted them and Julian turned on his heel and walked towards the aerodrome, lighting a cigarette as he walked, not looking back. The car's engine revved behind him, now barely distinguishable against the noise of the aircraft, and as Lucy drove away, he shrugged on his coat.

Stuart was giving instructions to a small group of pilots next to the flight line of BEs. The first machines clumsily taking off behind them. Their figures were lumpen and couched, ensconced in their heavy leathers, and the acrid smell of burnt exhaust swam about them. Julian marched up to him.

'The fuck have you been?' Growled the Captain.

'What am I doing?' Asked Canning ignoring the question.

'Rouex and Pelves, photos of the Boche defensive lines, here's the grid reference.' Stuart handed him a torn scrap of foolscap with some grey typeface, 'One of the replacements has been assigned as your observer, he's with the machine.'
Canning nodded and turned away.

'Leave the paper, Canning, for fuck's sake,' called Stuart, and Julian balled up the mission details and tossed them to the ground.

He neared the flight line, took one look at his aircraft, vomited, then lurched away from it in disgust. He staggered back and grabbed Stuart, hauling him aside and snarled at him, 'I'm not getting in that machine, give me another one.'

Stuart tried to push Canning away but he had the leather folds of his jacket gripped tightly, 'Why for fuck's sake?'

Canning tilted his head, eyes wide, 'Because it's still covered in *him*,' he hissed.

Stuart saw a feral look in the whites of Julian's eyes and nodded slowly, 'Okay, take mine.'

Canning nodded savagely and stalked off towards Stuart's BE. The replacement observer he had been assigned was sent across as well and he approached the BE tentatively, eyeing his pilot's wild, red eyes fearfully. But Julian didn't even acknowledge him, as the young airman climbed clumsily into the gunner's cockpit, getting tangled up in a flying wire, before settling into the low backed wicker seat as the wash of the engine blew cool around him. His tight leather gauntlets gripped the handle of the Lewis gun in terror as Canning hauled the BE off the ground with stomach turning aggression.

As they crossed the lines, Julian's head was everywhere but in the cockpit with him, and it was only the familiar bark of anti-aircraft that brought him back to some semblance of reality, where it became quickly apparent that the young observer in front of him was bundle of nervous energy. He was stretching and craning his neck at all sorts of unnatural angles in order to try and get a clear view of the sky from amongst the forest of struts and bracing wires. A French Nieuport passed them by, the pilot waving cheerfully, the white teeth of his smile visible against his dark flying gear. The grin quickly faded though, as the young lad in Canning's front cockpit grabbed his gun and sent a stream of dark tracer towards the

Nieuport, which banked away in panic.

'Hi!' bellowed Canning over the noise of the engine, 'Stop that, he's one of ours!'

Before having to duck out the way himself as the shower of bullets swept over his head, the observer swinging his gun around wildly in pursuit of his quarry. There was a tearing, ripping sound and the BE lurched drunkenly and seemed to slide across the sky. Julian turned in his chair to see that the replacement gunner had shot away their tailplane and rudder. Deprived of the tailfin's stability, Canning tried to bring the aircraft back under control but his rudder bar was now useless and his touch was too heavy to control the BE with the stick alone. It skidded horribly, the engine screeching in protest before falling into a dizzying flat spin. The observer in front of him threw up, his vomit carried away on the wind as the aeroplane spiralled down, until, in a final desperate bid for survival, Julian heaved back on the stick and threw it hard over in the opposite direction of the spin. Creaking in protest, the nose shot upwards and the machine flopped drunkenly over and hit the ground to plough a furrow across No Man's Land, the ground rushing past in a blur of brown and grey. Then Canning's shoulder blades cracked as the aircraft hit something solid, bringing it to a sudden, jarring halt and a momentary feeling of weightlessness seized him as the tail, still carried by the momentum of the descent, came up and over and the BE flipped onto its back to finish upside down.

Dazed but still conscious, Julian became aware of a slimy, wet sensation crawling across his cheek, and he peeled his face from a puddle of putrid mud. Something large and heavy was lying heavily across his back, but when he tried to move, he found it shifted easily enough, and he raised himself to his hands and knees, pushing what turned out to be the top wing off of him, and struggled to his feet. The brown expanse extended all around him, the shell holes punctuated with the familiar wooden stakes and spools of wire. A groan came from the wreck of torn fabric and splintered wood behind him and he saw the young observer, head and shoulders protruding from the front cockpit. His nose was bloodied but his eyes were open and alive and Canning was about to reach down and pull him clear of the BE when a hail of machine gun fire tore through the section of wing next to his head and he yelped in fear, leaping backwards and throwing himself to the ground. He watched, head down low, as another burst of fire raked the crash, punching through the canvas and whining off the metal of the engine. Then the first shell came down with a high-pitched whistle, to throw up clods of earth a few hundred yards away with a dull thump, as the German trench mortars started to zero-in on the crash site. Canning buried his head beneath his hands. His observer was calling out to him for help now, as a second explosion erupted closer to the stricken BE, the voice momentarily drowned out as a shower of dirt spewed up just short of the wreckage. Fuck it, thought Julian, if it hadn't been for the little prick shooting down his own aeroplane, he wouldn't be in this bloody mess in the first place. He turned away from the cries of the young airman, which were permanently silenced shortly afterwards by a direct hit from another mortar shell that flattened the remains of the BE with a crunch.

Canning started to crawl away from the shattered aircraft. He crawled through mud, muddy water and more mud. He crawled through things and over things, some of which were faintly recognisable, but mostly he had just crawled through interminable mud. He was so sick of it, he was seriously considering getting up and walking when he discovered what looked like an abandoned section of trench and he gratefully slithered into it, to sit with his back against the earthen wall, panting, wondering what the bloody hell he was meant to do next. The noise of battle around him had heightened and the crackle of rifle fire and thump of shells and grenades sounded worryingly close. He thought he could even hear the bark of men shouting. Julian decided it was better just to ignore it all, pulled his flask from his coat and drank deeply. The echo of gunfire was getting nearer still and he nestled into the bottom of the trench, swilling the rough whisky around his mouth to wash away the taste of dirt. He was stuck here, he supposed, until it got dark, then he would have to try and get himself out under the cover of the night. Then he realised that he had no idea in which direction safety lay. Well, he would just have to crawl until he hit the Front Lines. The worst case, he thought, was that he would reach the German trenches and be taken prisoner. Or bayonetted. Shit, maybe not. And the very worst case was that he struck a parallel course to the Lines and spent the night crawling across an endless stretch of No Man's Land. He started to panic, but it was short lived as a bellow of voices close at hand made him jump, and then a succession of bodies came flying into his trench to land with a thud against the opposite wall. To his instant relief, he saw they were wearing tin hats and khaki. But whilst the newcomers were in British uniform, he wasn't, and when one of them saw him hunkered down in the mud he suddenly found a bayonet thrust an inch from his gut and he threw up his hands.

'English!' he shouted desperately, 'I'm an English pilot!'

The sound of his accent relaxed the Tommy, who removed the sharpened steel blade and turned towards the final figure, who had barrelled into the trench a good ten seconds after all the other infantrymen had arrived and taken cover, and who was evidently in command.

'Pilot, Sir, one of ours,' said the soldier respectfully, pointing at Canning.

A tall but very youthful looking subaltern looked at him curiously, 'Hullo,' he said, rather formally, 'what are you doing here?'

Julian found himself at a loss. Too late he realised that the dashing, debonair air-warrior response would have been to welcome them all to his trench and inform them that he had just moved in himself. Instead his mouth just fell open and he shook his head uselessly and muttered, 'Umm.'

'Forced down, eh?'

Canning nodded in reply.

'Well I don't know if it's good or bad luck for you that we've rolled up, I think maybe good. You've landed in the middle of a little party we were throwing for Jerry, see, but unfortunately it's not gone quite to plan and we've rather outstayed our welcome. So we've just made our excuses and were making our way home, if you'd care to join us?'

Julian stared at the young Lieutenant blankly, then nodded.

'Excellent, in that case glad to have you on board, Lieutenant...'

'C-Canning,' Julian stuttered

'Splendid to have met you, Canning, I'm Forbes. Late of the Rifles but more recently assigned to this bunch of northern jackanapes. Bloody South Yorkshire, worse luck.'

The squad of Tommies grinned at Forbes's words.

'Right,' the young Lieutenant spoke with authority and purpose and clapped his hands, 'No time like the present. We'll split into two groups, I'll take the first. Lieutenant Canning, if you would be so kind as to lead the other.'

It wasn't a question. He shuffled across to Julian and began to draw in the mud wall with a spent cartridge.

'The Huns have got machine guns set up here,' he jabbed a finger onto the diagram, 'And here,' more jabbing, 'Giving full cover on our approach. However, about seventy yards up that way, near two burnt tree stumps is a defilade that should provide partial cover. I'll lead my squad round the back of this and offer covering fire.' His hand swirled in a circling motion, 'Lieutenant Canning can then make a run to the defilade and set up a sustained base of fire, allowing me to flank right before squad two follows in a pincer...'

The words and gestures washed over Julian and he stared blankly at Forbes, ducking instinctively as a shell landed nearby.

'Okay with that plan, Lieutenant Canning?' Again, it wasn't really a question, but the clipped words jarred him back to the present.

He nodded weakly.

'Right then, good luck, Canning.' He held out his hand, Julian shook it limply. 'Right,' Canning had noticed that Forbes liked that word, 'Let's go boys.'

And with that the young officer, followed by half the Tommies, vaulted out of the shallow trench, leaving Julian alone with eight muddy, dishevelled faces that looked at him expectantly.

'Sir?' A Sergeant, grimy and unshaven, who looked eminently competent, spoke in a broad Yorkshire accent.

Canning peered over the lip of the trench, saw the plain brown desolation, pocked and shattered, and slumped back down. He looked up at the Sergeant.

'Did you understand all that?' He asked, jerking a thumb in the direction the Lieutenant had left.

The tin hatted head nodded, confused.

'Will it work?'

'Yes. I mean, it sounded okay, Sir.'

'Good. You're in charge then Sergeant, go and do what he said.'

The Sergeant turned to his men, shocked, and was met with the same surprise reflected in their faces. They had never seen an officer so casually discard his authority before. He turned back to Canning, 'Sir?'

Julian looked at him, almost desperately, 'How long have you been fighting this war?'

'Two year', Sir.'

'I've been in it for just over five months and spent all of it flying, what the fuck do I know about all this?' He gestured helplessly to the brown expanse outside the trench.

The Sergeant turned back to his men. What the officer had said made perfect sense and had probably increased all their chances of survival. It could almost be considered magnanimous, yet there was something in the manner of the abdication that made it hard to respect. He looked back at Canning.

'Right, Sir. Phillips, Cooper, McCarthy, move now and move

quick. Rest of you, give 'em ten seconds then foller. You stay close to me, Sir,' the last word was almost sneered.

Three men hopped out of the trench and Canning made to scramble after them but a large hand hauled him back to fall into the mud. The strong, stubbled face loomed over him.

'I said stay the fuck close to ME! Sir.'

Julian scrambled back up into a crouch, any remaining vestiges of dignity gone. Then suddenly he was moving, following the damp, dirty khaki forms up and out. Bullets began to buzz past, kicking up clods of dirt, shells booming around them. Canning was breathless, gasping as he ran, still in his heavy flying jacket and trying to keep up with the Sergeant, who was then partially obscured by a shower of debris. One of the men beside him fell forwards, making a gurgling, choking noise that Canning could hear above the cacophony of guns and shelling. The fallen soldier rolled onto his back, clutching his throat which had been torn open and was pulsing thick, crimson blood into the soil. Julian froze, staring at him, the red mess of the neck, the white eyes as they rolled backwards into the sockets. Then a bullet hit the ground in front of him and he jumped back almost comically. Then something else went bang very loudly behind him, and he threw himself towards a huge crater with a frightened squeal, sprawling, scrambling down the side, and landing face first in the putrid slop at the bottom.

He spat the bitter, cloying paste from his mouth and used his scarf to mop the gloop from his face. Then he froze, stock still. Standing out bright against the dark of the crater wall were a pair of white eyes, wide with terror. Gradually, he was able to make out the shape of their owner. A small, huddled form, the same grey-brown colour as the shell-hole, sat with its knees drawn up, hugged tightly with both arms. On top of the head, sat the instantly recognisable curve of the coal-scuttle shaped German helmet and propped up alongside was the long barrel of a rifle. Slowly, like he was trying not to startle a small bird, Julian drew his revolver then lunged forwards and dragged the rifle away, throwing it into the mud at the bottom of the hole. The eyes never left his face as the figure cowered into the wall of the crater, burrowing into the earth. They belonged to a boy, surely no more than sixteen. He was dwarfed by the grey greatcoat that swaddled him and he was coated from head to foot in filth and grime. Julian covered him with his revolver but the boy didn't move and he was just starting to wonder what the hell to do next when a renewed burst of machine gun fire accompanied by the sharp crackling of rifles made him jump. It was followed immediately by a flying body that hurtled into the crater and splashed into the puddle at the bottom. The newcomer was up in a flash, unarmed and helmetless, his close cropped hair matted against his scalp. Without any distinguishing features, Canning struggled to make out if the new arrival was friend or foe and the man staring back at him was obviously in the same quandary, since Julian was also hatless and wrapped in his leather coat that concealed his uniform. He was however, holding a British Webley revolver and pointing it towards a German, something they both realised at the same time and the interloper threw himself at Canning with a guttural yell. Julian, utterly taken aback, was knocked off his feet and the pistol flew from his hand and over the lip of the crater. The man, now shouting wildly, struck him in the face and tried to fasten his hands round his neck. Canning was stunned. It had all happened so fast and now he was on his back, looking up into the face of a man, older than him, with a wild look in his eyes. Who was in the process of killing him. Killing him. Suddenly something snapped inside him, a realisation that this could be the end of everything. He was seized by a fierce desire to live and then a burning anger at the man who wanted to take it from him.

The German was struggling to get a grip on Canning's throat through the heavy woollen scarf and as he moved his hand to tear it away, Julian caught his index finger in his teeth and bit down hard. He could feel the gap between the bones and chewed hard to break them apart and tear through the sinews and tendons. The man screamed and tried to drag his hand free, but Canning pulled back with his neck muscles, and felt the joint dislocate then gnashed down with his molars on the shattered tissue. The German howled in pain and struck Julian round the head with his other hand, loosening his jaw enough for him to recover the now useless, flopping finger as Canning heaved him off his chest and into the mud. The two men faced each other on all fours like alley cats until the German soldier came at him again and Julian found himself fighting off hands that scratched and clawed for his eyes. He felt helpless, he had never fought like this, the odd schoolyard or drunken brawl, but never had he experienced the ferocity and sheer red aggression of killing up close with his bare hands. The German obviously had, and he fought with a brutal fervour, shouting and hollering, sweat pouring from his head and running in streaks through the dirt on his face. He was bigger than Canning and as they rolled on the ground, Julian could feel his hot breath and smell the dark shitty air that mingled with sweat and body odour as the German scraped a nail across the soft skin that bagged under his eyes. Julian reached down, groping for the other man's balls, looking to twist and tear, but the heavy grey material of his attacker's trousers was a thick barrier that stopped him from gaining any purchase. Dropping his hands resulted in another sharp blow to his head that knocked it sideways and he caught a sudden glimpse of the young boy scrambling out and over the edge of the shell hole, dropping the remainder of his kit that clattered across the floor. Both men lunged for a long bayonet that had fallen amongst the canteen and satchel of grenades but the German was faster and turned on Julian, trying to drive the knife into his chest. Canning kicked out desperately as he caught the hands wielding the blade and this time his boot hammered into adversary's balls. The soldier grunted in pain and Julian hurled himself forwards to bring them both crashing to the ground again, twisting the knife away from him. They writhed together in the slime, an undistinguishable, slithering grey morass. Canning was vaguely aware that he was shouting into his opponent's face, a hoarse, repetitive yell as he fought to turn the hands holding the bayonet, squeezing the shattered finger, and slowly, agonisingly he brought the wicked nineteen-inch serrated blade towards his enemy's face, driving it towards the German's right eye. Still bellowing, he forced it closer and closer. He wanted to see it sink in, watch the blood and jelly ooze, hear the cries. He had no idea these feeling could exist, it was as if something in him had broken as he brought all his weight to bear, inching the point ever closer to the white eyeball that widened in terror. The German was strong though, even with his damaged hand, and he managed to twist the Canning's grip so the knife sunk into his cheek instead of his eye. Julian saw the bright blood run red against the grey skin, felt the metal scraping against bone as the notches ripped and tore the flesh. He pushed harder, trying to break through the cheekbone but the blade slid off and buried itself in the mud. He had been screaming the whole time, staring deep into the German's dark brown eyes as he butchered his face, enjoying every twisted grimace of pain as the bayonet had ground out the gash that now flapped open ghoulishly. The next thing Julian knew he was reeling backwards, a deep, sickening shaft of pain cracked through his face as the German smashed his hand into Canning's still damaged nose, and he fell backwards, still clutching the knife.

Rolling to their feet and gasping for breath, they came together again, Canning swung wildly with the bayonet, the German jumped backwards, dodging the blade, then darted forwards at him as Julian overreached and struggled to regain his balance. A fist smashed into the side of his head, hard and stinging, making his ears ring and staggering him. Then he was falling, the German on top of him, brown eyes locked in hatred on his hazel. The great weal that Julian had cut in the man's face grinned and gaped evilly, dripping hot salty blood down onto him. He reached for it, groping with his black fingers, trying to push them under the skin to rend the flesh from the skull. The German howled in agony and pushed himself away with both hands. Canning, realising he was still holding the bayonet in his other hand swung it upwards, feeling it puncture cloth and meat and made to drag it sideways but it was torn from his hand as the German fell backwards. Then the man was rising again, using the wall of the crater to drag himself to his feet and pulling the knife from his side with an awful cry. He turned on Canning with a look of such tremendous hatred that Julian felt his bladder release, and as the warm piss turned cold on his thigh, he suddenly wanted to put his hands up, to stop this, to explain how stupid it all was and say sorry for hurting the man, but the German was coming at him now with the bloodied blade. Searching about in desperation Canning saw the barrel of the rifle the boy had left sticking out the mud. He grabbed at it, swinging it blindly like a club at the approaching German and the heavy wooden butt smashed the man across the jaw. Yellow teeth and red blood drops showered around him as the man pitched face first into the floor. Canning swung the rifle again, over his head this time, hammering the cropped head into the ground with a sickening crunch of skull. The force of the blow broke the butt and Julian tossed it away, grabbing the bayonet from the limp fingers and plunged it deep between the grey-brown shoulder blades, scraping and cracking through ribs. Again and again he lunged, screaming with fear, with anger, with relief, until he felt it all ebbing away alongside the blood of the mangled soldier at his feet.

He felt rotten and dirty, like some part of him had died. A wave of revulsion took him and he retched at the memory of what he had just done, sinking to his knees next to the fresh corpse. Only a couple of years ago he had been worried about revising differentiation, and now he was sitting in a hole, in the middle of the biggest battlefield the world had ever seen next to the mutilated carcass of a man he had just killed. The sheer lunacy of it all caused him to laugh out loud, cackling with the machine guns. Then he cried, sobbing and shaking.

Then he lay on his back, next to the remains of the German soldier and stared silently at the sky, where another BE was being slowly picked apart by a group of German fighters, and thought of nothing at all.

And in that BE, Stuart was in trouble. He slid his machine left before twisting in his seat to look behind, kicking at the right rudder pedal to make the aircraft skid the other way and the burst of tracer passed harmlessly between the wings. Marshall's limp body rattled from side to side in the front cockpit as another Albatros came screaming in off the right. Stuart threw the BE straight at it, startling the pilot who sheered of and almost clattered into the first German fighter that was repositioning itself. As both aircraft recovered, he took advantage of the brief respite to crank the BE round towards the Allied Lines and started to dive for safety. Marshall's corpse had slid down to the floor now, pulling the Lewis gun so it pointed straight up, revealing his helplessness, an open invitation to the Hun scouts who began to close in again. They were firing in short bursts but Stuart kept frustrating them by side slipping erratically, throwing the Albatros pilots off their aim. He was watching them closely, judging the moment they would choose to fire and then flicking the BE left or right. Too closely though, and he failed to see the third Albatros hurtling high out of the sun to send a stream of fire into the mid-section of the BE. Stuart heard the grunt of the machine guns an instant before his altimeter flew to pieces and his right leg erupted in blinding pain, kicking out involuntarily as the flying metal hammered into it. The sharp tang of petrol filled his nose and he realised that his legs were soaked in fuel, working its way into the bullet wounds, burning his tattered flesh. He could see torn strips of pale skin and khaki fabric mashed together into the bloody darkness of torn muscle. The engine cut out abruptly and the BE fell to the right as his now useless leg jammed against the rudder bar. Petrol was in his eyes, stinging and blinding but he slammed the flight stick over to the left and the aircraft groaned in protest, but righted itself and began to stagger towards the ground. The brown earth was getting closer and closer, the pits and pockmarking more distinct and with a last desperate effort, Stuart hauled back on the flight stick just before the BE struck, so it crumpled into itself like a soggy cardboard box. He was vaguely aware of the noise of tearing fabric and twang of wires, then an intense pressure on the back of his left shin, slowly pushing and pushing on it, and he screamed as he felt it bend and finally, agonisingly, splinter and snap as the cockpit collapsed around him and the world went black.

CHAPTER 26

15th April 1917

Canning awoke suddenly, knowing exactly where he was, and realised that he had fallen asleep in the middle No Man's Land. The sun was setting now, delicate ice cream pinks and peach creams sank softly into one another, the barbed wire silhouetted black against the failing daylight as he propped himself up against the wall of the crater. Was this what it meant to be a soldier, he thought. To find the level of hatred, the intensity, that had allowed him to kill the way he just had. And to do it on demand, any day, any time? He knew then that he just couldn't do it, that he would always be an also-ran, fodder for the real killers. Right now, he wanted to go to bed, but he was stuck in a shell hole. He wanted to tell Lucy about it but he had sent her away. He wanted to tell someone, but there was no-one left.

A few hours ago he had been wrestling for his life in this same pit, had tried to prise a man's eye out, and no-one would ever know. How could they? And what difference would it make if they did? A huge sense of wastefulness came over him. Nothing had been gained by what had happened, just one more corpse that wasn't him. In his head, he could see the face of the man he had killed, who now lay face down beside him, more clearly than he could remember Two Berts. His mind, stretched and distracted, couldn't see how it could ever be put back together again, how could he find the anger and hatred to carve a man's face off one day, then put on a suit and sit at a desk the next. Because at some point that could happen, and he couldn't see how there wasn't something fundamentally broken with the world.

But even as he stared at the crumpled heap in front of him, the dark, matted blood stains, the pulpy, purple mess that he had made of the back of the shaven skull, he knew that he still wanted to live. How else could he have done that to another person? Despite what had happened to Two Berts, despite the sheer fucking terror of what he was forced to do, day in day out. Despite his hated of the war, the world in general, he still wanted to live. And the realisation scared him. He wanted to see Lucy again, to hold her, have her back. He wanted to walk back down his home street. A pathetic, tiny minded sliver of a country swollen on ignorance and unearned pride. And still he wanted to be back there. It was routine, safe, and boring. And he wanted to be back there more than anything on earth. He needed a drink, something to quell the rising dread, but his flask was empty and he was horribly sober, the world around him was appalling in its sharpness and clarity.

High above him, the evening patrols were returning home, and he recognised the timorous noise of a BE as it tottered home. He started to crawl again, the aircraft's flight path had revealed the direction of the Allied Lines to him and he struck out into the gloopy, fetid soup of No-Man's Land, worming his way through more interminable brown mud, shit and detritus, back towards the relative safety of British territory. For two hours he crawled, well into the darkness of the night. Three times he got caught up in barbed wire that snagged on his clothes and ripped his skin, until finally and much to the surprise of the Tommies on watch duty, he rolled, gasping, into a forward observation post.

The next few hours passed in a blur. Someone gave him some rum, so rough it almost made him retch, but he drank it down, before somebody else pumped an injection of nevrosthenine, a potassium-magnesium compound, into a vein in the crook of his arm, which made his head buzz and his heart race. Then he was taken back through the trench network, given a cursory examination by a medic in a heavy blackout tent, who confirmed that all four of his limbs were still attached, then had the worst of the mud and blood cleaned away, before he was pushed onto a tender and shipped back to the squadron, so in a few hours time he could go out and do it all over again.

CHAPTER 27

16th April 1917

'Lieutenant Canning.'

Someone, somewhere was calling him, stretching out to him, tendrils through the dense fog of an alcoholic sleep. He forced the flicker of consciousness back down, back into the blackness where the world couldn't reach him.

'Lieutenant Canning.'

Distant yet clear, clipped and military. More insistent this time. His mind began to come to life. From the dark a momentary brightness faded into the colours of khaki and mud that was his world.

'Get up, Canning.'

Sharp now, impatient. His right eye opened a crack. The blur of khaki replicated in reality, the spark of a polished gold button. One final attempt to hold his ground and stay hidden.

'Get up!'

The water hit him, cold and jarring, bubbling in his ear and choking in his nostrils. He sat up in shock, trying to focus his bagged and bleary eyes. A panther's green death stare in the night.

'Get up please, Squadron Commander.'

Billington's lean figure swam into view, standing beside his cot, grasping a metal tankard.

'Wha...what?' His brain struggled to process.

'I said get up please, Squadron Commander, we need to confirm the day's assignments.'

'B..but...me no, not...commander?'

Billington sighed, long and low, 'Captain Stuart failed to return yesterday. We later received reports that he was rescued from the wreck of his machine by Canadian troops, albeit grievously wounded.'

Canning's expression remained blank.

'Which means, Lieutenant,' the adjutant continued, 'that you are the most senior and most experienced operational officer on this aerodrome and, therefore, de facto Squadron Commander.' Before adding quickly, 'In an acting capacity of course.'

'But what about...' Julian's protest fell to silence as he trawled through the squadron personnel in his mind.

They were all gone.

'Come on, Billy, they can't give me the bloody squadron...'

'If you would follow me to your new quarters, Sir.' He shot Canning a nasty look, 'Although I can't imagine they will be yours for very long.'

Canning felt grey. He sat slumped in a chair, at a desk, in a room, surrounded by other men's possessions. The tarnished, gilt framed picture of Frost's fiancée, ringed by glass shards, still sat next to the chipped ashtray, and one of Stuart's spare jackets was thrown carelessly onto a footstool where he hadn't had time to unpack. His head throbbed and pulsed from deep within his brain, and his face still felt greasy despite him having doused it with water three times already. The chill liquid had stung his nose, which was now cracked and red where the German had struck him the day before. At the bottom of his throat a queasiness persisted that rose slightly whenever he moved or shifted in his seat. His limbs felt sluggish and heavy and his hands had begun to tremble ever so slightly. A rumbling unsteadiness pervaded in his bowels. His whole body was rank with greyness. In his mind, his thoughts were brief and fleeting and he struggled to cling to or focus on anything in particular. His imagination was wrecked and unclean. Only the present existed and Canning sat there enduring every horrible grey second. Outside a cloying, moist mist had descended over the aerodrome and he was willing it to stay there with every tattered fibre. The last thing he wanted to do was fly. The thought of it made him physically shudder and the bile swelled in his throat. He gulped from the tankard of water that Billington had refilled and left with him, and lit another cigarette. The tankard smelt slightly of beer and made Julian want to heave.

The grimy black telephone trilled harsh and sudden, startling him, making his heart race and causing his armpits to break a sweat. He swallowed, letting it ring for a few more seconds, then tentatively picked it up.

'Hello?'

'Hello. Hello? Who is this?' demanded a clipped, peremptory voice.'

'Erm, Lieutenant Canning, 33B Squadron,' he replied, somewhat bemused.

'Canning, eh? Don't recognise your voice. Who are you?'
Julian felt that he was already starting to lose control of the situation.

'Well I'm…er…I'm Canning.' He offered, helpfully.
Silence for a second then the voice replied, 'I see.'
More silence.

'Put me through to your commanding officer,' it continued after careful thought.

'Who?'

'Your. Commanding. Officer.' The voice said slowly and deliberately, full of contempt, 'The highest ranking officer in your unit.'

'Right okay. Erm. That's me, I suppose.'

'You…Oh good lord. Okay then, listen up Channing. Do you have a pencil?'
Canning looked across the desk. There was a pencil in the far corner. He left it where it was.

'Yes, thank you.'

'Right. Nivelle is going over today but Jerry is pushing forwards in sector 34 and we are going to double up our forward guard with two half regiments from the 92nd, moving them up to K23 via F39. Therefore,' the voice continued, barely pausing for breath, and Canning began to suspect that the purpose of the call may not have been an enquiry into the squadron's stationery supplies, 'we need photographs of 66 and 612, the trenches that border N9 and 10 and sight of the terrain around the supply dump at Q4. Bit sticky that one, we think Jerry's moved some more fighters into the area and it's right next to their new nest, but I'm sure your chaps are up to it, eh Channing? Now, we are also going to need to keep the pressure up on any Boche artillery in Dog sector, so we will need art obs to work with the 112th, 3rd Canadian, and the 42nd. Going to be a hectic morning, what? Have you chaps got enough aeroplanes?'

'Err...'

'If I were you I'd put your best men on the photos, they're going to be critical over the next twenty-four hours, but the 49th is relying on you boys keeping Jerry's big guns quiet too, remember. So, got all that? Hello? Are you still there? Manning?'

'Yes.'

'Excellent, in that case I will call you at eleven hundred for an update on the morning's work.'

And then the line clicked dead.

Canning paused for a moment, considering what had just happened then slowly, deliberately, he replaced the receiver, removed his hip flask and took two long gulps. Then he walked slowly over to the sleeping alcove, climbed into the bed, pulled across the curtain, and went to sleep, pleased with how quickly he had picked up the knack of military command.

However, it felt like as soon as he closed his eyes, he was rudely awoken by the insistent buzz of the telephone. He staggered from the bed to catch a glimpse at the faded wall clock, which showed him that in fact, six hours had passed. A weak sun had broken through the cloud and glinted through the window. Without thinking, he instinctively reached across and picked up the receiver, instantly regretting it.

'Hello?' A familiar voice, but somehow even more terse and imperative than before.

'Hello,' he croaked in reply, dropping into his chair.

'Is that 33B Squadron?'

'Yes.'

'Who am I speaking to?'

'Canning,' he muttered.

'And who are you?'

A dreadful sense of déjà vu swept over him and he groaned out loud.

'You okay, laddie?'

'No.'

'Oh dear,' Came the response, then a pause, 'Put me through to your commanding officer, will you?'

'Who?'

'The chap I was speaking to before, Mannerly.'

'He's not here.'

'Well, where is he?'

'There is no Mannerly.'

'Oh, I am sorry, he seemed like a stout chap.' Another pause. 'Well anyway, listen here, who is your highest ranking officer?'

'I am.'

'I see. And you are?'

'Lieutenant Canning.'

'Right. Well see here Canning, I spoke with Mannerly earlier and gave him your squadron orders, did he pass them on?'

Julian sensed this was getting rapidly out of hand.

'Err, yes.'

'Well were the bloody hell were you fellows and where are my bally photos? Did any of you actually go flying this morning?'

'No,'

'Why ever the bloody hell not?'

Canning paused for a moment, judged that his new acquaintance was not an aeronautical man and confidently replied, 'Bad sky.'

Silence. Then, 'I see. Well, do you think you'll be able to get up this afternoon?'

'We'll certainly give it our best shot, Sir.'

'Good show, that's the spirit Herring. I'll call you back at seventeen hundred.'

Silence followed the click.

The situation had now become rather silly he decided, and unscrewed his flask as he began to search for a way out of it. Eventually he settled on flying to Switzerland. Truth be, he wasn't entirely sure where Switzerland was but he had a rough idea that if he just kept flying West while keeping eye out for some mountains he wouldn't go far wrong. He eyed the windsock. There was a good tailwind today too.

A knock on the door interrupted his musing and an enthusiastic, sandy haired, freckled face that he didn't recognise poked through.

'Begging your pardon, Sir, but me and the other chaps were wondering if we would be doing any flying today?'

Julian fixed him with an icy stare and took another swig from his flask, 'No,' he replied, 'bad sky.'

The youth looked puzzled for a minute, then shrugged, 'Very good, Sir,' and disappeared.

Canning leant back in his chair and steepled his fingers, deep in thought. He thought about going back to bed, but realised that would be a very short term solution. Then he thought about Switzerland again, but remembered he had been mortally afraid of his Grandmother's cuckoo clock as a child, and besides, the BE wouldn't have the range to make it in one hop. He started to panic. There was a very real risk that whoever kept calling him would eventually remember his name and he had realised that, whilst the military edifice seemed incapable of addressing relatively minor issues, such as the chronic obsolescence of its equipment or the woeful inadequacy of its pilot training, when it came to administering the ire of its senior officers, it could be incredibly proficient. His flask was empty and he got up to root around the office for the stash he knew one of the previous incumbents must have kept in the battered chest of draws, grunting in satisfaction as he pulled a half bottle of pre-war scotch triumphantly from under a pile of Frost's spare shirts. He looked closer, it was pre-war alright, pre-Boer War. Deciding it was too good just to dump in his flask, he found a chipped china teacup and saucer beside the sleeping alcove, wiped it out with the sleeve of one of the shirts, and poured himself a long, satisfying glug. Then sat back down and took a sip. A maelstrom of aromas hit him, deep oaky woodsmoke and burnt coffee, in a heady mixture that stung his senses but didn't strip his throat.

Billington burst in without knocking just as Canning had hit upon the answer. He glared at the scruffy figure that was sat with his boots up on the desk, head back and drinking from a willow pattern teacup, pinkie extended extravagantly.

'Canning,' he began.

'*Squadron Commander* Canning,' Julian interrupted.

Billington ignored him, 'Why the hell has no one been flying this morning? Did you get any orders?'

Julian nodded, 'Yes, I received some orders.'

'And?'

'And what?'

'What were they?'

Canning frowned at him, 'Never you mind, I'm just devising my strategy.'

'Canning, I am the squadron adjutant, and as recording officer I need to...

'There was a message for you as well.'

This time it was Billington's turn to frown.

'A request from Group Headquarters to testify at Major Frost's inquest.'

Billington's ears pricked up and a nasty gleam appeared behind his eyes.

'You've been asked to report to RFC headquarters in Amiens, full dress uniform, in readiness to give evidence at 1600 today.'

'But that's rather short notice…'

'There's a war on Billington! Do you expect the Army to send you a detailed summons?

'Right. Well...'

'What is it man?'

'Nothing. I suppose I had better get off then.'

He wanted to find out what the bloody hell Canning was planning, but the chance to attend an official inquest and spear Major Frost, whom he had despised for his softness, was too much for him. He turned on his heel.

'Oh, Billy?'

The adjutant looked back over his shoulder.

'They said to ask for a Captain MacAllen when you arrived.'

'Right.' The door slammed shut behind him.

Canning smiled to himself, out of everything he had just said, he was most surprised that Billington believed that anyone at Headquarters above the rank of Major would be still be either on duty or sober enough to hold an inquest at four in the afternoon. He dropped the empty bottle into the waste paper bin, glad the adjutant hadn't noticed the name printed on the faded yellow label.

* * *

Ripley had to run to catch up with Canning, who was striding towards the hangars in full flying leathers.

'He…Hey, Canning.' He panted.

Julian stopped and turned to him, all brown bulk.

'Is…is it true? Are you in charge?'

'Yes. For the moment.'

Ripley's face showed a sudden and total loss of faith in everything about the military institution, that he had hitherto believed in.

'Okay then. I, erm. Are you flying now?' He could see the

mechanics manhandling the drab silhouette of a BE from the hangars.

'Yes.'

'Shouldn't the rest of us be.'

'No, don't trouble yourselves, I've got this one covered.'

'Right. Don't you want an observer at least?'

'No.'

Canning started to walk away. Ripley chased after him, 'It's just that…'

'What?'

'Well, normally we, you know, have things to do.'

'And today I'm telling you that you don't. Now piss off Ripley, that's an order.'

He left the young pilot standing in the field as he marched up to the aircraft where the mechanics were starting to prepare the engine.

'All ready?'

'Yes, Sir.'

'Camera fitted?'

'Yes, Sir.'

'Plenty of plates?'

'Yes, Sir.'

He grunted his approval as he clambered into the rear cockpit.

Canning spent thirty minutes circling for height then struck off towards the Front, taking great care to stay well over the Allied side of the Lines. It didn't take him long to find what he was looking for, a non-descript patch of brown, potholed French countryside which he reckoned looked like every other bit of brown, potholed French countryside across the entirety of the Western Front. He then proceeded to fly over it repeatedly for an hour at different heights and angles, taking multiple photographs, stowing the used plates carefully in the cockpit. When he returned he beckoned the photographic Sergeant over and thrust an armful of exposed plates at him.

'Get those developed and sent off to headquarters. Quickly,

and before Lieutenant Billington gets back.'
The Sergeant did his best to salute whilst clinging on to the stack of photographs. Canning watched him in silent amusement before heading back to his office.

Billington's return was announced shortly after 2000, when the door to the squadron office flew open with a terrific bang, startling Canning who had just finished a telephone call where the voice had been warmly congratulating him on the quality of the reconnaissance photos the squadron had provided. He tried to compose himself.

'Something against my door, Lieutenant Billington?'

'What are you playing at, Canning?' Snarled the glittering green eyes.

'What are you playing at, *Sir*.'

'We're the same rank, Canning.'

'And I'm squadron commander, which makes me your commander, so you'll call me *Sir*.'
Billington sneered, 'Give me one good reason for not reporting you. Sir.'

'For what?'

'Dereliction of duty, disobeying orders.'

'Headquarters have just congratulated the squadron on a fine day's work.'
He raked Julian with his gaze, searching for the lie.

'I don't know what you're up to Canning but there was no inquest in Amiens.'

'Amiens? I'm pretty sure I said it was in Armentieres. It was a bad line though, water in the cables again, probably.' He met Billington's stare.
The adjutant dropped his eyes first, before they flickered back again with a flash of vicious amusement.

'I thought there must have been some...misunderstanding. Therefore, I collected the orders for tomorrow directly from Wing in person.'

'Give 'em here.'

'Oh no need. Sir. I took the liberty of making the assignments as soon as I got back. You have a low level reconnaissance twenty miles over near Lille at 1030. Told them that you'd handle it personally as the senior pilot.' A smile creased his spite filled face as he drank in Canning's expression, 'Thought you might appreciate that one. I know how you don't like early mornings. Sir.'

* * *

Billington sighed and scratched his pen across the bottom of a requisition form for new inner tubes, placed it carefully onto a neat pile on the right side of his desk and reached with his left hand for the next sheet of paper. A breakdown of mess costs for the previous month. Most of the names on the sheet were gone now, their bills would be settled out of their final pay and whatever was left sent home to wives and families. He sighed again. His leg hurt. Footsteps thumped unsteadily from behind the closed door as his eyes scanned the figures for errors. The thumping stopped and the door swung open. He saw Canning's silhouette swaying momentarily in the wan electric light, before stepping purposefully in.

'Lieutenant Billington,' he began formally, 'I am required to inform you that I am now conscientiously objecting to my continued participation in this conflict.'

Billinton's eyes narrowed as he tried to work out how drunk Canning was.

'I want to make it very clear that I am not deserting and I shall, of course, remain on the aerodrome until someone can arrange for the appropriate next steps.'

'Sod off, Canning, I'm busy. Go and finish your bottle.'

'Oh I'm stone cold sober, Billy, well, chilly maybe,' he grinned with satisfaction, 'From now on, I'm out of this war.'

Billington shifted uncomfortably in his chair. Usually he wouldn't take the bait. Would let the man bluster until he got bored and wandered off. But his leg ached and something about the smug smile on Canning's face grated.

'No, you're not. You're going to finish your bottle, go to bed and in the morning, get up and go to war. You, Julian Canning, will not conscientiously object. You cannot conscientiously object.'

'And why not?' the grin persisted, drunkenly self-satisfied, irritating.

'Because to really, truly conscientiously object, you need courage and conviction, and you have neither. You've been here a few months playing in aeroplanes, have spent a few hours at the Front Lines and discovered what war really is, and you didn't like it. And now you're drunk and you've made a decision that you have absolutely no hope of following through in the morning.'

'And what the hell makes you think that?'

'Because you are a mediocrity, you don't have the guts to be a hero and you sure as hell don't have the courage to be a rebel. You do just enough, and only just enough, to get by. To avoid being noticed. You balance up the risks, making them as small as possible and you survive. That's all. You do only what you have to do, and you survive.'

'Are you calling me a coward?'

'No,' Billington's voice was calm, cold and scalpel sharp, 'Anyone who gets into one of those contraptions every day is no coward. You're just not courageous, you have no conviction. No, wait, let me finish. You are like eighty percent of the soldiers in this army. You think about what you are doing. And because of that you drink.'

Julian flushed, 'Bollocks I drink because...'

'Because you struggle to reconcile what you have to do as a soldier with what you know and believe as a person,' Billington finished for him, 'You can't conceive of giving your life for a cause you don't believe in or care about. But what you don't realise is that it doesn't matter if you believe or not. As a good soldier, you follow the order, you don't need meaning or justification, you just do.'

He stood up from behind his desk, gripping the corner hard as a lance of pain jarred through a nerve in his thigh.

'Being a soldier is the easiest thing in the world. You do what you're told. Any conscience or morality, any doubts that you have are irrelevant. You follow orders without question. With obedience.' He had pulled back his shoulders and puffed out his chest, 'Except you're not a soldier. You're a jumped up schoolboy that they've dressed up in a man's uniform. Like so many of the others. You're too wrapped up in trying to save your own life, to realise that you've already given it to your country. And your country will decide when, if, you get it back.'

Julian's back straightened suddenly, 'I didn't give it.' He spoke steadily, 'They took it from me.'

His eyes fell to Billington's white knuckled hand.

'You speak as a man of experience, Billy,' He inclined his head, 'I've never asked just how did your leg happen?'

Billington paused, a little taken aback by the question, surprised that Canning hadn't risen to his provocation.

'A Boer sniper, hit me before I ever saw him.'

'Where were you?'

A pause, then, 'Volksrust.'

'I only know a little of the history, but I don't recall a battle at Volksrust.'

'I was on duty there, the bastards fought as guerrillas.'

Canning fixed his eyes on the adjutant.

'What was that duty, Lieutenant?'

Billington hesitated for a second, then snapped at him, 'I was on guard at the camp there.'

Julian considered him in silence for a moment, 'One of the concentration camps? Like Bloemfontein?'

'Yes.'

'Where you guarded women and children. And buried them when they died.'

'I was a soldier and I followed orders.'

'You watched women and children starve. Made sure they starved, maybe. Or worse'

'I followed orders.'

'You talk to me of war, of duty. You speak as if you know what it's like, about the reality, when all you ever did was get shot standing around watching women and children die? I bet you even gave some of 'em a helping hand. You malevolent bastard.'

Billington shot round the side of the desk and stood inches away from Canning's face, looking down on him.

'That's why I know how easy it is, Canning,' he hissed, 'I followed orders. I didn't think, didn't question, I followed my orders. It didn't matter what I thought, how I felt about what I had to do. It wasn't my job to think, they weren't my actions, they were my country's actions, and I bled for my country.'

Julian met his gaze and this time Billington saw something deep, deep within Canning's bloodshot, tired brown eyes.

'So you know then, what it's like up there for us, what it's like for the thousands of poor bastards in the mud a few miles away? What you did all those years ago means you understand us and means you can judge us? Makes you our equal, our elder, our better?'

Billington gave a twitching nod. A mirthless smile crept across Canning's face.

'I will fly that reconnaissance tomorrow, Billington. But I want to review the rest of assignments.'

The older man didn't move. Canning pointed past him at the pile of paperwork. Slowly, the silver-grey head turned and he retrieved a sheet of foolscap. Julian took it from him and picked up the recording officer's fountain pen. He crossed out some unknown replacement who had been allocated as his observer and, in his place, scrawled the adjutant's own name.

Billington's lean face greyed, 'I...I am the squadron recording officer, Canning. I'm retired from active duty.'

'We are short of men and I don't have a regular observer. And you know how to fire a gun.'

'But my leg.'

'I'm not asking you to run a fucking marathon, you just

need to sit in the front seat of my aeroplane while every Boche bastard within three miles tries to kill us. Then you can talk to me about courage.'

'But this is unheard of, I will have to report…'

'You will find some kit and meet me at the hangars in preparation for a 1030 take-off tomorrow, Lieutenant. That's an order.'

Canning walked back across the hallway and closed the door to the office. He reached across to the desk, picking up a manila envelope that lay on top of the blotting paper, and tucked Billington's service record back into the cabinet where he had found it, before flopping onto the bed.

CHAPTER 28

17th April 1917

Canning woke to the sinister feeling that someone was in the room with him, close by. He looked up in trepidation, only to be greeted by the faintly ridiculous sight of a man knocking on a curtain. It was the same freckled face with the sandy hair that had disturbed him yesterday. The young 2nd Lieutenant, Christ he looked about twelve, snapped quickly to attention as he saw Julian's one open eye.

'Terribly sorry, Sir,' he said formally, 'It's just Lieutenant Billington, Sir, he's acting rather strangely, been walking around in a flying jacket for about an hour now, muttering to himself.'

As Julian's memories of the previous night's exchange reconstructed themselves, a raw shaft of headache bored bluntly through his skull and he closed his eyes and groaned.

'Sir? Are you okay, Sir?' The young pilot shook his shoulder gently.

'Get the fuck off me.' Canning snapped, sending the lad scuttling across the office.

'S-sorry, Sir.'

'What time is it?'

'Oh-nine forty-five, Sir, the dawn show has just returned.' He offered helpfully.

Canning sat bolt upright and immediately regretted it.

'Who ordered them up?' He asked through a belch.

'Lieutenant Billington, Sir. Although he seemed a little er… subdued when he was detailing them.'

Good, thought Canning. Vicious bastard. At least if he copped it himself this morning that miserable arse would go down with him.

'Was that it?' He asked the blonde Lieutenant.

'Er...Yes, I suppose so, sir.'

'Piss off then, I need to get ready. Lieutenant Billington is flying with me so make sure he meets me by my machine. Oh, and get me a bottle of whisky.' He added as an afterthought. The freckled face bridled, something in the unwritten code of being an officer told him that he probably shouldn't be treated like a skivvy, but the chain of command worked wonders for Julian and ten minutes later, he had a fresh, unopened bottle in his hand. Five minutes after that it was only two-thirds full as Julian tried to steady his shaking hands and get the visions of stringy, red gore out of his head, the warm salt taste from his mouth and smell of blood from his nose and throat. Slamming the cork back into the bottle with the palm of his hand, he shrugged on his coat, dropped the whisky into one of the pockets and threw up twice into the waste paper bin next to the desk, before walking out the door. Canning emerged, squinting blindly into the daylight, to find Billington stood next to his BE. The adjutant's tall, lean frame was bloated and clumsy in a padded, full body flight suit that he had found. He already had his cap on and the googles pulled down over his eyes. He put Julian in mind of a child, ready for a day's outing, and he almost felt sorry for him. Then he remembered how much of a shit the man was and he walked up to him with his teeth bared in a mirthless grin.

'Lieutenant Canning, I really must protest.'

'Shut up, Billy, and get in the fucking aeroplane. That's an order.' Julian growled, dragging on his own cap and goggles and levering himself into the rear cockpit with his left leg. Billington lumbered up to him and grabbed the edge of the compartment with heavy-gauntleted hands, 'You can't do this, Canning.' He hissed. But Julian could hear the panic in his voice.

'I'm in charge, so I can do whatever the fuck I want, you

miserable piece of shit. And right now, I want you in that front fucking cockpit because we're going flying. Welcome to the war, Billington, be sure to give me a little wave when you shit yourself up there so I can hold my nose.'

The adjutant looked at him, bright green eyes helpless and pleading, but Julian simply extended a brown leather finger, pointing at the chair in front of him. Billington made a strange sound, something between a mewl and a whimper, then tried to get into the BE. He failed twice, falling backwards in his heavy flying gear and one of mechanics had to step forwards and help him in. Another handed him a Lewis gun and he held it out to Canning, hopelessly.

'Point that end at anything that tries to kill us.' he shouted, gesturing at the barrel. Then he unplugged the cork from the bottle of whisky and drank down three large gulps as his makeshift observer looked on horrified.

The smoky, sickly liquor dulled his senses and memories, quelled the bile rising in his chest and he closed his eyes. For the briefest of moments, he thought he heard a bird and then the aircraft rocked and he gripped the control column in a panic, before realising it was just the engine turning over. He necked another quart of the whisky, before easing the throttle forwards and the BE rose bumpily into the air.

As he climbed for height, Julian pulled the BE into ever tightening circles, until the struts creaked and he lost too much speed to climb effectively. But it had had the desired effect on Billington, who had turned a fascinating shade of puce behind his goggles. Canning struck out for the Lines, his own stomach now raw from the alcohol, and he found himself farting viciously as they puttered towards the front. He shuddered and clenched as one felt a little close for comfort, and for a second he panicked that he had shat himself, but when he massaged his buttocks against the wicker chair he felt no wetness and he settled back down, relieved.

When they reached the Front Lines, the first bursts anti-aircraft fire blossomed around them with resounding thumps and he laughed, loudly and bitterly as Billington threw himself flat in the cockpit in an attempt to take cover. He turned parallel to the trenches to draw out the amount of time they would be exposed to the German gunnery. The shooting was better than normal and Julian started to get a bit jumpy himself, but he still held a steady course, subjecting the adjutant to a prolonged barrage of shelling. The black airbursts continued to creep closer around them and Billington finally cracked, leaping up from the floor of his cockpit and started shouting, white-faced and wide eyed at Julian, his words carried soundlessly away on the wind. Canning thought he could see tears behind the glass of his observer's now grimy goggles and he laughed again, openly and emptily in the terrified face of Billington, whose rapidly cooling piss was now running down his thighs, as he stood there, six thousand feet above the earth, pleading for his life as his wildly drunken pilot mocked him.

'Sit down, you cunt!' Canning roared at him, his words also lost to the engine and onrush of air. He swigged from his bottle and swung the BE over towards German territory in a cavalier fashion, throwing Billington against the side of the aircraft. The adjutant was on his knees now, hands alternating between frantic gestures back towards the British Lines and being clasped in a desperate prayer. Julian ignored him and scanned the sky and ground around him. Below, he could see the plump, cushioned sausages that made up the German balloon line and here and there, the silver slashes of rivers and lagoons.

He saw it far too late. The dark flash across the blinding yellow of the morning sun, the death rattle, and as his whisky sodden brain fought to make sense of it all, bullets began striking the aircraft around him. A hail of shots punched through fabric and whined off metal, and in front of him, Billington went down, great red slashes torn in his padded suit, as he crumpled to the floor of the cockpit. Canning couldn't help but feel a pang of satisfaction, even as the flames billowed forth in front of him. He stared at them in bewilderment, bright orange and dancing, the heat of them starting to press on his face as he slowly began to realise what it meant. He backed away, pushing himself towards the rear of the cockpit, the drumming of the engine still roaring in his ears as the fire ate its way towards him. It still didn't seem real, like he was watching it happen to someone else. Even so, he found himself beginning to clamber out of the cockpit as the flames rose higher and the heat became too intense to bear. He swung a leg over the side of the cockpit and the slipstream took it, flattening it against the fuselage, the BE rolling dangerously as its balance shifted. His scarf worked loose to fly backwards and flap freely in the wind. And suddenly it was all terribly real and happening so, so fast. He wanted it to stop, to find something to freeze the moment, to step back and away from it. But he couldn't, it was happening to him, happening now. He was about to die. There was no stopping it. Now, right now, this was his end. Still his mind couldn't quite grasp the enormity of it. The other foot came out the aircraft, and he was lying back along the fuselage, clinging to the cockpit's leather rim, coughing on fumes, as the fire burned through the leather of his gauntlets. He watched helpless as the skin of his knuckles reddened and blistered, then the searing, scorching pain. And as his flesh bubbled, Canning let go.

CHAPTER 29

22nd April 1917

Stuart lay on his back and stared up at the ceiling. The yellowed, peeling paint and harsh electric lighting made him feel both drowsy and sick at the same time. Or maybe that was just the cocktail of drugs still swimming in his blood. From the corridor outside, he could hear the familiar squeak and rattle of the trolley. He levered himself up on his elbows, propping his back against the cold steel bedstead, and drawing the grey woollen blanket up to his waist. It was stained and blotchy, frayed at the edges with a hole in the far left corner where the moths had gotten at it. He caught a gust of scent as he moved it. It smelt, like everything else in this damned place, of blood, shit, disinfectant and, above it all, decay. A rotten, cloying smell of dead and dying flesh. He eyed the smeared streaks of brown that were strewn liberally across the cover in disgust, permanently dyed into the coarse grey weave that lay over the outline of his legs. Or rather it lay over the uneven stumps where his legs had once been. The left, taken off above the knee, finished some way short of the right, which had been amputated midway along the shin. There were no peaks in the blanket where his feet should have been. The puckered ends of his limbs, which he still couldn't bring himself to look at, ached unmercifully. They made him want to retch, and when he sat up, the top half of his body was now massively unbalanced and he struggled to stay upright, relying on his stomach muscles.

In the few hours following his crash, he had drifted in and out of a pain soaked consciousness, scraps of awareness melded with wild spiralling dreams until his eyes had opened to see rough green fabric and heavy stitching, memories of which had been quickly replaced by the surgeon's saw biting into his right shinbone. He could still feel the rasping, grinding of the teeth as it hacked through, then the sharp spike of agony as it sank into marrow and nerve. Then more jarring and the rotating of his crushed limb before it fell away where the muscle and meat had already been sliced through by a scalpel blade. The thought of it made him feel nauseous and the room rocked. The worst part had been when he had felt the knife being driven into the flesh of his left thigh to scrape on the bone above his knee and he knew what was coming again. He had cried out, until someone had mercifully jammed an ether soaked rag over his mouth and nose. Then a blurred, nightmare journey of bumps and jolts, of screeching horses and crying men, to wake up here, in a convalescent ward far away from the Front Lines, where similar cruel mutilations lay in narrow, steel-framed, shit-stained beds. A veritable fucking freak show, Stuart thought viciously.

As far as he could see from the confines of his cot, there were another three in the room who were missing both legs like himself. The man opposite him had seemingly lost half his face. Eye, jaw and ear had all been shot away to leave a head wrapped in bandages, yellowed from the weeping wounds, and a ghoulish open palate that dribbled constantly down his right shoulder. His one good eye was never still for a second and rarely blinked, as it flitted around the room in wide lidded terror. Those that could still speak seldom talked to each other, but Stuart learned that the young Corporal in the next bed, there was no separation of rank amongst the freshly butchered, had been a factory operator, tending to the great machines that smelted steel. He had lost a leg and both hands to shrapnel when he had raised them to protect his face from a hand grenade. The Scottish Captain had silently wept when he had first seen what had been done to his own bright, athletic body. And he had no idea what his life would now become. The thought of living as a cripple terrified him, but he still had enough self-awareness to be grateful that his family possessed a level of privilege. Whatever his future held, it would certainly be better than a one-legged northern factory worker with no hands, who would likely be swept away with the other detritus of war. The bed to the other side of him was filled by a huge, muscular officer whose right leg had been taken at the hip and when he was being tended and turned one night, Stuart had seen the bloodied bandages that covered where his cock and balls should have been, but which now lay flat along the curve of his groin. The man simply lay on his side, day in, day out, never saying a word. He had been told by one of the nurses that they would be shipped back to England in a week or two, when they were strong enough to move, and Stuart wondered if the same crowds that had waved him off would be there to welcome them back. Hail the conquering heroes.

The squeaking of the trolley grew exponentially louder as it entered the room, pushed along by the solidly built matron, making her way up the ward and handing out the newspapers. Stuart felt he should smile or thank her as he leant forward to take the cheap, inky broadsheet that had been proffered, but he didn't. It was a couple of days out of date and the front page was dominated by reports of the latest French offensive that the British attacks had been paving the way for. General Nivelle had lost, at a conservative estimate, over one hundred thousand men during the 16th and 17th April. The story spoke of the great sacrifices required to make great gains. Stuart turned the page quickly, sick to the stomach, there was just no fucking end to it. He scanned the despatches and the 'missing in action' lists on the back pages for reports of men that he knew, and his mouth twitched as his eyes fell upon a familiar name. Something between a smile and a grimace crossed his face as he folded the paper and dropped it onto his stumps, sitting back in the bed to gaze about him, wondering.

Canning, he thought, had been lucky again.

AFTERWORD

The First World War fighter pilot is a relatively well worn trope, at least compared to his erstwhile prey. Keen eyes will have picked up several nods towards the various works exploring his plight across the years, and which of course informed my own interests. And very often, it is the hard drinking, world-weary, daredevil warrior who cuts a common figure. Canning, I hope, is something an antidote to this, alcohol and world weariness yes, but dare-devil heroism somewhat less so. The very mundanity of the work carried out by the two seaters jars with the enormous risks they took, and the often decisive impact they could have on the infantry war, which in turn made them simultaneously so critical and yet so readily disposable to their lords and masters.

For a thorough overview of the Battle of Arras from the air, Peter Hart's *Bloody April* is an excellent source work, and proved invaluable to laying the historical foundation to Canning's story. David Baker's *Richthofen*, provides a fascinating study of the period through the eyes of the hunter. However, other than a quick drop in to visit the Baron and co., I have not sought to revive historical figures, for to pass judgement on select individuals over the course of a couple of weeks in the context of a global catastrophe would seem a little myopic (indeed the Arras offensive was one of the more competently orchestrated slaughters). All of my characters are, therefore, fictional constructs. I have tried to retain a manageable level of historical accuracy throughout the book, doubtless any aviation aficionados will tear holes in my technical details quicker than a pair of Spandaus, but then again, if your main concern is the mounting mechanism of a

Lewis gun, or the precise distance from Vimy Ridge to Farbus, then I wonder if you may have missed the point just a little. Regardless, any mistakes, omissions, errors and / or more general literary cock-ups remain utterly my own.

Canning himself is very much an anomaly, the majority of participants in the First World War went cheerfully and capably to their deaths, trusting in authority, eager to prove their bravery, and believing in sacrifice to a higher cause. But humanity is a spectrum, and somewhere in the millions there would have been a Canning, and for that matter, a Lucy, a Stuart and a Billington. They may have worn different colours and spoken different tongues, but fellow human beings, nonetheless. And when they started to sweep up the pieces of them on November 12th, one has to wonder what four years of unprecedented slaughter had achieved. This does nothing to diminish the courage and heart of the men and women, of all nationalities, who went to war, but it is everything against those that sent them to die. The higher cause betrayed them, and now our current generations, almost all of us fortunate enough never to have faced the bombs and bullets in our time, have lost that perspective. At time of writing, we are in a black and white world where petty nationalism is rife, politicians who have never known a day's discomfort liken their shabby bureaucratic wranglings to fighting on the beaches. Time has reduced remembrance to ceremony and spectacle. We seem incapable of debating shades of grey anymore and the true lessons of a hundred years ago are lost to rhetoric, polemic and appropriation.

We shall remember them. I am not sure that many of us really do now. But I think they were better than we can ever hope to be.

SJW

Printed in Great Britain
by Amazon

39386409R00179